SOON AND VERY SOON

Janice & Aki

SOON AND VERY SOON

A novel

By Sherryle Kiser Jackson

*No sooner they met
they married
then combined everything
Combine passion with faith*

Sherryle

URBAN CHRISTIAN

www.urbanchristianonline.net

URBAN CHRISTIAN is published by

Urban Books
1199 Straight Path
West Babylon, NY 11704

Copyright © 2007 Sherryle Kiser Jackson

All rights reserved. No part of this book may be repro-
duced in any form or by any means without prior consent
of the Publisher, excepting brief quotes used in reviews.

ISBN-13: 978-1-60162-949-4
ISBN-10: 1-60162-949-4

First Printing December 2007
Printed in the United States of America

10 9 8 7 6 5 4 3 2 1

*This is a work of fiction. Any references or similarities to actual
events, real people, living, or dead, or to real locales are intended
to give the novel a sense of reality. Any similarity in other names,
characters, places, and incidents is entirely coincidental.*

Submit Wholesale Orders to:
Kensington Publishing Corp.
C/O Penguin Group (USA) Inc.
Attention: Order Processing
405 Murray Hill Parkway
East Rutherford, NJ 07073-2316
Phone: 1-800-526-0275
Fax: 1-800-227-9604

Dedication

For Arvell and Nylah:
Two ways I spell love.

Acknowledgments

To God Be the Glory.

To my parents: Lewis and Delores Kiser, thanks for your unconditional tough love and support. I suspect you always knew I'd be a writer.

To my Big Sis, Monique P. Kiser, my first landlord, roommate and editor, I love you. After reading my entire first manuscript, hopefully I put in a few surprises for you. You're my Martha to my Mary. I hope my novels serve Him like your works do.

Arvell, I can't imagine taking this journey with anyone else. To Ms. Lolita Moses Jackson, thanks for your second born, your giving spirit and the macaroni and cheese.

To the late Pastor Floyd H. Gayles, Pastor Roy McCraw, and the St. James Baptist Church, thank you for helping to shape my foundation of faith.

To Pastor Anthony G. Maclin and the Sanctuary at Kingdom Square, formerly the Glendale Baptist church, especially the newsletter ministry, thank you for nurturing my further growth in my faith walk. Pastor, your pursuit to be like Jesus and manifest ministry is awe inspiring.

To my co-workers-turned-friends: Tiffani Whittacker, Khaisha Charles, Lydia Grier and Carole Rawlison who left me in the school's computer lab many days to begin this novel. Thank you for encouraging my vision. We have given so much to the children of Prince George's County Public Schools. We taught many students how to dream. Now, be fearless and go after your own!

Thank you to Sister Faye and Cassandra, formerly of Sisterspace and Books in Washington, DC. You are so supportive of writers and readers alike. Thanks for first giving a group of writers a space. To Valerie Jean, and the Writer's Workshop crew: JC, CN, EB, RN, RM, and RJ, you have created a safe and productive place for writers like myself to develop my craft.

To my Soulfood Sisters past and present: Andrea Phillips, Erica Dixon, Rhonda Carter, Stacey Bryant, Denise Moore, Antonia Johnson, Bridgette Buckner, Romica Brashear, Kijafa Parker, Aaron Hearn, Michelle Dacanay, Patricia Biela, Nichol Galloway, Giovonni Smith, Janulyn Lennon, Traci Price and Cecelia Toulson, our monthly meetings are like a subscription to a great magazine. It leaves me full of advice, tips and wisdom. The Bible says, 'iron sharpens iron.' You have all shaped my life. I am sharp because you are.

Finally, to my Urban Christian family, Kendra Norman-Bellamy and my Managing Editor, Joylynn Jossel, thank you for mentoring a newbie.

Epigraph

But by an equality, that now at this time your abundance may be a supply for their want, that their abundance also may be a supply for your want; that these may be equality: As it is written, He that had gathered much had nothing over; and he that had gathered little had no lack.

II Corinthians 8:14-15

Chapter 1

Go

Willie Green, the pastor of Harvest Baptist Church, watched as one of his most trusted deacons, Charley Thompson, loosened the loop of his striped necktie just enough to release the top button of his dress shirt.

"This is wrong! You can't go combining churches to suit yourself," said Charley over the chatter of personal opinion, that filled the room as Willie walked up the aisle of neatly divided folding chairs that were placed in the church conference room for the meeting.

Apparently, Charley had heard the rumor going around the church that his pastor and his new bride of two weeks, Vanessa Morton Green, had plans to unite their respective churches; Harvest Baptist and Mt. Pleasant Baptist. The union of the two churches was supposed to be taking place at the beginning of the new year. *I only told two people, one of the elders and the church clerk,* Willie thought as he relieved his arm of his Bible, note pad and random notes his members had passed him after service. He knew exactly who had spilled the beans.

When Pastor Green announced today's important Deacons and Trustees meeting which was to be held immediately after the day's services, he knew this would be the outlet for his officers to express their displeasure. Willie was surprised that Deacon Thompson had sat through the entire 11:00 a.m. service, which was not a part of his Sunday ritual since he usually opted for the sparsely attended Sunrise service followed by Sunday school. Facilitating service was a deacon's primary job; Sunrise Service was Deacon Thompson's shift. Willie figured Charley preferred to be in and out of church before most members rolled in for 11a.m. worship. *This meeting was inconvenient to Charley,* Willie thought, and probably so were these plans to relocate the church twenty minutes away from their current facility.

"We are all God's people, Charles. This is just a way to combine God's people," said Sister Mae Richardson, the church clerk at Harvest Baptist for the past 20 years.

"Pastor Green is a good man and he has married a beautiful woman; both in body and in spirit. We need to consider whatever it is our Pastor has to say," Mae continued.

"I thought this was a Deacons and Trustees meeting," said Charley.

"If you are referring to me, Charley Thompson, I will have you know that Pastor Green asked me to be here. I will be providing a summary of the minutes for the congregation." Mae was looking directly at Charley, who was trying his best to ignore her.

"Well it just seems as if things have already been decided without going through the proper procedures," he said.

What are the proper procedures for combining churches? Willie thought remaining aloof to their conversation. *Is it something the board should vote on if it's the will of God?*

Almost everything at Harvest Baptist Church had been

voted on since he had been Pastor. Anything of importance, that is, like the time Cree Anderson and her three
little ones were about to be evicted from their apartment.
The board decided to allow her and the children to stay in
the nursing room at the front of the church for three days
while she waited for her people up north to wire her the
back rent so she could at least get her belongings from the
landlord, who was keeping her things hostage. Willie had
to admit that his deacons had been conditioned to think
that it was their job to vote and to pray.

A processional of men began to fill the room signifying
the end to the unofficial meet and greet time after Sunday
morning worship. A church meeting wasn't official without
the six member Deacon board. As they entered, everyone
could hear the light banter that reflected the camaraderie
that has grown between them.

Clyde Simmons and John Ramsey, both from North
Carolina, came to the area after their tour of duty in
Korea in the late 1950's and had been with the church
nearly forty years. Phillip Brown joined the board after accepting Christ at the insistence of his wife to, as she put it,
"bring his lazy butt to church" in the first place.

Buster Johnson, the newest member of the board, was
an old neighborhood friend of the Pastor. At that time
they called him Conk head Buster for the lye-laced chem-
ical he would comb through his hair monthly to process
it. The unrelenting strength of this concoction left his
medium length hair with neither style nor body but rather
stripped it of any curl or luster of his hair's natural state.
So like many other conk heads, he slicked his hair straight
back.

Most of the deacons wore dark navy or black suits except Buster who adorned a royal blue suit. Willie knew
first hand that Buster possessed every color suit in the
rainbow with matching shoes, which was one of the rea-

sons Buster was considered a shade off. In their hands and over their arms, the deacons carried all-weather top coats accompanied by Dobb's hats that completed the Deacon look. The average age of these men was 60, which was ten years older than Pastor Willie Green. Despite the difference in the ages, these men loved and respected their Pastor and usually trusted his judgment.

Out of all of deacons, Charley Thompson had grown closest to the Pastor during his tenure at Harvest Baptist. Charley kept him advised and well informed about the happenings, not only at their church, but also at other churches in the immediate area. Since Charley lived only a few blocks away, he regularly maintained the grounds of Harvest Baptist during the week.

Harvest Baptist church was a small but sturdy brick front church built in the middle of Lincoln Avenue in Capitol Heights, Maryland, a town on the outskirts of the District of Columbia. The commercial part of this town was literally built up around the church after the construction of the subway station, a couple of blocks north. Narrow streets and restricted parking was a fate they shared with their DC counterparts. A string of gated, split level homes sat in the next block away from the church. Parishioners had to share parking with the other establishments that occupied the street—a laundry mat, a dollar store and a Quick Mart .

The church did not have many other places besides the conference room to hold a meeting this size other than the sanctuary. This room like the other rooms in the rear of the church was built to serve many purposes in a time when living rooms and store fronts were being converted into sanctuaries to have worship services. This was the same room Mae Richardson brought the new members who joined the church to receive information and schedules of the next baptism. This is also where the four members of the Pastor's aide committee met every second Saturday. On any given Saturday, one may find the Woman's Auxiliary planning their next shopping trip or the Willing Workers planning their next service project. The only other rooms in the church included the pastor's office, a nurse's room, a fellowship hall and kitchen.

Willie had spoken to Deacon Pace, the chairman of the Deacon board, over the phone to explain his position and form an alliance with him. Although this was a joint board meeting, the members of the Mother's board were also asked to stay for the meeting. Willie had figured out long ago that it was important to have the women of the church on his side.

There was never any discussion about the seating arrangement for meetings like these. The members usually took the seats from front to back according to the level of importance their title carried in the church. Paul Grant, who looked up to Willie as a mentor and the next likely candidate to be considered a young deacon or trustee-in-training, was sitting in the middle of the room and took the lead by giving up his seat to one of the mothers. A few of the Deacons began to follow suit in Paul's gentlemanly act. Deacon Charley Thompson remained seated.

Willie took a seat on the edge of the old rectangle table and began fidgeting nervously with his gold engraved writing pen that he always wore attached to the collar of his robe like he may need to jot down a note or make a last minute change to his sermon outline. His robe that he now wore unzipped was black, trimmed in purple. The fact that he still wore it showed that he did not take the time to retire to his office after service.

Willie could only remember being nervous like this one other time; a time when he had sat before this very same board ten years ago and gave a speech of intention as a pastoral candidate. The church required him to preach four consecutive Sundays and teach Sunday School, which lead him to the intention speech, which he prepared like a lawyer's closing argument. He was still a minister at his home church, Gilead Baptist, with growing responsibility, but not yet a Pastoral Assistant. *No church is going to elect a nearly 40-year-old, unmarried minister, basically straight out of college,* he remembered thinking. Being full-time in school made him inexperienced at the day to day operations in the church, and being single, in some people's opinion, made him inexperienced in a whole different facet of life.

Willie had been preparing for ministry since he was in his thirties. That is when he had announced to his family at a family reunion that he wanted to be a minister to almost no support. Preachers didn't bring prestige to an immediate family of doctors and college professors. Everyone in his immediate family took the long path through school and usually stayed there to teach something. The higher up they went in academia, the farther they seemed to get away from the teachings of Christ and the church. They could not see why he wanted to waste his time in a black church that did not want to pay their minister an hourly wage for his time.

Willie had what many in this area considered a good federal government job in the District of Columbia. It didn't matter what a person did for the Federal Government in those days; the steady check and benefits were enough for many to build their hopes and dreams on. Willie knew the Lord had called him to preach and he spent nearly ten years processing grant applications to pay his monthly bills and have enough money to one day pay his way through seminary.

At that time, Willie carried a torch for the secretary in his building named Kay. They spent many work hours talking about everything from sports to religion. Kay was a bold, often brash, woman on the exterior that wasn't romantically interested in the straight-laced Willie, who worked a nine to five job and dreamed of attending seminary at night. They became friends sharing lunch together throughout the work week.

Willie was fascinated with how this statuesque beauty wrote loving and nurturing words to her imprisoned boyfriend who she admitted had been abusive to her on more than one occasion in the past. He wished someone like her would speak the lover's language to him one day.

Willie didn't entirely understand the attraction he felt toward Kay. He only knew he loved being in her presence, which scared him, because aside from his puppy love days, he had only felt that way toward God. He chased Kay while running from his call to preach figuring he had plenty of time to do what God wanted him to do. Many of his close friends and relatives thought Willie and Kay were an item because of the amount of time they spent with one another; Willie said nothing to persuade them otherwise. He started accompanying her to bars and seedy dance clubs after work, watching with a knot in his chest as she drank and danced herself into a hypnotic state; yet he was always there to make sure she got home safely. He felt the more time he spent with her, the more she would eventually care for him in the way he cared for her. He thought their relationship had changed when Kay eventually stopped talking about her boyfriend, at least in his presence.

One day he told her he loved her. It was nothing that he had planned; it just popped out of his mouth one night. She just kissed his nose and patted his cheek as she often did and said, "You're a good puppy, Willie Green, but in no way do you and I add up to be right. You shouldn't even be with me now. Some of us were meant for better. You don't want to share my hell."

Kay haunted Willie. It wounded his heart as well as his ego to hear that she didn't feel the same, but he knew she was right about their relationship not working. She became more vocal about her plans to be married after her boyfriend's release from jail. As much as Willie enjoyed his time with her, that knot in his chest that he always felt when he was with her was a physical sign of his conflict in desire. Willie realized he had wasted enough time trying to make something out of nothing. Kay had her boyfriend and he had his studies to attend to.

Willie eventually went to seminary. Afterwards he left the government and attended Howard University School of Divinity full time and heard his lover's voice. It was the Lord telling Willie to wait on Him. The voice of the Lord was speaking to Willie more than ever during his time in graduate school. He became confident not only in his gift to interpret scriptures and preach the gospel, but also to counsel those in need; all the characteristics of a good pastor.

The Lord allowed Kay to cross his path again as she attended his home church on a Sunday that he preached in his Pastor's absence. This time instead of trying to possess her, he tried and succeeded in saving her soul. Willie followed his heart and continued his studies receiving a Master's Degree in Divinity. He was ready to go into ministry full time.

"Can someone go get the Trustees, please? I promise to keep my announcements brief," Willie said.

Charley got up to retrieve the Trustees from the Nurse's Room where they counted the money the church had taken in during collection each Sunday. He was considered a member of the Trustee board as well, partly because he was Treasurer of Sunday School, but mainly because he wanted to know at all times what went on with the church's finances. As the Trustees began to align the back of the room and Charley regained his seat in the front, Pastor Green began his monologue.

"As the Pastor of the church, I am responsible for your souls, and committed to winning more souls for Christ. I am dedicated to Ministry for the Lord, and I will go where the Lord tells me to go. My wife and I would like to thank you all for the gifts and sentiments that we received during our wedding season. You can imagine that it is a challenge for both of us to foster our new marriage leading hectic lives of being Pastors to our own respective churches. Early on, the devil brought about fear and doubt about our decision to marry. It was hard to pick a date for the wedding around preaching engagements and ministry meetings. We knew we had to sacrifice time with each other to maintain our vows to God's church. It took some serious prayer." He took what seemed to be his first breath since he started. He sat still, scanning the faces in the room for their understanding.

"While in Hawaii on our honeymoon, the Lord spoke to me saying basically that I have answered your prayers and addressed many of your church's needs. Strengthen your ministry now, minister together." Willie continued before anyone could question or comment. "We all know we must sacrifice; and we should be willing to go where the Lord leads. He told me as clear as the Hawaiian sky that we should combine our congregations over at Mt. Pleasant."

Willie continued listing the benefits of uniting churches. The hour was getting late and Deacon Thompson looked as if he would burst if he didn't speak.

"This just seems like you are bringing this on us all of a sudden. You and your wife have been courting for months before now. You mean to tell me that this discussion about what to do with your churches never came up while you were dating?" Deacon Thompson sighed loudly, trying to think and fill the air with sound so not to lose his space in the conversation. "This just seems like a personal decision made by you and the misses."

"We knew a change was imminent," Pastor replied. "We prayed about whether Vanessa would step down as pastor of Mt. Pleasant, or if we, as a couple, should start another church. This was a decision we were not going to make hastily. We had planned to continue the pastorate of our separate churches until everything calmed down after the wedding and the Lord helped us decide. Call us selfish, but we just wanted to get married first. If anything, we were sure we loved one another and wanted to be married."

Paul Grant cleared his throat loudly and fidgeted as if he felt the conversation was getting too personal. "What does this mean for us, Pastor Green?"

"I want Harvest to know that I haven't hidden anything from this church. As a church we have prayed for financial relief. The Lord blessed us in the past ten years since I have been Pastor here to pay off the mortgage. Then we prayed for much needed repair and renovation. We have been trying for seven plus years to accumulate a Building and Maintenance fund. We wondered what was the problem. Why were we not reaching the goal? Face it, the building is old and in need of some major repair. Everyone thought I was crazy when I asked everyone to begin to pray for a ministry that would glorify God, and not just for a physical building we could boast about. That was the right direction; He has answered us." Pastor Green declared, standing to his feet. "The Lord wants us to strengthen our ministry and expand our sanctuary beyond Lincoln Avenue in Capitol Heights. He has met our need but we must do it His way."

"Pastor, I hear what you are saying," Deacon Thompson said. He looked toward his fellow deacons for support.

"But are we going to vote? I personally think we are fine where we are," he continued.

"Pastor Green, I've been at Harvest Baptist for most of my adult life," Mae spoke up. "Raymond and Louanne Bell owned a tailor shop right here. He was a tailor and she was a seamstress. When they got up in age they gave their property to Reverend Ignatious Harris, the first Pastor of Harvest Baptist church; God Bless his soul. He came all the way from Kansas in 1931 with his wife, Ellen, and their two children. They say he used to be a street preacher on the corner of Lincoln Avenue until the Bells heard him. Changed their whole lives," Mae said, reciting the history of the church. She had committed it to memory after reciting it year after year on the church's anniversary that one would have sworn she was a member back then. "Sister Mae, we all know the church's history, but God wants to add another chapter," Willie said.

"I'm devoted to my church," Mae Richardson said. "I'm just a little concerned. We got our own way of doing things. We got our own Deacons, ushers and choirs. I'm sure the big old church up on that hill got many choirs, boards and committees. They surely must have several clerks, maybe even secretaries," Mae Richardson said.

"See, I'm not the only one who don't think this is right," said Deacon Thompson. He had new fire in his eyes. "We all have been dedicated to serving in our positions in this church."

"That's not it. I'm not concerned about my job here as church clerk and I'm not saying I won't go with Pastor Green," Sister Richardson said. Willie knew she did not want to appear as defiant as Deacon Thompson. "It's just that we may not fit in. I mean, we may not find opportunities to serve like we have here."

Mae Richardson had been church clerk at Harvest the

entire ten years Willie Green had been Pastor. After the death of her husband, Frank, and as her retirement from the school system, she spent most of her time in the church. Her son, Albert, knew when he couldn't reach his mama at home, she would be at the church. She even had a small desk in the corner of the Pastor's office. She wrote down his appointments and set up the calendar of events for the church. She was the one who fixed his tray of water and orange juice for Sunday service. She was the one who made sure one of his three robes was laundered and ready to wear for preaching engagements. She was the liaison between the sick, poor, battered, homeless, and bereaved and the man they called Pastor. So in a way, she was a little displaced when he told her he was going to get married, and yes, she was unsure about the move to Mt. Pleasant. Willie thought that she probably felt the way a mother does when her children leave the nest.

"Pastor, what can we do to prepare our hearts and minds for where God wants to take us?" Paul said to an audible sigh by Deacon Thompson.

"I hear all of your concerns," Pastor Green stated. "There is a place for us all in the combined church. The Lord spoke to me with this vision. I'm sure He will speak to you also; just pray. It will take some getting use to, even for me. I know we have thoughts and I know we have questions, but the hour is getting late. It being the first Sunday of October, we have three good months to prepare. We don't plan to start our combined services until the first of the year. Until then, we will have services here as usual and regular church meetings to address your concerns. Before we go, let us hear what our chairman of the Deacon board has to say."

Deacon Pace leaned forward to propel himself out of the chair. At 71, Deacon Pace was the only one who dated back to the Bell era. He continued to drive himself to church, kneel for every altar call, and help with the service of communion. He was a man of quiet wisdom. When he spoke, everyone listened to hear the knowledge that years of serving the Lord faithfully had to offer.

"I support our pastor in his judgment. If he tells us that the Lord wants us to go to that church on the hill, well sir, I'm going." Deacon Pace took his seat, which signified he had finished what he had to say.

"Let us pray now, and when we go home, continue to pray." Willie said. "I plan to call a special church meeting for the whole congregation no later than the end of next week to say the same thing that was said here. We'll discuss things more then. Deacon Thompson, why don't you close us out in prayer."

Usually when Deacon Thompson prayed it was like running a marathon. He would pace himself, making sure to count every blessing and petition God to bless everyone. He'd ask for God's traveling grace over the congregated souls and for a space in God's kingdom. In the midst of his prayer, he would compliment God on His grace, mercy, forgiveness and power. But at 2:30 that afternoon, Deacon Thompson prayed a short prayer, "Lord, help us."

Chapter 2

Home Training

Twenty minutes down the road, Pastor Vanessa Green, still in the glow of her honeymoon, met with the members of her own staff: Luella Banks, Vanessa's secretary; Keisha Morton, her sister in real life and in ministry; and Mt. Pleasant's two deacons and four trustees. The sum total of their church's executive board, met their Pastor for an emergency meeting early Sunday morning before service. Most of them, ready to brief their Pastor on what she missed while she was away in Hawaii, were surprised, but not stunned, when Vanessa shared with them the vision to combine churches over at Mt. Pleasant. Some thought that the way Vanessa ruled the pulpit would surely translate into her marriage. Her announcement was met with applause and a hug from Luella, who feared that Vanessa would surely leave their church to be with her husband because to her, a woman's place was with her husband. Vanessa felt that if her board was so agreeable, then she was ready to let her congregation in on the news.

"So you see beloved, this is God's plan for our church. Mt. Pleasant shouldn't have a problem with God's plan.

We just got to move over a little closer in the pews. How many people in here realize that you either move over or God will move you out the way? You can't stop the will of God. It's like a mighty steam roller. GlorytaGod." Vanessa's face began to flush with a tremendous heat that engulfed her. It was the Spirit filling her soul. Most ministers took advantage of that energy to drive a message home by "hooping" a passionate, sometimes sing- songy, conclusion to a sermon. In Vanessa's case, she usually spat the words at her congregation like a fire breathing dragon.

Vanessa fit her announcement to the church comfortably within her sermon. She preached about Abraham's willingness to sacrifice his son, Issac, at God's request, and in doing so proved himself faithful to God. She equated his obedience to God's will and his personal sacrifice, to the obedience and sacrifice they would have to make as a church when they combined with Harvest Baptist. It was dramatic but effective. Despite the slight hum from their Hammon B-3 organ at certain points of the sermon, one could hear a pin drop where there were usually a chorus of "amens." She was satisfied, now that everyone at Mt. Pleasant knew. Those who missed this sermon would have to get the tape or wait for the news on the gospel grapevine, she thought.

"Let's look to the Lord to be dismissed," Vanessa said, offering blessings and benediction over the congregated souls.

Vanessa stood in the middle of the wide isle greeting members after service. Out the corner of her eye she was searching for her younger sister, Keisha. As much as Keisha tried to convince Vanessa that she was ready to follow in her footsteps, she was never around when real ministry was going on. At that moment, she regretted not mentoring more ministers for her ministerial staff, but it wasn't like the people at Mt. Pleasant were exactly jumping over pews to accept the call from God either. The only people she routinely relied on to take her place in the pulpit when she needed a break was her now husband, Willie Green, good friend, Benjamin Rawls, and a 78-year-old retired minister and friend of her father's, Reverend Owens.

Reverend Owens had taken over her duties as pastor for the past three Sundays while she had tied the knot and had gone on her honeymoon. Reverend Owens was very conservative with a very low voice. He repeated his sentences over and over again as if to try and stretch a thirty minute message to at least an hour. Many felt his services lacked emotion. Vanessa's own sister shared that in her opinion Reverend Owens made the Good News seem like a bad lecture. You didn't need a line graph to see the decline in attendance anytime the congregation knew Vanessa would be away or not preaching.

Vanessa Green needed help with the receiving line of members that snaked around the altar. She desperately needed to escape to the bathroom to relieve herself, but she knew there were some people who had been waiting for the past three weeks since she had been away for a chance to talk to her. Then there were the well-wishers whom she and her sister have often jokingly referred to as the Pastor's Paparazzi because of their nature to hound her. The paparazzi wanted to be seen with and recognized by their Pastor. Several members who have come to see Vanessa during office hours have often remarked that they have wanted to shake her hand after Sunday service only to find themselves behind Sister So-and-So who wanted to show Vanessa a scrapbook full of vacation pictures or someone who wanted to cry on Vanessa's shoulder about one thing or the other instead of making an appointment to see her privately themselves.

Vanessa gave the woman's hand in front of her a reassuring pat and turned to Luella, who was never far from her side. "Get Sister Masiri's full name and assign her to the Watchcare Ministry. She needs to get a call and Godly encouragement about Bible study and upcoming activities." Vanessa leaned in further. "And I don't know what you're going to tell the rest of these people, but I got to go to the ladies room badly."

Vanessa kissed her fingers tips and waved good-bye with a look of regret to those in the line before taking off down the side aisle. Members congregated in groups parted like the Red Sea when they saw their Pastor trying to get by. They couldn't help talking about the news. Some were taking the announcement in stride like her executive board, while others were outraged and couldn't wait until they were at least outside to gossip about the Pastor's motives. Vanessa heard one woman say to her husband, "If Mr. Green had been handling his business like he should have on a honeymoon, they wouldn't have time for any visions." Then he replied to her, "That's just like a woman though, as soon as you get a man you can't wait to combine everything. I mean, I know they are married and everything, but their churches are not common property."

Vanessa cleared her throat loudly. She had to smile at the look of sheer horror on their faces when they realized that she was behind their barricade across the aisle and could have possibly overheard what they were saying. *That ought to teach them about gossiping in the church,* Vanessa thought, *and lead their butts to repentance.*

Before Vanessa could turn the corner into the side hallway that led to her office and personal bathroom, she came face-to-face with one of the mothers of the church. Mother Thomlin, like her own mother, always gave Vanessa the feeling that she wasn't quite grown yet. Vanessa could not figure out how to get around her expansive backside without being rude or around her cane without disrupt-

ing it, so she decided her bladder could stand the imminent interruption.

"Excuse me, Mother Thomlin," Vanessa said.

"Pastor, I was going to find your number and call you
tonight," Mother Thomlin said.

"Why Mother Thomlin, is something the matter?"

"How do you know for a fact that God wants you to
change your daddy's church again?" Mother Thomlin said
as if to remind Vanessa that the church wasn't hers to do
with as she pleased.

There were rumors that Vanessa Morton ran out the
founding members of Mt. Pleasant Church, who served
under her daddy's leadership. The truth was that a lot of
them had left in droves when she, as they put it, "tried to
change Jesus' style" or accused her of becoming too contemporary. Vanessa didn't like the contemporary label.
Mt. Pleasant was huge in stature but had a transient popu-
lation since Vanessa became Pastor. She consistently maintained a membership of close to 200 members though, of
which eighty percent were women. These women came to
Mt. Pleasant hardened by life and didn't get offended by
weekly reality checks in the sermon. For a while, she felt
she was running a refuge s for abused women Sunday to
Sunday. She had come to accept that as her ministry
focus.

Vanessa knew where all the contention between she
and her more seasoned members began. She started a re-
molding project after hearing a guest preacher from
Philadelphia lead a seminar on financing church renova-
tions. To Vanessa, she was just doubling the size of the
sanctuary to fit the land God had blessed them with and
to prepare for the members that were sure to join after
coming to Mt. Pleasant and hearing her preach. Now she
realized it was hard enough trying to please the members
she had.

"Like I said, Mother Thomlin, we've been praying for a long time. God revealed His will to my husband during his daily devotion time and I received confirmation. I woke up with the Valley of Dry Bones on my mind, the very same series I just finished preaching before I left to get married, but with new revelation. My husband was meditating on those same scriptures."

The woman was shaking her head as if Pastor Green's explanation would not suffice. "But how did you know that it was God saying to combine churches instead of just a regular ole dream?"

"Mother Thomlin, by now I should know how the Lord speaks to me," Vanessa said, losing patience. "Willie and I both felt that each of our churches was losing zeal. We are content at Mt. Pleasant to just come to church, hear the word, and go home. That's why I've been pushing outreach, missions work and evangelism. My husband's church is a small church, but they are used to giving their time to help others. They can be a great influence on us. Read Ezekiel 37 when you get home. It showed us a solution to breathe new life in our ministry. Verses eighteen through twenty-two describe some of the confusion you are going through right now. The Lord told us to join our churches into one, alright, Mother Thomlin?"

Mother Thomlin nodded and hobbled away as well as the few in her entourage, as if homework verses added to Vanessa's usual prescription of verses from each sermon were more than they bargained for.

"See you next Sunday?" Vanessa called out.

"Lord willing and the creek don't rise," Mother Thomlin said.

Vanessa hugged another member at the entrance of the hallway then made a dash for the pastor's lounge.

After using the facilities, Vanessa walked to the adjacent conference room to find Keisha standing with a man that

Vanessa remembered accepting into the fold at Mt. Pleasant recently during one of her altar calls.

"Hi, Vanessa, I mean, Pastor Green. This is Darryl
Miller. He joined Mt. Pleasant not too long ago," Keisha
said, standing just off the gentlemen's shoulder with such
a wide smile that suggested to Vanessa that she was interested in more than his salvation.

Vanessa widened her eyes as to say, "That's nice, but why
does Brother Darryl merit a personal tour of my conference room?" Besides a few officers, no members were allowed in the back on Sundays.

"Have you met with the new members, I mean the ones
who joined today?" Vanessa asked her sister.

"Oh yes, they filled out the information cards, right
here," Keisha said raising the folder in her arm. "We
prayed with them, made sure that they were sure about
their salvation and sent them on their way."

Vanessa didn't have the energy to be mad with her sister
right now. She wanted to say, "When did *we* have the responsibility of meeting with new members?" Vanessa had
told her many times she was too distracted. Keisha shared
with her sister a year and a half ago that she was called to
ministry but hadn't committed to any formal training
since. Vanessa thought that after all God had brought her
sister through, He could really use her if she wasn't constantly on the prowl for what she wanted, which right now
was a husband. "Therein lies the problem," Vanessa had
told her many times. "You shouldn't be the one searching." Vanessa looked over Keisha's latest prospect. He was
just her sister's type; tall and lean. He had such a smooth
complexion that looked more like poured milk chocolate
than skin, but as far as they knew, he was a babe in Christ
that didn't need the distraction of a new relationship either.

"So, Darryl, how do you like Mt. Pleasant?" Vanessa asked.

"The services are great. I haven't made it out to Bible study yet, but like I told your sister, we are so blessed to have a pastor whom the Lord speaks to."

"You say that as if the Lord doesn't speak to you as well," Vanessa said.

He swallowed hard. "I'm sure he does. Sometimes it's a little hard to tell. I guess what I meant to say was, that we are blessed to have a pastor who follows the lead of the Lord and I support the vision the Lord has given you."

"Well thank you, Brother." Vanessa said, thinking, *Isn't he the charmer?* "You've blessed my soul. Now we have to get you into Bible study class to bless your soul. Studying the word of God will help you to hear his voice. Tell me about your family. Do they attend Mt. Pleasant with you?"

"No, It's just me. My parents never really attended church much, but my grandmother on my momma's side used to make sure I attended church with her occasionally. She attended Redemption Baptist. I got baptized there."

"Thank God for grandmothers. So you're single?" Vanessa said, noticing a frantic look from her sister as if Vanessa was hounding the man.

"Yes ma'am," he replied.

"Single to serve. Praise God. We could use some dedicated single brothers in the service. We have an excellent Single's Ministry, don't we Minister Morton, led by my sister here. I'm sure she has told you all about it. Her sessions will let you in on why you should dedicate your life to the Lord and trust in Him to reveal your mate."

Once again, Keisha shot her sister a look that she ignored. *That will teach her to entertain guests in my conference room,* she thought. Vanessa gave him her best welcome to

Mt. Pleasant smile. "Minister Morton, I'll talk to you later. Are you coming over my house?"

"No, I think we are going to take in a bite to eat," Keisha said.

Good, Vanessa thought, she was tired and ready to go home.

Vanessa entered the foyer of her house and dropped her keys, purse and Bible bag on the table before hanging up her coat in the hallway closet. She relaxed herself on the leather couch in the living room and closed her eyes in an attempt to adjust her mind to the stark silence of her house as opposed to the noisiness of the church. She flipped through a mental roledex of members with whom she spoke to during the course of the day to determine which ones she would have to follow up with. There were no deaths, hospital visits or any other catastrophe that needed her immediate attention. She thanked the Lord that she could stay in her lounging position a while longer.

Vanessa couldn't help but think about her sister, Keisha, and how they were very different growing up, but led by God to the same place. Keisha was in her mid thirties, which Vanessa thought was the prime of her spiritual purpose. Vanessa thought a person's spiritual life had stages just like their physical and emotional growth and development. They start out with home training. That's where their spiritual roots were established by the people around them. Either a person was brought up in the church or not; either they saw examples of true Christians or not. Then there were the BS (or back sliding) years; the time Vanessa figured was between high school and middle adulthood when a person feels immortal and live like they don't need Christ. Those who made it out of the BS phase and went through a personal restoration period were ready for their Godly purpose.

The Morton sisters were naturally brought up in church being the daughters of a pastor. Vanessa and Keisha would go to church with their Grandma Cecily, her father's mother, while her father tended to the congregation at Mt. Pleasant and her mother tended to him. Keisha, nearly ten years younger than Vanessa, hated church and blamed the institution for her parents' long hours and lack of attention, but Vanessa loved it. At that time the actual church service wasn't the exciting part, but the occasion of church was the ritual Vanessa looked forward to so much.

Grandma Cecily lived with them after her Grandpa Miller died. She was a thin and spry older lady that was so accustomed to doing everything for her husband, that she couldn't imagine living by herself when he died. They lived in a three bedroom semi-detached house in Forrestville, MD, which at that time was considered upper middle class for an African-American family. Grandma Cecily took on the role of a nanny for Vanessa and her sister and a house keeper and maid for the family as her way of paying for her board and keep.

Saturdays would be spent preparing for Sunday church service and dinner. The Saturday before the first and third Sundays, Grandma Cecily, Vanessa and Keisha would walk two blocks to Inez Beauty Salon at the corner plaza and spend all day receiving a shampoo, blow-dry, and press job. Despite the head full of natural curls on both Vanessa and Keisha's head, they were made to sit through the absurd process of pressing it straight just to curl it again. Despite all that time spent at the hairdresser, Grandma Cecily never let the sun set before preparing the bulk of Sunday dinner so that she wouldn't dishonor the Sabbath Day by slaving in the kitchen after church.

Sunday morning had its own special atmosphere. Everything seemed calmer, kind of hushed and still, as opposed to the week where the girls had school followed by various church activities. Grandma Cecily would wake and shower before Vanessa and Keisha even awoke. Then she would wake them up and usher them to a tub of Mr. Bubbles bubble bath. While they bathed, Vanessa could remember smelling breakfast being prepared downstairs and hear her grandmother singing Mahalia Jackson style to the Sunday morning spirituals on the radio. Before they were allowed to come down and eat, they had to have on their undergarments, which included underwear, tights and a slip. Vanessa always remembered wearing some type of pantyhose to church even in the summertime because her grandmother could not stand women or girls to go bare legged in the sanctuary. Their plates would be waiting at the round kitchen table where Grandma Cecily would inspect the girls' face, ears and hands. Breakfast could not have lasted more than ten minutes because they spent so much time grooming.

Vanessa would grudgingly fling the chosen garment over her head and sit on the bed to watch her grandmother. From then on, Vanessa's appearance was not her own. She knew her grandmother would twist and pull and tug and fuss over her appearance for the rest of the day until she was allowed to change clothes. She thought all the accessories her grandmother picked out for her were silly, but on Grandma Cecily, they were glamorous.

Her grandmother had a handbag to match every pair of shoes. She always had a fresh handkerchief and several starlight mints in her bag. Grandma Cecily wore hats that made her look like a movie star. She had lots of hats from the wide brim styles to the stingy brimmed pill box styles. Even after spending hours in the salon, her grandmother would press the hat in place over the crown of her head and affix it with pins. Vanessa was hard on a hairstyle. Although Grandma Cecily would tie her hair with a scarf at night, it always seemed scattered about in the morning. Her grandmother would relentlessly brush her matted curls into ponytail combinations over her head.

Church was one of the few occasions that Vanessa's grandmother would take the car cover off and drive the Oldsmobile. The Oldsmobile had been her husband's car. Vanessa did not remember her Grandpa Miller because he died when she was an infant. At that time, Mt. Pleasant was half the size it is now. Grandma would march Vanessa and Keisha proudly to the third pew where they were expected to sit still until the end of service, which was nearly impossible. Her grandma was on the Mother's Board, the older and well respected women of the church who dominated devotion time with testimonies that years of living afforded them. Back then, Mt. Pleasant had huge stained glass windows that were apparently sealed shut because Vanessa never remembered them opened or the circulation of air conditioning. Church fans with advertising from various cleaners and funeral homes were persistently fighting the heat like the continuous fight against the oppression of Hell itself. Those summer services seemed endless to Vanessa then.

Vanessa got the worst spankings in her life for misbehaving in church. Like the time she was caught playing in the bathroom with Emma Thomas or for what her grandmother considered playing church while in church. One day while the deacon prayed during devotion time, Vanessa began to feel the Spirit move within her like a bird fluttering in her chest. It was something about the deacon's promise to meet Jesus face to face when everybody got to heaven that made Vanessa want to flap her wings. She let that bird inside her chest soar to heaven, and in doing so, she came to know the freedom her grandmother and the other men and women of the church felt when they got "happy." She began to respond to that feeling like everyone else by calling out, hallelujah and by rocking back and forth and waving her hand. Her sister, thinking her outbursts were a part of a game, mimicked the Spirit-filled shrieks and began jumping around, which alerted their grandma who was caught up in prayer herself. Grandma Cecily usually would only have to stare at Vanessa and her sister or swat their leg with her purse strap to get them to behave. There were rare occasions when her Grandma would yank her down the isle to the doom in the ladies bathroom.

Keisha immediately stopped when Grandma Cecily set her gaze upon her, but Vanessa didn't. Before Vanessa knew it, Grandma Cecily had her down the isle. She barely got Vanessa through the bathroom door before she exposed her bare bottom for a "whopping." She didn't have the words to explain then what she didn't completely understand herself so she accepted the punishment. Afterwards, Grandma Cecily brought her back down the isle as if nothing had happened and drew Vanessa close to her. In the cradle of her grandmother's shoulder, Vanessa settled down and her Grandmother resumed fanning both of them.

Vanessa and Keisha had special training as the Pastor's daughters to smile on command and greet complete strangers and pray in front of the congregation. Everyone could tell 11-year-old Vanessa had a special gift when she prayed. She could move the emotions of the crowd with the modulation of her voice like a lot of preachers. When her grandmother passed, both she and her sister were asked to do a tribute. Vanessa's tribute ended up being her grandmother's eulogy as she spoke about how special her grandmother was to her. She talked about how when she was feeling down, or had a fight with her sister, or when her parents said she couldn't do something, that all she had to do was get a hug from her grandmother and everything seemed to be okay.

Vanessa knew more than anything that her grandmother was blessed and had found a place in God's kingdom but she also knew that her grandmother's favor in the sight of God didn't automatically cover her. She admonished everyone to press to the Lord the same way she did to her Grandma Cecily. By the time she was through, there wasn't a dry eye in the house, including her father's.

Adolescence hit Vanessa hard. At age sixteen, she had a face full of pimples, was tall and lanky, and very aggressive. Vanessa had an obsession with being a deacon at Mt. Pleasant. Her mom immediately told her "no", putting her in more suitable activities for girls in church, such as the Babes in Christ Choir as well as the junior debutantes. Vanessa enjoyed the choir but refused to be presented as a debutante, feeling that a bunch of girls marching around in white evening gowns had nothing to do with church. Her father, thinking Vanessa would be a far better deacon than some of the ones Mt. Pleasant had presently, and who had reduced the office to a few standard pew prayers, made Vanessa a deal. She could sit on the Deacon Board as long as she wrote a report telling him what was required by God of a deacon to the church. The catch, Vanessa soon would find out, was she also had to be presented in the Junior debutante ball as her mother wished.

It was hard for Vanessa to balance school, Bible study, long debutante practices and her pursuit to become a deacon. To top it off, her father was dragging her along to help him with his duties. She thought that he might be trying to discourage her from writing her report like some of the other deacons who kindly refused to sit down and talk to her about their office. One day while they were serving the Lord's Supper to an elderly man who needed assistance just holding his cup, Vanessa's father told her why he had been taking her with him for the past month.

"This is what ministry is all about, Vanessa," he told her. "You can't serve with your head in the books all the time. I'd love to study God's word also and read my books and commentaries all day and all night. It's not about what I'd like to do half of the time, but rather what God has called me to do all of the time, which is serve His people. I do believe you have a calling on your life. Your grandma told me she saw something special in you when you were very small. Now it's time that you pray about it until you are clear what it is you are called to do."

Vanessa still wrote a report on the office of deacon, studying books in her father's library, although she told her father she didn't know if she was called to be a deacon. She told him Mt. Pleasant wasn't ready for a female deacon anyway, and he told her if it was what she was really called to do, no one would be able to keep her from it. Her report read more like a manual, dispelling myths about deacons in the black church. Her father had her present her report to his current deacon board and to those in training. Even the deacons could see, once they got pass the fact that a young woman was training them, that she had a knack for teaching.

By the time Vanessa turned eighteen, she was sure of her calling to preach the Gospel. She had even preached at Mt. Pleasant, but many saw her as a novelty preacher, only to be enjoyed on special occasions. Although many in the congregation had that attitude, her father encouraged her. Vanessa knew people doubted her calling because she was a female and she always faced her doubts by studying more to affirm her confidence. She went off to college and majored in divinity with a minor in theological research and graduated at the top of her class.

Vanessa returned home an even more powerful orator

and a well versed theologian. She had also grown into the fullness of womanhood with a wildly exotic look of deep glossy brown skin, full lips and a nest of thick curly hair, which she always wore pulled back. When anyone at her home church asked what she planned to do with her degree, she would tell them that she wanted to become Pastor. Rumor spread like wildfire that little Vanessa Morton had returned to Mt. Pleasant from college to take over the pastorate from her daddy, who was now 73, like she was a part of some hostile faction looking to overthrow a government. The one thing her high priced education didn't prepare her for was the whims of church people.

The same people who loved her before she left for college didn't know what to make of her sitting in the pulpit every Sunday. She went to her father and announced her intentions to join his ministerial staff made up of a few traveling ministers, who had come by letter of recommendation from their home church to sit under her daddy's leadership while they were in town, and her daddy's friend, Reverend Owens. She told him that she eventually wanted to become pastor of Mt. Pleasant and asked him to help prepare her. Her father was proud of Vanessa's accomplishments, and from what Vanessa learned later was that he took a lot of criticism about encouraging his daughter to become a preacher. He expected that Vanessa would follow in his footsteps and agreed to teach her the finer points of the family business before he turned over the pastorate.

Despite her duties at the church, Vanessa felt amiss; she was not happy with Jesus alone. Sometimes loneliness was so real for Vanessa that it felt like a cloak weighing her down. Men at Mt. Pleasant wouldn't touch the Pastor's daughters with a ten foot pole. She never really imagined herself being more than a preacher of the Gospel. Seeing couples daily with their children opened up a floodgate of yearning that she never knew was welled up inside her. Although the Apostle Paul relished in the fact that he was single, she felt that being single hampered her ministry, especially when dealing with married couples and their relationships.

By the time Vanessa became the prime pastoral candidate when her father announced his retirement, she prayed that God would suppress her desire for a mate and help focus her attention on getting the position. Even though she was an almost certain heir to the Pastoral throne, the church required that a pool of candidates be presented when the office of Pastor became vacant. So, Vanessa prepared her Bible study lessons and sermon outlines, as well as studied the style of the only other candidate—a male. She had a gnawing feeling that this would be the perfect time for Mt. Pleasant to maintain the status quo of most Baptist churches and elect a male preacher. Instead, the recommendation was accepted by the joint board and congregation that Mt. Pleasant give their outgoing pastor a last and final gift of making his daughter the new pastor-elect. Her father became Pastor Emeritus and remained a vital Part of Mt. Pleasant until he died at age eighty-two. Her mother died six months later of an almost certain broken heart.

Vanessa and her sister grew close after the death of their parents. Vanessa hadn't seen her sister in over a year before their father's funeral because Keisha had found every excuse under the heavens to occupy her time, which included her then live-in boyfriend, Chris. No one could reason with her as she left Mt. Pleasant church altogether on her own carnal journey. At that time M-E-N spelled relief for her.

What Vanessa didn't know was her sister had sunk into a depression when she found out that Chris had fathered a child by another woman. Her circumstances led her to see

first hand the emptiness trying to live by the world's standards could bring. The combined weight of the lost of her
parents and bruises of a relationship gone sour led her
back to church. Keisha also returned to their childhood
home where, once again, she and Vanessa lived together.
Vanessa noticed her sister was a shell of the vibrant and
spunky person she once was. They prayed, cried and reminisced together. In six months time, God used Vanessa to
restore her sister's confidence in herself and faith in God.

Keisha felt that in return for her spiritual make over
that Vanessa needed to be made over physically. She encouraged Vanessa to lose the librarian look by getting rid
of the wing-tipped glasses and getting contact lenses. Keisha
felt that although she was too fragile to date, it didn't stop
Vanessa from finding a suitable mate. So she went to work
matching up credentials and interviewing candidates like
she worked for a dating service. Vanessa felt like a guinea
pig and urged her sister to stop the mad search for her
perfect mate. Vanessa thought something had to be wrong
the way Keisha was obsessed with Vanessa's social life. Finally, Keisha emerged with a candidate and Vanessa was set
up with a real estate agent named Montgomery Bennett.

Vanessa found Montgomery very kind and very attractive, but something was missing. He was accommodating
at first to Vanessa's position in the church and her preaching schedule. He was also good for lunch dates in the middle of the week or an occasional evening out . It was that
kind of tedious dating where they only talked on the
phone enough to arrange another date out of obligation.
There was no, "so how was your day or what are your plans
for the future?" Vanessa wished she could catapult their
rut into a relationship or something more heartfelt because she was way too busy for just an arbitrary date on
her calendar.

Montgomery must have felt the same way, because after

dropping her off from a preaching engagement, he decided to call it quits. Vanessa must have appeared stunned because he offered an explanation that has always stuck with her.

"Do you ever separate church from your personal life? You are a very beautiful woman that I would love to get to know, but it is as if you're always preaching. Your hands are swinging and your voice is modulating like you're in the pulpit. I go to church on Sundays, but there is not that much religion in the world that would make me want to sit through a sermon each time we go out, and I don't know too many brothers that will."

Vanessa took what he said to heart. She had taught herself to be bold in order to be taken seriously as a woman preacher, and now she found that same authority was intimidating to men. Vanessa wondered as she climbed through her thirties to her early forties, was it her, or was God singling her out to remain single? She was a preacher that was passionate about the word of God; that's who she was. Vanessa clung to the literal interpretation that God would give her the desires of her heart, so she prayed to God to take away her desire for companionship or show her the brother that wouldn't mind a matinee sermon every once in awhile. He sent her Willie Green.

Chapter 3

A Spiritual Hook Up

Vanessa Morton met Willie Green during the 50th anniversary celebration of Dominion Baptist church. Pastor Benjamin Rawls and longtime friend, First Lady Pat Rawls, had invited Vanessa to their small church in Ashton, Virginia to preach the Consecration service that would kick off a week of services to celebrate the church's golden anniversary.

Pat was the only real girlfriend Vanessa still had from young adulthood that always looked out for her and prayed for the frailties of her human side. Other friends were immediately intimidated by her when she became the pastor of her own church. With Pat, she could be real, letting her in on the loneliness that sometimes plagued her soul when the doors of the church weren't open.

After the service was over that Sunday night, Pat and Pastor Rawls convinced Vanessa to stay over to hear the week's guest preacher, who by their description had the "most countrified city church" they had ever visited. Pat went on so much about the integrity and laid back preach-

ing style of the Reverend Willie Green that Vanessa became intrigued and made arrangements to stay over another night.

Vanessa immediately knew it was a set up when Pat introduced him as " the very single Willie Green" at the next
evening's dinner before the service. Willie smiled and
said, "That I am," before helping Vanessa pull out her
chair. Vanessa practically kicked her girlfriend under the
square four-seater table they crowded around. What had
they told him about her? Vanessa wondered. For the first
time in a long while, Vanessa felt nervous, almost antsy.
She was not sure how to act. She thought about what
Montgomery had said about her being too authoritative
in social settings; she was not in the pulpit now, her internal monitor warned.

Pastor Rawls and Pat shared with both of them their
church's plans to build or buy a new church. Vanessa
found herself muting her usual strong views on what she
called "the Mega church complex." Although she knew
her friend's church was busting at the seams, she also
knew that some pastors were tricked into believing that
collecting more real estate was more pleasing to God than
gathering more souls. One of the first things she did when
she became Pastor was to take her rustic church that was
sitting on two acres of land and start an expansion project
that doubled the size of the original sanctuary without
counting the cost. *Been there done that,* thought Vanessa. Instead of bringing all that up again, she steered the conversation to raising the funds for such a project.

"If your congregation is not tithing above the church's
current operating budget, then don't even start a building
project. Now Pat and Ben, you know I know what I'm talking about," Vanessa had told them.

"That's why we are leaning toward buying a church, but

we want to stay within the same general location," Pastor Rawls said.

"If I can just be real," Willie interrupted, "sometimes only ten percent of your members are giving their ten percent. Then all your best laid plans for renovation on the church go out the door. So you start another campaign drive." Willie looked at Vanessa who was listening intently. "What do you think, Pastor Morton? Ben tells me you have that big church that I drive by all the time. How do you keep the lights on and the plumbing fixed?"

"Well the Bible says to give the ten percent. I preach and teach tithing as a Biblical principle. We don't have all those other funds, drives or special offerings." *No strong gesturing,* she told herself. "That's a promise I made to my congregation. Just give your tithes and I won't have to ask you to come out of your pocket for anything extra."

Willie radiated warmth like the candlelight and variation of earth tones on the walls of the restaurant. If he was nervous, he didn't show it. He stood briefly to take off his suit jacket and roll up his sleeves. He looked ready to dig into the meal that had just been served by their waitress, as well as the conversation. He held Vanessa's glance through the steam that rose from their entrees before they both looked away deliberately to make sure they were engaging the others at the table.

"I guess you have to know your congregation. My folks would be heartbroken if they couldn't get in that kitchen we got at the church and sell their dinners or plan a bus trip to someplace or another to add to our building fund," Willie told her.

"I don't give my people that option. Some folks will feel that just because they raised x amount of dollars by sponsoring a fish fry, that they have done their share of giving.

I emphasize that they are still obligated to give ten percent of their earnings."

"I wouldn't call it an option to tithing, Sister Vanessa. If you're teaching them what is right, which obviously you are doing over at Mt. Pleasant, then they will know their obligation." Vanessa noticed that he had shifted to a familiar first name basis. "I think when my church raises money by other means, it is more about the fellowship and the sense of accomplishment that the members feel raising money to dedicate to the church. Everyone in my church is not going to tithe and I am not going to turn down the money that they raise. Each one of my auxiliaries has their own fundraising efforts."

"Well, if you don't expect everyone to tithe, then they won't," Vanessa said softening her words with a smile.

Pastor and First Lady Rawls had been forgotten. Willie and Vanessa were enjoying the debate as they continued to make points and ask questions just to hear each other speak. Vanessa's internal monitor had been turned off now and she felt as if she didn't have to hold back her opinion.

"Bringing an offering to church is part of serving God," Pastor Rawls interjected.

"Exactly, but bringing your tithes is Biblical law. Going to church Sunday after Sunday without tithing from your income and expecting to be abundantly blessed is like praying and expecting something from God without repenting from your sins first. There is a Godly order. Bring ye all the tithes into the storehouse, then he will open the windows of heaven and pour out a blessing," Vanessa said.

"I don't want you to think it is all about the money at Harvest. My missionaries prepare meals to feed the hungry and maintain a dry food closet for the homeless in the community. What they don't give the church in money they more than make up for it in time and talent."

"That's great. I guess we can agree to disagree on this issue because I still feel that everyone can and should give their tithe, no matter what. I teach tithing from the pulpit during Sunday morning worship, in Sunday School and in Bible Study. I figure the Lord will convict my members to do what is right," Vanessa said

"That's right. We can preach, but the Lord will convict. I always say the Metropolitan area is a great place to be a Pastor. That is why I accept every invitation to preach because you can always learn so much from other ministries. How about you, Vanessa?" Willie said, changing the subject.

"I don't get many invitations to preach unless it's from my good friends such as these good folks here in Ashton," Vanessa said.

Willie looked perplexed as if he didn't know why. Vanessa left the obvious unsaid. Although they lived on the outskirts of a major city, there were still ministers that didn't accept her ministry because she was a female. She didn't sit in many pastor's pulpits. Didn't he see she was a woman, because she definitely noticed he was a man; a very good looking man. He had a slender build with a freshly manicured hairline that tapered into side burns that were slightly grey at the temples, which gave him a distinguished look.

Pastor Rawls reminded Willie and Vanessa that they were on a schedule, which put a halt to their conversation. Pastor Rawls wanted to get back to church to provide meditation and prayer time for his guest preacher before the service. Willie and Vanessa traveled in separate cars back to the church with Willie riding with the Rawls' and Vanessa driving her own car. Already she was feeling the void of her dining companion.

After arriving at the church, Vanessa wished she had gotten a seat on the front pew while Willie was preaching instead of sitting behind him in the pulpit. She scoped out a seat on the front row with the deacons, and another in the very next row where a few ladies were sitting a comfortable two person width away from one another. Other than that the church was packed. Vanessa wanted to see the same passion on Willie's face that she heard in his voice. It was amazing how he was saying so much with very little words. He slowly walked a circle around the text until he reached his listeners and then brought it back to the center of the text. He was for real, Vanessa thought. She had been holding her breathe ever since dinner ended thinking, *Lord please let this man be more than just a preacher in title only.* She was ecstatic at how well he could preach and didn't know why.

Vanessa was shocked when he called on her to have several scriptures ready to read on his cue, which was a trademark of his preaching style. She stood beside him when she had the last of the three scriptures marked and was handed a mobile microphone by one of the deacons. He started to continue with his point until the feed from the microphones being so close together caused a blare of sound from the receiver. The unexpected noise sent a gasp of alarm through the congregation. Vanessa quickly clicked her mic off.

"Chemistry, brothers and sisters," Willie said throwing his hand up in a Hallelujah wave. Pastor Rawls and a few members who caught Willie's innuendo, including his wife, Pat, were on their feet screaming, "Amen." Vanessa could not help but blush with joyous embarrassment. Willie leaned away from his mic and whispered to Vanessa, "Sister Morton, now, you need to take that microphone and go stand waaaaaaaay over there so I can concentrate on my message and not your perfume. Amen."

In one word, Willie had summarized why Vanessa had been feeling antsy and ecstatic earlier and now embarrassed—Chemistry. He was for real. Vanessa stepped back still shaking her head. Wisps of hair escaped from the bundle of her natural curly mane she had captured with a jeweled hairpin. Willie did a brief recap of the point he was making. He deferred to Vanessa, not only to read a related scripture, but also put her spin on its relevance. He allowed her to give the congregation a prescription of verses to study at home, which was a trademark of hers. They were like a spiritual tag team. By the end of the message, she felt as if she had reached a new level of happy.

After the service, Vanessa knew she had to head back home. It was already 9:30 p.m. and she had a two hours drive ahead of her. Several of her members, including her secretary, had accompanied her to the service that she preached the previous day. When she decided to stay over, she promised them she would be okay coming back alone. She gathered her things in the pulpit. Willie was still doing his victory lap, moving through the crowd accepting praise and passing out encouragement. The night was coming to an end and she didn't know what to do next. She didn't want to leave without talking to Willie, but she kept her distance and allowed him to minister. She wanted feedback on their chemistry before they went their separate ways.

Vanessa knew that pastors could spend hours held up with members after a good sermon. Although Vanessa had preached the night previous, people came over to her to tell her how powerful their message was tonight. Many thought Vanessa and Willie's collaboration in the pulpit was planned because of how natural it came across.

Like a God send, Pat Finally pulled the both of them away to the Pastor's study. Pastor Rawls was still in the sanctuary. Willie and Vanessa were left alone momentarily while Pat attended to a knock on the study's door.

"It's been a pleasure meeting you, Pastor Green. You

are truly an anointed man of God," Vanessa said, extending her hand.

"Tell me you're staying all week," he replied, shaking her hand and holding on.

"I'm afraid not. I've got a church on the other side of the bridge that I have to get back to."

"I have a serious problem then. What prescription can I get for that?"

"Well," Vanessa said, "I always start off with a dose of John 3:16, then . . ."

"Then, Vanessa 301 322-2343," Pat interrupted coming from the door and handing Vanessa an envelope that enclosed a check for the love offering that the church had collected for her the previous night. Then she walked away. Willie pulled out his pen from his shirt pocket and wrote Vanessa's number on the edge of his sermon outline.

"I tell you what, you show me your church and I'll show you mine," Willie said, an easy smile sliding across his face before flaring into a full grin.

"Why Reverend, are you asking permission to sit in my pulpit?" Vanessa asked, returning the smile.

"Look, Vanessa." He paused, appearing to weigh his words." I'm a straightforward man. This had been a wonderful evening with the fellowship dinner and the service, but I feel especially blessed to have met such a lovely woman of God. I could care less if I sit in your pulpit. I just want to see you again real soon."

"Same here," she said, suddenly feeling hot. "I'm going to hold you to your promise to visit." Vanessa felt like a school girl caught up in a whirlwind romance. "I keep office hours everyday except Wednesday."

"I'll call for an appointment to come see your church, and I'm going to call you tonight to make sure you got home safely and I'm going to ask you out to dinner as soon as I get back across the bridge."

"I'd like that."

Willie kept his promises. Every night the two of them stayed on the phone until one of them fell asleep. Vanessa had never met a man like Willie who was so generous with his time and attention. She felt they both were ready to share with each other what was most precious to them-their churches.

Vanessa didn't sit in Willie's pulpit the first time she had attended Harvest Baptist Church for a service. She sat in the fourth pew surrounded by the rest of the congregation for the annual Deacons and Trustees day in early December. After a representative from each group gave their gracious donation to the church's building and maintenance fund and other presentations, Willie came to the podium. He recognized a few friends and the rest of the visitors.

"I see we have one of this county's most esteemed preachers with us tonight, Pastor Vanessa Morton," he said. All eyes landed on her followed by a weak round of applause. "She is the Pastor of Mt. Pleasant Baptist church, right off of Ritchie Highway. Let me tell you, saints, she can preach." A few more people smiled after that personal endorsement from their pastor.

Vanessa stood at the mention of her name. She wore a simple camel colored dress that accentuated her small waist and the matching shoes and purse. Some of the women stared a little too long evaluating if Vanessa was wearing the outfit of an esteemed pastor. A large scarf embroidered with a cross fell by her side that she used to cover her legs as she sat.

"Escort Pastor Morton up to the pulpit," Willie said to one of the ushers.

Vanessa shook her head and mouthed to the crowd that she was fine where she was. Willie knew she never sat in the pulpit unless she was wearing all white, all black or her robe. They had orchestrated this little stunt so that the congregation could get used to seeing her face. They had done the same thing at her church the week before where Willie also sat in the congregation. What the congregation didn't know was that they were on a date that would continue after the service and that the couple had been dating now for over a month. To them it wasn't being dishonest. They just wanted to ensure that their relationship was what they both wanted before dating in the public and often critical eye of the church.

"Sister Mae, make sure you put Sister Morton on the calendar to preach. I'm in the mood to sit back and listen to some good preaching around here," Willie smiled, that adorable wide tooth smile Vanessa loved so much.

Everyone said amen as Vanessa took her seat to enjoy the rest of the service.

Taking Willie up on his invitation, Vanessa preached her first message at Harvest to the seven women of the nurses' Unit, their family members and the Harvest twenty four-seven saints that came out to every service. She had fumed about it ever since Mae Richardson had called her with the formal invitation extended from the church. She didn't tell Willie she was mad, although she knew he could sense something was wrong when they prayed together before the service in his pastor's study.

By the time he met her in the study after service, she was ready to explode.

"Willie, I think that we need to be perfectly honest in this relationship," Vanessa said, sitting in the chair across the desk from Willie.

"I agree one hundred percent. Is there something on your mind?"

"You know I really thought that when we met and when

you invited me to preach that you took my ministry seriously."

"I do." Willie stopped jotting down a memo he was writing to himself. "What is this about, Vanessa?"

"When I invited you to preach at Mt. Pleasant, you preached to my entire congregation. When I come here I get the nurse's Unit Anniversary?"

"I told Mae to give you the next available preaching engagement which just so happen to be their annual day. But what does it matter? We're talking about edifying souls and proclaiming the infallible Word of God."

"You're right," Vanessa said, shaking her head in an attempt to silence her internal monitor that was telling her to shut up. "I guess I just misread your intentions."

"Wait a minute, we are talking about honesty here. I'm confused. Talk to me. Tell me what this is all about." Willie rounded the desk and pulled her to her feet so that he could look her directly into her eyes.

"I guess I just figured you got the woman preacher to preach to a woman's auxiliary because you didn't think I had a word for the entire congregation or you knew that I wouldn't be accepted by all of your people." She cast her eyes downward, hoping they would not betray her by shedding a tear.

"That's just not true."

"You don't know what it's like being a female preacher and seeing half of my Daddy's faithful members leave the church when I took over the pastorate because they didn't think I had the authority to share the word of God with them. It hurts to only get invitations to preach for a Women's Ministry, or a First Lady's Prayer breakfast, or Deaconess Day," she confessed, pinching the bridge of her nose. "It hurts when I preach to my own congregation and the men don't even try to listen to see if anything ap-

plies to their life or shy away from you in general because
they perceive you to be too aggressive. It isn't any wonder
why I'm not married yet," she said, suddenly wishing she
had kept that last comment to herself.

"You have a lot to offer to God, his people and some
very lucky man."

"I'm sorry. I guess this issue has always been a scar that I
have carried with me. I should be over it by now."

"Let me write you a prescription for this scar," he said,
pulling her into an embrace and whispering the balm of
God's word in her ear. "Isaiah 61:1 says, 'the Spirit of the
Lord is upon you; because the Lord hath anointed you to
preach'."

"Thanks," she said, breaking from his embrace to wipe
her tears. "That's exactly what I needed to hear. It's not
that I doubt my calling. It's just sometimes I wonder am I
being effective."

"That same scripture says that he sends us preachers to
bind up the broken hearted. That's what you have done
for me. We all have scars. Before I met you I had an infin-
ity for being interested in the wrong women; strong women;
but they were wrong for me. I've dated two women in my
adult life. I didn't want to be one of those single Pastors
that go from woman to woman like some kind of Pulpit
Playboy. I had more insight in God and what he wanted
for me to be that kind of man. Now I believe with all my
soul that I have found the right woman in you and I am
easily, and rather quickly, falling in love with you."

Vanessa closed her eyes and thanked the Lord that he
felt the same way about her that she did about him. When
she opened them, Willie had leaned in for a kiss. It was
like someone had turned on a blow torch. They stood in
the middle of his study kissing as Mae came in the door.

"I'm sorry; well, I just wanted to see if there was anything else you may have needed," Mae said, as flushed as if she herself had just been caught kissing.

"No, Mae, I got everything I need," Willie said squeezing Vanessa's hand that he refused to let go. "By the way, you need to schedule Pastor Morton to return and preach Communion Sunday at 11a.m."

"Yes, Pastor Green," Mae said. She was so stunned that she almost ran into the door post when exiting. Willie and Vanessa laughed and shared one more very long kiss.

The only thing left to do was come clean to their congregations. Mt. Pleasant seemed overjoyed and a little relieved that their Pastor had found love with a man of God. Vanessa was relieved as well. She was tired of the two women on the Mother's Board that dated back to her daddy's time as pastor asking her, "Ain't you got some nice man courting you?" She knew that some of her members held on to the misconception that a single woman past her thirties and unmarried was one to be pitied.

A few members at Harvest embraced Vanessa as tightly as they did their pastor, especially his Pastor's Aide Committee. Vanessa had to get use to being zipped into her robe, given a special seat in Willie's pulpit and served hand and foot by a few ladies at Harvest that were so old that Vanessa felt she should be waiting on them. Most members, on the other hand, were skeptical of her motives. Willie's church was a close-knit family that could really pour out the hospitality on a visitor that they knew wasn't staying long, but like with any other host of an unwanted guest, rudeness was a tactic they used to try and get her to pack her bags.

Willie's congregation had become comfortable with his being single and consuming himself with their needs and wants. Since he was spending more time with Vanessa, they saw their relationship as a threat to their own relationship with their pastor. Willie and Vanessa knew that they were being watched very closely for impropriety or any signs of breaking up.

Willie and Vanessa made it a point to make time for each other without the pervasive thoughts of church concerns, which was harder for Willie since Harvest Baptist had many more dates on the calendar then did Mt. Pleasant. Every weekend it seemed as if there was one annual day after another at Harvest. They both had to make sacrifices though and they often attended each other's church to get some time in. Vanessa told him that she felt a little uneasy visiting his church. She didn't want to point the finger, but she had to let him know that the same folks that were smiling in their faces when they were together were jeering at Vanessa behind his back.

After being together for only six months, Willie addressed his relationship with Vanessa in front of the entire congregation during his tenth anniversary as Pastor. Vanessa sat beside him and Pastor Rawls in the pulpit wearing a cream ensemble and a yellow corsage for the occasion. Willie wore a dark suit with a yellow tie. Pastor Rawls, the guest preacher for this celebration, wore a classic black robe with black tassels.

"Saints, I've tried to be all things to all people in the last ten years, and you all have been equally as giving to me," Willie stated. "I appreciate it greatly. How many people know that it is impossible to be all things to all people?" He waited for a show of hands. "The Lord said it's not good for a man to be alone. He has granted me a divine companion that is by my side tonight. She cannot take the place of my church family and you all can't take her place in my life. The same love and respect you've shown me over the years, I expect you to extend to her. She is my help mate and I love her very much."

Willie walked away from the pulpit and began to address Vanessa. He did not ask her to stand beside him, but rather approached her seat. She knew him to be a very direct man and braced herself for what he was about to say. He knelt down beside her and offered her the contents of a blue velvet box. He proposed to her and she accepted, like mostly all of their other encounters, publicly and in church.

Chapter 4

Let No Man Put Asunder

Vanessa was still reclined on the couch when Willie arrived home. He sat the brown grocery bag in his arm down on the floor, flung his coat on the back of the easy chair, and leaned over the couch to give Vanessa a kiss.

"How did it go with your Executive Board? You're getting home kind of late," Vanessa said, moving her feet so that Willie could join her on the couch.

"I don't know," Willie said.

"You don't know?"

"I don't know, Vanessa, some folks that I didn't expect were very disagreeable to the move. It's like they understood what we are trying to do, but they had questions as to why."

"The why?" Vanessa replied.

"I know, they want to know why we are uprooting their church."

"I thought the why was apparent; the deal sealer. God said it, and He out ranks us all; that's what I told my congregation," Vanessa said, checking the condition of her manicure.

"Wait a minute, you told your entire congregation? That wasn't the plan," Willie said, bolting straight up.

"I know, but what is the big deal? They are all going to know eventually." Vanessa rose up from her lounging position as well.

"It is a very big deal. I wasn't planning on telling the whole congregation until next week sometime. Sure, some will find out through the grapevine, but at least the leak will come from inside Harvest. Your church is less than a country mile from mine. My members deserve to hear news like that from me, not on the street." He began to tug on the knot of his necktie to loosen it, but after several attempts to unravel it, he let it hang lopsided around his neck.

"I doubt word will travel that fast," Vanessa said, thinking he was being melodramatic. "Think about it. I knew very little about your ministry and you knew even less of mine before we met in Ashton. Our churches are close in proximity but worlds apart."

"Yeah, well it's that gap that I'm worried about," Willie said pausing as he stood, retrieving the grocery bag and entering the kitchen via the hallway. He called to her, "Think about this; we decided on something together and you changed that plan."

Vanessa couldn't help but feel that it had only been one day back with their congregations after their wedding, and the honeymoon stage of their relationship was already over. She wanted to tell him that her sermon topic was a perfect way to weave in their announcement, but who was she kidding? She was so excited after her morning meeting with the executive board, that her mind was set on telling everyone. She would have found a way to announce it even if she was preaching the death, burial and resurrection of Jesus Christ. A person can weave anything if they have a big enough needle.

Okay, this is the part where I apologize, Vanessa thought. They did stay up late the night before discussing how they would tell their members about combining churches. Vanessa wondered then why they had to have one uniform way to tell their churches. He had his way with his people and she had hers, but, they had decided it would be proper protocol to tell those closest to them in ministry first, and then hold a special meeting to tell their entire congregation.

Vanessa entered the kitchen and found Willie at the counter unloading the bag he had brought home with him. She walked up on him close and hugged him from behind. She felt him inhale deep into her embrace and knew he was amicable to what she had to say.

"I'm sorry. I guess you feel as if I pulled rank on you. I'm so use to making these spontaneous decisions as a pastor and a single woman, that I temporarily forgot I am married now and these decisions affect the both of us."

Willie spun to face her, circling his arms around her waist to keep her close. "And now that we plan to combine churches, we have the congregation to think about as well."

"So am I forgiven?" Vanessa asked.

"Yeah, I guess; you are a novice at this wife stuff."

"Woo," Vanessa said buckling at the knees as if she were about to faint.

"What is that for?" he said, bearing her weight.

"We survived our first fight as a married couple."

"Hopefully it's our last one for awhile."

"What are we going to do next?"

"I'm going to eat. Are you hungry?" he said, exposing a Pyrex dish of fresh fried chicken and various containers of side dishes. He pulled out two plates from the cabinet.

"I mean with our congregations silly. Mt. Pleasant has got several special dates left on the calendar for the year, plus we promised to preach in Ashton. We need some time to get our people together." She spooned heaps of macaroni and cheese on both of their plates before replacing the plastic lid on the seal-top container.

"I know. Don't worry; God doesn't give you a vision without a way to make it work. I say we plan for a retreat before the Christmas holiday. Got to be cheap too, 'cause people are going to try to find an excuse not to come. I'm going to get Mae to call around to some places close," he said.

"Wait a minute, let me guess, all this food came from Mae Richardson right?" Vanessa said, dangling a drumstick as if she contemplated tossing it back in the container from which it came. "I told that woman she could stop fixing your food and pressing your clothes."

"I don't see where you have started dinner, and you were home before me. Remember our rule; the first one home starts the meal, a pot of soup, peanut butter and jelly—something. I'm still waiting to taste your cooking," Willie said, looking around the kitchen. The wide smile he wore expressed more jest than sentiment. He noticed her less than enthused expression and softened his comments. "It's okay dear; Mae loves to cook for us."

"She loves to cook for you."

"Well, I see plenty in here."

Vanessa had to admit she wasn't exactly domestically inclined, but all that would change now that she was married to the Pastor. In her mind, cooking for her husband would be a welcome obligation when she found the time. Following her mother's example, it would be an offense to have someone caring for your husband the way Mae had, and cause for suspicion.

Vanessa knew early on in their relationship that Willie was well taken care of by the sisters of Harvest Baptist Church even when they were dating. Every night of the week he could get his meals home-cooked and home de-livered. Vanessa was told explicitly by the head of Willie's Pastor's Aide Committee, "We know you're too busy to cook and we can't have our Pastor wasting away." *That was the difference between male and female preachers*, Vanessa thought, *people figured if she could preach, then surely she could cook her own meals.*

"That's another thing, your Mae and my Luella might be like oil and water. It will get confusing with two secre-taries for one ministry," she said.

"Correction, Mae is my church clerk, so that makes one church clerk and one secretary."

"Mae Richardson is more than a church clerk, dear. Bless her heart. She is more like a mother." Vanessa hesi-tated before taking a couple of pieces of Mae's fried chicken from the dish as if by talking about Mae at the same time might put a hex on the food she was about to consume.

"Does Mae really keep any of the church records? You told me yourself that the courts are waiting for Harvest to file a years worth of marriage certificates with the state to verify that the couples who filed for the license actually did get married."

"Mae keeps my appointment calendar and the church calendar, thank you," he said, deciding it would not be in his best interest to belabor the point. He moved toward the dinning room table.

"I can agree to one church clerk and one secretary. Their roles just need to be defined," Vanessa said, follow-ing him. Vanessa felt embarrassed that she felt a bit jeal-ous over Willie and Mae's relationship. She knew Mae was too old to pose a serious romantic threat. It was just the way that Willie would just as soon turn to Mae for advice than he would her that bothered Vanessa. And for every

matronly Mae, there had to be a couple single seduc-
tresses lurking, Vanessa was sure.

"I'm sure, being women of God that they will grow right
fond of one another and work out their duties. You might
come to rely on Mae as much as I do and vice versa with
me and Luella," Willie reasoned, chewing loudly. "Mae
has never been paid for her services though. She volun-
teers her time to the ministry."

"I guess that is the difference between a clerk and a secretary," Vanessa responded, stabbing at her chicken leg
with a fork in an attempt to pull the meat off the bone. "I
have several paid people on staff that help keep things
going. The world is paying folk for their labor, why not the
church? These people are not just laboring in the field of
the Lord on Sunday, they are like my administrative team.
Now I only have part time people, but I have been considering paying Luella and a new custodian full time wages
for the full time work they do at Mt. Pleasant. As the ministry grows, we will need to accommodate maybe even
more help. I'm sure there will be some people from Harvest Baptist who wouldn't mind working for the church."

"I'm sure you're right," was all Willie said.

Vanessa knew that Willie had a hard enough time
breaking up disputes between Charley and Mae when they
were helping him at Harvest once a week. In her experience, both of them were always trying to be more helpful
than the other when Willie was around. It takes special
people, who can put aside their needs and dedicate themselves enough to minister to others. Vanessa had many
more people to manage. She even had a small security
ministry to serve as a buffer from overzealous saints who
mistook getting close to the preacher with getting close to
God. Willie thought that was a good idea at first when she
had preaching engagements away from Mt. Pleasant, but

he did not know if it was necessary when she was among her own people.

Willie and Vanessa completed the rest of their meal in silence; each pondering the reactions of their church members to the news of the union. Vanessa considered another challenge or possible problem in uniting their congregations, but kept it to herself when she noticed Willie's stoic expression. She imagined that if this move was a mild irritation to some members of Mt. Pleasant, like Sister Thomlin, it would be a harsh abrasion to some Harvest members. After all, they were the ones packing up and physically moving. Her suggestion to Willie would be to tell his congregation that this is the will of God for their churches. They need to put aside all personal opinion and pray about it. To her, it was not a question of will they be able to combine churches and minister together, but how will they make the transition easier so the work of the Lord could continue.

Vanessa started clearing off the table when Willie said to her, "I can sort of empathize with our congregations having to deal with yet another change so soon. The union of our churches is coming on the heels of our ten month courtship and marriage."

"That should let them know that we are open to God, and with his help and each other, we will pull through anything," Vanessa said on her return visit to the dinning room to pick up the leftovers that needed to be refrigerated.

"They don't know all the problems we went through," Willie said.

"They should know, they caused some of them. We weathered quite a bit during that time." She pushed through the swinging door that divided the dinning room from their kitchen.

"The rumor mill was definitely up and running."

"But what gets me is the same people from both our churches who are now acting like they cannot share a pew in the combined church were the same ones starting gossip on the both of us." Vanessa said, emerging from the kitchen for the last time. She took her seat back at the dining room table and reclined as much as she could in the high back chair.

"How about the one that said we were living together before marriage," Willie said with a half grin.

"I wish I knew who started that one."

Vanessa and Willie's new house together was the model home for a development that completed sale on their entire lot. They went to the closing two months before they were to be married and began moving stuff into the house before the big day. Despite rumors that ran through both of their churches that the couple had actually moved in and were living together "in sin" before the wedding, the house sat empty for little over a month until after their nuptials. It was like opening a present to come to a brand-new house after the wedding and get use to it together.

"I think that had to have started in your church," he said, tossing an abandoned dinner napkin at her playfully.

"It wasn't funny then. It was hard during that time. I'll never forget the luke warm reception I received from your family."

"Come on, Vanessa, I'm their son and I still receive the same treatment at family gatherings. We're preachers. That profession didn't fit into their bourgeoisie lifestyle. That didn't automatically give us a six figure salary or qualify us for a platinum Visa card."

"Unless you are blessed with a congregation of over a thousand members or you are a jack-leg preacher," Vanessa said.

"I never heard of that one, Vanessa."

"My father used to always talk about jack-leg preachers.

That is a preacher with one hand wrapped around a Bible and the other hand in the offering plate; just crooked."

They both laughed at the recollection of someone who partially, if not wholly, fit that description. "Go figure, Willie Green wanted to be a preacher and help save souls. Doesn't he know he is going to have to struggle with stubborn folks who just don't relinquish their souls as easy as they do their minds in the classes she and daddy teach over at the University?"

"There are a lot of people with a head full of knowledge but a soul full of hell."

"Watch it; those are my parents you are talking about."

"Hey, you said it yourself; the minute your dad started teaching evolution, Christianity became irrelevant to him."

"But Mommy and Daddy are saved, in theory. They met and fell in love in college and got saved the same Sunday, or so the story goes. They came up to a preacher at the right hour, in the right church on the university campus. Got saved and managed to get out at the right time," Willie said, his playful attitude getting a little more serious. "Can you believe the last time my parents visited Harvest, other than our wedding, all they had to say about the service was how long it was."

Vanessa took one of his hands from across the coffee table and gave it a long stroke up the forearm. "Well, I guess that is what happens when people get saved in theory."

"The process doesn't end when you get saved."

"You know you're preaching to the choir." She let some time pass before saying, "You care too much about what people think of you and your ministry, you know that?"

"Yeah well, they're my parents," Willie said, shifting in his chair, causing Vanessa to drop his hand.

"Not just your parents though. It's your members too.

I've seen them get to you on many occasions. You're going to be consumed if you don't lay some of that burden on the Lord," She said, getting up from the table. "I'm going to get a piece of cake, want a slice?"

Vanessa left him with that thought as she went into the kitchen. She knew he couldn't deny the truth of her statement. It was almost intuitive the way they knew each other so well. Every now and then they pointed out each other's idiosyncrasies. Like the time Willie told her that in some ways she was like his mother. Everything was either black or white with her. Her attitude with her congregation was, "the Lord told me this, here it is, and here are the verses to prove it." He knew she would much rather preach and teach the word than deal with the emotional haywireness that comes along with churches and church folk.

Vanessa re-entered the dinning area with a triple layer chocolate cake that Willie brought home earlier in the week from another donor of his church; this one unknown. She placed a cake plate in front of her husband before sitting down. He waited until they had both downed a good portion of their cake before he said, "You know one sure fire way you can get in my mother's good graces is to offer her a grandchild."

Vanessa smirked nervously, showing front teeth tinted with chocolate frosting. "Don't go there, okay? We've discussed this before. I'm forty years old. Besides, I have close to two hundred children in my congregation that keep me busy. They would really think I've lost it waddling to the pulpit pregnant. Then what would happen to our vision?"

"Leave it in Daddy's hands. I'll take care of the church and you'll take care of home," Willie said, patting his chest triumphantly.

Vanessa tried to conceal her horror. She felt as if she was on a swing her parents created for her out of an old tire that was wound tight and left to spin out of control. At this point, she couldn't read his expression nor his intentions. She knew Willie was the old-fashioned type, but he had to know she was far from traditional. Vanessa believed it was their differences that fueled their attraction and created a balance in their lives.

"Now Willie Green, you can't be serious. I don't know where all of this is coming from, but you have got to know that I just am not the mother type. I mean, in this stage of my life my purpose is to help lead this combined church. God hasn't even begun to equip me on a maternal level."

"Calm down, don't have a heart attack," Willie said, slow to shed that smile that matched his usual sense of humor. "You can't blame a guy for trying, right? I have always known that with God all things are possible, but not until I met you have I felt like I could have it all." Willie held Vanessa's trembling hand.

"You're sweet, but God, you had me scared." Vanessa slapped him on the arm.

They remained quiet for awhile, hoping their quiet reflection would lead them to a more neutral topic of conversation.

"What do you think will be the most difficult part of this whole combining process for you? I know we've talked about me and my members, but I have neglected to ask my wife how she is feeling," Willie said.

Vanessa had to smile at how nice the word wife sounded to her and how easily it rolled out of his mouth. "I keep," she started. "I keep thinking back to when I was called to preach. Daddy was in the prime of his ministry and I was a young woman off to college. I knew then that I would be a pastor. I thanked God, and I praised Him for the mere privilege. I knew I couldn't fail because He had appointed me. My faith was unwavering then. Now I wonder if I have failed in some way for Him to send me help with my flock," she said. "You are blessed help, but help none the less."

"Baby, don't you see He wants to do great things with us now? Forget about the past. In fact, we ought to be praising Him now for the blessings." His voice trailed off as his thought patterns for conversation were distracted. She knew it was the prompting. The prompting of the Lord left a lot of their conversations incomplete.

There were many times when they would start a conversation on the telephone and one of them would have to leave immediately. She knew he would be grabbing a Bible and retreating to their office for quiet meditation, to ask for clarity and interpretation of the Holy Spirit. The prompting from the Lord was more than an urge; it was urgent. It was like a beckoning from a friend who wants to let you in on an important secret. They yielded their lives as pastors so that the prompting of the Lord could come upon them anytime and anywhere. Vanessa watched Willie go behind the closed doors that led to their office.

Vanessa gave her husband two hours alone before checking on him in their home office. Out of all the rooms in their new home, the office was their sanctuary. This single room was the subject of many planning sessions and compromises. The couple had consented to share a home office out of practicality. The Greens' office was a converted den with a fireplace and all the resources of a small lending library. Around the perimeter of the room were mounted degrees, special photos and a crucifix over the brick fireplace. Under these mementos was a wrap-around desk and a hutch joined with a wide work station that would accommodate both chairs. Willie selected a traditional, executive style chair upholstered in cherry vinyl. An Italian, swivel chair for Vanessa could be moved easily to the opposite end of the writing area in the unlikely event they both would be sitting at the desk at the same time.

A huge cherry oak and black wall unit supported their collection of more than two hundred reference books. It contained commentaries, concordances, philosophies, books and study guides from their combined years of Bible college. The Devotional, New American, New International, New Living, Parallel and King James' versions of the Bible took up two shelves alone.

Vanessa found Willie on the couch in the center of the room writing on a yellow legal pad that he used to outline his sermon notes for Sunday. She brought in two steaming mugs of coffee on a bamboo serving tray given to them as a wedding gift.

"What are you working on?" she asked.

"Actually, it's something we both can use for our people," he replied. He motioned for her to join him on the ivory couch. "I've been looking for a theme for our vision and trying to look up scriptures. Something to combat the spirit I feel that threatens to attack our vision." He leaned back on the couch, leaving the legal pad on the couch between them. He propped his feet up on the coffee table.

"Mmm." Vanessa said as she threw back her head, quick to release the coffee she had just sipped. She mirrored his position on the couch, Resting her head back on the overstuffed pillow. " 'What therefore God hath put together let no man put asunder'." She reminisced with a smile.

"I was thinking about Corinthians, 'Ye all speak the same thing, and there be no divisions among you; but that ye be perfectly joined together in the same mind and judgment'."

Willie and Vanessa continued this volley of scripture quoting back and forth as they stared at the ceiling of the office. They had recently referenced some of the same scriptures in preparation for the union of the churches.

The other verses just came to them while they continued this banter. All of the scriptures referred to parts joining, combining and working together. They sat in silence beside each other until one of them would speak a phrase that came into their minds. Neither of them got up to reference a Bible. If one could not remember the exact wording or a complete verse, the other would chime in with the missing pieces. To an onlooker it would appear as if this was a drill that they used to prepare the other for their Ordination.

"'Many members in one body and all members have not the same office'," quoted Willie.

"Yeah, I like that one," Vanessa said. She sat up on the sofa. She slid her hand slowly down the length of her face to help her concentrate on the meaning.

As if being orchestrated, they both finished the verse together. "'So being many, are one body in Christ and every member one of another'." They both instinctively emphasized the words "one body".

"We will accomplish this move," Willie declared looking at his wife to assure her. "The devil has tried to trick us by making us worry over each step we take and even made me anxious to approach our people. We should be celebrating the fact He chose us for his plan."

"Glory," Vanessa said, waving a single hand in the air. Willie's words were refreshing to her. They confirmed notions God had dropped in her own spirit about reorganizing the church through the Valley of Dry Bones series she just finished preaching to her congregation.

"I think we have a theme for our Unification service. Out of the book of Romans, 'many members in one body,'" Willie repeated. He grabbed his legal pad and jotted down the scripture. "How does that sound?"

"Great. Sounds like a campaign. I was thinking on the way home about how we need to get members from both churches to serve on the Unification Committee. We can't do all the planning ourselves starting with the retreat on up until we unite at Mt. Pleasant. We know who can do the work. We need to get us a core group together who loves the Lord and believes in the vision," she remarked. She began making a list of people at her church to call for this special committee.

Head in hand, Vanessa stared around the room trying to locate the small digital clock. The couple decided a clock was necessary but should be small enough so not to preoccupy them with how much time they actually spent in the office. The clock read 9:30 p.m.

Vanessa turned to her husband who was adding names of people from Harvest Baptist to her list. "What is left to do?" she asked.

He locked eyes with his wife. "Go to bed."

"I'll race you," she said, getting a head start.

Chapter 5

Blessed Assurance

Willie pulled his blue Lincoln Mercury directly behind the church into the space designated for the Pastor and sat there. He took out the key chain with three interlocking rings—one set for his house keys, and the other two for the internal and external locks of the church. The only other person who had access to the church building was Charley Thompson. They met at church each Wednesday at 11:00 a.m. Charley usually walked the premises to check for vandalism and clean up around the property, and then they would grab lunch at the neighborhood McDonald's. Willie would then meet with Mae Richardson and go over the church schedule around 1:00 p.m. Charley never stuck around for this meeting, preferring not to aggravate himself with the likes of Mae Richardson. Willie could never understand how two people with such devotion for their church did not have the same for one another. Willie then spent the rest of his Wednesdays dealing with various church matters until prayer service was held at seven.

The two old men of Haitian decent that owned the convenience store on the corner had often said that the Harvest Baptist Church surely must be doing the will of God to have been fortunate to remain intact over the years since every other establishment on their street was constantly subject to theft and vandalism. In the wake of a sudden tropical storm the previous night, the rumor around the Lotto machine this morning when Willie stopped in for a cup of coffee was that the church, which was the hardest hit, had lost favor with God. Willie Green, on the other hand, saw a rainbow illuminated in a puddle on the sidewalk from his open car window as he sipped his coffee that reminded him of Noah after the flood.

The first sign of damage that he could see was a tree limb dangling precariously from a power line connected to the back of the church. This prompted Willie to get out of the car. He knew Deacon Thompson needed help cleaning up the debris from the storm if the church was to be ready for Bible Study that night. He walked through the alleyway divided by a chain link fence that fit loosely into a crack in the concrete which separated the church from the repair shop beside it. The gate gave way to the sidewalk on Lincoln Avenue at the front of the church. The alley that usually became littered by passers by during the week was now dotted with shingles from the church's roof.

Willie looked for Charley in the alley. Most times Charley collected nearly two bags of trash during his weekly collection. This gave him less to pick up on Saturday before Sunday service. He couldn't understand what was keeping him. Charley was usually so emphatic about keeping to a schedule that he would rather call a whole meeting off than come late.

Leaves crunched under Willie's feet as he approached the front of the church. Not many trees lined this street, but the storm blew in reminders that the leaves were changing according to God's plan and left a multicolored carpet at the base of the church's front steps. Willie turned the key in the front door of the Harvest church only to find it already unlocked. He could hear Charley humming faintly from the back of the church. Willie decided to set up the small podium in the center aisle for those who wanted to lead the church in a prayer or a hymn during Prayer Service later that night.

"Hey Charley, I didn't see your car out back." Willie called to the back like a man announcing his arrival at home after a hard day at work.

"I grabbed a spot out front. Did you see how Tropical Storm Roberto made a mess out there? I thought I'd come a little early. I'm going to put up some heavy plastic to sure up the windows. One of them looks as if it is about to shatter."

"They didn't look that bad to me as I walked up from the car," Willie said, plugging in the portable podium and turning the knob until he could hear the hum of the small microphone attachment before cutting it off again.

"You came through the alley?" Charley said making an appearance from the back. "The alley side had a buffer from the storm but the street side took a beating."

Willie was shocked to see Charley in denim overalls as opposed to casual slacks and button down shirt that he usually wore. He had come prepared to do more work than just trash collecting. He hauled a huge ream of plastic that they kept in the storage closet to winterize the basement windows in an attempt to save a little money on heating. Willie looked at his own attire and decided to lose the sports coat and change into a more comfortable pair of shoes that he had in the back to help out a little.

"I told the board that we should have gotten bars put on the basement windows, but no one listens to me," Charley said stoically.

"I know, I'm the one that vetoed that idea. I just don't like the church looking like a prison. We put bars over our windows and gates around our church to protect it, but we must remember that God wants us to be inviting to his people," Willie said, checking the mail Charley had placed on the front pew for him. "I'm going to change and help you a bit."

"That won't be necessary, Pastor."

"I know, but there is a lot of work to be done before tonight."

"Now how will I look allowing my pastor to plaster windows with plastic and pick up trash?"

"How do I look letting an old man clean up around the church each week?" Willie smiled at their ongoing joke about Charley's age, which never stopped him from helping out around the church. He waited for Charley's usual light-hearted response, but didn't get any. "This is extenuating circumstances though, Charley. I need to assess the damages. We may need to call someone in to help."

Willie walked to the back. He noticed how stiff the conversation had been between them and felt there was more on Charley's mind than damage left by the storm. Willie wondered did it have to do with his reaction to the announcement of the move at the joint board meeting but decided to wait to breach that conversation with him later. He got an old button-up shirt and a casual pair of shoes from the closet in his office and walked next door to the adjoining bathroom to use the facilities and change. As he unlaced the shoes he was wearing and slipped off the right one, he stepped in a small pool of water. Willie immediately looked up to find a bulge in the ceiling's plaster and paint with a drop of water that barely missed his face as it hit the ground. Willie placed the empty trash receptacle under the spot in the ceiling and made a note to call someone about it.

Willie was almost afraid to see how the church looked on the street side. He saw more missing panels of roofing tiles above the gutter that seemed suspended in air from the side of the building. Charley had stacked a few of the tiles to the side and was using a clear packing tape to seal the basement windows. He grunted and held his right knee a bit as he pushed his body up from a crouching position. Willie picked up a few branches here and a couple of bottles there, then worked his way to the other side where he continued to do the same.

Willie met Charley at the Harvest Baptist Church sign just outside the church in the patch of grass at the top of the landing. The sign, which was in a metal case, now read *H vest Baptis Ch rch*. The second and third rows that usually displayed the schedule of services was indistinguishable. The door, made of heavy plastic, used to keep the retractable letters in place, was blown open, causing a buckle in its hinges. Charley tried to get it closed with the force of his hands.

"That darn Mae Richardson never closes this thing tight when she is through in here," Charley complained.

"It probably needs a new door," Willie said. "How much money is in the Building and Maintenance fund?"

"Three hundred, twenty six dollars," Charley said, temporarily putting a halt to his fight with the door to the sign post, "and fifty three cents."

Willie was trying to estimate the cost of the repairs that the church would need. He couldn't believe that for the past five years all they had accumulated was three hundred some odd dollars. Then something dawned on him and he smiled.

"Thank God we're moving to Mt. Pleasant," Willie said. He watched Charley hammer away at the hinge with a look of determination on his face.

"Can I get you to hold this door in place while I try to

wedge the nail out?" Charley asked, not looking up at him.

"Don't worry about the sign," Willie said. "If people don't know that this is Harvest Baptist Church by now, they got just under three months to find out."

"I got it," Charley said placing the fork of the hammer head under the bent nail and jerked it back and forth like a mad man.

"Charley, stop," Willie said, holding back his arm. "You've picked up around here and sealed the windows, now that's more than anyone can ask. I guess you were planning to cut the tree out of that power line also. We will call someone for the sign, the power line and the leak inside the back bathroom. We'll use the entire three twenty for anything the insurance won't cover if we have to. Now let's go and get some lunch. I have something to talk to you about."

Charley reluctantly placed the tools inside the church and locked the door behind him while Willie pulled the bags to the dumpster. They walked pass the corner of Lincoln Avenue and Main Street to a small strip mall just a short walk from the church. They arrived at the McDonald's to find it crowded. They usually ordered separately but instead Willie asked Charley to secure a table. Charley pulled out a precise $5.25 for his value meal that he had loose in his pocket and gave it to Willie.

Willie had noticed that it was a habit of Charley's to separate his lunch money from his wallet in the morning and check it several times during the day to make sure that neither the bill nor the quarter had fallen out. Charley was probably disappointed that he couldn't face-off with the cashier who was identified as Evelyn by her name badge, Willie thought. He seemed to enjoy the power he felt when he ordered his cheeseburger with ketchup—no pickles or mustard—and paid for it without requiring change. Willie watched Charley wait for a family of four to finish their meal and vacate their usual table by the window while he waited a few extra minutes for Charley's special order.

"I got you an apple pie for dessert," Willie said, sitting down facing the window.

"An apple pie?"

"Yes, an apple pie. You get two on the dollar menu."

"So that's fifty cents I owe you." Charley grabbed his wallet as if he hoped he had enough change so he wouldn't have to go into his refill money that he tapped lightly in his left pocket. "What about the tax?"

"Charley please, It's on me."

"You sure?" Charley asked with fifty three cents in hand.

"Put your money away." Willie handed him the pie. "I wanted to talk to you about Harvest merging with Mt. Pleasant. Have you had a chance to think about it some more? At the meeting you seemed a little upset." Willie said draping his jacket over the back of the seat.

"You know, Pastor, I got out of bed this morning, drove down to the church house to pick up trash. The same thing I did today, I have done for nearly fifteen years. I always take care of God's building," Charley said, checking his burger.

Willie paused to say grace over their meals then resumed, "God's got many buildings Charley, but you haven't answered my question."

"I love Harvest and I know there are many that feel the same as I do and just didn't say anything at the meeting. If you were to call every deacon or trustee when we get back and tell them that the church was damaged by the storm, they would all come down here for one reason. That is to help return things to normal. So, don't tell me I'm being irrational. I was being honest at that meeting; it is going to be hard for me to pick up and move just like that."

"Now, no one is saying you're irrational. I completely understand, but we've wondered on many occasions how long our building is going to last. For each thing that goes wrong, we have a special collection that immediately goes to fixing that problem, nothing ever accumulates. So the next time we have a problem we are back to square one. We reached an all time low when we needed to replace that furnace. Do you remember what we did?" Willie said, pinching a few fries between his fingers and dipping them in a mound of ketchup on his tray.

"We had a special service to raise money."

"We had two services under the guise of a Gospel Choir concert and a Miss Harvest Baptist Church pageant," Willie said, temporarily losing his appetite for a lump rising in his throat. "My God, we had deaconesses toting around lists of patrons to their co-workers and friends so that they could wear the title of Miss 'We-Need-A-New-Furnace' Baptist Church."

Willie watched as Charley swallowed hard himself. He appeared to brace himself as if he knew the subject of the move would come up and had prepared a response; but it didn't come. Willie thought that maybe Charley was finally getting it.

"You were there, what was wrong with those services?" Charley questioned.

"Tell me, were we more concerned that the service glorified God or that the service met our financial goal?"

"It is the way we have always done things, and God has made a way for us each time," Charley said.

"He has and is continuing to make a way with this vision. I'm convinced more than ever that this move is right for Harvest, especially after this storm. I'm not going to continue to nickel and dime this church to death to keep a dilapidated roof over our heads. You know good and well that if this was your house causing you this much money every time you turn around, you would have put it on the market and cut your loses. Raising money for renovation has taken our focus off of ministry. We used to pray more, and praise Him more; we used to serve the community."

"So it doesn't make sense that now we are packing up and leaving this community. What's going to happen with the church building?"

"We control the fate of this building. In fact, Vanessa and I have talked about selling the building to some nonprofit organization that will provide services to the people in this area or we could run a community center and continue to do missionary work out here since so many of you live out this way."

"The Mrs. has a plan, huh?" Charley said, checking the change in his other pocket.

"Yes, just talking about this makes me more sure that this is the direction God wants us to move in."

"But c'mon, Pastor, January first is just around the corner, "Charley said, playing with the carton of the apple pie before sliding it out and taking a bite. He returned it into its container. Charley took the top off his cup and placed thirty three cents out on the table for his medium refill. He took a break from the conversation to get his refill while Willie finished his soda.

"I know, that is why we need everyone on board."

"I think we need more time for this transition. I mean, the packing alone will take the next three months. No one has even thought about starting that. Some of us have some strong ties to Harvest. I'm surprised you expect us to deal with this individually. We don't know what they are planning over there at Mt. Pleasant and vice versa. We may want to consider pushing back the date."

Willie could feel the wheels of change turn and began to gain momentum. He knew now that Charley was ready to throw a rock in the way to slow it down or even stop it.

"You've given me something to think about while I'm in my office waiting on people to give me estimates on the repairs that need to be done around the church. But right now, we need to get back," Willie said. He wasn't even going to suggest that Charley stay and discuss his ideas. He knew Charley had a schedule of game shows and an evening nap ahead of him.

Willie also knew Mae Richardson would be pulling up to the church soon to go over the schedule with him. He was glad he was able to talk things through with Charley. Hopefully he'll mill over what has been said and change his mind. Now he would get Mae's opinion. They walked back toward the church. The street was bright from the glare of the sun reflecting off the beads and puddles of water left by the storm. Willie waved to a few people he saw every week when he and Charley made this excursion.

"I know you have things to do before prayer meeting tonight. Promise me you'll give this move a chance. We are all praying that God uses us as He sees fit."

"I think the church needs a new gate. It's wobbly," Charley said.

"We'll take care of that too," Willie said. "Give the move a chance."

"I will," Charley said muffled within a cough. Willie walked him to his car and Charley got in quickly. He could see Roy Jones, a homeless man in the neighborhood that usually took up residence in the alleyway beside the church, approaching from the driver side window he was standing near.

"Excuse me, Pastor Green, uh Deacon Sir. I wonder if I sweep up in front of yo' church, would it be possible to get a couple of dollars to get something to eat?" Roy said, bowing his head in a reverent gesture.

"Stay right there a minute, Roy," Willie said, turning to say goodbye to Charley. He wanted to say one final thing that would make a difference in Charley's opinion. It looked as if Charley wanted to say something too, but Mae pulled to the curb in front of Charley's car, barely missing his front bumper.

"Holy moly," Mae said, eyeing the church as she got out. "Well, don't just stand there gentlemen, I have boxes. It's never too early to start packing."

Willie and Roy immediately began helping Mae at the trunk of her car. They realized that Charley was leaving by the sound of his tires pulling away from the curb. Willie wondered had anything he said permeated Charley's thick and stubborn skull. Whatever was going on in his head, Willie knew there were probably others like him who were filled with doubt in his congregation. The signs were clear to Willie. The minor repairs and non-existent Building and Maintenance fund was like a pebble sized warning from God; the damage from the tropical storm was like a brick. Willie rubbed his head; he didn't need a wall to fall.

Chapter 6

Decently and in Order

"Pastor, are you ready?" Deacon Buster Johnson said, knocking on the door outside of the Pastor's study.

"Come on in, Buster. I'll be just a minute," Willie said. He folded his notes into his Bible to mark the page of his message text and looked for one of his many handkerchiefs that he carried with him into the pulpit out of habit in case he needed to wipe his brow, but mainly just to hold while he preached.

Buster Johnson was the charge deacon that week, which meant one of his responsibilities was to escort the pastor into the sanctuary. Usually Pastor Green remained in his study through devotion time to pray and meditate until the service officially began.

"Why did you want to come out so early? Devotion has basically just begun." Buster asked.

"I know. I asked the Lord last night to show me what I can do to help the congregation prepare for the transition we are about to undertake. He told me to watch and see," Willie said, settling on a paper towel from the adjoining bathroom that he immediately began to fold into a square. He held the paper towel in his hand trying out the weight and feel of it. It wasn't like Mae to forget his handkerchiefs with the weekly laundry.

"Watch and see? Huh. Boy there's going to be some ripe testimonies this morning with you out there."

Willie tried to figure what Buster meant by his ripe testimonies comment. It was if he suggested that some people would embellish their experiences in order to put on a show just for him. Willie placed the folded paper towel on top of the Bible and indicated to Buster he was ready to go with his hand. Buster took the Bible from Willie at the door with one hand and used the other to go into his pocket. He pulled out a handkerchief already folded in fours and handed it to Willie for his approval. Willie smiled; he was comfortable with cotton.

"So, what did I miss out there already?" Willie asked.

"Oh, Deacon Simmons started with the scripture reading. Then Mother Lane sang a hymn and fell out." They rounded the bend into the hallway that led to the sanctuary door.

"My goodness, why on earth didn't you tell me that at first?"

"She does that nearly every week Pastor, every time she sings "Oh, How I Love Jesus." We just figured she is deep in the Spirit every time she sings that song." Buster said, perched at the sanctuary door, waiting to finish their conversation before proceeding.

"I didn't know that. I see Sister Lane walk down the isle just as fine every week."

"That's after she has laid down in the nurses' room. The nurses have her now."

"Nearly every Sunday? Seems like she would ask the Lord what he was trying to tell her or sing another song. Mother Lane is not a young woman. She shouldn't be falling out in the floor every week. She could hurt herself.

See this is the kind of stuff I miss. I can't wait to get out there. Let's go worship, Buster."

Buster led the way to the base of the altar and extended an arm to usher Willie up the four steps into the pulpit. Willie had to motion for the few members to sit who had stood automatically at the sight of their pastor, thinking time had slipped away and it was time for the beginning of service. He sat on the front pew with the other deacons, not wanting to take authority away from those that were leading the devotional period by sitting higher than them in the pulpit. A few people stood to share their short testimony followed by a song. The deacons served as the Amen corner, encouraging everyone with a hearty round of amens at the end of their song, prayer or significant point in their testimony. Willie tapped his finger and sang along with Deacon Pace who led the congregation into one of the easiest devotional songs with basically one word—Amen, and a few Hallelujahs thrown in.

Willie was enjoying his view from the front pew. He never understood the architecture of most churches where the pastor's view was partially if not wholly obstructed by his podium stand in the pulpit. From here he could see everything written on the faces and the body language of his people. He could see some people in earnest praise singing "Amen" as if it was a testimony by itself. He could also see pain on the faces of others who were desperate to hear a word of hope. Then he spotted Sister Tandy waving at him as he made his observations. She couldn't wait for Deacon Pace to bring his song to an end to pop up and share her testimony.

Even as she stood, Willie knew exactly what she was going to say. Sure enough she talked about taking in her sisters' kids, ages eleven, nine and five, because their mother was on drugs. She also talked about her eldest daughter who was only nineteen and was, as she put it, a slave to the world, who had two children, one age four and another age two, that were also with her in a three bedroom townhouse. This was the reason that her blood pressure was sky rocketing every time she had a doctor's check-up. Willie had heard this all before. Members had offered to help, but she turned them down. Willie had also advised her to tell her daughter to take and care for her own children, but another year had gone by and nothing had changed about her testimony except the children's ages.

"Saints, I ask you to pray my strength in the Lord," Sister Tandy said, taking a seat.

Willie remembered a conversation he and Vanessa had that revealed why Mt. Pleasant didn't have a devotion time. Vanessa said it was just an open mic for people to promote themselves. Willie argued that the Bible said we are overcome by the words of our testimony, to which she replied, "But who said a testimony had to be given in an open forum?" Vanessa just put that on a long list of topics that she would have to teach her congregation about before she could let it become a practice in her church.

Willie remembered her saying it as if their uncensored testimonies would do more harm than good. He thought about the testimonies he had heard today. None of them left him with a sense that the person had actually overcome something through the power of Christ. He heard the voice of the Lord saying, "New mercies but no new praise." Willie had to wonder to whose testament was it that they continue to have the same problem without the hope of change. He and Vanessa never revisited the topic since deciding to combine churches. The fate of devotion time when they got to Mt. Pleasant was up in the air and falling fast.

Finally Deacon Brown came up to say the closing prayer. He was the nicest man anyone would ever want to meet; a grandfather figure to all the kids at Harvest. But he surely could get tangled up in a prayer. The more words he uttered the more he seemed to keep spiraling back to the beginning.

"Gracious God, our Father, it's once more and again that I come before your throne of grace, thanking you for another day you didn't have to give. You touched us with a finger of love and told our golden moments to roll on a little while longer. Yes Lord, you woke us up in due time and not into eternity and we say thank you that our beds were not our cooling boards. All these and other blessings we ask in Jesus name we pray, Amen."

Willie kept his eyes closed a little while longer to pray his own strength in the Lord. Their ceremony or way of doing things was more entrenched than he thought, down to the same prayer, the same song, and in the same order. He knew everyone was waiting for him to transition them into morning service. He usually prayed before coming out that his sermon would be delivered with power and that souls would be saved. Now he prayed that the congregation would be flexible enough to withstand the transition he was about to take them through.

The Sunday School had dismissed and those members staying for morning worship were being allowed to enter the sanctuary by the ushers. Willie saw Charley behind the glass door check his watch. Willie suspected that Charley's curiosity as to what was going on led him to join the congregation that was waiting for service to begin instead of going home. The choir was in place just outside those doors. Buster was back on duty at the base of the altar. They all waited.

Willie was ready to mix it up a bit. "Oh give thanks unto the Lord for He is good," Willie said once he reached the microphone. For tens years, Willie had entered the sanctuary saying, "The Lord is in His Holy temple," which became the official signal for the choir to march in and for service to begin. "Oh come on, church. It's worship time."

The choir swayed into the church while singing "Soon and Very Soon", then remained in position for the opening prayer, responsive reading and the singing of the doxology. Gregory Johnson, the primary musician, played this musical prayer with the formality and tempo of a funeral dirge. Although it was a congregational song, Alice Jones' true soprano voice stood out with the high notes at the end while everyone else fell short in their delivery.

Then came the welcome, reading of the sick list, announcements and pastoral recognition or what he and his wife called intermission. Besides being the second most popular time to go to the bathroom for members, other than offering time, Willie liked this time where he could talk candidly with his congregation. This time had to do more with fellowship then worship, per se. Willie was always impressed how Vanessa wrapped her intermission up in five or ten minutes tops while he waited on Mae Richardson, the church clerk, to pass the piton off to him like the last man in a relay race. To Harvest, intermission could be a twenty to forty minute pit stop.

"When you come into the house of the Lord you ought to automatically feel welcome. The Harvest Baptist church extends to you an official welcome from our hearts. Welcome once, Welcome twice, you're welcome in the name of Jesus Christ. If we have anyone visiting with us that wish to make a response, you may do so," Mae said.

"Hello saints, I'm Floral Henry and I bring you greetings from Covenant Baptist Church in Nashville, Tennessee where the Reverend Henry J. Starr is my pastor. I used to live in this area and visited here quite a few times, but I'm retired now. I heard you all were fixing to relocate yourselves and combine with another church. Since I was coming this way with my niece, I figured I'd come over here and visit and see this church one more time. Pray for me and I'll pray for you," Sister Henry said, taking her seat.

Word travels fast, Willie thought. There were a couple of people he could see in the congregation that were like Sister Henry and visited Harvest all the time but just hadn't taken the step to make Harvest their church home. They didn't even stand anymore when Mae called for visitors. He wondered if they were going with them over to Mt. Pleasant at the first of the year. Mae read the list of the church's known sick and shut in like a memorial to those fallen in battle. Quite a few of those names that were read every week weren't actually sick, but rather pregnant, bereaved or had found another place to worship like Sister Mable Scott, who was the widow of one of the late deacons of the church and moved to Tallahassee.

Willie had to prepare himself to address the congregation but he was caught up in every detail of the service. He couldn't believe all the things he missed while meditating on his sermon text each week. He was sure that just like the Lord was showing him what to observe, the Lord would show him what to emphasize in the text. This was important to see what he and Vanessa would have to discuss later about the order and flow of their combined service.

Mae read off the announcements. She had a folder containing all announcements church members handed her throughout the week. Each were written on their own slip of paper. She left the podium to get her purse for her glasses, which she must have left at home because she came back to the podium without them. An usher came up to her and handed her an announcement on a little strip of paper. Mae struggled to make it out so the usher whispered the announcement in her ear. Willie took his place at the podium to bring an end to this delay in the service; everyone knew that Mae was too stubborn to have someone help her read the announcements. Willie had created a monster and he didn't know whether it was out of respect or fear, but everyone left it up to him to tame her.

"Souvenir booklets from the Pastor's tenth anniversary are still on sale for five dollars," Mae read with ease because it had been a standing announcement each Sunday since the event. "See me or any member of the Pastor's Aide Committee."

"Sister Mae, just give those things away. That was four months ago. Anyone wanting a booklet or to find out about any of the announcements need to see Sister Mae," Willie said. "Thank you, Mae, but I have something important I need to talk to the congregation about in regards to our move."

"But Pastor, the Willing Workers have a presentation to make to the church."

Willie saw those members of the Willing Workers scrambling to put their funds together from a recent fundraiser as Mae was talking. A choir member put on her travel signal, sticking one finger up in the air to indicate she was leaving the choir loft to find her team captain and hand her the money she had in her robe pocket. He saw an usher, who was also suppose to be on duty in the service, counting money so she could calculate the final total. That same woman made her way to the altar despite what Willie had just said, money in hand, no envelope. They all were out of order, Willie thought, and it was about time he addressed it.

"Ladies, return to your seats. You can turn in your money to a trustee later. We will make sure the amount of money you turn in is noted for the bulletin," Willie said. "This is the way we are going to do things from now on— decently and in order. Turn in all money before Sunday.

There will be no grandstanding at the microphone. I thank all ministries for working so hard to raise money for the church; really I do, especially since the tropical storm tore through here this past week. And again, if you're concerned that everyone will know what amount your group has turned in, we will have totals printed in the bulletin. The Bible says in the Gospels that Jesus despised the moneychangers in church. He thought they were turning his church into a den of thieves. Our primary function as a church should be prayer, praise and worship."

Where was his Amen corner now? Willie thought. Everyone was stunned at his deviation that the deacons were silent. Latecomers who normally came in time enough for the message found themselves in the middle of a church chastisement. Willie thought about what Charley said the other day about the move being a lot to deal with emotionally. They needed more lessons like the one he was giving at that moment and more information about the process. He saw Paul Grant enter with the latecomers and got an idea.

"Saints, if you were here for the special church meeting, you know that the Lord had chosen us to be an important part of a powerful church he wants to raise up. He could have chosen Bethlehem Baptist, Revelation or any of the other churches in this area. That means we have to be prepared. We must sharpen our focus on God and leave a lot of Harvest Baptist ways behind."

The ushers allowed a woman with her young son to enter that made Willie temporarily forget what he was talking about. She couldn't have been more than thirty, but her thin face looked more weathered than the slightly ripped and soiled clothing that she wore. It wasn't unusual for an occasional homeless person to find his or her way into the church from the main street, but Willie couldn't shake the fact that this woman looked familiar.

She took a seat a few rows from the front on the corner seat and sat her son on her lap to quiet him.

"I want you all to be involved in the process as much as possible. I saw Brother Paul Grant come in. Brother Grant, come up front here," Willie said. He waited for Paul to reach the base of the altar after basically just getting settled in his seat. "This brother here came up to me when I first got to Harvest Baptist Church ten years ago and asked me: 'How can I serve the church'? That told me right there that he has a willing spirit. I've taken him under my wing ever since. I have a position for you, Paul. Paul Grant will serve as our liaison between this church and our new church, Mt. Pleasant Baptist. He will bring back information about where we are in the unification process and get as many of you involved as possible." Willie nodded his head at Paul as if to certify if this new appointment was okay with him. When Paul returned the nod, Willie went on to say, "Thank you, Paul."

Paul was dismissed to his seat, no doubt, wondering what his new position would entail as the officers prepared to collect offering. Willie hoped he wasn't being overzealous in adding this new responsibility on Paul. He knew that Paul was settling in his career, which sometimes put him in a tussle with time and the management of it. He was a genuine good guy with no apparent hidden agendas like some church members Willie had come across.

Members of the Deacon board seated on the front row congratulated him by shaking his hand and patting him on the back except for Charley Thompson who pretended that he was filling out his offering envelope. Charley was probably wondering why Willie didn't think about appointing him for the new position. Willie wondered that as well. Reporting to the pastor about the affairs of another church or church entity was right up Charley's alley.

But then again, Willie thought, are those hidden agendas that he had ignored over the years?

The officers were back on their post of duty setting up the table for offering and Willie was back on watch. The trustees held the baskets while the deacon prayed, "Bless the gifts and offering we are about to receive. May they be used for the furtherance of your kingdom, Amen."

Willie wondered why all this time they prayed before the offering was collected. He thought for sure Vanessa's church did it afterwards. He didn't know if it made any real difference.

The young woman that sat three rows behind Paul was now being led to the basket by an usher that was unloading the assembly from their pews from the back of the church to the front. The woman went into her purse and found a few crumpled dollars and gave her son one just in time to put it in the basket. She clutched the money close to her before releasing it into the basket, and as soon as she was in the center aisle she dropped to the ground sobbing.

The deacons kept the members who were approaching the basket at bay. The usher posted at the choir loft helped to direct the remaining pews behind the deacons and the basket- holding trustees to merge with the opposite side so the congregation could continue giving. By the time Willie made it down the steps of the pulpit, the nurses had her up on the front pew with her son seated beside her.

"I'm sorry," she said at the sight of Willie. She stood burying her face into his robe front, "I didn't mean to break down like this."

"It's okay; we all have to cry sometimes. What ever it is, you can take it to the Lord," Willie said. This time the Amens were right on time from all those that were listening.

"I know, that is why I came here today. I knew this was the place for me to be because even when this church was damaged by the storm, like my house was, someone brought a bunch of food in a basket and left it on my door step with a tag from the church."

It dawned on Willie that he had seen this woman and her son in the neighborhood living two doors away from the church. "And the Lord brought you here today for a purpose."

"I have nowhere else to go. Part of my roof caved into my living room and we can barely move around in the house," she said, taking a deep breath to hold back the sobs so she could continue, "and this was Section-8 housing provided to me by the government. I had to wait two years on a waiting list. I could finally enroll my son in school and make sure he went everyday. If I call them and tell them what done happen to the house, I don't know where they are going to put me. I ain't been to work in three days since the storm hit so I could watch my house and my belongings."

"Honey, do you have any money?" Mae Richardson said, standing in her pew on the opposite side of the aisle.

"No, the devil tried to take everything I got so I made sure that I came today to give what little I did have to the Lord before he took that too."

"That was a tremendous act of faith, but the Lord wants you to surrender your life to him also. I know you have some immediate needs now that we have to try and figure out. When you're ready to do that we will be there for you."

"It seems to me that your house should be insured through the government, which means that it is only a matter of time before they fix that house of yours up. We had to call up the insurance on this church building also.

You might have to be displaced until they fix your roof. Let me put in some calls tomorrow to see what I can find out," Deacon Simmons said.

"Pastor, she and her little boy can stay with me for the time being," Eursela Banks said, embracing the woman. "I don't live too far from here. You can continue to send your boy off to school and you can get to work."

"Are you sure, Sister Eursela?" Willie asked "You might want to go home and ask Brother Banks first."

"Brother Banks better not have anything to say after his good-for-nothing brother just moved out after staying with us for nearly two years. This child is in need and we got plenty good space from the addition on our house built for my mother before she died."

"Well let me tell you what I'm going to do today, church. We have just finished taking up collection. I want you to take my portion and divide it up between this sister here and Sister Banks for her living expenses. Anyone else willing to reach in their pockets and give according to what God has put upon your heart should come now."

The nearby Trustees handed Willie the offering plate from each side, which was always reserved for his weekly living allowance and he held it in the center aisle. He beckoned for the woman, her son and Sister Eursela to stand by his side as a reminder as to why he was asking them to give yet again. Members left their pews to bring money to the plate or directly to either woman and whispered words of encouragement. This time there wasn't an usher to lead them orderly around. Willie could see that this was not the traditional disorder of the day, but rather the traditional outpouring of charity from the people at Harvest Baptist Church. The Usher who was collecting money from other members for the Willing Worker's presentation turned over the entire wad to the cause. After the long winded prayers and testimonies, impromptu presentations and a family in need, the Lord was telling Willie to forgo his message that Sunday. He had showed him that the Harvest Baptist Church members had always had the most important kind of service down pat.

Chapter 7

And the Man Shall Lead

Willie often watched television evangelists on cable television much like a person would watch an action movie. He wanted to be taken on a ride and contemplate the plot all at the same time. He tried to experience God through the worship experience as if first hand like the congregation sitting in front of the preacher. Vanessa, on the other hand, was too analytical. She tried to figure out where the preacher was going before he got there. She was concerned with style while he concentrated on the message. He found himself watching Bishop Robbie Robinson and the Generations of Hope Church from both perspectives while he waited for Vanessa to arrive home.

Bishop Robinson, known for his tear jerking testimonies and lengthy sweat-soaked pleas for salvation, called his wife, Corina, to the stage. He paused as the cameraman captured the First Lady's regal ascent up the stairs. She stood at the edge of the stage as if she awaited additional permission to enter the sacred space of the pulpit. An associate minister seated slightly off camera offered a hand to help her mount the final landing that set Bishop Robinson above all others in the service.

"Beloved, as I prepared this series, God's church, God's family, I was reminded of many stages in my thirty nine year marriage to Sister Corina here," Bishop Robinson said. "Today we discussed Godly order. My wife can testify to the fact that we didn't always have the Godly order in our lives or in our marriage."

At first glance, one couldn't imagine the couple old enough to have been married so long. Bishop Robinson especially looked great for his age, if a day over fifty. Bishop Robinson, who always kept a little length to his hair and a clean shaven face, showed no signs of graying. He wore a burgundy robe similar in shade to his wife's tailor-made suit in the event that they would be captured together like this for a photo; they wouldn't want to clash. No doubt their apparent good health and Hollywood appeal was due in part to the Lord blessing them with a pastoral covering to over 10,000 nationwide, which helped contribute to the best doctors, nutritionist, trainers, public relations specialist and wardrobers for their first family.

"My wife told me the day that I proposed that she would follow me as I followed Christ and she has stayed true to her word. I remember a time when I wasn't working. This was early on in our marriage, early on. Braxton, our first born couldn't have been no more than six then. After twenty years of working for the steel mills after high school I found myself out of work. The whole Labor Movement brought about unions, and guys like me who weren't signed up were let go when the union secured higher salaries and benefits for their people." Sister Corina patted her husband's back, apparently only called to the stage for moral support.

"Brothers you can imagine how I felt. I had asked for

my wife to leave the stability of her home with her parents to the uncertainty of life with an out of work steel worker. My wife went back to work at the beauty shop. We lived in a roach infested apartment, hear me now, days away from being evicted. I dreaded the thought of having to go to her parents for money, or worse, a place to stay," Bishop said, his wife closing her eyes as if the memory was painful.

"But God was with us. There is no doubt in my mind that it was the prayers of my wife and her constant support that helped me get back in line with God's will. Before then, I began to sink in a depression that kept me immobile for awhile. It kept me from taking the position God wanted me to have as the provider for my family."

The cameraman did a pan of the crowd that stopped at about the fifth row. There were men and ladies up front urging the Bishop on with the traditional church speak. Willie suspected those seats were filled with the Bishop's faithful following, the associates that had stock in the success of the Generations of Hope ministries. A good preacher played toward the back of the house where the less than devout Christians sat. He had been watching Bishop Robinson long enough to know when he was about to cast the net to reach those beyond the cameras lense and even those sitting in their living rooms like Willie. Any time a minister puts this kind of time in a personal story, especially air time that cost per second, Bishop Robinson was going for the big catch.

"Every week we would sit down with the money my wife had earned. She would turn over the check to me and ask what we should do with the earnings; what bills needed to be paid? It wasn't as if she didn't know, but she remained meek, humble and submissive to her husband and allowed me to keep some dignity."

"How many people know that she could have been like

some women today; 'you've got to have a J-O-B if you want to be with me' mentality. My opinion would have counted for nothing because I wasn't bringing home the bacon. God is saying, stop using the shortcomings of that man in your life as an excuse to step over him and take over. Next thing you know you have a wife who doesn't respect her husband. There is a Godly order. Don't step on your man when he is down. Help that man get to where he needs to be. If you help him up, he can help shoulder the load. Then you sistahs can return to the home and raise the generation of wayward children. Get your house in order."

Bishop Robinson was ready to reel them in. Willie knew exactly how it felt to be led by God to disclose a portion of your life with a congregation, and have it resonate with so many people. Bishop had them primed and ready for the call to discipleship.

"So we ignore all the comments about our relationship. We figured out a long time ago that it doesn't help our relationship any trying to conform to what others think we should be. We've heard all kinds of things from people, even people who use to work for us. Notice I said used to work for us. Some had the nerve to refer to Sister Corina as a slave because she takes care of her husband. Some take offense to the way she calls me Bishop or wipes my brow at altar calls. But guess what? She is exactly what I need. Let me tell you something, Sister Corina is a strong woman who is partially responsible for our family ministry here at GOH; but I am the man. I am in charge. God said, 'and the husband will be the head'. We have no problem in our relationship with our roles. If this family or our ministry goes astray, God will come to me like he did Adam and say, where are you Robinson? I see you hiding. What happened? I can't blame it on my wife then, like Adam did. It didn't work then and it won't work now, men. She is your wife, your gift and your blessing. Do not be afraid to tell your wife how you feel, what you need from her and what you expect from your family. "

Willie found himself saying amen aloud. He pondered the implications of the Bishop's message on the union of his church with Mt. Pleasant and his marriage. He felt he and Vanessa had an open relationship, but she was strong willed and was used to being in charge. He thought about how Vanessa quickly changed the plan of when they would tell their congregations about the vision to combine churches. There were some issues that had to be discussed before coming together over at Mt. Pleasant. Although her church had been pastored by a Morton for two generations, he was coming over to help lead it in a new direction. He didn't want to come across as an overbearing chauvinistic tyrant, but he had to be clear with his wife that he did not intend to get lost in the shuffle.

"We show God we love him by serving him. We show our husbands and wives we love them by meeting their needs. I realized I couldn't let my wife work herself to death to support our family alone and that any job was good enough as long as I was helping. God rewarded me," Bishop Robinson said. His wife Corina lifted holy hands in agreement. "He took my faithfulness and faith and gave me favor. He placed a call on my life and here we are today. He took care of our family. Let him take care of you."

The service was abruptly interrupted to allow time for an announcer to solicit seed offerings into the Generations of Hope ministry. Willie looked at his watch that was creeping up on six thirty and wondered where his wife was at that moment. It was their date night. He had given in to Vanessa's demand of keeping a weekly slot of time open for them to go out and have fun much like when they were dating. It was suppose to keep the relationship fresh.

Mondays were suppose to be their date night, but because of a meeting at her church the night before, she pushed it back a night. As it stood they were 0 for 1 for date night since the honeymoon. Willie was starting to realize that although he wanted a wife in ministry, he needed his wife home in the evenings, if not merely to establish a set dinner time.

Willie used the remote to turn the volume down when he heard Vanessa approaching. It wasn't until she had the door open that he realized she had her sister with her. It was rare that he allowed his emotions to get the best of him, but his anger at Vanessa's apparent disregard for their agreements had him on his feet with his arms crossed like a father ready to confront a child who broke curfew.

"What's up, bro?" Keisha said, giving Willie a hug before taking off for the kitchen.

"I guess we aren't going out tonight," Willie said curtly.

"Good afternoon to you also, Willie Green," Vanessa said, kissing his cheek before hanging up her coat. "Keisha caught me in the parking lot of the church as I was about to leave. She was like a little puppy dog that followed me home."

"I heard that."

"What's she doing?" Willie said, lowering his voice.

"I guess using the phone," Vanessa said, also whispering.

"I mean what is she doing here, tonight."

"She said she wanted to talk about some Singles' ministry stuff. Yada yada yada, you know Keisha. We will probably end up talking about some guy."

"What were you doing at church so late?"

"Stuff. You know how you go in to take care of a few things, and you wind up doing other stuff. I had a member who was in a car accident and I was waiting for someone to get back to me as to whether or not I had to make a visit. We couldn't locate her all day. Come to find out the ambulance had taken her to a hospital way up there on Capitol Hill and she had been released with a few scratches.

"I'm glad everything turned out all right," Willie said, ashamed of his insensitivity.

"While I was waiting to hear something, I decided to order you a chair."

"A chair?"

"For the pulpit, you know to match mine, but Ethan Allen must have stopped making the style I have. So I started looking through some catalogues and lost track of time."

"Don't I have a say in what kind of chair I'm going to sit in?" Willie said, determined to make an issue of something.

"When have you ever been concerned about picking out furniture? Besides, I already have a chair. I was just trying to get one that matches. What is with you?" Vanessa said, walking a wide curve around her husband as if trying to get around the tension filled space. She tossed the newspaper to the opposite side of the couch before sitting down.

"I just want to make sure I know about everything that goes on. I mean that, Vanessa, anything that has to do with the combined church, I want to know about—no surprises."

"What's for dinner?" Keisha said, interrupting. She pranced past Willie and plopped herself on the ottoman across from her sister. She looked up at Vanessa who looked to be taken by surprise and then she looked at Willie as if wondering why he was still standing.

"You didn't start anything?" Vanessa directed at Willie. "This time you were the first one home."

"I thought we were taking in dinner before the movie. It's date night, remember?" Willie said sarcastically.

"That's right. What time is it?"

"A quarter to seven."

Both Willie and Vanessa looked at Keisha as if to give her a hint. Keisha, in obvious oblivion, looked through a manila folder, preparing to spring some new idea on Vanessa.

"What are you guys going to see?"

"*The Preacher's Wife* with Whitney Houston and no, you're not coming with us," Willie said, finally taking a seat in his arm chair. "In fact, we need to leave in fifteen minutes."

"It seems like your brother-in law is trying to kick you out. This shouldn't take long, right, Keisha?" Vanessa said.

"I'm not paying him any mind. I love you all, but I don't want to go with you on your precious date night. I do want to see that movie though. I guess I'll just have to get someone to take me," Keisha said, sticking her tongue out at Willie. "I think Whitney Houston would have made a great first lady, don't you? I mean, when she first came out on the music scene, she was so positive—and so beautiful. You know her mother, Cissy, was a gospel singer. She was brought up in church. Yeah, Whitney should have married a minister."

"It takes more than that to be a first lady. First ladies are reserved and usually don't sing secular music for a living." Vanessa said.

"First ladies have a ministry to their husbands. They make sure his needs are taken care of," Willie added.

"Yeah, like Mom, gosh, she did everything for dad. First ladies keep a clean house and plenty of food in case company comes over," Keisha said, lingering a hand in the air.

"How about that?" Willie said, lifting up in the chair to slap a high five with his sister-in- law."

"Sounds like Bro-man wants a first lady like mom, sis."

"Well, he's getting something better. He's getting a co-pastor," Vanessa said after an awkward moment of silence. She then turned to Keisha. "Isn't it time for you to go?"

Willie wished someone could make his wife see that she could be both. "No, let your sister talk. I imagine we have a little time as long as we catch a quick bite."

"Remember when I was dating Rex Herman, that minister over at Trinity AME? I always used to think, what if God sees fit to give him his own church and we get married? What kind of first lady would I be? I guess I was rushing the relationship just a little bit. It never dawned on me that a minister could be a lying dog. He had a nerve to say he didn't know if a couple of dates could be considered a relationship."

"From what I've heard, both of you didn't in the least bit know what you were doing with yourselves, let alone each other," Willie said.

"Amen honey," Vanessa chimed in.

"How do you know, Willie?" Keisha said to him then immediately turned to her sister. "Gosh you don't have to tell your husband everything, do you?"

"She doesn't have to. You're always over here blasting your business yourself."

"I know it was a disaster," Keisha said, ignoring him. "I almost choked, on a communion wafer no less, when I went to his church to surprise him and found out he had been dating an usher there."

"I'm glad you didn't get mad at the usher. I hate it when the women get mad at one another instead of at the man that was stringing you both along. She probably didn't know about you either."

"Well, as long as you live, God will allow you to learn."

The key, is did she ever learn anything? Willie thought. He knew Keisha admired their relationship. He could just imagine the two of them when they were younger; the little sister looking to follow in the footsteps of her older sister. Keisha wasn't patient enough to wait for the man God wanted for her though. So she called herself helping Him out by dating everyone who asked. Then she wants to sit in their living room and ask for advice that she was sure to ignore. *Go figure, that this is the woman leading the Single's ministry at Mt Pleasant* Willie thought.

"I wanted to show you my work on the Singles Conference. I know it's in January, but I wanted to be prepared for the new singles that join our church after the churches combine; especially the single brothers," Keisha winked. "You guys should be so proud that I have something to report at the next Ministry Heads meeting."

"She's never ready with a report, so this is a plus for her," Vanessa said.

"The conference is at the end of January, thank God, so it doesn't interfere with Unification. I was thinking you and Willie could lead the first day, you know, set the tone for the year. Then maybe Pastor and First Lady Rawls could come up and teach on Saturday," Keisha suggested.

"No," Willie said.

"No?" Vanessa and Keisha said in unison, eyeing Willie suspiciously.

"This is a singles conference, not a marriage conference. Correct me if I'm wrong because we don't have a Singles Ministry at Harvest, but you're leading a ministry of individuals who want to learn how to make Christ their mate. Remember, not everybody wants to be married, like you do Keisha. Some are satisfied with their single status and want to live a life pleasing to the Lord. I sure wouldn't want some married folks talking to me about singles issues like abstaining from sex, when they are sanctioned by God to have that kind of family ministry. I would want to hear from someone who is living through the struggles I can relate to."

"Well," Vanessa said in an apparent lost for words.

"But I already discussed this with my committee and roughed out an itinerary with topics and everything." Keisha looked at her sister for help the way a child would who was playing both parents against another.

"Tell your committee thank you for being so diligent about ensuring a successful conference, but Pastor Willie Green thinks you all need to go back to the drawing board. It's called coming under the authority of your pastor."

"Excuse me," Keisha said, dropping her presentation papers on the floor.

"Get used to it, this man will lead, not be led," Willie said before realizing how corny he sounded.

Keisha let out a squeal like a balloon sputtering with a slow leak of air. Willie looked at his wife who was also muffling a laugh. Maybe he was going a little overboard. He knew they had been used to running things since their daddy had been gone. Willie had sat through many conversations like this one where the Morton sisters made a decision about some aspect of Mt. Pleasant. Willie would just remain quiet because at the time it didn't involve him. They would see that he didn't intend on taking a back seat.

"I will be co-pastor by then, and I will be more than willing to give the welcome or say a prayer at your conference. Matter of fact, give me a call tomorrow and I can give you the name of a minister over at Morning Starr that is single and leading a strong ministry in the Suitland area."

Willie could tell the prospect of meeting another single minister brought a smile to Keisha's face, but he didn't know what to make of Vanessa's expression. They would just have to get use to him putting his foot down every now and then. Vanessa wasn't the only one with a strong opinion. This was ministry, not two sisters party planning.

"We'd better get ready to leave. Don't you want to change?" Willie asked.

"What's wrong with what I have on?" Vanessa said, looking down at her purple sweater dress and black boots.

"You've had that on all day. Besides, would it hurt you to go out with your husband in a pair of jeans?"

"Jeans, huh? Good luck," Keisha said, placing her conference plans back in the folder.

"Baby, we're going to the movies, not on vacation," Vanessa replied.

"And?" Willie said, going to the closet for his jacket in an attempt to give Keisha yet another hint that it was time for them to go, therefore it was time for her to leave as well. "I like the way you look in jeans."

"That's why I wear them at home for you. We are going to the cinema down at the mall; anyone could see me— someone from my church, someone from your church, someone from the Baptist conference."

"Let me break it down for you," Keisha said, standing beside her sister to illustrate her point. "A woman of your wife's stature must be seen by her public with a tastefully made up face, very little foundation, definitely not a lot of rouge; a basic dress, not too form fitting, feminine, but not too business like either; and at least a two inch heel."

"And let me show you to the door," Vanessa said to let her sister know that she didn't need her help.

At that moment, Willie thought that his wife and her sister bore a slight resemblance to one another as they stood there smiling. Maybe it was because they both had their hair pulled back. Keisha, who had recently hacked her hair off, according to Vanessa, in an attempt to gain a new attitude around her thirty-fifth birthday wore her hair pushed back with a headband. Vanessa, on the other hand, had her length pulled back tightly and wrapped around itself at the nape of her neck to create a bun.

Once both Vanessa and her sister had their coats on,

Vanessa asked, "Is there anything else, Mr. Green, or can we leave?"

"Yes, as a matter of fact there is. Tonight . . ." Willie said, taking the opportunity to do something he had wanted to do since being married. He walked up to her and ran both hands along the wisps of hair along her hairline as if to smooth them back in place. He continued to run his hand through the crown of her hair, getting snagged a few times in thick masses of curls and finally the pins that secured her bun at the nape. One by one he dislodged the pins until her hair fell below her shoulders in the back. He took one hand to tousle her hair so that it fanned out on either side. "Your husband wants you to wear you're hair down."

Willie titled her chin slightly just as Vanessa tried to lower her gaze. She cleared her throat as if to let him know her sister was still in the room with them.

"I think that's my cue to leave," Keisha said, unlocking the front door. "The way the two of you are looking at one another; I doubt you guys will even make it to the movies. You might decide to engage in family ministry." And on that note, Keisha was out the door.

Chapter 8

The Choice is Yours

Mt. Pleasant sat at the edge of a city by a similar name in Maryland. Pleasant Heights was among many Maryland suburban cities in Prince George's county whose name suggested modest elevation. Towns such as Capitol Heights, Fairmont Heights, District Heights, Hillcrest Heights, Marlow Heights and Forest Heights ran north to south along the inner loop of the beltway. This area sat on a plateau above the District of Columbia and allowed each of these towns a ten to fifteen minute access to the capitol city.

Paul Grant drove up the incline to the parking lot on the side of the church. He rounded the corner to the back lot because he was nearly twenty minutes late and all the front spaces were taken. After his mother informed him that she would not be accompanying him to Harvest Baptist as usual, he decided to go to Mt. Pleasant Baptist to experience their service on the first Sunday since being named the liaison. The first thing he noticed was the size of this church. He could not figure out if the church looked so huge because it sat on a hill or because it really was that big.

Mt. Pleasant had unique architecture for a more modern church. It had two huge columns on either side of the building that supported a wooden trellis that created a covering over a stone walkway to the front entrance. A concrete steeple surrounded a circular pane of stained glass in its middle. Additional panes of glass were set inside the walls throughout the sanctuary. Brass fixtures and handles highlighted the huge oak doors.

Church announcements were being read as the usher led Paul down the center aisle. He tried to walk in unobtrusively and find an aisle seat on the right side of the church. The usher, an aggressive female, blocked the way and stuck an insistent palm towards the center aisle. This aisle separated the large church in half. On either side were twenty curved pews that got longer toward the back of the church. The arc of the pews formed a semi circle that nestled the altar and pulpit.

The usher secured Paul a seat between an elderly gentleman and a lady with two children. The church announcer was reading an invitation to a unification retreat for both Mt. Pleasant and his church. She rattled off several dates for the planning committee for that retreat. *Here comes a round of meetings,* Paul thought. He wondered why Pastor Green hadn't mentioned anything about a retreat to him and figured that he probably was waiting until today's worship service to spring it on him, just like he sprang the liaison appointment on him.

Paul's focus was turned to the choir stand that ran along the sides and back of the pulpit platform. A tall thin man stood to direct the close to fifty member chorus in a song. The choir members stood as directed. They had on deep burgundy robes that were a couple of shades darker than the covering on the pews.

The choir sang a version of "I'll Fly Away" that Paul had not heard before. It had the same words but a decidedly funkier baseline. It added another dimension to the old classic. The lady beside him was on her feet immediately. Her two children, both boys, bopped and swayed along side her. The younger one did a side step and clap combination that landed him on Paul's foot every other beat. Those who remained seated clapped along with the choir.

The choir director, who wore a cream colored robe, sang lead in a raspy voice while moving his right hand to signal the choir. The choir was accompanied by what sounded to Paul like a small band. A brother in a black suit played the organ. A bass player, keyboard player, and drummer were behind the singing ensemble and could not be seen from where Paul was sitting. He was surprised to see no one on the piano since that and a tambourine were the instruments of choice at Harvest.

Harvest's Combined choirs could not compare to this, Paul thought. Every Sunday, Sister Richardson would beg members to come out and join the choir during the announcements. The same handful of people that were in one choir appeared in the other choir as well. Paul could not imagine Sister Jones or any soloist at Harvest Baptist singing a rift over this melody. To them, any song with this much percussion must be a sin. He thought if they were singing like this at Harvest, there would be no problem attracting people to the choir.

The second song was a slower selection that Paul didn't recognize. The harmony was finely tuned. Paul could hear the distinct parts within the richness of sound. It was like riding a roller coaster. The song seemed to escalate its pace as each part reached a note higher. Once again the director sang lead, pointing a bony finger upward as the singers went higher with each chorus. The song ended as each section reached the initial note of the part above them. Tenors belting out alto, alto's wailing at soprano and soprano's reaching for the heavens. The majority of the congregation was standing and reeling in the climax of praise. Paul took in the awesome experience like a spectator at a ticker tape parade.

Deacon Thompson, who also decided to check out Mt. Pleasant, had a funny feeling sitting in another church service other than his own. He seldom visited other churches unless his pastor was preaching. And here he was sitting in a strange church. He could not get comfortable knowing a woman sat behind the preacher's desk waiting to address the crowd with the word from the Lord. Men were the only preachers in the church where he grew up in Louisiana. There were lady faith healers and voodoo priestesses that could manage to draw a crowd under their tents during Festival season, but you couldn't call them preachers. Charley was always told that they were full of sin.

Charley's mom was one of them. His dad had told him for years that she was very sick and eventually died in a hospital far away from their home when Charley was five. One night during Festival, Charley had wondered into the tent of Sister Gertrude, who was known for leading a group of gypsy women through the south, praying for the sins of men. They were known as the Daughters of Eve and literally blamed Adam, and all men for that matter, for what they called hell on earth. No one exactly knew where these women lived before and after Festival in Lake Chamberlin except for the fact that the location excluded all men. That night Sister Gertrude had women lined across the front of a milk crate altar rubbing something on their foreheads. She started chanting something so fast that it seemed to put them all in a trance. A few women came up to the front as the chant got louder.

"Join the chain of converts, sisters. Leave this man-made hell hole behind. God doesn't want us to live like this. It is the evilness of man that has the world in the shape it is in now." Charley was suddenly focused on one of Sister Gertrude's assistants—his mother. He had studied the picture that was framed in their living room and was sure that the woman he saw was her. She was walking along side Sister Gertrude, co-signing every statement Sister Gertrude made with a nod or a verbal agreement. She held an old container of Crisco oil which Sister Gertrude dipped her finger into to anoint the new converts. He watched her go behind the curtain backdrop that separated the makeshift sanctuary from their sleeping area. Charley left his spot behind the back flap of tent and circled on the outside. He waited for the next time his mother took a break. He tried to dodge the track lighting of beeswax candles that cast his shadow on the tent. If he was going to approach her, it had to be then.

Had he gotten her attention that day, he would have asked her why she left him and his father. Charley's dad had grabbed him, though, before he could put his plan into action. He had tried to tell his father that he had seen his mother. Charley couldn't understand why his father wouldn't want to see his mother well again and why he was so upset at him. Finally his father had said, "Any woman who would run off from her responsibilities to her family and pretend to preach the gospel, just as well be dead."

In time, Charley adopted his father's philosophy about his mother and women in general which was that women were put on this earth to build and take care of her family. There was no need to pretend anymore. The framed picture of his mother came down and a picture of his aunt, who had helped raise Charley ever since his mother left, went up after her marriage to Charley's dad. Charley's Aunt Agnes was different from her older sister. She had no outside interest other than dutifully looking after both Charley and his dad. His mother was never mentioned again.

Pastor Vanessa Green stood silently at her podium, allowing the Spirit that filled the crowd after the musical selection to die down. She was 5'8 and of slender build. She wore her mane pulled tightly back in a bun. Her soft, leather bound Bible stood open to the text for the morning.

"Thank you, Morton Memorial Choir, for those selections," she said. Charley was shocked at how powerful her amplified voice sounded.

He became disturbed as Vanessa directed her congregation to the book of Joshua for the morning message. She really felt she had authority to preach the Gospel, he thought. He thumbed through his own Bible to the sixth book. He considered walking out then but he wanted to make sure he saw a whole service. He would then be able to give full report to his wife when he returned home. He just hoped the service wouldn't take all morning. In his mind, he couldn't figure out how this woman could pass herself off as a pastor and how this church board would allow her to take on the appointment of a man. Not to mention, his own pastor married this woman and believed in her ministry enough to change everything and combine churches with hers. Willie had shared with him that his wife had assumed the duties of her late father. Clearly the church wanted to keep the church within the Morton family.

The passage Vanessa directed the congregation to came from the twenty-fourth chapter, fifteenth and sixteenth verses. She read it aloud to the congregation.

"And if it seem evil unto you to serve the Lord, choose you this day whom ye will serve; whether the gods which your fa-

*ther served that were on the other side of the flood, or Amor-
ites in whose land ye dwell; but as for me and my house, we
will serve ye the Lord."*

She intoned, "The choice is yours" as a sermon title. "I
can feel that I got the right message for you this morning.
The choice is yours. Turn to your neighbor and tell them
that the choice is yours," she said, stamping her foot with
each syllable. Charley ignored the middle-aged woman
who turned his way. His eyes were locked on the preacher.

"The Lord always gives us free will; even from the beginning in the Garden of Eden," Vanessa preached. "The
lesson we must learn is to stay within the will of God. See,
we are being used daily. Say Amen, the choir is always
singing, 'Use me Lord.' That should be our divine purpose, but the devil has the same thing on his mind. Sometimes we allow the devil to use us for his purposes. I don't
know about you, but I don't want to help the devil out
with his plan." She paused dramatically, shaking her head
back and forth.

"Let's see what these verses have to say to us. The Word
says if it seems evil unto you to serve the Lord. Why would
it be evil to saints? Some of us cannot discern those things
that are of God from those that are not. So we end up
bucking against the direction of God. Lordhamercy!" She
exclaimed, hunching her shoulders up and down.

"The Lord says you have a choice. You can serve me, go
in my direction or stay in the land of your fathers, that old
backward land with old backward ideas and ways. Some of
us are struggling with whether we are going to stick
around when our church unites with Harvest Baptist, as if
the change in churches, changes our God!" she said,
smoothing her hair with the flat of her right hand.

"The choice is not between Vanessa Green and Willie
Green; or between Mt. Pleasant Baptist and Harvest Bap-

tist. That is why it is important to stay focused on Jesus, and learn of him. Ask him to direct your path and follow him," she yelled, pounding a fist on the podium.

"I wish we could bring Harvest Baptist here right now via satellite to hear this."

Deacon Thompson sat in awe. He felt as if Pastor Green was speaking directly to him the whole time. She did not know him or the situation. There was no way he could come here, he thought. Vanessa Green was too outspoken. Didn't the Bible say women should keep silent in church? And to think his pastor had seen how this woman preached. Charley thought back to when Harvest Baptist came to fellowship with this church. He had decided not to go because he knew Mt. Pleasant had a female pastor. He never figured his own pastor would marry her. There would be no way Charley would allow his wife to rant and rave in church or anywhere in public for that matter. He huffed, picked up his coat and prepared to leave.

"As for me and my house, Willie and Vanessa's house, Harvest Baptist and the Mt. Pleasant Baptist churches, we will serve the Lord. I have got to close, but, what happens when you make the wrong choice? Write this prescription down so you can read it when you get home, Deuteronomy 30:19. The choice is yours," Vanessa finished.

Deacon Thompson wrote the verse down and retreated as the call was made for Christian discipleship. *Dag, it's 1:30; the football game has started*, he thought. Mt. Pleasant could never be his church home with a woman at the helm. It was a mockery to Charley. He wondered how many deacons at Harvest had seen how their pastor's wife carried on over here. He would call every one of them and tell them this move was not right. *Apparently our pastor is blinded by love for this woman*, he thought. There were many Biblical examples, Adam and Eve, David and Bathseba, Samson and Delliah, of how women have corrupted great men. Willie Green is another example. He remembered how she could barely contain herself in the pulpit today. How is Pastor going to come over here in her territory and lead?

Meanwhile, Paul Grant was blown away by the powerful preaching of Vanessa Green. He could almost see why his pastor had fallen in love with her so quickly. She didn't bite her words. He always liked strong women who knew what they wanted and could articulate it. She had a way of mixing words for effect that he could relate to since he was a writer.

Paul thought he should at least talk to Sister Green about his newly appointed position and ask her what he could share with the people of Harvest Church. He found her at the base of the altar after service.

A woman who was standing alongside Sister Green stuck up a finger to indicate it would be a minute before he could speak with Sister Green who was praying with a troubled member. Their prayers got louder at times, causing Paul to lower his head out of respect. After a few moments of hearing nothing but silent sobs, Paul made eye contact with Sister Green.

"Amen, It is so," Vanessa said, ending her prayer while extending a hand to Paul. The woman who appeared to be Sister Green's assistant, walked away with the woman who they had just finished praying over.

"May I help you?" Sister Green said, apparently use to sorting through the needs of her members after service.

"Hello, I'm Paul Grant, from Harvest Baptist Church. Pastor Green appointed me liaison between our two churches."

"The liaison, huh?" Sister Green said, appearing to be thinking. "I'm sorry Brother Paul, but I wasn't aware we had a liaison."

"I think it was kind of a spur of the moment thing to help Harvest Baptist Church members feel more comfortable with the changes and get them involved in the process."

"Don't get me wrong, I think it is a good idea. My husband just neglected to tell me. But as you can imagine, things are getting more hectic by the day. Three more months and the craziness will be over. That is the hope. How can I help?"

"What are some things Harvest members can do to prepare to blend with this ministry?" Paul said, feeling more like a reporter than a liaison. He was beginning to regret putting her on the spot like that, but he just wanted to have a clue as to what he could do to help in his new position. He got the feeling that neither Sister Green nor his pastor had any idea of how they were going to pull this move off themselves.

"Well I think by doing exactly what you did today, visiting Mt. Pleasant, can make them more comfortable. It's much like anything new. You got to research and find out if it is the right match for you. Let me put it to you like this: if you were going out to purchase a new car or shop around for health insurance, you would go out and research the company, read the literature on it, go to the dealer or health care provider. Likewise, when making the decision of a church home. You need to read up on the role of the church in the Bible, and visit the company which is the local church. If one dealership is rude and nasty or is not meeting your needs, you go to another one—in this case, another church," Vanessa said as if it were that simple.

"Well, I thank you," Paul said.

"Are you available this coming Tuesday?"

"Umm, I'm not sure."

"The eighth? The fifteenth? The twenty-second?" Vanessa asked.

"Ma'am?"

"Did you get the dates for the Retreat Committee? The retreat committee is meeting every Tuesday of this month to plan our combined retreat in November."

"Ah, no ma'am. I'm not sure of my prior commitments right now to even say for sure if the retreat is even feasible for me."

"Hmm," Sister Green said, "Let me do this, let me talk to my husband—your pastor, 'cause I definitely have some ideas about making the move a smoother transition. It would be great to have some Harvest members involved. We're going to have to get on the ball with our communication though. If you have any further questions or suggestions, you can tell him or call me here at the church.

"I sure will," Paul said, noticing that she was already pulled into a conversation with another member.

Paul at least felt as if he had something to hold onto. He couldn't wait to tell his mother, who had also been worried about the move herself and if she would like such a large church. He would reassure her because he figured that was part of his job as a liaison. The services were longer than what they were used to at Harvest. He didn't know if he could get his usual four hours of work in that day. He usually spent that time in his home office on Sunday afternoons to finish up a manuscript after church and have dinner with his mother.

Paul looked at his watch. It was already quarter after two. He knew that if he visited with his mother and started going over the details of his visit to Mt. Pleasant that he would not complete the Montana recall project. Paul was a technical writer by trade working for ISC Communications, a corporation of writers who were contracted out to write proposals, brochures, and manuals in layman's terms for the mainstream public. This project was his first level two research project. Montana, a large car manufacturer, let thousands of new Transports, their sports utility model, off the assembly line with the old gas caps that did not allow enough pressure to release from the gas tank. It was more economical for the customer to self install the new cap and have a mandatory inspection than to recall 125,000 cars. His job was to convince the customers that this was an added safety measure by Montana as opposed to a manufacturing mistake. Then he would work with the Montana team to write simple installation instructions.

Paul wanted to proofread and edit his own manuscript, which wasn't necessary because they had an editing team at ISC. A flawless manuscript is what he strived to produce before submitting it to editing. *Sorry mom,* he thought. He opted for an hour conversation with his mother instead of a two to four hour visit.

Sundays were usually spent with his mom, Thelma Grant, for healthy portions of good food and a dose of her wisdom. He wished he had his cell phone to call his mom on his way home. He wanted to get their conversation over with so he could concentrate on his manuscript when he got home.

The phone was ringing when he entered his townhouse. Paul assumed it was his mother and was surprised to hear a man's voice on the other end.

"Hello, Paul. It's Deacon Charley Thompson."

"Hello Deacon. What can I do for you?" Paul said, standing by his kitchen extension with his suit jacket still in hand.

"I wanted to talk to you about this move our pastor and his wife have planned for us. I went over there to pay the new church a visit and I don't really think there is enough room for us there."

Paul could not believe his ears. Deacon Thompson couldn't possibly be talking about the same place he had just visited. Paul wondered why Deacon Thompson was calling him with his concerns. He never recalled Deacon Thompson calling him before.

"I just visited a service at Mt. Pleasant today as well and talked with Pastor Vanessa Green. In my opinion, they have plenty of space with a good twenty rows of pews on each side of the aisle," Paul said, taking a seat on his counter side stool.

"Uh, I don't mean physical space," Charley said. "Look, since you've been over there, you know and I know that a woman pastor isn't right for our church."

"I don't have a problem with a woman preacher. I found Sister Green to have a very warm spirit," Paul said.

Paul didn't think that the move was an option. He had honestly never given the fact that Sister Green being a woman preacher might be an issue to some people. He personally had been more concerned about the distance of the location and length of service at their new church home.

"This move has to be stopped," Charley declared.

"Whoa, wait a minute. This is something you should discuss with pastor."

"You're the liaison, right?"

"Yeah, but . . . ," Paul said.

"Yeah, well, you're supposed to make sure the congregation is ready for this move and I say we aren't. I have been calling other members and I got a group of them who feel the same way I do. Now, what are you going to do about it?"

Paul had never heard Deacon Thompson so agitated and irrational. He really didn't have a reply because he wasn't aware that answering to disgruntled members was a part of his job description.

"I'll let the pastor know," Paul managed to say before Deacon Thompson hung up on him.

Chapter 9

Can I Get a Witness

Charley had to go out to the store to buy some quick relief for his pounding headache after making several phone calls like the one he had made to Paul Grant. Many people dotted the sidewalks of the plaza going in and out of stores. He remembered a time when commercial establishments were closed on Sunday with respect for the Lord's Day. If someone needed something like medicine, they would have to borrow from a neighbor or wait until the work week. But everything was made for convenience these days, like the combining of his church with Mt. Pleasant. It couldn't get any more convenient for Pastor Green and his wife.

Charley met the gaze of a familiar woman coming out the store as he was entering. He wasn't young anymore and he couldn't recall names as well as he did faces.

"Hello Deacon Thompson. Harvest must have let out kind of late today," she said, noticing his church attire that he hadn't taken the opportunity to change out of yet.

"Hello, nice to see you again," Charley said, holding the door for another woman waiting to go into the store.

"It's Blanche."

"Of course, Blanche Seward," Charley said, saying the woman's full name. Blanche Seward had attended Harvest Baptist for about two years. She was the kind of woman who wore the hem and neckline of her suits shy enough to let men know she was single and looking. Charley hated women who would blatantly display themselves just to snag a husband with some importance in the church. Blanche was one of those women. He remembered when Blanche's sights were set on Pastor Green. If it wasn't for the deacon's board, he was sure Blanche would have sat right up in the front row so Pastor Green would have a better look at what she had to offer. Willie, being a man, fell for her single, saved and sanctified routine. Charley knew Willie was interested in pursuing a relationship with Blanche by the way he would offer to give her a ride home after Bible study instead of instructing one of his deacons to do so. Charley told Willie she was working her way through all the Baptist churches with single pastors. Charley had thought that someone had to put a stop to it. Besides, to Charley, it was good that their pastor remained single. It kept the old women baking and the young women meek with hopes of getting Willie's attention. Blanche left the Pastor's Aide Committee of Harvest Baptist church less one member when her overtures to Willie Green were no longer returned. That was not before Blanche tried with all her womanly wiles to change his mind.

Charley let Vanessa Morton fly under his radar though. He never thought Willie could possibly take her ministry seriously. Now he was about to lose his entire church because of it.

"Don't tell me you joined a new church," Blanche said. "You and Willie are still friends, right?"

"I was just visiting Mt. Pleasant Baptist Church this morning. You know Willie just got married. His wife is preaching over there. He and his wife have plans to join churches next year."

"If that don't beat all. It is a small world."

"You're familiar with Mt. Pleasant and Vanessa Morton?"

"I guess you could say I worked for her a bit. Well, well, Willie and Vanessa Morton got married. That's great," she said, not looking half as happy as her sentiment.

"Yes they did. What did you say you did at Mt. Pleasant?" Charley said, stepping out of the doorway, suddenly interested.

"Oh, I am an auditor. My company was contracted to get the churches books straight so she wouldn't lose that big church of hers."

"Really?"

"I'm sure they are straight now. She and her father were receiving a living allowance from the church, you know, to pay for their mortgage and daily expenses. It was stipended out maybe four times a year, I guess, so it wouldn't be considered a salary." Blanche shared. "Harvest was used to taking up special offerings for Willie because he was taken care of by his retirement checks from the government. When Vanessa became full time at Mt. Pleasant, the board approved her position to be salaried. I don't know who the church accountant was then, but salaries and benefits need to be taxed, and they weren't at first. You know, she got to pay Uncle Sam like the rest of us. We told her it's either one or the other, allowance or salary. That, on top of remodeling the sanctuary so that it was state of the art, nearly broke the church," Blanche said shrugging her shoulder. "I suppose, that could put a damper on a stewardship message if you come one Sunday and the church's lights are out, don't you think?"

"Interesting," Charley said.

"I guess Willie will be on salary now too. Better be prepared to start giving more than you did at Harvest," she laughed.

Charley felt like he did when he was a kid and had just finished the Ranger Rick puzzle in the newspaper that revealed a piece of the plot on his weekly radio show. He had to go tell everyone. "Blanche, I don't want to take anymore of your time. Do you have a card? I got a meeting coming up with Willie and we may be able to use your expertise."

Charley noticed how her eyes lit up with the prospect of talking to Willie again. *This might work out well,* Charley thought, *because Blanche Seward doesn't mind playing the vixen.*

"Sure," she said, retrieving a business card from her clutch purse. "Tell me more."

Charley changed directions to walk Blanche to her car. He suddenly had no need for the medicine.

Chapter 10

A Cause for Alarm

Willie stood dumbfounded in the walk-in closet after throwing his starched shirt into the dry cleaning pile and putting on an army green polo shirt. He was trying to figure out what could have happen to Charley that would make him neglect his duty as the designated reader during his sermon. Buster Johnson had worked out surprisingly well that morning when Willie went to him out of desperation. Although he stuttered a bit out of nervousness, he came in on cue to reread the passage each time.

Vanessa came in the bedroom humming a familiar tune. Willie had been so deep in thought that he failed to hear her come in the house.

"Blessed be the rock of my salvation," Vanessa sang out. "Hey, hon." She greeted him smacking a kiss on the side of his face.

"Got some chicken and rice with peas in the kitchen from Sister Richardson," Willie said.

"Great," Vanessa said. Willie had not expected that response.

He watched as she substituted a heather gray sweat suit and all white Keds for the purple a-line dress and black patent leather pumps she had worn to church before going downstairs to the kitchen. He followed down the steps behind her.

Maybe Vanessa was thankful for Sister Richardson's home cooked handouts today, Willie thought.

"If this woman can prepare the meal, the least I can do is heat it up and serve it properly to my husband," Vanessa said as if reading his mind.

It occurred to him that she may have a lot on her mind too. Willie had learned in the short amount of time that they had been together that Vanessa had a strange and irritating way of glossing over conflict until she had stewed over it for a while. She's a woman who speaks her opinion, but Willie had to admit that sometimes he had no idea how strongly she felt about an issue. She took on an, "if-you're-okay-with-it-I'm-okay with-it-too" mentality the first time she preached at Harvest for the Nurse's Unit anniversary until afterward when he found out differently. Then, she was ready to explode.

Willie wanted to tell her about some of the points of his sermon, but he wanted to give Vanessa a chance to unwind. That was shop talk and they were off the clock. Willie sat down and allowed her to serve him since she seemed so determined to get the food out of Mae's bag and into her dishes that she ripped the bag in the process. Every plate had its run through the microwave oven. She pulled fork after fork out of the drawer to carefully match the silverware as if with each detail she could claim more ownership over the meal. Finally, she set the small circular table at the bay window of the kitchen with two steaming plates of chicken and rice, two small bowls of peas and a pitcher of iced tea.

"Tell me about your morning in church," Willie said, sipping his tea as she situated everything on the table.

"Tell me about the liaison you appointed between our two churches," Vanessa said so casually that Willie reasoned that this was what was troubling her. She bowed her head to bless the table quickly before getting a reply.

"Charley had suggested to me that the congregation might have a harder time than I thought leaving Harvest, you know, for sentimental reasons. So, one day during worship service, I saw Paul come in and just thought, here is a way to get him involved in ministry. He's very likable in our congregation, so I thought he would be ideal to champion our cause."

"You say cause as if there is a revolution going on over there at Harvest," Vanessa said with a raised eyebrow.

"Uneasiness," Willie said. "How'd you hear about the liaison job?"

"Surely not from you," Vanessa said, taking another stab at her point and the piece of chicken in front of her. "Brother Paul came to my church today to ask for clarification on his role, for which I couldn't give."

"Oversight," Willie said nonchalantly.

"I'm sure it was," Vanessa said sarcastically. "I don't like being left in the dark any more than you do. I mean the other night you went on about a pulpit chair that I didn't talk to you about and the Singles Conference thing, but I don't know about something as important as a liaison to my church."

"I know sweetheart, my fault. So what do we do, bring an alphabetical listing of our members with roles and responsibilities to the dinner table?"

"That may not be a bad idea. Or how about two lists labeled the laborers and the troublemakers," Vanessa said smiling. "I'm kidding, but it just feels weird. Here we haven't been married three weeks yet and already I miss the times when we didn't allow our church business to spill over into our relationship."

"I know what you are saying, but we can't continue to operate as if our churches are two separate entities. Maybe that's the problem. We should be making joint decisions. After the retreat, it will get better. We'll have it all ironed out."

"Yeah, they say He's coming for a church without spot, nor wrinkle," Vanessa said.

"By then, you'll get to know my spots and wrinkles and I'll get to see yours."

They rested in that notion as they began to really eat the food that they had only picked over before. Willie got up to go to the pantry. He knew what they needed to lighten the mood. Willie and Vanessa shared a love for board games. Even when they were dating, the couple could be found setting up and playing Clue, Jenga, Scrabble, Monopoly and their favorites, Checkers and Connect 4 on evenings, days-off and holidays. They kept their collection in the pantry along with the canned and dried foods. The more strategic the game, the better the game was to them.

Willie pointed to the battered checker board as he took his seat. He placed their drinks and condiment shakers in the window seal to allow room for the board in between their plates.

"Ooh, you must want to take a beating today," Vanessa said.

"Keep dreaming sweetie, keep dreaming," Willie said, setting up the board.

Before they could begin the game, the telephone rang. Willie jumped up thinking it might be Charley calling. For some reason, Willie could not sway his mind from thoughts of his friend. Charley would have called Willie by now. It

was a ritual for Charley to call on Sunday, even after seeing him during early service and say, "Do you need me to
come by and pick up the trash around the church on
Wednesday?" To which Willie would say, "I can use the
help. Afterwards we can catch a bite to eat."

"Willie, it's dinner time, let the machine catch it,"
Vanessa said, anxious to get started.

"I know, hon, just this one, I am expecting a call about a
member," He said, going through the swinging doors to
the kitchen to pick up the nearest extension.

It was Paul Grant. Willie listened as he explained how
Charley was calling people from church opposing the
move. Paul had been trying to talk so fast, but from what
Willie could figure out Vanessa and the manner in which
she conducted her services were the reasons for his dis-
sension. Charley had taken it upon himself to do some in-
vestigating at Mt. Pleasant. Willie was angry just imagining
Charley reporting every detail to the other members, especially those on the deacon board instead of coming
straight to him. Charley could be quite dramatic when he
wanted to prove a point.

So it was Vanessa that got Charley in a tizzy, Willie thought
with displeasure. What was it with him? Could he earnestly
believe that his choice of a mate was unholy? Did he doubt
their ability to keep their home life separate from church?
Willie thought all this time that Charley was concerned
about leaving the community. It was one thing to have
strong opinions about female pastors, and quite another
to try and persuade others to take on his viewpoints.

Willie felt defensive, as if a case were being tried against
him. The burden of proof was on him that this move was
actually the will of God. Charley was on the opposing side,
contending that the pending union was just a whim of a
newlywed couple and the congregation was the impres-
sionable jury waiting for the evidence to be presented. He

was use to stepping out on faith when most of his congregation couldn't see the move of God, but, this situation with Charley felt different somehow.

"Is everything alright?" Vanessa asked as he returned to the table.

"Yeah, everything will be okay," Willie said, forgetting everything they had said previously about sharing information about their churches and church members.

They could hear the phone ringing again. It was probably another deacon from the church who received an infamous call from Charley. But why had they called on this phone? He had a separate line installed in the office for his board members to call him about church business. Vanessa didn't afford her board members that privilege and only select members had her home number. He imagined before the night was through that both phones would be ringing off the hook.

"I'll let the machine pick this one up," Willie said, making the first move on the checkerboard.

They proceeded to alternate between moving red and black pieces and taking bites of their dinner. Vanessa was able to diminish his side on the checker board to half the pieces. She approached the corner spot and ascended a claim to Checker's royalty while the machine played their outgoing message. It was a cheerful message Vanessa recorded the day they got back from Hawaii. That could be interpreted by anyone that heard it as, we are in love and glad to advertise it—oh, and by the way, leave a message. This was very different from the vague message Vanessa recorded on her private line when she lived with her sister intended to preserve her anonymity.

A female's voice could be heard after the beep. "Hello, Willie, this is Blanche Seward. Look, I need you to give me a call. There is something I need to discuss with you. I ran into Deacon Thompson today. I was surprised when he told me that you and Vanessa Morton had met, fell in love and got married all inside of a year. I told him this is truly a small world; especially since I worked at Mt. Pleasant for a short time and had gotten to know her. Of course you and I had gotten close as well while I was at Harvest. Tell Vanessa I said hey. I'm happy for you two."

Everything seemed to stop as they listened to the message—the eating, the game playing, and all other sound. What could Blanche Seward want and how did she get their new number? He could tell that Vanessa was wondering the same thing, and since Blanche wasn't there, he had to try an offer an explanation.

"Is there something you want to tell me?" Vanessa said, eyeing him suspiciously.

"Apparently she just found out we got married from Deacon Thompson and called to congratulate us," Willie said, not wanting to put much credence into the call. He leaned toward the checkerboard to study his next move, realizing that one careless move could cost him the game.

"But she wants *you* to call her back."

"Blanche used to go to Harvest. Honestly, I have no idea what she might be calling me about now," Willie said, making a safe move to a corner spot. *That part was true,* Willie thought. It just wasn't their complete history, which he didn't think was necessary to reveal.

"Well, she was a part of an auditing team that worked with the trustees and our church accountant after my first year as pastor."

"Is there anything you want to tell me?" Willie asked.

"I just did," Vanessa said, raising her voice a notch. "How long were you two dating?"

"Huh?" Willie said.

"Like I said, I know Blanche. In the short time that she was at our church I could tell she was just a little too loose around every man in the office. I just thanked God that she was a contract worker, not permanent staff, and definitely not a member because then it would be my job to bind that Jezebel spirit before it ran through my church."

"We went out a few times but nothing came of it."

Vanessa looked at him as if he had a disease, "I knew it. You jumped up earlier to get the first phone call. How do I know this wasn't the message you were waiting for?"

"I'm telling you it wasn't," Willie said, matching her stare, almost pleading with Vanessa to be reasonable. He watched doubt drift in like a cloud and hang like a sheet between them.

"When I heard her voice, I knew a woman like Blanche didn't just casually call unless she had her eyes locked on a target. I hope she doesn't think—"

"That was a long time ago," Willie said, cutting her off.

"But you never told me."

"C'mon, Vanessa, can you honestly tell me that you have told me about every man you've ever dated. Because if I want to know, I can call your sister right now and she would be more than happy to fill me in. This is ridiculous. The mere fact that she calls out the blue and on top of everything else that is going on should be an indication that the devil is behind it. The question is, are we going to fall for his trick?"

"What is everything else that is going on?"

"The uneasiness," Willie said, raising his voice slightly. The truth is he didn't want to admit he didn't know what was going on. He was tired of feeling like he had to justify himself at church and now at home. He was not on trial. "You said yourself that things were starting to feel weird with all our roles overlapping. We just tossed a hell of a lot of things up at our churches. It's going to be a mess until we sort it all out."

"You're right, you're right, "Vanessa said. Willie wondered was she really agreeing or just harboring a volcano.

Her attention returned to the board. She jumped three of his men with the spot he had just left open.

"Now c'mon, let's finish enjoying our evening," Willie said, surveying the checkerboard. He had no move left.

Although Willie knew he wouldn't call Blanche back, he was awfully curious as to what she wanted. That would be like opening the door and letting the devil walk right in. He wanted to hear from the man who started all this ruckus. How had Charley and Blanche crossed paths? Willie had to shudder at the thought of that duo—major spots and wrinkles.

Willie knew he would have to deal with this matter in the coming week when Vanessa went out of town to preach revival. Vanessa would, with her best intentions, simplify the situation by telling him to let go and let God handle it. That is exactly what he would have done with any other member, but he knew how Charley's brain worked, in an all or nothing mentality. Turning away from Harvest might be the same as turning away from God to Charley. He knew when he met Charley that he had walked that fine line between serving God and serving the church. Every message about commitment and dedication to Christ were for members like Charley, as well as the non-believers.

They had made all these grandiose plans to combine churches and now it seemed as if Harvest was crumbling under the weight of that decision. For the time being, they were his people. He was the pastor and he would handle it. Willie decided to function on cruise control at home until Vanessa left for Virginia the next morning. Then all his efforts would be concentrated on retrieving the Prodigal son.

Chapter 11

A Friend in Need, is a Friend Indeed

"This feels like a scene from an old movie," Vanessa said, holding Willie's hand as he escorted her to the Amtrack train platform.

"I guess this is the part where we kiss and I pledge my undying love," Willie said. He watched a few others bid loved ones farewell. "But don't expect me to run alongside the train."

Vanessa leaned over to give him a peck, but when Willie pulled her into him, she surrendered to the intensity of his kiss. This was the first time the two of them had been separated for any significant amount of time since being married. Pat and Ben Rawls had suggested that Willie come along with Vanessa for the week so that they could fellowship. Ben had even given them joint billing in the program to share the series of messages which they had come to be known for in Ashton, but Willie insisted that he was working on a project related to his congregation and the move and promised to join them Thursday in Virginia. Vanessa was not at all surprised that her husband couldn't manage to pull himself from his church, but she was disappointed. She was resigned to the fact that they would have distinct roles in the combined church; they would both pray, preach and teach; but he had the added duty of coddling the members.

Willie and Vanessa kissed a final time before she boarded the train. The passenger car was almost completely empty so she took a seat and placed her travel bag in the seat beside her. She relished in the silence and used it as an opportunity to listen to a recording of her series called "Preparing for Pentecost" that she preached last year. The Holy Spirit was leading her to revamp the series for the people of Ashton during their revival. She had tapes made at the audio library at Mt. Pleasant so that Willie could listen to it and add his own interpretation when he joined her in the pulpit for the last two nights of the revival, but since she was traveling alone, she decided to start listening from the beginning.

Vanessa had barely turned the first tape over to side two before she was asleep. She awoke from the slight screech of the train's brakes and gradual halt at the next station to find the car had halfway filled with people who had apparently started their trip with a bite to eat in the adjoining dinning car. She was troubled by a dream about Willie being locked in his study at Harvest with no one there to help him get out. She wondered was there any symbolic credence to that dream. She decided to make the phone call to check in with Willie at Richmond where Pat would be waiting for her.

A young woman got on the train just as it was about to depart for its next destination. She plopped down in the seat across from Vanessa and heaved her heavy duffle bag topfull with clothes on the seat closest to the aisle. She was crying, but her tears were muffled by her hand held over her mouth and nose, leaving only the slit of her eyes brimming with tears and very long lashes showing on her face.

Vanessa figured she could be no more than sixteen or seventeen. She must be a runaway, Vanessa's heart told her. "Lord watch over her and bless her," she whispered.

Vanessa, the consummate fly on the wall, was always observing people's behavior and sending up intercessory prayer instead of getting involved directly. She felt the familiar gnawing of the Holy Spirit pushing her to do something, interact somehow with this young girl. She didn't think an introduction of, "Hi, I am Pastor Vanessa Green from Mt. Pleasant Baptist Church," was in order for this situation. The truth is, she could make a plea to a congregation for salvation in the pulpit, but she had to work on reaching out to those who do not asked to be helped.

The girl scrunched down in her seat so that the top of her head was level with the window. Her knee sent her bag that had been teetering next to her into the aisle. She scrambled to the floor trying to recover the possessions that were in her reach. One shoe, an oversized clog, tumbled near Vanessa. Before she could bend down to get it, an older woman came from across the car with tissue in hand extending it as a sign of peace. She moved the girl's bag that was now on the floor to the side and sat beside the distraught woman. The older woman whispered something to her and patted her lovingly across the back like a grandmother. Vanessa picked up the shoe and tapped the older woman on the back. The woman took the shoe from Vanessa and smiled as if Vanessa were returning her shoe then turned her sole attention back to the young girl.

The woman and the young girl started a conversation and it wasn't long until they got up and moved to the dining car; the older woman carrying the girl's duffel bag. *That would have been my husband,* Vanessa thought. *He would have found an in so he could minister to the girl in need or at least he would have offered to help her.*

Willie was always coming home telling her about the

people he had met or helped during his everyday routine. It was typical for him to say, "I met the most interesting man from El Salvador today at the gas station. I noticed he was just wondering around so I went up to him." Vanessa used to think that by studying human behavior she could acquire a knack for interacting with people until she watched her husband with the members of his congregation and realized he had a gift.

The train arrived at her station shortly after noon. Vanessa got her things, left the train, and took the escalator up to the street level where her good friend, Pat Rawls, was waiting for her. Pat wore a brown and cream pinstripe pantsuit with a chocolate brown leather jacket and a fuzzy brown scarf to match, that looked more like a feather boa that a show girl might sport, only thinner. The heels of her cream colored boots were so thin and so high that Vanessa wondered how she walked on them. Seeing Pat made her rethink everything she had packed to wear for the week. Shoot, she knew she should have packed her best when she was in the presence of Diva First Lady, Vanessa thought as she dropped her bag to hug her friend.

"Lord knows it's good to see you, Vanessa," Pat said, "Honey, you're looking good."

"Not half as good as you," Vanessa said, linking arms with her as they began to walk toward the parking lot.

"Where is Reverend Do Right?"

"Ben didn't tell you? Willie can't be here until Thursday. So he left me to lay the foundation and he'll roll in time to finish the week off."

"Isn't that just like a man to show up after the real work is done?" Pat laughed. "Seriously though, is everything alright?"

Vanessa hesitated. She thought about sharing her dream about Willie with Pat but decided against it. "Yeah, you know Willie's church has always got something planned, and since they are preparing to move, it seems like they have even more meetings planned. I'm going to call him once we get to Ashton to give him the hotel information."

"Well, Ben can't wait to show off the church to him." Pat said, pressing the keyless remote on her keychain to automatically open the doors of her Mercedes 350 sedan; another push and the trunk of the car popped open for Vanessa to place her luggage. Vanessa joined Pat inside the car.

"Well, I can't wait to see it myself and brag to my husband that I got to preach in the new pulpit first."

"You two are just alike. Do you all still taunt one another when you beat each other at those board games?" Pat said, navigating the maze of levels in the parking garage before paying the fee to exit to the street.

"All the time," Vanessa said. "There is nothing wrong with a little friendly competition."

"So are you hungry? We can swing past a restaurant before I take you on a tour of the new church."

"First, can we swing past the mall? I need for you to help me pick out some shoes to go with a winter white suit I brought with me to wear. Usually I wear my black heels because I wear the shell of my suit underneath my preaching robe."

"Oh no," Pat said, shaking her head as if the ensemble she just mentioned was unacceptable. "What happens when you transition out of the robe? You'll be horribly mismatched. Black and white only looks good on a zebra. I'll have to hook you up."

Vanessa only thought about fashion when she was with Pat or Keisha. Both fashion mavens were responsible for most of the clothes she presently had in her closet.

Instead of stopping at the mall, Pat took Vanessa to a boutique in Crown Plaza midway between Richmond and

Ashton. The store was any well-dressed church lady's dream come true. They had a section for suits and dresses, shoes and hats; there was no casual wear to be found.

"Let me make sure they have my hat before we go back to the shoe department," Pat said, stopping at the alterations counter. A short woman with a measuring tape around her neck came over to assist them. Pat handed her a ticket that had been ripped at the bottom from the perforated holes. The lady matched up the ticket to one of the many stored in a box. It had a swatch of pink material at the bottom. This time she matched up the numbers with those written on hat boxes until she found the right one towards the bottom. The lady brought out the hat for Pat to examine. It was a pink hat with silver trim that seemed to spiral upward like a staircase. On the side were two tiny feathers. It was beautiful; it was Pat.

The back of the store held a modest shoe section of mostly satin shoes that could be dyed to match any of their suits. Vanessa now knew the secret to Pat's perfectly matched ensembles.

"I guess now you have to get the shoes to match," Vanessa said, looking at styles in the sectioned marked classic pumps.

"Oh, girl, I got the suit and the shoes in my office at church."

"At church?"

"Yeah, I keep them in my office. It's harder to hide an incomplete outfit at home from Ben according to the way I have my closet set up. So I wait until I have all three pieces then I sneak it in the house."

"I can't even imagine, but I'll pray for your obsession, "Vanessa said and they both laughed. "Which shoe?"

Vanessa was shocked to see so many white shoes out in late October until Pat informed her that women are wearing white year round. She went down the aisle as if she was a police officer sizing up suspects in a line up. She pulled down four pairs by the time she reached the end of the aisle. Vanessa eliminated two immediately because of the extremely high heels. Her choice was between a two inch pump with a matte finish and a pair that was a pearly white. Vanessa picked out the latter.

They walked up the aisle towards the register when Pat spotted an outfit for Vanessa. It was a periwinkle suit with iridescent piping throughout the bodice that gave it a metallic look.

"This suit is so bad, you could preach in it," Pat said, pulling the jacket aside exposing the almost floor length skirt, "You should get it."

"Are you serious?"

"This would definitely be making a statement. What size are you? A twelve?" Pat said fishing for her size.

"What statement would that be? I'm very particular about the statements I make in church."

"You would be saying, 'don't try to out dress me in my house'," Pat said, hunching Vanessa with her elbow in a half serious gesture.

"How about in the Lord's house?" Vanessa said.

"Okay, don't try to out dress me in the house the Lord blessed me with," Pat said, handing the dress to Vanessa to try on. "But seriously, I know vanity is sin. I dress my best for the Lord and my husband. They both treat me too good to be walking around playing the pauper role. Besides, when was the last time you dazzled Willie with an ensemble like this?"

"September twenty-second, at our wedding," Vanessa said seriously. She held the outfit up to her to see if it suited her. She felt like one of those female television evangelists that preached on the national stage in some of the most regal suits and shoes Vanessa had ever seen. *Why not?* Vanessa thought. Maybe she'd wear it Thursday when she and Willie took the pulpit together.

By the time they left the store at a quarter after two, Vanessa had the suit and two pairs of shoes: a white pair and a pair that resembled a glass slipper. They arrived in Ashton, at the newly built Dominion Baptist Church, a little after two. Pat pulled into the parking space marked for the First Lady and led the way into the atrium of the church that had several pictures of the First family and a cross-shaped skylight that flooded the main entranceway with natural light. There was a hallway on either side of the wait area that led to classrooms and offices.

"Pat, this is absolutely beautiful," Vanessa said. "God is good."

"Wait until you see the sanctuary," Pat said, taking her through one of the doors that led into the sanctuary.

For Vanessa, there was something about walking into a sanctuary that immediately brought praise to her lips. They stood in what Pat described as the usher's post beneath the overhang of the balcony and viewed the layout. The church was divided into four sets of pews that curved around the pulpit. Pat pointed out architectural details that showed knowledge obtained from months of working with contractors. Vanessa was fixated on the pulpit where a huge rock was mounted to form the preacher's desk. As they moved closer, Vanessa could see where Matthew sixteen verse eighteen that says, "Upon this rock I will build my church," was chiseled into the rock's face.

Pat urged Vanessa on to show her the office suites that contained a lounge where she used her Counseling degree to guide members to a solution through the word of God. The Dominion Baptist ministry was truly a team ministry except Pat was more behind the scenes. Vanessa couldn't wait to join the ranks of strong husband and wife ministry teams.

Ben Rawls was in conference with Dominion's chief musician, Pearl "Peaches" Harvey, when Pat and Vanessa knocked on the door to his office study.

"Pat, Vanessa, where have you all been? I expected you hours ago," Ben said, extending his arms to hug Vanessa.

"Good to see you, Ben," Vanessa said.

"We had to make a stop," Pat said mischievously.

"Oh boy," Ben said. "Vanessa, you remember Peaches Harvey?"

"Sure I do. Nice to see you again," Vanessa said.

"Your key is still C, right?" Peaches asked, referring to the straight chord Vanessa preferred in the background when she started to "whoop" at the end of her message. "Peaches and I were discussing the need for the choirs to join the Gospel Music Workshop Symposium in Atlanta, Georgia at two hundred and fifty dollars a choir, if, of course, the church could foot the registration fee. That's not including airfare and hotel accommodations. Ask the First Lady her opinion before I go, I'm sure she will agree with me about the restriction of church funds since we have been blessed with a new edifice."

"Oh no, you've come to the right place for an opinion, right here to see the pastor," Pat said, taking a seat. "I'm not getting in the middle of anything."

"Peaches, I'll get back to you. I have to make sure my guest preacher is ready for tonight."

Pat remained in her defensive stance until Peaches left the office.

"What was that about?" Vanessa said. Her question was aimed more at Pat.

"Church politics," Ben answered. "Some people will try all avenues to get their way. Last month she thought our choirs needed new choir robes that the church had to pay a hefty advance for before the seamstress could even come to measure folks."

"Well, you handled it very well. I was just thinking on the ride down here how, like you, Willie is the one that has the gift of negotiating with people."

"He sure does. I've learned a lot from your husband," Ben replied. "So, Vanessa, we have got you a room at the Colonial Suites hotel. You nearly broke the budget for guest preachers, but at least we get a two for one when Willie comes. You can go rest. Lord knows what Pat has had you doing this morning." Ben looked at his wife who had turned the silent treatment on him. "Please join us for dinner before service. I guess we can manage to rustle up something between the two of us."

"I don't miss an opportunity for free food," Vanessa said, suddenly hungry for the meal she passed up to go shopping.

The Colonial Suites was a half a mile from the church. Pat made sure Vanessa was squared away in her room before she left for home. Vanessa ordered room service after laying out her clothes for the evening service. She called Willie but could not reach him at home or at church. That was unusual, Vanessa thought. She called the house again to leave the hotel information on the answering machine just in case he ran out. He was probably outside the church meeting with the contractors that were making repairs, she reasoned, trying to halt the visions of her dream about Willie from earlier. She decided to stop giving into the eerie feeling she had been feeling lately; act like a woman of faith, and pray.

The prayer worked wonders for her soul as she started to relax. She lounged on the bed listening to her tape series until a waiter from the hotel's restaurant arrived with her room service. She ordered a chicken salad sandwich that was served on a large plate with a pickle that had more garnish than substance. Vanessa paid the hefty price for the convenience to the waiter before she ate her sandwich and set her Bible to the text for her sermon later on that evening. She called the lobby to request a wake up call for five-thirty as she laid down for a nap. All she needed was to hear from Willie.

Vanessa didn't know how tired she was until the wake up call that came from the front desk seemed to come only minutes after she drifted off the sleep. In actuality, it was-five thirty and she still hadn't heard from her husband. She dressed for the evening and met Pat in the lobby at six where her friend informed her that Willie had called their house looking for her. Obviously, he hadn't received her message with her hotel number. In the past, while they were dating, they relied on second-hand messages like this one through answering machines and secretaries to communicate with one another when their schedules were hectic. Somehow this was different; she was perturbed that he hadn't done more to try and contact her personally.

The congregation at Dominion Church was, as her daddy used to put it, empty pitchers before a full fountain. Vanessa could tell as she presented the word of God that they still had praise-filled spirits full of thanksgiving for their new church edifice. The series was going better than she expected and she felt as if they would reach Pentecost in sermon and in spirit before the end of the week.

That night Vanessa had another dream about her husband. This time Willie was on a ledge like many dramatic scenes played out on television where someone tries to take their own life. Vanessa could not tell whether Willie was going to jump or was there to save someone else because she jarred herself awake. She had become so used to having him around in the short time they had been married, but it did little to lighten her mood. Even when Pat called the next day to ask her if she wanted to ride out to their old undergraduate college, she declined. She stayed in her hotel room all day. She refused to call Willie, thinking that if he was satisfied with leaving a phone message rather than talking to her directly, than it was okay with her as well.

On day three, like a ritual, Vanessa ate room service, prayed, listened to her tape series and napped until Ben and Pat came to get her for service. She could honestly say she didn't feel up to preaching until she stepped to the sacred desk, called her scriptures and began to preach. The Dominion Church gave off an energy she had not felt all day. Much like a performer, she fed off that energy and reciprocated it. Her topic was "On One Accord." As the Bible states, when the church was in one accord, in one place, the Holy Spirit filled the place and gave them extraordinary power. Vanessa emphasized the need for congregations to unite in order to receive the power God has for them collectively. She added this portion to her previous series to help Ben combat church politics and ulterior motives of his people, but the message rang true for her as well. She couldn't help feeling, as she settled into her hotel room that night that it was time for her and her husband to come together as well.

Vanessa Green pulled back the tightly tucked hotel sheets later that night to pick up the ringing receiver in her room.

"Hello," Vanessa said.

"Hey baby," Willie Green said from the other end.

She sat up in the bed so she could see the clock on the night stand. "Willie, honey, it's nearly two o'clock in the morning. What's the matter?"

"Nothing, I just missed you, that's all. It's a cruel thing pulling a newlywed wife away from her husband in the first months of their marriage."

"Well, I miss you too. I've been waiting to hear from you."

"I've been waiting to hear from you too. How is the revival?" he asked.

"Powerful. The Lord is blessing. Everybody all right at Harvest?"

"Yeah, everything is fine. I just forgot that we had an important meeting at the church planned for Friday night to tie up some loose ends," Willie said.

"Does that mean you're not coming down?"

"I'm afraid not, but I figure you're in good hands with Ben and Pat."

"Wait a minute, Willie Green. How will I get home? The train thing was cute and nostalgic on the way down here, but I know you don't expect me to get a return train ticket too."

"Well, Keisha and Luella are still driving down for the last night. I will arrange with them to bring you back if that's okay. It will give you time to visit with your sister."

"Alright then, I guess you're off the hook."

There was a hesitation. "Well, I just wanted to tell you that and to hear your voice. Go on back to sleep. I love you."

"Love you too, Willie," Vanessa said before hanging up the phone.

Vanessa laid in the bed starring at the ceiling. She wondered why Willie was being so evasive. She was mad at herself for letting him off the hook so easily, but she was just happy to hear from him. She could tell from his voice that something was wrong with him, which probably meant it had to do with a member of his church. Vanessa knew that her husband was like a lifeguard that monitored when his members were going too far. His compassion for people made him want to rescue everybody before the waves of life came crashing down on them. He did not consider the fact that some of the most skilled rescuers got caught under the breakers themselves.

The next day, Pat prepared brunch for Vanessa and

served it in the sunroom addition to her home while Ben
went to the church. Vanessa usually ate a moderate lunch
so she would be hungry enough to eat dinner when she
got home. It was 1:30 p.m. and Vanessa knew that after
eating generous portions of thick slab bacon, potato
rounds and Belgium waffles, that this would be the only
meal of the day.

Vanessa was still concerned about what could possibly
have Willie so occupied. She knew Pat could tell something was bothering her as well. Pat warned her this morning that she wasn't taking no for an answer to her brunch
invitation because being First Lady has made her a gracious host to any guest of the church, especially her best
friend. She waited until Pat had her plate and sat down before sharing concerns about her husband.

"Willie is unable to make it this week. He sends his re-
grets. He told me to leave it up to him to call Ben at the
church and apologize," Vanessa said.

"I'm sure it can not be helped," Pat said, buttering her
waffles. "Oh boy, Ben wanted the two of you to anoint us
on the final day of the revival. I guess you can do the hon-
ors. You've been holding it down. Everybody has been
singing your praises."

"Well, I'm going to let Mr. Green have it when I get
home."

"What? Why?" Pat said. "You're acting like his schedul-
ing conflict is on purpose. Vanessa, what is going on?"

"That's just it. I don't know. I keep having these dreams
that Willie needs help or is in trouble," Vanessa said, trying to put into words her once vivid dreams that now
seemed hazy.

"But sweetheart, you've talked to him. Does he seem alright?"

"Yes," Vanessa said, "I just wonder if the dreams are true
somehow and he's not telling me."

"Then you know what you must do. Ask the Lord for help," Pat said, using a fork full of potatoes as a pointer. "Now, eat, I didn't ruin a $40.00 manicure chopping up potatoes and onions for nothing."

Vanessa began to eat her waffles that were now room temperature. Vanessa couldn't understand why Willie wasn't sharing information that would probably affect them both. Pat has always been her confidant and prayer partner. Maybe if she shared her suspicions she could help her with a solution, because right now, Vanessa was frustrated with Willie.

"I think the devil has already begun to attack our unification plans. I mean, ever since we announced the vision with our congregations, Willie has been under pressure, he's always uptight, his members call the house every day, and now this mysterious meeting this week."

"Gosh, Vanessa, maybe this wasn't a good time to invite you two to preach revival when you all have plans of your own with your churches uniting soon."

"It's Willie. You know he's always been so wrapped up in his member's lives, but now his members will be my members. I know it is hard leaving their church, but they're going to have to get it in gear to get to where God wants them to be. I tell my people all the time, you can't do battle in street clothes. I guess I will have to teach them, including my husband, that they must put on the whole armor of God. If I wasn't due to preach here I'd show up at this mystery meeting."

"Do you hear yourself? I haven't heard you use the word "I" so much. Even before you were married it was always you and the Lord. Now, God has made you Willie's wife, and not just his co-pastor." Pat paused. "I can't presume to tell you what you two will go through as pastors, but I can tell you a thing or two about being married. You are now one. You should speak with the same voice."

"It's kind of hard when my husband is not sharing with me."

"That should be telling you to go into your prayer closet and pray for your husband. I hope you have enough faith in Willie that in his own time he'll come to you. The Lord may be dealing with him, and I know you have enough sense to stay out of God's way."

"I got to wonder though, is it the move or is it me? Sometimes I feel like I'm not meeting his needs as a wife."

"Well, do you hear him complaining?"

"Sort of," Vanessa said, thinking.

"Take your cue from Willie. What does he say when he 'sort of' complains?"

"Silly stuff like, there is nothing cooked in the house."

"The man's got to eat," Pat said, pointing to her apron embroidered with the word Diva. "Take up your apron and start cooking."

Vanessa had not thought of it that way. Ben performed their marriage ceremony and when he heard the news about the vision the Lord had given them concerning their churches, he had a long talk with both of them about the dual roles that they would play in each other's lives. The key was to know when to switch roles. The advice from both Pat and Ben seemed to come from a place of personal experience.

"I guess you all must have had your share of trials building the new church from the ground up."

"Yes, girl," Pat agreed. "It is so important in those stressful times to be more attentive to our mates, because I'll tell you, if you're not meeting your husband's needs the hell-bound, home-wrecking hounds can sniff it out."

"I know what you're talking about. One of them has already surfaced. Willie's ex, who already thinks she has license to his attention. I told Willie to handle that because if she comes to my door with some mess, I don't know

what I'm going to do, but it's not in the Beattitudes."
Vanessa put two hands up in surrender.

"Say no more, that's why I pray like anything that your
desire would match with Willie, because if it doesn't, the
devil will use that division to destroy the work of the Lord,"
Pat said, dabbing the corner of her mouth with her napkin, " and even your marriage."

"You don't mean you and Ben?" Vanessa said, reaching
across the table for Pat's hand. "Oh Pat, you never told me
you two were having problems or anything."

"When was I supposed to tell you, during your monthly
premarital sessions with Ben? Besides, God handled it."

"What happened?"

"Well, you know we were meeting weekly with the archi-
tect and other building contractors for the church. We
had these big plans for a foyer fountain and stadium-style
seating for the choir stand. At that time, Peaches and I
were really close and we would discuss the progress of the
new church. Well, when you get to the point where you're
matching plans to dollars and you're adjusting for their
miscalculations, things have to be cut."

"Girl, you know that I have been there when we reno-
vated Mt. Pleasant."

"Well, I got to bragging with Peaches and the other sisters and it seemed like every week I would have to eat
crow and tell them about a change or two that we had to
settle for to stay within budget. Lord knows I can not
blame anybody, but I was convinced that Ben was being
too passive with these contractor guys. I felt he wasn't listening to my input and that he considered this his project,
when in actuality, I was the one making it personal. I was
so angry with him back then."

"Like I am with Willie," Vanessa said.

"So on top of him having to answer to the joint board,
he had to answer to an unsupportive wife. Our relation-

ship was so strained, girl. Some nights we weren't even speaking—not even sleeping in the same bed. Now you know that was nothing but the devil to have me pouting in the guestroom instead of on my five hundred thread count sheets." Pat began to tear up. "Then he told me that it would be cheaper to build a regular choir stand on the pulpit level, and all I could think about was how embarrassed I would feel having to tell Peaches. So I got all big and bad and invited myself to a progress meeting, taking all authority from my husband, and told those contractors we would accept nothing less than what we planned for in our preliminary meetings."

"No you didn't," Vanessa said. "That's bolder than me thinking I can tell my husband how to pastor his people."

"I think now about how embarrassed Ben must have felt having to pull me out of that meeting. He had to show me the loan statement from the bank and the estimates from the contractor to shut me up," Pat said, tossing aside her fork as if it was hopeless trying to complete her meal now.

"I compromised my marriage for a choir loft. Ben had to tell me that God promised us a church, not a fountain and a choir stand with stadium-style seating. Now I'm telling you, God promised you that your churches would combine; he did not say it would be smooth. Take your cue from Willie, continue to pray for the promise, and be prepared to support your husband through the hard times."

Vanessa had come to Ashton to deliver a message, but ended up learning a valuable lesson herself. She had to admit she had a lot to learn about marriage. She hugged her friend who could even admit she was wrong with a lot of grace and style.

Vanessa brought the power of Pentecost to the people of Dominion Baptist by Thursday afternoon and couldn't wait to expand the series for the last day to include the ministry that sprung forth after that time. She led the congregation in a corporate prayer and anointed the Pastor and their First Lady for the work they were put in Ashton, Virginia to do. Ben, in turn, anointed Vanessa and gave her a vial of blessed oil to take home for her husband.

Chapter 12

God is Trying to Tell You Something

Willie had been waiting for an opportunity to speak with Charley all week. He decided to pay him a visit after he had spoken to Charley's wife, Elaine Thompson, on the phone, who sounded nervous when asked about her husband's whereabouts, like a suspect ready to crack in front of a grand jury. Willie was sure she had been coaxed to be just as evasive as Charley had been since his, now infamous, Mt. Pleasant visit and tabloid version of his experience. Charley had not come by the church on Wednesday so Willie figured he'd go to him.

Elaine Thompson answered the door and announced Willie's arrival to her husband. Willie didn't wait to be escorted back to their family room, having been there many times previously. Charley, who sat in front of the television with the remote, popped up when he saw Willie. Willie could hear the rattle of change in his pocket. Charley pretended to be on his way out and even went so far as to grab his jacket and keys and head for the door, leaving a tray of uneaten food on a side table. Willie walked the distance with him to his car while Charley assured him that he and a group of concerned members would meet with him at church to iron out any problems they had with the move.

It just so happens that they set up this meeting on the day Vanessa was due back to town. He felt bad that he had to ask Vanessa's sister to drive her back from Virginia so that he could tie things up at church. He just hoped the whole thing could be smoothed over in a short time so that he could give his wife a proper homecoming.

The day of the meeting was one of those fall days in the Metropolitan area where the seasons seemed to be in a tug of war. The lingering warmth of summer that tried to hold on for most of the ever shortening day time hours, now seemed to be overpowered by fall's chilly grip in the evenings.

The lights from the church and the crowded narrow street indicated that Charley's group weren't the only people there. It looked like a church meeting gone awry once Willie got inside. Members crowded the front of the sanctuary and appeared to be yelling at one another, at the altar no less, which if anywhere should remain a place of peace.

"Good evening everybody, I'm surprised to see all of you out on a Saturday night. Brother Charley, you brought out more people than were in attendance at our last church-wide meeting," Willie said, trying to lighten the mood.

"Willie, tell these people we have an appointment," Charley said.

"Oh, he is Willie now? You don't have any respect, Charley Thompson, not for Pastor Green or God. How could you plan to sabotage your own church?" Mae Richardson said, clutching her chest.

This was more serious than Willie had thought. Whatever was at the root of the problem had his church divided. He braced himself to rebuke a spirit that had worked its way into his church. "Wait. Before we start, let's pray. Charley, do you want to lead us in prayer?" Willie said.

"I don't trust him to pray. We don't know whom he is serving these days," Mae Richardson said.

"Now calm down. Maybe it would be best if I just meet with Charley and his group alone."

"No, we aren't leaving you alone with them Pastor," Clyde Simmons jumped in. "If he can call around to rally folks against the move, we decided to do the same in support of you and Mrs. Green."

Willie searched the sea of faces. Some were already angry, some looked surprised, and others looked uneasy. What had already transpired before he arrived? He tried to tell which ones had come with Charley from their stance and position in the room. He grabbed Sister Richardson's and Deacon Simmons' hand and closed his eyes out of habit.

"Let us pray. Gracious God, our Heavenly Father. We thank you for life, health and strength," Willie prayed. "We need you, oh Lord, to come into this gathering. Lord, we know the devil is a liar. He comes to steal, kill, and destroy the vision and the victory that you have for us here at Harvest and later at Mt. Pleasant. Let us not lean toward our own understanding, but on the everlasting arms of your son, Jesus Christ. Now Lord, remove anything that is not of you; take us out of self, for we struggle not with one another, but, principalities, powers, and spiritual wickedness. You made us more than conquerors over these things. Send your Holy Spirit to help us be about your business decently, and in order. This we ask in the precious name of Jesus, Amen."

Willie looked at Charley from the corner of his eyes. Charley had not bent his head in prayer. Willie had never seen Charley look so cold. It was as if he had been replaced by this gnome whose mouth was drawn up in a knot. Willie could also see a single stream of tears rolling down Elaine Thompson's face. Charley was now a fugitive facing the firing squad. The chilling thing was that when Charley put himself out there to prove a point, he wouldn't surrender.

"Pastor Green, we didn't mean to stir up any confusion. Some members and I wanted to express our disagreement," Joe Morton said. He held out a piece of paper.

"If that were true, then why did you all call everyone you could to sign your ole petition?" Mae Richardson said. She wobbled backward from a sudden pain. She held back her arm to brace herself against the back of the pew. That arm buckled from the pain racing through it and she went crashing onto the pew.

"Mae? Sister Paula, why don't you and Clyde take Sister Richardson home to lie down. This is getting out of hand now." Willie said.

Deacon Clyde Simmons and his wife helped Mae up despite her efforts to mouth that she was alright. Willie turned with mounting anger to the side where Charley and Joe were standing. "What are your complaints? I have told you all that come January, the churches are combining." Willie said snatching the petition out of the young man's hand. "It's not up to you. It's up to God."

"You and your wife plan to co-pastor the church when Mt. Pleasant and Harvest combine?" Charley said.

"That's right," Willie replied.

"I think that there are a few things this church should know. I've asked Sister Blanche Seward to be with us this afternoon to share some startling news about the financial dealings of Mt. Pleasant Baptist church," Charley said, signaling for Blanche to stand.

A murmur ran through the crowd; apparently everyone was so involved in the conflict to notice her sitting in the third pew. Willie had to admit seeing her took him by surprise as well. He could tell that Blanche loved the attention. She raised up from the pew and slowly drew attention to her curves by smoothing the skirt of her suit down her hips. She brushed past Willie in an attempt to get to the very center of the crowd.

"First, I'd like to say, I'm sorry to have to do this." She leaned over exposing an eye full of cleavage in an attempt to talk directly at Willie. "I tried to call you so that we could go over these details privately. Something just told me that you had no idea about what you were getting yourself and this church into. But, I felt it was in the best interest of everyone to know."

Blanche brought a whole different kind of demon, Willie thought. All eyes were on her and all sidebar conversations ceased. She was the kind of woman who went to great lengths to get noticed but donned a humility cap when the attention was finally on her. False humility was a form of pride, Willie thought. Everything she did was exaggerated, from the way she tilted her head, to the way she put on the glasses that were dangling from a string around her neck. Even to the way she referred to the paper notes that Willie knew she had memorized. That told him Blanche was prepared to sell a line; and sex appeal sells, even in church.

"I was contracted to get the financial records straight at Mt. Pleasant. Your wife was on salary and receiving a living allowance. The first couple of years that she was pastor, she started a very costly project of remodeling the sanctuary, having to pay out rent to the local high school so they could hold service until the project was complete there. You might want to find out if Mt. Pleasant has paid off their bills, including the one for the back taxes the church neglected to take out of Sister Green's paycheck. I'm sure the church is still paying for that mistake. Not to mention the legal trouble the church was in for giving *Daddy*

checks from a retirement account that he didn't contribute to while he was working," Blanche shared.

"Sister, you're out of order." Willie said knowing how
much satisfaction she was receiving for sharing this information with the church. The crowd was eating this new information up. Even though many in the crowd didn't
understand the particular implications of what Blanche
just shared, Willie knew impropriety of any kind, especially for a preacher, was viewed as a double sin. Blanche
turned and returned to her seat.

"Are we going to have to pay two salaried positions to
one household?" a young man in the crowd asked.

"I'm not prepared to discuss the financial matters of
Mt. Pleasant or Harvest Baptist tonight. What we can discuss is what we can do to prepare this congregation to
combine with Mt. Pleasant under the leadership of my
wife and I," Willie said.

"A woman pastor has not been sanctioned by this
church body nor by God," Charley said.

"Who are you to say who is called by God? If you have a
problem with God's messenger, take it up with God."
Willie turned to address the spectators. "This seems like a
personal matter between Charley and me. He's just stringing you all along, and because some of you have not been
rooted long enough in this church or in Christ, that you
are willing to follow anybody. Who else on this list has a
personal problem with me or my wife?"

A silence fell over the church. Many members lowered
their eyes as Willie looked over the list. Most of the names
on the list were those of relatively new members to Harvest. The names of Trustee Bill Case and Gregory Johnson, the primary musician, came as a complete shock to
Willie. They never expressed displeasure with the decision.

"Greg?" Willie said.

"Pastor Green, I really don't have a problem going to Mt. Pleasant if I can be assured to play at the same rate. That church has a Minister of Music, but if I can play a couple of Sundays a month, I'll go," Greg Johnson said standing at his seat in the second pew.

"I can't assure you of anything. If you're going to leave, you're going to leave." That statement showed that this was nothing but a gig to him anyway, Willie thought.

"Let's get back to what this petition means," Charley said.

"Look at us, Charley. Don't you have more faith in me than this? More faith in God? Matter of fact, take a look at your wife. She is torn up. She is torn between a church and a husband she loves."

"What about your wife? Have you seen her preach? I have, just last week. She prances back and forth proclaiming she can preach the word of God. She tried to put a curse on me preaching about curses. She stood up there that Sunday morning basically saying anybody that didn't follow her would be cursed."

"What on earth are you talking about?" Willie put his hands up in desperation.

"I came to you because I've known you a long time. I think you are being misled by this woman and you're using the church as an excuse. Your wife is pulling you down."

Willie slapped him across the face. He couldn't believe Charley was humiliating him in front of his congregation like that. Willie knew he would have kept hitting him had they been alone. It was one of those slaps that shocked the mind, as well as the system. Charley grabbed his jaw in disbelief. Elaine Thompson could not control her sobs now. Spectators began responding over her loud wailing.

"Get out, Charley. I will not sink to your level anymore and I will surely not allow you to disrespect my wife. You are so bound in your own insecurities and lack of control that you can't see God anymore," Willie said.

Deacon Thompson pushed past his wife and walked to the exit of the church.

"Someone stop him before he leaves and get the keys to church," Willie yelled.

Sister Thompson started to follow her husband, dropping her purse and spilling its contents. Her loud bawling silenced to weak weeping. No one helped her to retrieve her things. No one said goodbye. Blanche, who was also visibly shaken by the assault, grabbed her clutch bag and left behind them as if she might be the next target. Willie stared at the entrance of the church long after they had gone. Long enough to see the less dramatic departure of a third of his membership.

Chapter 13

In Abigal Mode

Vanessa had not been home a good thirty minutes before she was writing down telephone messages for her husband from the members of his church. She knew Willie would be terribly concerned when he heard the last message from Paula Simmons that said that they had to take Mae Richardson to the hospital after she continued to complain about chest pains.

She camped out in the kitchen waiting for her husband after going throughout the house looking for any changes that might indicate what Willie had been up to all week. It was getting late, which made her think that maybe Willie would want a snack when he got home. She got up with the glee of a school girl at the prospect of having a snack prepared for her husband. She filled the kettle for some tea. Pat's diva apron hanging on her pantry door came to mind. Vanessa figured she needed one that read novice because she couldn't even decide on something simple enough to throw together from the sparse selection of food in the refrigerator. A package of Lorna Doone cookies were on the counter. She emptied the box on a serving tray to serve with her tea before she realized how sad it was. Her attempt didn't even make a right dessert, Vanessa thought, it was more like an offering a 4-year-old sets out for Santa Clause on Christmas Eve.

It never occurred to Vanessa to even go to the market for her husband before she left for the week. The pantry and refrigerator were running low on the groceries they both bought together a couple of days after their honeymoon. She was a Divinity Diva, but the worse wife when it came to cooking, she thought. Even when she lived alone or with her sister, she ordered out a lot and even considered hiring a personal chef. She sat down at the kitchen table as her thoughts made way with her enthusiasm.

Willie came in and greeted his wife with a brief kiss as if he had just seen her that morning. She didn't know what she expected, but it was definitely more affection than that. Vanessa noticed subtle changes in her husband's appearance. His usually taunt chocolate skin gave way to slight indentations at the eye and cheek area. Either he wasn't eating right or a lot had transpired since she had been away, she theorized. It worried her that it was becoming a habit of his to be withdrawn when he had something on his mind, which was the very thing he had warned her not to do.

"You've had several calls from members. I didn't expect your meeting to run so late tonight."

"I stayed over. People are still a little anxious because it's so close to the move. I wanted to get some things out of the way before service tomorrow."

"Well, I had a glorious time, if you care to know." Vanessa said. "I'm sure Ben has told you about their new church. It is remarkable, to say the very least. Ben says now if they can just get their members to continuing tithing like they are supposed to, he would have no prob-

lems paying for the project, maybe even burn the mortgage in fifteen years."

"Everyone has a problem with members tithing, except,
I guess, Mt. Pleasant Baptist Church pastored by the great
Vanessa Morton Green. Maybe that's what has gotten
some of my members up in arms. You all are just too perfect over there." He smirked as if cracking a personal joke
with himself.

"What is that supposed to mean, Willie?" Vanessa said,
not knowing how to take his comment.

There was a knock at the door before he could reply.
Vanessa looked at her watch. It was nearly eleven o'clock.
Willie rolled his eyes with a heavy sigh as if he had an idea
who might be on the other side of the door.

"Are you expecting anyone to come over tonight?"
Vanessa said.

"No," Willie said, taking the hallway to the front door.
Vanessa followed close behind him. Buster Johnson along
with Clyde and Paula Simmons crowded the doorway. "Hello
Pastor, Sister Green," Clyde Simmons said with a weak
smile. Vanessa immediately thought about the phone message they left earlier and thought for a moment they
might be carrying a message of grief.

"Buster, we don't have to go all through this. I'm fine.
I'm about to prepare for Sunday worship. I'll be okay,"
Willie said.

Vanessa realized there would be no negotiating of the
truth while they had visitors. She grabbed her bags from
the foyer and took them toward the bedroom. "Excuse
me, I'll make some hot tea."

Buster waited until she was way down the hallway before
he started to speak again. Vanessa could not help but over
hear the conversation as she prepared the tea in the
kitchen.

"I just want you to know th . . . the . . . there are more people at the church that love and support you than there are against you. Charley is a st . . . stubborn like an old mule," Buster said.

"And you all are just as foolish. You had no business up there tonight," Willie said.

"We didn't want you to be alone," Clyde Simmons said in their defense.

"None of this would have happened if you all didn't take it upon yourself to bring people up there tonight. I could have handled everything peaceably. So they had a group who signed a silly petition. This wasn't a gang fight. It just caused more confusion," Willie said harshly. "You all are my leaders now. What we seen and heard coming from Deacon Thompson was nothing but an evil spirit. We just railed it up, entertained those who came to see a street fight, and drove off about thirty members in the process."

"We didn't mean anything like that to happen," Clyde said.

"Pastor, is there anything you need us to do to help?" Paula Simmons said.

"I could read for you ta . . . ta . . . tomorrow. I'll meet you after Sunday school, like Charley did, for the text."

Willie grunted. "I probably won't have a reader any more now that Charley is gone. I won't put us through the embarrassment with your stuttering and all. No, I guess I won't have a reader."

"I suppose," Buster said, obviously insulted.

"Pastor, Mae is in the hospital. They couldn't tell us what was wrong by the time we left, but her son is with her now," Paula said.

"Well, I got to go work on my outline," Willie said as if he didn't just hear what she said. "It's nothing we can do now but pray." His voice trailed off at the end. "Vanessa, Buster and the rest of them have got to go. Is that tea ready yet?"

Vanessa, who was listening intently, was rattled at the call of her name. She had never heard Willie talk so abruptly to anyone, not to mention how he spoke to her earlier. She heard Willie walk up the stairs and down the hall towards the master bedroom.

Buster peeked his head in the opening to the kitchen. He stood outside the entrance. "That's all right, Sister Green. We don't want to impose on you for some tea. We need to be heading home."

Vanessa stopped his retreat into the hallway by pulling him inside the kitchen door. Then she returned to the door frame to signal for Clyde and Paula to join them. She led him to the kitchen table where her cookies and tea from earlier served as just the right welcoming gesture.

"Thank you so much for dropping by," Vanessa said quietly. "You will have to excuse my husband. I'm not sure that I know exactly what is going on at Harvest, but I do know Willie is taking everything so personally. You've got to know that the members of his church mean the world to him."

Clyde and Paula nodded their heads in acknowledgment. Buster had a faraway look in his eye as if he wasn't so sure.

"Is there something going on?" Vanessa asked.

"The church is falling apart, that's what's going on," Paula said. Buster and Clyde looked as if they were ready to muzzle her.

If that were so, Willie wasn't helping matters by being rude to those who cared about him, Vanessa thought. She felt both compelled to make amends on behalf of her husband and helpless as to how to do it. She barley knew Willie's members. Why should they tell her anything that Willie hadn't?

"You can help me to help your pastor by telling me what went on tonight," Vanessa asked in a caring term.

There was a long pause. Paula looked from her husband to Buster before beginning again, "Pastor had a meeting with Deacon Thompson and some other people. They had a petition against the move of the church. Clyde thought it would be good if we could be there to support Pastor Green. Everyone was shouting and carrying on. Then Sister Richardson fell out."

Vanessa looked around the table to see if there was anymore to add to the story. Both Clyde and Buster seemed reluctant to speak about the specifics of the night's events. Vanessa sipped her tea and waited. It seemed to have a calming affect on everyone, especially the threesome who looked haggard, the way someone would who had been out all night.

"What do you think is the matter with Deacon Thompson and the rest of them? I mean, what's their issue?" Vanessa asked.

"Well . . . It's you, Sis . . . ter Green," Buster started. "I mean y . . . you were the topic of conversation. Charley told Pastor that you are bringing him down and that you were not a real messenger of God. P . . . pastor Green slapped him. I have never seen him that angry before and you know we go way back. Charley disagrees with females in the pulpit, I guess."

"Lord Jesus, I should be used to this. What about you all, how do you feel about female preachers?" Vanessa asked.

"Well, where I come from, you d..don't see any women in the pulpit but I wouldn't say I'm against it," Clyde said.

"I see. Tell me something, are you married, Buster?" Vanessa asked him.

"N . . . n . . . no, Sister Green. W.w.why do you ask?" Buster stated.

"At the age of 43, I married for the first time to your

pastor and I'm still learning his ways. I'm sure Brother and Sister Simmons here have been together long enough to finish each other's sentences. I can now tell by Willie's voice what kind of mood he is in and sometimes what he is thinking. Even before my relationship with Willie, I've had that kind of intimacy with God. Although, I can never know what He is thinking. I know His voice and I've harkened to His calling to preach the Gospel. That means I am called to walk after the spirit, not the flesh. Some people can only see that I am a woman. That's my flesh. God knows my spirit. I've stopped trying to convince people of my calling."

They could hear Willie's footsteps on the hardwood floors above them. She looked at the ceiling wondering what her husband was doing, and more importantly, what was going through his mind.

"Don't be mad at your pastor. He doesn't mean any harm. It just occurred to me that he may be having just as hard a time letting go of Harvest as some of you," Vanessa said stretching against the back of the chair. "You know, I always liked the way the reader would come in throughout Willie's sermon. Tell you what, Buster, when you get to Mt. Pleasant, I would like you to read during my sermons sometimes. How would you like that?"

"That would be nice. Are you sh . . . sh . . . ure you don't have anyone at your church to read for you?" he replied.

"It will be our church," Vanessa said, clearing away their cups as her guests rose to leave.

Everything will be unified for the ministry of the Lord. Everything that both churches need will be within its doors."

"It's been nice talking to you again, Sister Green," Buster said.

"Same here. Oh and Buster, maybe God will have a sister waiting for you over at Mt. Pleasant also."

"That surely would be nice," Buster said.

They walked the short hallway to the front door. Vanessa clicked the light switch on for the front porch and watched as they got into their cars and drove off. She then made her way up stairs.

Vanessa saw Willie close his eyes as she approached the bed. She wondered had he been listening to her every move. Did he hear when Buster, Paula and Clyde left, or the door to their office close after she had been in there for an hour working on her own sermon outline? She fell comfortably into the fold of his arm and could feel the rapid rhythm of his heart and breathing. He never slept on his back, and probably, if he could clear his mind to sleep, he would have changed positions. He wanted to pretend like he was sleeping so she didn't start a conversation with him. They both lie meshed with their eyes closed deep in their own thoughts, both aware of their spouse's sleeplessness, yet trying to conceal their own.

Chapter 14

A Serenity Prayer

It was one thing to be in a service where the Spirit leads a pastor to discard their sermon topic and notes, and quite another thing not to have any notes to begin with. This was one of the few times Willie did not feel like being at church. Everyone and everything showed the aftermath of the church meeting the day prior. He noticed several empty pews where members normally sat and the choir sang accappella because there was no musician.

A full heart is all Pastor Willie Green brought with him to the sacred desk and one topic: "Change." It was not something he wanted to preach about, rather, it was put upon him. It was one of those occasions when the Lord spoke to him while speaking through him. At first, he danced around the premise of the concept without getting specific, never mentioning the events of the previous evening directly. Then the Spirit took him into the opposite direction like a shell being delivered on the shore from a wave just to be taken back again. He took his text from a familiar passage, Matthew 10: 14-15, and read the passage in a somber manner.

"And whosoever shall not receive you, nor hear your words, when ye depart out of that house or city, shake off the dust of your feet.
Verily I say unto you, It shall be more tolerable for the land of Sodom and Gomorrah in the day of judgment, than for that city."

Willie looked up only occasionally during the entire sermon. He read the passage over again and illustrated how one can never really change a person who isn't willing, even in ministry. Willie never felt the word needed embellishing. It was powerful and purposeful in itself, but today he shared his testimony.

"It's funny how you can be surrounded by people and still feel alone in the ministry," Willie said, "Your human side wants you to be accepted by everyone. Church, I've come to tell you that I have been called to preach the Gospel. I stay before the Lord and I resent any implication that I don't. I guess the Lord allowed me to see how my wife has felt all these years being a female preacher and having people doubt her call and ability to preach. After yesterday, I felt like saying the heck with Harvest Baptist Church; the Lord has graced me with another church. But soon I realized, I have an obligation to the people here. When you spend the majority of your time on your knees praying over the souls in *this* church, then you can try and tell me what the church should do in January."

When he was done, a pin drop could be heard. He left the pulpit immediately after the sermon to disrobe. He didn't stay after church to fellowship with well wishers as usual. Instead, he decided to visit Mae Richardson at County General. If anyone was on his side, Mae was. He wanted to hear her familiar opinion of any situation that had to do with Deacon Thompson. "That Charley Thompson burns me up," she'd say. He claims to be God's foot soldier, but he don't want to advance."

Mae could not offer her pastor an opinion as she lay in and out of consciousness in her hospital room. Her face sloped dramatically on the left side due to a stroke she had experienced the night of the church meeting. Her son, Albert, who had taken up vigil at her bedside, gave Pastor Green some time alone with his mother. She was asleep, and despite her disfigurement, she looked quite serene. For an instant, Willie thought she might have been dead, the way she laid seemingly motionless, until he noticed the slight rise and fall of her chest. Willie's eyes began to mist up as he grabbed her hands. He prayed a prayer of a loved one, not that of a pastor. It was a selfish prayer that Mae would be healed and well enough to complete this move with him.

Pray without ceasing, Willie thought. He tried to separate his needs from his wants in his mind as he drove home from the hospital. He had prayed for Mae, but how could he pray for Charley if he did not know what it is he wanted? It took him unusually long to get home. Vanessa was home before him and was in their office working. Willie had forgotten that they were supposed to work on the agenda for the final retreat meeting and the schedule for the retreat itinerary.

They ended up working well into the night offering Willie a distraction from the trials at his church. Vanessa was excited with all they had accomplished and looked forward to the trip fast approaching in two weeks. Vanessa and Willie began packing up the paper work for the night.

"You know, after looking at this roster, only forty of my people pre-registered. You would think we were doing all this planning in vain," Vanessa said.

"I'm not surprised; they probably don't see a need to

go. Your people seem a little self-serving," Willie said, leaving the office. *She's one to complain,* he thought. Forty people was about all he had left in his membership. He could feel himself getting angry and didn't know why.

Vanessa followed her husband up the stairs to the bedroom. "Well, from what I hear, your members are cynical and stubborn," she said lightheartedly as if this were one of those times where they joked about whose congregation was the best.

"You told me yourself that the words evangelism and outreach are foreign to your congregation," Willie said louder than he had wanted.

"And your so called fellowships are just an excuse to get in each other's business at Harvest," Vanessa replied, taken by surprise by his tone.

"All churches have their problems, even yours, Vanessa." He sat on the bed waiting for her reply. He had her on the defensive, which made him think maybe they could drop the pretense and have an honest conversation; maybe get her to admit that she wasn't so perfect.

"I can accept that, but, I don't accept the way you have been speaking to me the past couple of days." Vanessa put her hands on her hips. "So, I guess all your people signed up for the retreat?"

"The majority of them," Willie said.

"Except the Thompsons, and all the other members who left the church because we've planned to unite our churches."

He immediately stopped undressing at the mention of the Thompsons' name. Then he resumed pulling off his shirt to get ready for bed. He didn't know how she found out about the events of the previous night. *Since she knows about the situation at church,* Willie thought, *why isn't she supporting him?* "I don't know what the Thompsons plan to do."

"I talked to Buster yesterday about the church meeting, Willie. Am I not supposed to know something is bothering you?" She went to join him on the bed.

"Am I not supposed to know that your church was nearly broke because you and your daddy were on the payroll, and you wanted to redo the sanctuary to make Mt. Pleasant the envy of all the Baptist churches in the area?"

"Wait a minute, Willie Green, we haven't exactly set aside time to talk about ministry failures, past and present." Vanessa stood again with her arms extended in an exasperated gesture.

"You have any idea how embarrassing it is to have Blanche Seward, of all people, to share the irresponsible dealings of your wife in front of almost your entire congregation," Willie said before he had time to censor it. He could tell his comments came as a blow to Vanessa as she took a seat on the bed as if to brace herself.

"What is with the condemnation?"

"I'm not condemning you."

"Oh really? You're snapping at the members of your congregation, and snapping at me. You've lost that fire and excitement for the move. Then you think I don't know you haven't been sleeping nights. I'm supposed to be your wife, remember?"

"I know that," Willie said. "I just wonder if you know that sometimes when it comes to cooking and cleaning."

Vanessa dropped her head and shielded her eyes for a minute. Willie wanted to go to her and wrap his arms around her, but he couldn't, as if he was locked in his position. They had tip-toed around the feelings for awhile. Now it was time to have this very real conversation. When she lifted her head Willie could tell she had new determination.

"The Bible says . . ." Vanessa started.

"Quit with the prescriptions, okay, Vanessa? I know what

the Bible says; I'm a preacher remember. It says you're my help meat. It says he who findeth a wife, findeth a good thing. What else are you going to tell me it says, huh?"

"It says we struggle not against flesh and blood. All I know is what you're communicating to me. So maybe you think our vision was doomed from the beginning and maybe you're thinking I'm not the woman that can meet your needs. Maybe the only way this whole thing can work is if I take a backseat and let you lead," Vanessa said, rising from the bed. She was preparing to leave the room with a pillow and a spare blanket from the closet, which left him very little time for rebuttal.

"Now you're going to take everything I've said out of context."

"What other context is there when you tell me that I'm a second class wife because I don't cook or clean, which I take exception to. If I didn't clean this house would be filthy."

"I admit the comment I made earlier was out of line," Willie said. "I was just frustrated."

She walked the bedding over to Willie and thrust it in his mid section and then stood her ground so there would be no misunderstanding. "Well, I'm not going to continue to argue with you. I'm going to wait until you realize we have a fight ahead of us and I'm not your enemy."

Chapter 15

For Everything, There is a Season

Mae Irene Richardson had another stroke and died on the Sunday before the retreat. Her body laid in wake for viewing on Tuesday night at Harvest Baptist Church. She was eulogized and buried on Wednesday by her beloved pastor. Deacon Charley Thompson was not present.

Willie Green was very particular about the arrangements. The funeral would start on time, the music was to be upbeat and the repast would be catered by the Women's Auxiliary. It was to be an Estate funeral, with all the formality usually reserved for someone of the cloth or a founding member of the church. Willie wore his clerical collar under his black robe that Mae had laundered and ready for such an occasion as this. The altar was draped in floral sprays of every variety courtesy of the Flower Club for which Mae was a member.

Her eulogy was based on text, in an attempt to prevent the emotional breakdowns that would come from basing it solely on memories. It was apparent that Mae affected many people from the forty five minute tribute that various organizations in and out of church gave to honor her memory. Vanessa, who sat in the pulpit with her husband, read the old and New Testament scriptures. Then Alice Jones led the opening song. Everyone sang along to the lyrics, "Well done, well done. Oh, I want my Lord to say well done." Mourners kept time to the song by clapping their hands and tapping hard bottom shoes on the wooden floor.

In all that had gone on in their church, Harvest needed the reassurance of the eulogy as much as the immediate family. Willie was emotionally spent from the whirlwind week that began with the church meeting with Charley and his group and ended with the death of his church clerk. He wondered if he could provide solace to anyone with the way he felt. He looked at Albert, Mae's only son, holding his baby girl in his lap, and felt as if he should be on the front pew with them. Willie knew he would mourn later. He had to be pastor now and lead this family and his entire congregation in rejoicing in the full life Mae was blessed to have.

"For we can be assured that Mae will be there in Glory when we get there. The Bible says, 'for if we believe that Jesus died and rose again, even so them also which sleep in Jesus will God bring with him'," Willie said. "Then Paul ends that chapter of Thessalonians by saying, 'Comfort one another with those words'. May you find comfort in all that was said here today."

Lean not to your own understanding, Willie thought in an attempt to comfort himself. He was fighting an irritation he had with God. He couldn't help thinking that out of all his members, why God would decide to call Sister Richardson home, especially after the Charley fiasco. Was he meant to go at this move alone? Willie had helped a few mem-

bers who had called him on the phone this week to see
what he didn't completely believe himself; That Mae didn't
die because of the incident at the church meeting. He
wanted to say, "You're right, Sister Simmons, none of this
should have happened."

"Sister Banks, Mae shouldn't have been at that meeting
that night trying to defend her pastor. None of us should
have been there." He was angry because Charley Thompson was not there right now, helping out like he had done
so many times, directing the family and standing in as a
pallbearer. Everything was changing so drastically. Deep
down in his heart, he knew this was the will of God.

After the repast was over, Willie shook hands with Harvest members who thanked him for the lovely service but
could not help but ask, as an after thought, if the retreat
would go on as scheduled. To which he replied, "Definitely, the will of God must go on."

He carried that philosophy into the remainder of the
week. He decided to go to the church the next day to
begin packing up part of his office to be moved over to
Mt. Pleasant. Vanessa urged him to take it easy until the
retreat, but he felt he had to do something productive.

Willie could see Roy Jones in the alley beside the
church when he drove up. When he cleared the corner,
he could see the man in the knit cap hovering over Roy
Jones. Instead of Roy cowarding in the corner, he got up
from his cardboard pallette and said, "I'm not going to do
it anymore. That's what got me where I am today."

Willie immediately jumped to Roy's aide. "Leave him
alone. If you don't get away from this church, I'm going to
call the police."

Knit Cap thought about Willie's threat a moment. "You
know where to find me," he said to Roy, and then he released the grip he had on him. Willie watched Knit Cap

walk down the street slowly and cross over at the convenience store into the next block before he addressed Roy.

"Are you okay, Roy?" Willie said. "Let me help you get
into a shelter. It's safer for you there than being out here."

"I got kicked out the shelter a week ago. They weren't
ready to hear my message there. I've been waiting to tell
you, Reverend; I found Jesus."

"That's great, Roy, but where will you go? I bet if I call
the shelter I can explain that it was all a big mistake."
Willie said.

"But it's not a mistake. You know how I know Jesus?
'Cause he shown me things," Roy said, closing his eyes real
tight as if making a wish. He then continued. "I used to always sit in this alley and think of where I been. Just imagine a whole day in my head, in real time. A day in the life
that I couldn't go back to anymore 'cause I destroyed it
with my habits. Isn't it like that, Reverend?" Roy opened
his eyes and waited for a response.

"Isn't what like that, Roy?"

"How God will touch you. He'll help you release the
past. It's like when my cousin and I used to go swimming;
we use to dive in over our heads." He grinned at the memory. "I would close my eyes real tight on the way in and
only open them when I was near the bottom of the pool. I
wanted to see what the bottom looked like. It was nasty
down there; like every impurity done settled right at the
bottom. It's like that. You know, God took me from a three
bedroom house, a wife and a child to nothing in less than
three years and I'm okay with it."

"And now?" Willie asked, trying to make sense of what
Roy was saying.

"Now, Reverend Green, he has let me see the bottom.
Now all I can do is go up. I think he wants me to share my
message. Ooh, can I share it in your pulpit, Reverend?"

Willie got real close to Roy and grasped both his shoulders like Knit Cap man had done before. He didn't smell of liquor like he usually did. His once red eyes were now wide and clear. Willie noticed he was wearing a new suit a couple sizes too small under his blue windbreaker with thick sports socks and tennis shoes.

"Roy, the church is moving to Mt. Pleasant the first of the year. That is why I really want to make sure you're settled before then."

"I'm settled. Don't you see, he left me to carry on. So you don't have to worry about Lincoln Avenue or all of Capitol Heights for that matter. I'm going to share my message," Roy said with a childlike enthusiasm.

"Well, you don't have to worry about that. We're not just picking up and leaving this community. We're going to do something for the community right here."

Roy scrunched up his face. "I thought you would be happy for me, Reverend. You don't believe God can use a man like me?"

"Oh no, I believe God can use anybody that is willing."

"I'm going to share my message," he said, bending to fold his pallette.

"Roy, I just worry about you, that's all. I can see you're getting your life together and I'm happy. What can I do for you now?" Willie asked.

"Just pray for me," he said gathering his things into a tattered suitcase.

Willie watched him carry his suitcase and makeshift bedroll to the stop light and in the direction that he had watched Knit Cap Walk. He couldn't help but think how Roy made a lot of sense. Was he touched by God or just suffering from insanity that plagued a lot of homeless people? If Roy's calling was true, he had an even harder lot to deal with bringing his message to the people on the street than Willie did combining his church with Mt. Pleasant.

Willie walked up the front steps of the church and tried

the door handle as if he expected it to be unlocked. He turned on every light in the church between the front door and his office in the back. He couldn't wait to share with Vanessa what God was doing in Roy's life because he had told her about him hanging around the church when he wasn't in a shelter. He felt melancholy at the thought of leaving in this manner. Now the move seemed to be coming too soon and he couldn't help wondering was it the right time. Mae's death and Charley's departure should be a time for a church to rally together, not pack up and move. Willie would gauge the feelings of his members over the retreat weekend. Maybe the date would have to be moved back.

Willie's desk was clear but there was a small stack of papers on Mae's desk in the corner. He noticed she had a tiny notepad with the retreat date scribbled on the top card. Under that on the stack, there was a reminder of a board meeting the week after they were to return from the retreat. This led Willie to look at the appointment book Mae kept for the church. He flipped the pages of each week to see only the words Prayer meeting, Bible Study, Sunday school and Worship service written on their appropriate days each week in the calendar. Other appointments didn't grace the page, but rather were written on colored note cards and stapled to the week that the event was to occur in the calendar. Mae was planning on stapling in the retreat note card for this week. She was even scheduled to go, Willie thought. Before the grief could rise in his chest like gas, the telephone rang. It was Paul Grant calling about the retreat and the possibility of obtaining one of the last slots since his work schedule now freed him up to go. Willie wrote a note to himself using one of Mae's note cards to add Paul to the retreat list. He had to work something out for his liaison.

Willie decided he would deal with the file cabinet and other drawers he did not use everyday. This would give him time to purge a lot of things he didn't need. He was surprised to see so many folders in use in the bottom cabinet drawer. He pulled out the last folder on the end and read in Mae's shaky script, Pastor's 10th anniversary. Immediately a picture of Mae escorting him down the isle on that day popped in his head. He replaced the folder and pulled out another discovered drawer full of file folders with a single church program in each one—anniversaries, weddings and funerals. He laughed to himself as he thought of the timeline Mae had unknowingly started for him. Willie thought about condensing the system Mae had set up by putting all the programs together for the sake of packing, but couldn't bring himself to do it. He noticed that the last drawer had folders to spare and he knew this collection would not be complete without the program from her funeral.

Willie walked to the main sanctuary to see if by some chance an extra program would be lying around from the previous day. He walked up in the pulpit and got an eerie feeling looking out at the twenty empty pews. Then sadness engulfed him as if one by one the members of his congregation had either died or left the church and he was left to preach to an empty church. He sat in his chair behind the pulpit and closed his eyes to collect his thoughts.

Lost in his own thoughts, Willie envisioned the church full like it was for his 10th anniversary as Pastor. He had stood below the pulpit platform while Mae had pinned a pale yellow corsage on his suit lapel. Everyone had clapped and stood to their feet. He could see through his mind's eye people in the congregation mouthing accolades. The service continued and he had taken his seat in the pulpit.

"Christian Friends, we are certainly glad to be in the house of the Lord one more time," Deacon Charley Thompson had said before giving the invocation.

The choir sung. Then each organization had come up to pay tribute to Willie for his service to the church. Mae Richardson had approached the altar and refused to use the microphone like everybody else. Willie had extended a hand to help her up the stairs into the pulpit.

"Pastor, we cannot pay you for the many services you provide to our church family. Let me tell you, church, I know, this man works all the time. I declare if I didn't cook him a meal every now and again he would forget to eat for worrying about the members of this church. I just want to give you this as a token of my appreciation," Mae had said, shaking Willie's hand firmly and standing there as if she knew a handshake would not be enough. Then he had grabbed her small frame into a full embrace as the congregation applauded.

Then, as if a director had said, "Take two," Willie's mind replayed scene after scene from the previous week. The church was still full, but this time it was the night of the church meeting. He watched the scene play out as an observer up until the part where he slapped Charley. The force of the blow made him jerk where he sat in the pulpit. Next, he was in his own living room telling Buster Johnson he couldn't use him as a reader because of his stuttering. He was now able to see how letdown Buster must have looked that night. His argument with Vanessa replayed in his mind and his visitation with Mae in the hospital. That was the last time he saw Mae alive.

Willie opened his eyes to let the tears roll freely down his face, or maybe he opened them because he wanted to see his personal bottom. He looked up to find Vanessa sitting in the usher's pew in the back of the church. Her eyes were glassed over with tears also. Seeing her reminded him that it was time to rebuild relationships and move on. Vanessa stood as Willie left the pulpit and walked to the back of the church to meet her. He grabbed her hand and pulled her down into the pew with him. Both of their tears seemed to intensify as his eyes communicated how grateful he was that she was there—how grateful he was that she was his wife.

Willie began to think about Charley. He turned to her looking like a wounded lamb. "What's going to happen to Charley?" he asked his wife.

"It's not for us to know. He has to take the road his faith leads him to," Vanessa replied.

"But I struck another man of God. I had no right."

He braced his head in his palms, ready to pour it all out before his wife and the Lord, ready to listen, ready to be healed. She began whispering as if the normal tone of her voice would cause more pain.

"This situation with Charley is something you will have to make right with the Lord, and make right with Charley later if the Lord allows your paths to cross again. Come on, Willie, stay focused on the vision. I can't do this without you," she said.

"He's actually got people following him and others doubting their choice to go. I'm sure I helped them make the decision by my actions the other day. I'm tired, Nessa. I'm tired of defending myself, tired of praying for folk who aren't praying for me—with me. Maybe this is a sign."

"Listen to yourself, you know better than that. Any vision of God's will be a target for the devil. That's why we can't lose our focus." Her pleading turned into a prayer. "Oh Lord, we can't lose our focus on you."

Willie wondered what Vanessa was doing as she unzipped the side pocket on her purse and took out a bottle of what appeared to be oil. She turned slightly in her seat to face him and outlined a cross on his forehead and then her own. With her hand pressed firmly on the crown of Willie's head, she began to address God on their behalf. *Now, we can only go up,* Willie thought.

Chapter 16

A Charge to Keep

When a pastor needs to plan something big, they know on whom in their church they can depend. The Unification Retreat Committee was just the right mix of people from both churches to get the job done. They were given the task to plan buses, accommodations and sessions to help foster the fellowship between the congregations. The committee was comprised of the members from the Women's Auxiliary, Missionaries and Men's fellowship from Harvest Baptist and the Pastor's Aide and Willing Worker's Club from Mt. Pleasant. All their past experience planning bake sales, bazaars, dinners and services made them no strangers to orchestration.

Keisha Morton was drafted onto the retreat committee by her sister. That was the downside of being the pastor's sister, Keisha thought. Vanessa was an expert at delegating tasks and Keisha was the first to receive her orders. As far as Keisha was concerned, she served her commitment sitting at the registration table Sunday after Sunday tooting her sister's expectations.

"Pastor Green expects Mt. Pleasant to register for the

retreat in good number. Welcoming Harvest into our church is like welcoming the move of God into our lives." Keisha also wanted to enjoy herself on this retreat like all the other participants instead of working like a behind the scenes gopher. She had been feeling that it was time for her to step from behind her sister's shadow. She got her hair freshly styled and packed her best Christian casuals. She wanted to meet the new people from Harvest, especially the singles, and recruit them into her ministry once the churches combined.

Keisha thought back to when her sister was thinking about starting the Singles Ministry at their church, even before Vanessa and Willie started to date. Keisha remembered how cynical she was about the actual purpose. They were having a conversation about how and where to find good Christian men.

"Maybe I should start a Singles Ministry at Mt. Pleasant," Vanessa said.

"Not after the way you scolded me about fixing you up, and now you are condoning your members fixing each other up on dates in the church?" Keisha said.

"This will not be a dating service. A lot of churches are instituting this ministry as a viable way to teach sexual purity and morality."

"Yeah, help those brothers see they have gotten intimacy all wrong; trying to sleep with a sister after one or two dates," Keisha said, speaking out of personal experience.

"And help the sisters see they don't need to sleep with the brothers period just to get him to love her. The ministry will also help you know what to look for in a mate."

"Well, if they don't know what to look for in a mate, than they are in bad shape."

"Within the word of God, girl, some of us don't notice that we are drawn to the same type of person because we are not spiritually preparing for God's will in our lives,"

Vanessa said, pointing a finger at Keisha. "The ministry will also help you feel comfortable with the fact that you are single."

"The only comfort you can provide a 30-something female like me is one of the tall, dark and handsome variety," Keisha said.

When Vanessa later charged Keisha with the Singles Ministry, after she accepted the call on her life to ministry, Vanessa made sure to point out all the pain Keisha had been through making men her savior and the standards of the world her Gospel. She didn't have to worry about Keisha going down that road again. The same hindrance that kept Keisha from her call to God was prohibiting other singles to grow in faith as well. Keisha didn't take it lightly that she was now the instrument that God used to educate his people and possibly keep them from falling. She just hoped God had it in his plan to hook a sister up with one of His best.

Keisha wondered had her roommate arrived as the line of late arrivals was dwindling down. She now considered the hastiness of the no questions asked, no money down reservation that she took from a relatively new member at Mt. Pleasant. The woman, Lenora Rodgers, told Keisha that she didn't know anyone on this trip, so Keisha slid Lenora into the slot as her roommate. She wanted someone to hang out with since her old hanging buddy was serving double duty as wife and Pastor. Keisha could see women counting their bags and checking on items as husbands made themselves useful, inquiring about route and travel times from the drivers. She found Lenora Rogers smiling apprehensively at the end of the check-in line. Lenora's face registered recognition as Keisha walked her way.

"You made it," Keisha said, rising to give her a half hug across the table.

"Yeah. Do you know what bus I'm assigned to?" Lenora asked, trying to juggle her weekend bag, with the retreat facility map and itineraries handed to her at the table.

"We are riding on the first bus with Pastor Green and the Reverend."

"Thank you so much. Can I get on the bus now?"

"Sure, my stuff is already on the bus. I'll show you," Keisha said, leading the way, anxious to get away from the restriction of the registration table. "Have you met Reverend Green, Pastor's husband, yet?"

"No, I haven't."

Lenora followed Keisha out to the bus area. Willie and Vanessa took position between the rear and front bumper of the two coaches. They looked like the President and First Lady on the campaign trail shaking hands trying to win approval before an election.

Keisha spoke introductions. "Pastor, Reverend, this is Lenora Rodgers. She is a member of Mt. Pleasant and my roommate on the retreat," Keisha said as if the latter description qualified Lenora for a door prize.

"I thought I recognized you. I'm sure my sister will take good care of you on this retreat and share with you how you can get involved," Vanessa Green said.

Lenora smiled politely. "Okay," she replied.

Keisha and Willie painted on knowing smiles, fully aware that Lenora was about to be drafted onto the dreaded Unification Committee. It was not that Keisha wasn't a supporter of the union between Harvest and Mt. Pleasant; it was just that the Unification Committee would have you tied with them in meetings from Thanksgiving to New Years. That is why Vanessa was hard pressed to find committed people.

"I don't have my list with me, but let me ask you this, would you be willing to work on the Unification Committee after the retreat is over?"

"Sure," Lenora said pensively.

"I guess first I should ask, will you be in town over the Thanksgiving holiday?"

"Yes."

"Great, that's great because many of the Retreat Committee members have family commitments during the holidays. See me at the end of this retreat so I can remember to put you on my list to call for our next meeting."

Keisha and Lenora boarded their bus. Keisha had claimed a seat directly behind Willie and Vanessa's seat. The bus was almost completely filled so she and Lenora took their seats and waited for departure.

Paul Grant hoped he did not have to flag down the buses on their way to the church. He had left work in plenty of time to pick up his mother. Of course he knew she couldn't just leave home until a series of chores were complete. She cleaned up as if guests were staying at her house while she was gone. In thirty-seven years Paul had never been able to shake the role of mama's boy. Ever since his father died, he had been his mother's companion and chauffeur. Even after he moved out on his own, he still picked her up for church. So she was delighted when Paul told her that he took time off from work to go on the retreat, because if it wasn't for him going, she wouldn't be going either.

Paul and his mother were loading his Isuzu with his mother's luggage when he had noticed a group of traveling evangelist that often passed out literature about their church. He could not believe they were making their rounds this late. They parked at the entrance of the development and began dispersing over the unsuspecting neighborhood. Pamphlets in their hand, determination in their heart, and rhetoric on their lips, they descended the hill. One had to admire their tenacity. It gave his mother great pleasure to be as persistent about her beliefs as they were with their own. She went in the house to retrieve her church fliers that she kept for her regular visitors. This was Thelma's evangelism.

"Come on, Momma. It's a quarter until five. The buses are supposed to leave at five-fifteen. We don't have time for this now," Paul said. "How will it look if I am late and I'm on the committee?"

"I want to see if they come back to my house. You think any of them came to the Fall Revival I invited them to last month?"

Paul shook his head. He was finally able to get his mother into the car when the group turned the corner to an adjacent street at the top of the hill.

The streets were filled with vagrants and visionaries selling their wares to anyone who had compassion enough to patronize them as they drove to the church. Paul raced up East Capitol Street passing T-shirt and incense stands. Paul contemplated the route to the retreat center as the inevitable consequence to their tardiness. He stopped at another light at the base of the subway station. Window washers and Muslim brothers weaved throughout the motorists holding up their goods as a silent sales pitch. The lights worked against them as they encountered the entrepreneurial efforts of the street florist and over-aged paper boys. His mother did not seem to recognize the time as she summons a man for the day's daily just as the light turned green.

"Lord Jesus boy, slow down. Are you trying to break the sound barrier over the Maryland line?" Thelma said as she barely got her paper through the open window before Paul took off. All Paul could think about was sitting back on the bus and relaxing. He had factored these days as a mini vacation and reward for completing a difficult research proposal for a pharmaceutical company. They could hear the roar of the bus engine as they entered the parking lot. A wave from Pastor Willie Green signified that Paul had made it just in time.

Paul loaded both arms with their bags and lagged behind his mother while she greeted other members. The driver motioned them toward the back of the bus by the bathroom facility where the only available seats were left. He indicated that their suitcases would have to be carried on the bus with them. Paul sighed a breath of relief as he took his seat and thanked God for the loose time schedule of Harvest Baptist Church.

The buses arrived at Seaport shortly after seven-thirty p.m. Although Paul was tired, he wanted to show his face at the welcome reception listed in the itinerary because being the liaison made him an immediate member of the retreat committee. The Wildfowl lounge seemed deserted. Paul and Thelma stopped at the entrance of the lounge and read the sign that confirmed the reserved space.

"I'm not going in there. This looks like a bar. I'm going up to the room, I'm tired anyway," Thelma said.

"The paper said Wildfowl lounge," Paul stated.

"I don't know who picked this room, but it's not proper for a church group to fellowship in a bar."

"I'm going to stay here for a while, get something to drink and see who shows up."

She leaned in close. "All right, Paul, I know you're grown and all, but please don't go drinking any alcohol. This is a church trip. We are representing the Lord down here and you are representing our family."

"Don't worry about it, Ma." he laughed. He couldn't believe she would actually think that he would down a couple of beers on a church retreat. He knew in his party days he had given her cause to wear out her knees in prayer, but all that had changed. The mere fact that he had returned to church more committed to serve like his father had in the past should have been an indication to his mother how much he wanted and needed the Lord in his life.

"I'm serious. I'm going back. Do you have a key?"

"Yeah, get some rest, Ma," Paul said.

Two people were leaving the lounge as Paul entered. He could see complimentary snacks being put out by the lounge attendant. He approached a woman who was obviously waiting for them to set up the table as well along the back wall.

"Hello," Paul said.

"Hi," she replied.

"Are you from Mt. Pleasant?" Paul said, pointing to the retreat badge.

"Yes, Keisha Morton. So, I take it you are from Harvest Baptist."

"Yep."

Paul clasped his hands together. Now he felt obligated to stay at the table with her until the man finished his arrangement. She was petite but attractive, he thought. If this were several years earlier, he would have really ordered himself a couple of beers before kicking her a line to see if she would bite. They looked up every time they heard people in the entrance way of the lounge, but no one came in. The snack table has been temporarily abandoned by the man and his cart.

"This isn't a line, but you look familiar, as if I've seen you before," Paul said.

"If you tell me I look like my sister, I'll kick you," Keisha said, pointing a heel toward Paul's knee where they sat. "Vanessa Green is my sister."

Paul smiled. For some reason he remembered her face as the lone bridesmaid at his pastor's wedding. "Right, small world. You were in their wedding, right?"

"That's right. I'm surprised anyone could see me the way Vanessa was beaming all over the place."

"Are you here alone?" Paul asked, shaking his head at how generic his idle conversation sounded. "I meant do you have a roommate?"

"She's upstairs unpacking; something I never do on a trip. She's a little on the shy side."

"I see."

"Your name is?"

"Paul"

"Paul what?"

"Grant."

"Was that your mother with you earlier?"

"Yeah, she did not want to come in here because she says it looks like a bar, and that it sends the wrong message for us to assemble in a bar." Paul could imagine the saints from Harvest thinking the same thing and fleeing the scene.

Keisha smiled. "Oh is that it? I was wondering where everybody was."

"I'm sure everyone is tired from working all day and the drive up here. Those motor coaches are not the most comfortable."

"Yeah, I guess, especially for someone as tall as you." She glanced down at her hands and began to pick at her nails. "I wonder where Pastor Green is."

"Yeah, he was at church pretty late last night when I went up there to pay for the retreat. He was beginning to pack up the main office to be moved."

The confused look on her face made him realize the misunderstanding. They both smiled.

"You almost didn't make it. I saw you pulling in from the bus window," Keisha said, looking at the service entrance of the lounge for the missing attendant.

"My mother almost made us miss the bus. You wouldn't believe my afternoon," he said.

Paul began filling Keisha in on his race to make it to church on time beginning with his mother's cleaning spree. Keisha laughed as he imitated his mother counting out twenty-five cents in assorted change for a newspaper at the stop light. They both stopped laughing when the attendant returned and began placing sodas back on the mobile cart. Before either of them could ask, a woman from Mt. Pleasant came in the room.

"They said the reception has been changed to suite 207. Do you think someone should put a sign out front?" The woman asked.

"I guess I can do that. It's the least I can do since I'm on the committee," Keisha said fanning off the lady who immediately left when she was relinquished of the responsibility. Keisha got up from the table. Paul got up from his chair and walked with her to the entrance.

"Me too, I was appointed liaison from my church," Paul informed her.

"I didn't make too many meetings." Keisha said as Paul echoed his own simultaneous explanation for their not meeting sooner at a Retreat Committee meeting. They laughed again. They paused as they reached the threshold of the lounge to write the change of room on a piece of paper she found on the corner of the bar. She folded it to form a tent and propped it on the table in front of the sign. She watched for a moment to see if it would stay pitched where she left it.

Paul asked, "Shall we?" He squinted as his eyes got readjusted to the light of the hallway. His watch read a quarter after nine.

"Nah, I'm going to bed so I can get up in the morning. I have a ministry session and I'm sure my sister has a million things for me to do tomorrow."

"Same here, Pastor already asked me to help him with a session. Maybe I'll see you tomorrow at breakfast." Paul said, walking toward the elevator, no longer interested in attending the reception himself.

Keisha was so tired when she got back to the room that she laid across her bed fully clothed prepared to do a quick prayer just in case she fell asleep in the next few minutes. Lenora startled her when she flushed the toilet and came out of the bathroom in her nightgown and head scarf. She hoped Lenora didn't plan to talk her to death, because she sensed Lenora was one of those types content to latch on hard to one person instead of branching out and meeting many people. Keisha could have gone to the welcome reception with Paul if she wanted a lot of conversation. She felt bad because she promised her brother-in-law that she would come to the reception with a few icebreakers in mind, just in case people only wanted to mingle in their current church groups. Willie would be okay, Keisha reasoned. Besides, he was married to Mrs. Congeniality, and Keisha sort of needed the icebreakers for herself because she hadn't quite figured out what she was doing for her early morning ministry session.

She had a hard time interpreting what it was that God was trying to tell her lately. She felt He was trying to reveal something, pushing her forward into something, but she hadn't managed to steal away in prayer and study amidst the retreat and unification frenzy that seemed to have overtaken her church and everyone in it. She couldn't help thinking that participating on this retreat was a big distraction.

"Did you enjoy yourself?" Lenora asked, hovering over Keisha's bed.

"Yeah, but I didn't stay long. They moved the location of the room."

"I think you all did a good job of planning. Check-in ran so smoothly. I've already met some nice people."

"Me too," Keisha said, not feeling up to much conversation, but remembered a Morton family rule from when she and Vanessa were girls; they were always to be good ambassadors of the church and their family. What she needed most was to talk to God in prayer.

"I invited this guy and his mother from the other church to eat breakfast with me. You can come too if you plan on being up that early."

"That would be nice, thank you," Lenora said as she began to fold up the outfit that she wore on the ride up to the retreat center. "How is it being the pastor's sister?"

Keisha almost screamed, but realized Lenora wouldn't understand the promise she made to herself the next time she heard that question. She didn't mean any harm, Keisha told herself. "I imagine it is like being a sibling to any other person. You fuss and fight, get on each other's nerves and then call each other up to apologize."

"I can't imagine talking to Pastor Green on the phone," Lenora said. "I don't even know where she lives."

"We used to live in Forrestville until she got married and moved to Temple Hills."

"Wow, that's good to know, I guess," Lenora said while looking through her options of outfits hanging in the closet.

"She is a person. You act like you're afraid to talk to her." Keisha rolled over on her side to face Lenora and propped her head with her hand.

"I guess I don't want to bother her. She's got to be awfully busy," Lenora said, pulling down the ironing board to prepare her clothes for the next day.

"What if you have a spiritual concern? That's what pastors are for."

"I don't know. I would try to be strong in the Lord and pray for myself. If it were a real emergency, I would call the people listed in the bulletin for Watchcare."

"You don't allow yourself to be pastored to. Forget all that Watchcare stuff, I'd go straight to the top."

"Well, of course, you're her sister. I figure she has a life separate from church that I shouldn't interrupt. As well as your sister preaches, I should at least have garnished enough faith to keep me in bad times. I don't want to grieve the pastor with something I can take care of on my own, with a little prayer."

Keisha thought that either Lenora was a real mature Christian or a naive one. Keisha had never given much thought about interrupting anything when she visited her sister's house or needed to talk to her until now. Heck, she took it all to Vanessa; everything from what she should do about her career to relationship concerns.

"I can't imagine calling Pastor unless my mom was dying or something. What if she is busy or just doesn't feel like talking?" Lenora droned on.

"She just says to me, 'Keisha, we will talk about it later' or 'I'll talk to you at church,'" Keisha said in her best Vanessa impression. She swung her legs over the side of her bed to get up. She took her toiletry bag from the zipper compartment of her suitcase. "I'm going in the shower. I've kept you up long enough."

Once inside the confines of the bathroom, Keisha sat on the lid of the toilet stool, bent at the middle and began to pray. "Lord, thank you for the blessings you've bestowed upon my life and the life of our church. You've allowed Mt. Pleasant to enlarge it borders, but God, I can't help feeling as if that is my sister's ministry and you have something different in store for me. We were both uniquely made and saved for a purpose. Help me to clearly define my calling, and my ministry. I'm ready to be more dedicated and committed. In Jesus' name I pray, Amen."

The next day, Keisha and Lenora dressed and walked together to the lobby for breakfast. Lenora dropped in to buy a newspaper at the gift shop while Keisha requested extra towels from the front desk. Keisha saw Paul and his mother leaving out the front exit and called to them.

"Hey," Keisha said.

They walked over to her. "Mom, this is Keisha. This is my mom, Thelma Grant."

"Skipping breakfast?" Keisha asked.

"I'm not," Thelma stated.

"I was going to see if there was a store around." He turned to show Keisha the charred outline of an iron print that showed after a failed attempt to tuck it into his pants." The expanse of his back and shoulders were massive in comparison to his small waistline.

All Keisha could do was laugh which in turn made Paul laugh also. "Who did that?" Keisha said, looking at Thelma.

"Not me, I got sense enough to take a hot iron off clothes after they been pressed. He lucky it didn't burn a hole straight through it," Thelma said.

Keisha turned to Paul. "Why don't you just put a suit jacket over it?"

"That's what I said," Thelma stated.

"I only brought one for Sunday service, besides, I don't want to eat in a jacket," Paul said.

Keisha circled him to get another view of the damage. "You need a bigger belt, or cummerbund or something." She couldn't help but laugh.

"Don't start in on me. Look, why don't you and my mom go in and eat. I'm going to check nearby for a shop that sells shirts. If push comes to shove, I'm man enough to handle it."

Lenora had already found an open table when Keisha and Thelma came in to the banquet hall. They waited to be called to the buffet before helping themselves to generous portions of brunch entrees. Paul appeared ten minutes later in the same ivory shirt. Almost everyone in the dinning area had already filled up on second helpings. It took only minutes for Paul to fill his plate and make his way to the table. Keisha was being entertained by Thelma's back home stories.

"No luck, huh?" Thelma said to her son.

"No. I'm kind of mad because it is one of my favorite shirts," Paul replied.

"What's the matter?" Lenora asked.

"Iron mark," Keisha whispered.

"That's a shame. Yeah, it's ruined," Lenora said.

"There was something we used to use to take care of iron marks," Thelma shared.

"I never heard of anything to take out iron marks," Lenora said.

"Back home they had what you called a salve," Thelma said.

"Tonic," Paul reminded.

"You heard this one?" Keisha said.

"I heard them all." Paul rolled his eyes.

"Anyway, it was a Goodman product," Thelma continued. "You know the kind they sold door to door back in the day; that could take out any stain known to man. It was strong too, and smelled like turpentine. Almost killed my Aunt Nettie, left her sterile instead."

"How did that happen?" Keisha said. She looked at Paul as if he could deliver the answer quicker. He just shook his head as Thelma continued her story.

"She drank it," said Thelma. She left everyone hanging while she ate her French toast.

"Why in the world did she do that?" Lenora said.

"Aunt Nettie was known for being out of her head. Like I said, we used to use that stuff for every stain. Momma used to order a special bottle for us girls to wash out our undergarments; you know, after our monthly. I mean, that stuff was like the blood of Jesus; it would wash everything white as snow. So, crazy Aunt Nettie thought if she drank it that it would make her monthly clear or at least white," Thelma said.

Keisha wanted to laugh out loud but Thelma was so serious. She looked at the expressions on everyone's faces. Paul smiled at her and said, "You asked."

"Well, everyone got someone in the family that is a little off," Lenora said. Everyone shook their head in agreement to that.

Thelma Grant was the type of woman a person wanted to adopt into their family. She shared several stories throughout their meal and imparted a lesson learned from each one. Keisha knew for sure Paul had not heard all of his mother's stories.

They did not notice that they were among the few remaining people left eating breakfast in the dinning room. Willie and Vanessa made their way over to the table to urge them on to the morning sessions. Keisha jumped in hospitality mode and began introductions around the table. When she got to Paul and Thelma, Willie took over.

"Honey, this woman is the true meaning of the title willing worker, Thelma Grant and you know her son, Paul," Willie introduced.

"Hello, you all seem to be enjoying yourselves over here. We don't want to rush you, but the morning sessions are about to begin," Vanessa said generally, then turned toward her sister, "That means you, Session Leader."

"Remember, Brother Paul is meeting with all those participants who haven't committed themselves to a ministry before and after lunch. We made up a card on the computer where they can check off a ministry they might be interested in," Willie said.

"That's right. Get everyone involved. God is calling everyone here to be laborer."

"Speaking of preaching, who is preaching tomorrow?" Keisha said.

"Does that matter?" Vanessa said, gently bumping into her sister. "She thinks she is privy to that kind of information just because she is my sister."

"And part of your ministerial staff," Keisha reminded.

"Oh really, we could have used your ministerial assistance last night at the reception." Willie chimed in.

Keisha opened her mouth to offer and excuse, then thought better of it. She would have to make it up to Willie. It was one thing to disappoint her sister, with her sanctimonious self, who from their past, halfway expects her to foul up. It was another thing to disappoint Willie, who usually cuts her some slack, and as of late had been putting her sister in her place.

"We are trying to keep it a surprise who will preach tomorrow. I assure you, either way, the word will be from the Lord. Willie and I are going to preach when the Spirit gives us the message. Follow us as we follow Christ, Sister Morton," Vanessa said, checking her watch. She and Willie decided they ought to be hastening on themselves. Vanessa followed Willie through the maze between the circular banquet tables to the exit.

"Well, you heard the pastor," Thelma said, struggling to her feet.

"Nice to meet you, Sister Grant," Keisha said.

"Same here, darling. Paul, I'm going up to the room before checking out choir rehearsal."

"I'll go upstairs with you," Lenora said to Thelma.

Keisha and Paul were the last to leave. "So, you are a minister?" Paul said.

"Yep, Minister to the Singles. I'm not licensed to preach, but I teach sessions on purity and what God expects of us. Single to serve, that's the slogan Vanessa came up with, but I'm slowly working on making it my own. Soon, I'm going to take it to a new level, right after Unification." Keisha said, suddenly curious about Paul's single status but afraid to ask for fear of him getting the wrong impression.

"I see," Paul said looking genuinely interested.

"I think you mentioned last night that you're a writer? What have you written? Do you have anything in the mainstream?" Keisha said.

"Of course, manuals, travel brochures, handbooks for non-profit organizations."

"Oh, I was thinking more on the lines of poems, stories or screenplays."

"I write a little of that, too. I'm afraid to do the creative stuff full time though. I have bills to pay, you know. And, what do you do professionally?"

"Work like a dog," she said. "I am a data processor, but I'm thinking about going back to school soon. With my duties at the church though, I don't know when I'll have the time."

"Well, this is as good a time as any while you're still young." Paul said.

"Thirty-five," she said, without prompting.

"I got you by two years."

"Well, I could use a creative brother like yourself on my ministry. We're meeting in room 215."

"And I'd love to get involved, but like you said, I don't know when I'll find the time. My work schedule is a little hectic right now."

"I understand," Keisha said.

There was a brief silence. "If you have a short term project that I can help you with for your ministry, I'm your man," Paul said, flashing rows of perfectly aligned teeth. "Now, I better let you get to your session. I've got to go upstairs and get my itinerary," he smiled.

"I guess I'll see you later."

Keisha watched him walk to the elevator and smiled when she saw the top portion of the iron print. She felt as if she had inherited a new family on this retreat. She was glad she had met Paul and his mother. Most of the time she felt isolated or like a third wheel in her sister's circle. Today, she felt like she wanted to break the cycle.

Chapter 17

Time and Talent

The retreat schedule was exhausting. It didn't look that bad when it was written out on paper, Vanessa thought. She and Willie would have to spread themselves thin if they wanted to make sure that one or the other attended each session to observe the dynamics of the groups they were asking to combine. Any and every foreseeable ministry that needed to be reorganized was asked to send a group to represent them at the retreat. At the last meeting, Vanessa and Willie were very specific about post retreat outcomes which were: affirm faith in the move of God and unite with one another in fellowship.

There were workshops and fellowships scheduled around the clock for Saturday, including two mandatory rehearsals for choir members that were asked to render two selections for worship service. Vanessa walked in the auditorium for choir rehearsal and was surprised to see Willie saunter in ten minutes later. She tapped his thigh when he sat down beside her and leaned in to whisper something to him. "I though I left you with the trustees."

"I figured those guys know what they are doing," Willie

whispered while tapping her leg back. "Plus I wanted to see the choir; you go check on the trustees."

"You know how important it is to me that the musicians set the right atmosphere for worship."

"These are your musicians. They play for you all the time. I need to check them out to see if they meet with my satisfaction. For all I know they could be like most churches playing that gospel disco stuff you hear on the radio now."

They traded licks again in a fruitless effort to get the other to move. Vanessa hoped they weren't causing a scene but couldn't help show her playful side when Willie was around. That was another reason why they needed to split up. Willie would be whispering and having her giggle like a school girl on a date. Vanessa had a no-nonsense image to maintain. She also felt each group needed supervision and they would regret the fact that they left the trustees to their own devices during the critical combining stage. She tried one more time to convince him.

"You know music is in my blood. I moved my way through the ranks of the choirs growing up here at Mt. Pleasant," bragged Vanessa.

"I've seen the devil wreck a choir by making talented people high on themselves. I've seen choir members at odds with choir musicians. You know like I know, we do not need any additional headaches," said Willie.

"Well, I can assure you that we won't have any of that here."

"We both shall see, won't we?"

Keith Fischer, the choir director, stood at the microphone in the large auditorium. Willie hushed Vanessa before she could say another thing and held her hand as if they were about to view the opening act of a Broadway show.

"We will both observe and go right into combined session afterwards," Willie whispered. "Don't think 'cause Mt. Pleasant has big time musicians that Harvest doesn't have some sisters who can blow. I bet you that Sister Alice Jones, A Harvest Baptist Church member, gets a solo. She can sang. I hope your guys can recognize talent."

Vanessa waved him off. She was not about to make a bet over a retreat choir soloist. Willie would just have to see how some of her choir members threw down on a microphone. Keith pushed play on his compact disc player and positioned a microphone in front of the mini speaker. An audio assault of shouting over a tremendous amount of bass and percussion startled some and entertained others.

"You see, that's exactly what I was talking about earlier," Willie whispered.

This time Vanessa shushed him with a pat of her hand. She had trust in her musicians.

"This is considered today's gospel music," Keith said. "but what many of these artists don't know is that gospel music has its roots in the Negro spirituals that the slaves would sing and even farther back in the African tribal songs. Every kind of popular music had it's derivatives from good, old fashioned church music. We don't have to borrow from the world's music to get our point across. The soulful belting of gospel soloist and the stories that accompany a song innovated the jazz chant, the R&B rift and even the rap freestyles," Keith said, as if teaching a music seminar. "Popular music seems to take the lead from gospel style. While Christians were singing, "Precious Lord, Take My Hand," the world was singing, 'Loverman, Oh Where Can You Be'? There is an overlap between the message of Gospel and the Blues, just looking for different saviors."

Vanessa looked at her watch. She realized there was a flaw in the schedule. How could they have not seen that the morning session had less time then the afternoon session? That left Keith a short amount time before the group session with her and Willie scheduled to take place in the same auditorium after rehearsal. She hoped the other groups were being productive.

Keith asked Vanessa to go over expectations and the breakdown of the four newly structured choirs they had agreed upon before the retreat. Disapproval came over the disbanding of the Morton Memorial choir for a combined choir to which she replied, "If Pastor Vanessa Morton Green isn't upset, than why should you be?"

Vanessa could tell Willie was relieved that Keith chose two standard songs: "What a Friend we Have in Jesus" and "I Really Love the Lord." Willie kissed Vanessa on the cheek before dismissing himself. No doubt, he was now going to check on the trustees. She pulled him by his back pocket, "Hey what about our bet?"

"You keep tabs for me. We'll settle up later."

Keith directed the group to sit according to their voice range in three point harmony. Keith showed that his own voice had range as he sang the tenor, alto, as well as the soprano part for each song.

Vanessa also noticed Sadie Briscoe sat in the alto section. Sadie sat upright, not allowing her back to rest in the folding chairs set up for the choir to the right of the pulpit stage. She often led songs in the Jubilee singers at Mt. Pleasant and was known to get the church "happy" after one of her solos. She had a definite ear for music.

"Keith, can you play the alto part again? I can hear all three parts over in this section," Sadie requested. Keith plucked the individual cords of the first song real slow on the piano. Sadie took it upon herself to accompany him so that everyone in her section was sure to hear her perfectly pitched voice.

"Now, I want just the altos from the beginning. I really love the Lord," Keith instructed. As soon as the altos started to sing, Sadie's hand went up immediately. Vanessa could tell Keith's patience was wearing thin. Sadie was definitely one of those divas they were talking about earlier, Vanessa thought. Sure, even she could hear that some of the singers were flat even from where she was seated. What did Sadie expect them to do, hold auditions for a retreat choir?

"Yes, Sister Sadie," Keith said when he came to a pause.

"Someone is still off." Sadie turned around as if she was trying to pinpoint just who it was. "Some people are singing soprano and then some are just tone deaf."

"No one is perfect Sister Sadie," Vanessa said. "It sounds fine to me for the first go around. Let's get through it a couple of times."

Everyone tried to concentrate on their part and not on Sadie. Vanessa could hear Sadie's voice dominating the section. The next refrain Sadie yielded her voice, singing just a few beats behind everyone else, emphasizing the key words.

"Sister Sadie, grab the microphone," Keith said. Sadie sprang from her seat and pulled the microphone from its base. This time she led the choir into each verse. "Sister in the first row with the red blouse, please join her at the microphone. I'm sorry, what is your name?" Keith said, pointing to the soprano section.

"Alice Jones from Harvest Baptist Church," the woman replied.

Sadie seemed reluctant to place the microphone back in the stand so that Alice could share the spotlight with her.

"I want to open the song with the both of you singing the verse before the choir comes in." Keith said, playing the introduction. Alice started in with "I really love the Lord." Sadie paused as if she were rating Alice's voice.

"Both of you," Keith said, signaling Sadie to join in.

"You don't know what He's done for me. Gave me the victory. I love him. I love him. I really love the Lord," they sang in perfect harmony.

"Great, Ladies. I trust that you will practice your parts tonight. Let's give both of them a hand, choir." The applause seemed to make Sadie feel better about sharing the spotlight. "Hopefully everyone knows, 'What a Friend We Have in Jesus'. If not, you need to get with a fellow choir member to review the words before tonight's rehearsal.

Keith was forced to stop as people began filing in the auditorium from their opening ministry session. Vanessa took her place on the platform and shook a few choir member's hands that were on their way down the stairs. Willie walked in with Perin Jones, the head of the combined Trustee Ministry, and joined her on the stage.

"I want to make sure everyone is here before we begin. I saw the deacons, trustees and Paul's group come in," Vanessa said.

"I see Miss Lillian and the other Sunday school teachers; they met with the Bible study leaders. I think this is it."

"Oh, there is Luella. She has the master schedule, "Vanessa said, ready to get the session started so that it didn't run into lunch. She waved her secretary over. "Luella, is this everyone?"

Luella looked between her list that was clamped to her clipboard and the room full of people waiting to hear from their pastors. "The Singles are missing. I bet your sister's session is running overtime. Do you want me to go get them?"

Vanessa waved her off. "We can't wait anymore." She was fuming and now trying to get her anger under control before they started. The last thing she needed was to see her sister's smug face. This was not the first time Keisha had done her own thing and totally disregarded the time frame they had put in place for church activities. She barely turned in her ministry reports on time. Any other officer would have been reprimanded or removed from office by now. She would have to talk to Keisha seriously before people began to believe she was getting preferential treatment.

Willie and Vanessa both planned to address the crowd in their own way. It was important to them to remain themselves and not try to conform to a cookie cutter mold of what ministry couples should be. Willie Green, in his quiet and friendly manner, explained the vision bestowed on them on their honeymoon. Then he ended with hope for the unified church. He implored the crowd to devote themselves not to the effort, but to Christ. Vanessa could tell he had to suppress the urge to preach as he asked everyone to present themselves as living sacrifices unto God.

Vanessa Green abandoned the microphone to get closer to the crowd she was addressing. She knew she was under particular scrutiny because most of the audience was from Harvest. She got everyone on their feet to give God praise for the vision God gave them for the combined church. She set the tone with the scripture reference for the retreat and explained that every member present was there to perform their part in the work of the Lord. She shared her firm belief that no one signed up for this retreat by chance, and how she couldn't accept anyone present to be, as she called it, "a pew-warming member" of the unified church. The retreat was the catalyst for finding a particular calling. She read from the list of sessions with ministries that had already met that morning and others listed in the itinerary for that afternoon, so that those who woke up late or planned to skip the afternoon sessions and go shopping, might consider changing their plans.

Vanessa was about to dismiss individuals to their sessions, but several people had questions. Clyde Simmons asked, "Sister Green . . . , I'm sorry. Pastor Green, if you belong to more than one ministry, how can you make it to more than one session?"

"Of course, you can not split yourself in half. You need to pick one meeting. I would go to the one that I hold an office for because new guidelines have been established. Deacon Simmons here brings to mind another point without even knowing it, and I think we need to discuss it here. Willie and I plan to share the pastorate of our church. I am your pastor as much as he is your pastor." She looked about the crowd for the familiar face. "My good friend, Deacon Johnson, Willie and I were talking at the reception. Anytime he wanted my attention, he called me Sister Pastor, and anytime he wanted Willie's attention he called him Brother Pastor. I thought that was great; it is endearing and still gave honor to the man and woman of God. Beloved, I invite you to do same."

Willie came up behind her and grasped her shoulders. "Call me anything you want, just don't call me late for a meal. They've just informed me lunch is ready to be served in the main dinning area. If Vanessa and I don't get a chance to come around to your table and greet you, go to your sessions and be blessed."

Chatter spilled into the hallway as the members filed out directly across the hall to the dinning area. Vanessa knew she had a half an hour to forty-five minutes before she was expected at the Women's Auxiliary session. After that, Vanessa knew she would be unavailable herself; facilitating Budget and Finance sessions. They had hired a new accounting firm and Vanessa invited her lawyers to be present as they discussed the legalities of transferring funds from one entity to another, as well as ensuring salaried positions for both her and Willie.

Vanessa walked the thick carpeted halls of the retreat

center with a copy of the master schedule she had gotten from Luella as if she was following a map through the forest trying to find the break in the trees that led back to civilization. She wanted to catch her sister in action and ask her just what did she think she was doing rearranging their carefully planned out schedule. Willie always joked that Vanessa was the Captain and Keisha was the Social Director at Mt. Pleasant as if they worked on a Cruise ship. Keisha just needed a little reminder every now and again that she was aboard her ship and not the other way around.

Naturally the room would be at the far end of the hall, Vanessa thought as she noticed the room numbers descending. The lights were out in room 202 where the Singles were scheduled to meet. She pressed her face to the glass as if she would find her sister hiding inside and almost missed the note posted on the door in her sister's script. The sign read, Singles have gone out to lunch. That was it—no destination, no estimated time to arrive back.

Vanessa retreated. She tried to see the situation for what it really was; an attempt for her sister to get to know those who want to be a part of her ministry; not a heinous plot to cause division amongst her retreat participants. It was a good thing Vanessa didn't find them, she thought. She could just hear her sister explaining herself as if it were perfectly logical that her entire group miss the combined session with their new pastors in order to get a good table at TGI Friday's. Whatever the motive, it was irresponsible.

Once Vanessa reached the first floor she nearly bumped into Luella, who appeared to be looking for her.

"Did you find them?" Luella asked.

"No," Vanessa said, still moving, as if she was trying to walk off her frustration. Luella was forced to change direction to hear a reply. "They went out to lunch. Let me know the minute they get back," Vanessa said over her shoulder. She got a few more feet and then stopped. Luella was now at the opposite end of the hall waiting as if she anticipated a last minute thought from her pastor. "As a matter of fact, don't tell me when they get back. I don't want to know. I've got more important things to worry about."

The next morning, Seaport experienced an early November frost. Inside suite 402, Vanessa's nerves were rattled as Willie Green seemed to be enjoying a rare treat of his own: watching his wife get ready for Sunday worship.

Harvest had a Sunrise service that usually put Willie up and out of the house before Vanessa prepared herself for Sunday School at Mt. Pleasant. Now maybe he could see why he was always left waiting when he used to pick her up for a date, Vanessa thought. Most men don't realize how much is required for a woman to get all dressed up.

Willie laid across the bed having already used the facilities and watched. His navy blue suit, white shirt and paisley tie were draped across the chair.

Vanessa was methodical and knew she would be fully dressed in the twenty minutes they had left before breakfast ended and worship service would begin. She floated back and forth from the bathroom, to the closet, to the suitcase.

"You don't need to stay out of my way. You need to get dressed yourself," Vanessa said.

"I'll be ready. I'm just watching you."

"What?"

"Nothing."

Vanessa made use of the bathroom, bathing, brushing and flossing. Then out to the suitcase where she girded herself with undergarments and a slip. After that she made a follow-up visit to the bathroom with her cosmetic case for foundation, a light powder and eye make-up.

"Answer me this, Nessa. If you were in the bathroom earlier, why didn't you put on your makeup then?" Willie said.

"I had to let the steam out of the bathroom. It would have just made me hot and made my makeup run."

"Why do you put your makeup on before you get dressed anyway?"

"What is this, twenty questions?" Vanessa said. She went back to the suitcase where she made a choice of shoes. "I put on my makeup before I get into my dress because I've had my compact forever," she said, showing him the tattered chocolate covered puff. "The pressed powder gets all over the place because the makeup is old. Plus, I have a chance to see if I like my initial application or if I need to start again.

Vanessa went to the closet and stepped into the periwinkle suit she bought in Ashton and made a last visit to the bathroom to run a brush dampened with water and gel through her hair. She appeared in front of her husband transformed. She slipped on two-inch crystal pumps and simple diamond studs before reprimanding him for not being ready.

Vanessa couldn't help thinking, if Willie was trying to drive her crazy as well. First it was her sister. Then Buster Johnson called their suite several times in anticipation ever since he talked with Vanessa at the welcome reception about reading during her sermon. She knew he couldn't help thinking about the stuttering that has plagued him since grade school. He shared with her that the more fervent he felt about something, the harder it was to get the point out without repetitions and hesitations. From what Willie told her, she gathered that he had no problem making people laugh when they were younger, and the stuttering added to his routine. He played up his outlandish image with a colorful wardrobe and outrageous antics to camouflage his insecurities. She did not give him a passage of scripture until this morning, shortly after midnight. When he asked her the format she told him to be in prayer as if she was going into the unknown.

Vanessa was nervous about ministering to the semi united congregation as well but she did not want to show it. She had gotten up an hour earlier than Willie to meditate and pray, knowing they would pray again before going to the platform. Willie suggested they have a private breakfast sent up by room service, but Vanessa preferred the noisiness of the fellowship hall. They got downstairs with a few minutes to spare. All she needed was a bowl of fruit and a cup of tea. She was ready to show the participants what the Divinity Diva does best.

After the choir sang, Vanessa instructed Buster to stand at the microphone on the ground level. She greeted everyone as if seeing them for the first time. The congregation was asked to focus on Matthew 25 with the sermon title: Hidden Talents.

"Beloved, this passage tells a story, a parable of a man and his servants. My husband always says there are no gimmicks in the Gospel. There are no tricks. It's straight forward. Jesus uses the parable purposefully. In the previous chapter of the same book of Matthew, a disciple asked Jesus, 'why do you speak in parables?' The Lord replied 'because the seeing see not; and the hearing, hear not, neither do they understand.' What we don't understand today is that God gave us talents and gifts to use in the world for His glory. But some of us got them hidden, buried down deep and afraid to use them. Vanessa turned to Willie on the platform.

He gave her a nod of agreement. "Take your time." he said.

Vanessa Green always started a sermon with the context

of the passage she chose. It was like a pattern to start with historical background and then finish with present day applications. That way of preaching gave the Bible relevance that the congregation did not get from just reading a few scriptures each night before going to bed, she thought. She was also sensitive to the Holy Spirit when she studied a passage, as well as the impromptu teachings from the Spirit during the sermon delivery. That's when the message got personal. Those were the words that changed and saved lives.

A major part of her preaching style was passion. She believed anyone could get up and regurgitate some scriptures and any half educated person could paraphrase its particular meaning. Behind each verse was life, she often thought. How else do you present life except lively? She was a preacher's daughter and had sat through thousands of boring messages. In her mind, if you can rant and rave over a favorite team or musical group, then Jesus Christ can surely get a hearty hip, hip, hurrah.

"Basically he spoke in parables for those who were ignoring the simple facts. We are wonderfully made by God," Vanessa said, sticking out a finger to indicate each point. "We are fashioned in his image with the purpose to glorify him and bring others to him. How do we do all that? One way is by using our God-given talents. Lordhavmercy. Brother Buster, pick up Matthew 25 verse 15 for me. Real slow now, we want to get it."

Buster had to even himself on both feet from a leaning position. Vanessa saw him stare at the scripture with wide eyes as if all of a sudden his pocket-size Bible became difficult to read. His chest began to heave with trepidation as he fumbled through the first verse and began the second.

"And unto one he gave f.f.f.five talents, to another two, and to a.a.nother, one; to every man according to his several ability. Straightway took his journey," Buster read.

"Stop right there, Brother," Vanessa told him. Let me make my point of teaching. The man passed out talents. Now he was passing out money. But, like we said before, a parable is a story, sort of like a children's tale where the character represents true life situations with a moral at the end. For our understanding, a talent can be a calling, gift, or in this case, financial. He passed them out much like God gave each of us talents; some one, some more than one. All right, read, Brother Deacon."

Once again Buster appeared to be caught off guard. The pause seemed to be forever as he searched for where he left off. Vanessa could hear the faint sounds of the mothers in the second row calling out verses. When he located his place, she heard the familiar catch in his speech. He struggled through the next five verses, stopping and restarting, repeating and self correcting like a person driving a stick shift for the first time on a sharp incline. Each verse was like a light in which he revs up to, then drifted backward while alternating between the pedals to prevent from stalling.

Vanessa was patient as she stopped him at the twentieth verse to make several points that made up the bulk of the sermon about investing time in one's talent, being rewarded for their time and talent, and bringing the harvest to the Lord. Buster regained his composure as he began to think about the message. Pastor Green called in other scriptures, which she read herself about purpose, cause and calling. Buster called out to bless the Lord when Vanessa told the crowd, don't let anyone tell you that you are a mistake. She disclosed how she felt she had to defend her calling to preach for years.

When Buster was called upon to read again, a cloud of expectation hung over her statement. "This is the important part, the promise, the victory. Read Brother, verse 21."

Buster started off slowly. "His Lord said unto him, well d . . . done thou good and f . . . f . . . fai." The second and third syllable would not come. He looked as if he wanted to curse his affliction and sit down. Vanessa wanted to help him through it, but knew that he could do it, that God wanted him to get past his affliction. He looked up at her as if he had failed her by not finishing the statement, especially one so critical to the message.

Vanessa broke in, "Brother Johnson."

He peered up to the podium. "Yes, Sis Pastor."

"God wants to use your talent. Do you believe that today?"

He thought about her words. "Yes Pastor."

"God hasn't given us the spirit of fear, Deacon. I believe the word is in your heart. I don't say all this to embarrass you. We are all family. I have a feeling you have been praying about this for some time. In the New Testament Jesus healed a man with a speech impediment. It was the man's faith that gained him favor. You're about to get your breakthrough in this place today."

She detached the microphone from its stand and walked down the steps with the aide of her husband. "The Bible says speak with boldness. Although anyone can read this passage, I believe Brother Buster was called to proclaim the word," she said.

Vanessa pressed his forehead with such force that her ring began to make an indentation. "Speak boldly without fear, not because I stand before you, but because the Lord, our God stands with you. You said in your word, 'Be opened.' In the name of Jesus, loose your servant's tongue and grant him articulation of speech." She gave his head a slight shove with the intonation that marked the end of her short prayer. "What is the Lord saying to us in that passage, Brother Deacon?" Vanessa asked.

Despite all the excitement and focus of the entire gath-

ering on him, he found his place instantly. "Thou good
and faithful servant: thou hast been faithful over a few
things, I will make thee ruler over many things. Enter
thou into the joy of the Lord," he said clearly, and leapt
for joy in spite of himself.

"Enter the joy of the Lord, Brother Buster. You've been
set free. How many people in here want to enter the joy of
the Lord? Lose those bonds? Use your talents? Enter the
joy of the Lord, say yeah!" Vanessa lifted her dress to right
above her knees and started in a dance.

Keith Fischer jumped on the organ and intensified the
jubilation with lightening quick syncopation from the
organ. The spirit came in like a mighty tornado sweeping
over the crowd and touching people in a sporadic pattern.
A woman jerked into motion with arms and legs flailing as
if being controlled by a mad puppeteer. The Spirit left behind a trail of His presence throughout the sanctuary.
Some were left standing, some flattened level to the
ground in praise, but everyone was happy.

Vanessa grabbed the microphone. "Use your talents for
God, for it is pleasing to the Lord. How many in here want
to please God? Deacon what did the passage say that God
will tell us if we are faithful?"

"Good and faithful servant, enter the joy of the Lord!"
he screamed.

"Woo, GlorytaGod," she shouted at his continued clarity of speech. She replicated her dance from earlier.

The choir kept up the rhythm with clapping. The Nurses
Unit sent mini brigades to form a barricade around the
praise filled members.

"Wait, they don't need anyone to hold them," Vanessa
informed them. "They are not sick. They're praising. You
better get your praise on yourself."

Vanessa hugged Buster and rejoined her husband on
the platform.

"I got sense enough to let the Lord have His way. I'm done," Vanessa said. Willie handed her a cup of cranberry juice that she sipped before sitting down. She left him with the hard task of closing out the service and retreat without quenching the Spirit.

Showered and refreshed, the participants boarded the buses. Although Seaport was a mere 2,500 feet above sea level, all aboard the two motor coaches felt as if they had reached a peak that weekend. From this mountaintop experience, Vanessa felt Willie had risen above the previous obstacles that presented themselves at Harvest and was on the fast track to the move of God over at Mt. Pleasant.

Chapter 18

Sibling Rivalry

"What have you done for me lately?" Vanessa asked rhetorically, but quite literally of her sister's request over the phone.

"Girl, what are you talking about? I do things for you all the time, Keisha replied."

"Really?" Vanessa said, wanting so badly to remind her of her antics on the retreat a week ago, that they had yet to discuss.

"Can I borrow your clear pumps or not? I would go out and buy my own pair, but you said you bought them in Ashton. As much as I need them to complete my outfit, I am not about to drive that far. C'mon."

"I guess," Vanessa said. "I'll bring them over later."

"You don't have to do that, sis. You know I'll come over and pick them up."

"What's the matter? Can't I drop by and visit my baby sister every now and again?" Vanessa said, pausing to think when was the last time she had been to her sister's apartment. She never had much of an opportunity to visit since her sister was accustomed to camping out at her place. "Plus, we need to talk," Vanessa added.

"About? Wait a minute. I don't believe I asked that question. Of course it's about ministry. How unlikely you'd be coming over to my house to shoot the breeze. I forgot, everything is about ministry with you."

Vanessa was surprised by her sister's comments. "We shoot the breeze plenty. What about our little excursion to the mall?"

"That was so you could pick out a dress for a service you were invited to minister."

"And the time we went to that charity basketball game?"

"Vanessa, you can't be that old. You made me think we were just hanging out, but then you made me introduce you to one of the managers of Heaven 1580 radio station so Mt. Pleasant could get a plug or you could get a show or something."

Vanessa had to laugh at her sister who could be quite the comedian. "Every weekend you are over my house and I welcome you with open arms," Vanessa said, knowing she couldn't deny that.

"Yeah, and if it wasn't for me coming over, you would have no idea what's going on with me."

"Well, I hope you've got dinner prepared, because we will have plenty to shoot the breeze about. And if church or church related topics should come up, sue me. I'm a pastor for goodness sake."

"It's cool though. You can't get to where you are in your ministry without being driven. I've been thinking a lot about my own drive lately," Keisha said. "So, I'll expect you in an hour or two?"

"Maybe sooner," Vanessa said, resisting the urge to comment about her sister's drive.

Vanessa felt instantly convicted by her sister's commentary on their post-marriage relationship. She knew the fact that she was extremely busy was a poor excuse to offer her baby sister, with whom she used to live with. She was actually too busy to be taking the time out to visit her sister now, Vanessa thought as she stacked the folders of retreat initiatives in front of her that she and Willie needed to approve.

Willie was orchestrating the packing, moving and overall close out of Harvest Baptist. There seemed to be a million and one decisions that Vanessa needed to make right away. She felt near to tears after spending half the morning weighing the pros and cons of Sunday school materials used by both of their churches that needed to be ordered for the winter and spring sessions. Each initiative, each dilemma or crisis that came up, there could only be one choice, one decision; decisions she was finding harder and harder to make on her own.

That's why Willie and Vanessa needed to maintain their current operations and only blend those things that didn't require a lot of work. Some things can be mixed together manually and others needed to be broken down by the aid of a whip, beater or mixer. That is why this talk with Keisha was long over due. Lately Keisha had been testing the waters and doing her own thing. In lieu of how Keisha was feeling, it would be trivial to bring up the events of the retreat, Vanessa thought. That was water under the bridge. What she needed was for her sister to know how crucial it was for her to be consistent in her current role of hospitality, acclimating new members and teaching. Unification was a church-wide effort; she would have to share with her sister that the singles ministry may need to take a backseat for awhile.

Vanessa arrived at her sister's door within thirty minutes to be welcomed to an apartment filled with robust aromas. Her sister had rearranged a few things since she last visited. Vanessa relieved herself of her bags and coat before taking a seat on Keisha's couch.

"What is that I smell?" Vanessa asked.

"A beef roast," Keisha replied.

"Did you do the carrots and potatoes like grandma used to?"

"You know it," Keisha said, walking into the kitchen to check her meal.

Vanessa sprang forth from the couch and followed her. "You got a hold of Grandma's recipe?"

"More like Great-Aunty Helene's recipe that grandma perfected. You know Grand didn't write those things down," Keisha said, clicking the switch to light the oven compartment so they both could view the roast-in-progress. "I just remember a lot from sitting in the kitchen with her and watching her cook."

"I didn't pick up a thing. What was I doing?"

"Being a busy body and trying to help Daddy run the church."

"Well, it must be nice having all this time to prepare these elaborate meals," Vanessa said, opening a pot of water with a pat of butter dissolving in the middle, no doubt for rice, Vanessa thought, until she spotted the mound of peeled potatoes on a cutting board. "I feel so privileged that you went to all this trouble to cook for me."

"Girl, this is my dinner and leftovers for the rest of the week. You just don't up and prepare a meal like this 'cause your sister decides she is coming over to pay you a visit," Keisha said as she sliced each potato down the middle before dropping them into the pot. "It takes time and it has quite a ways to go before it will be done. So let's go in the living room and let the roast do what it's going to do."

Keisha and Vanessa went back to the living room where

Vanessa unzipped her boots to relieve the pressure on her calves. Taking off her boots reminded her of the shoes her sister had asked to borrow, which she almost forgot and had to run home for. Vanessa went into her carry-all bag to get the shoes and started to hand them over then asked, "What are you going to do with my shoes?"

"I'm going to wear them to Morning Star Baptist. I talked to Willie's single minister friend; a Minister Henry Holmes."

"I knew somehow this had to be about a man," Vanessa said, handing the shoes across the coffee table before sitting with one leg crossed beneath her in the middle of Keisha's couch.

"How do you figure?"

"With me, it's all about ministry. With you, it's always about a man."

"Give me some credit. It's not even like that. This time it's about my ministry. I told him about the Single's Conference I wanted to do at Mt. Pleasant and asked if he would be interested in teaching. Then, he asked me about my ministry. He said he was looking for a guest minister to teach a session to his singles as well," Keisha said. "He invited me to teach a seminar at his church. And if God should see fit to hook me up with a Willie and Vanessa love story in the process, then so be it. I faxed him my lessons on the wedding of Christ and he really liked it."

Vanessa remembered the series of lessons and how she felt so proud of her sister for preparing and presenting the adult session at last year's Vacation Bible School. She taught how singles and married people alike are the bride of Christ. Each day she instructed the congregation on how to adorn themselves spiritually as opposed to how a bride adorns herself physically for an earthly marriage. Those lessons made available on cassette and video added validity to Keisha's ministry to many people at Mt. Pleasant who previously wondered what her role was other than the pastor's sister.

"And you just accepted without consulting me?" Vanessa asked, wither hands out on both sides to emphasize her question.

"I consulted with you about the shoes."

"I'm serious; when is it?"

Keisha hesitated, "Next weekend."

Vanessa couldn't pinpoint off hand anything special happening at Mt. Pleasant, but it didn't matter. This was the same selfish behavior her sister got away with on the retreat. Now that they were back from the retreat, any date until the unification was complete was just bad timing.

"Hello, your church is going through unification. Did it ever occur to you that your pastor may need you?" Vanessa said, pointing both index fingers toward herself.

Keisha crossed her arms across her chest but immediately dropped them to her sides when she noticed Vanessa in the same defensive stance. "I can't believe how selfish you are being right now."

"Likewise," Vanessa said, sliding to the edge of the couch. Keisha had got her started and she felt like she did when they were kids ready to do anything to prove a point. "First it was the retreat where you purposely took a group of participants away from the retreat site."

"It's called fellowship. Remember, retreat goal number one?" Keisha said, letting her sarcasm slide into anger.

"But you made them miss the joint session with me and Willie. Oh, I guess that's not important as long as your fellowshipping. We should have let each ministry leader make their own schedules."

"You're the one that told me, and not so nicely I might

add, to get it together with the Singles Ministry or pass the mantle."

"I meant with the late reports and last minute activities. It's what you needed to hear, because people were beginning to talk."

Vanessa knew that her last comment stung and wished she could retrieve it. "Unification is not something that's just happening to me; it's happening to our entire church. I just happen to be in charge. And to think I wanted to bless you with the honor of being the Unification Day Chairperson."

Vanessa didn't know where the offer came from. It just sort of came out of her mouth, but it was perfect. If Keisha wanted to do ministry so badly, she could do it at home, Vanessa thought. That would be one last thing she would have to think about.

"Don't even act like that's an honor. I know you, sis. You just don't want to do it or nobody else will."

"The meeting is next week and there are plenty of people from Willie's church who would love to handle this. Ask yourself, why would I trust such an important day as this one to anyone that I didn't trust as a capable leader?"

Vanessa could tell that Keisha was thinking about it. "I'm going to Morning Star next weekend," Keisha said, jumping up and stamping off to the kitchen as if her roast or pot of boiling water was calling her.

Vanessa could hear her mumbling to herself while opening the oven door before allowing it to slam back closed. Vanessa got up from the couch to move closer to the kitchen door to see what she was saying. Vanessa, who loved to have the last word, used to hate when Keisha would go off mumbling instead of completing an argument. She never wanted her sister to raise a point or serve an insult that she couldn't reciprocate. Vanessa could see

the bottom half of her sister's bent frame behind the refrigerator door. She heard her say, "It's all about you, isn't
it Vanessa?"

"No, but it's not all about you either," Vanessa said, startling Keisha with the closeness of her voice.

"Gosh, Vanessa, sneaking up on me like that, " Keisha
said, rolling her eyes and leaning on the open refrigerator
door as if she needed a minute to get herself together.
"I'm about to eat in a minute, right after I mash these
potatoes. I like my beef rare, so if you want yours cooked a
little more, you'll have to wait about twenty minutes.

Vanessa came over to the refrigerator door to catch
some of the condiments her sister stubbornly piled into
her hands without asking for assistance. Vanessa set them
down on the counter within arms reach of Keisha's boiling pot. She watched as Keisha poured the water off the
potatoes, lightly mashing the potatoes that already appeared to be falling apart and then adding a few ingredients to the mixture before whipping it together with a
fork first, then a whisk. *It's that simple?* Vanessa thought. It
would do her good to learn a few things from her sister.

Keisha stuck her two insulated hands inside the oven to
retrieve the main dish. She signaled to Vanessa to get the
kitchen door so that she could carry the roasting pan to
the dinette table to cool. She was back in the kitchen without stopping to spoon the mash potatoes in a serving dish.
Vanessa went to the cupboard to piece together a service
for two. They sat at the table without proceeding any further with the meal.

"You didn't answer my question from earlier about Unification and being the chairperson," Vanessa said, wondering what they were waiting for. She was starving and
the roast looked too delicious to pretend it wasn't on the
table.

"You didn't comment about my teaching engagement at Morning Star, other than how upset you are that I didn't consider you first," Keisha said as if she was waiting for Vanessa. "Carving knife, serving spoon?"

"I didn't grab either," Vanessa said. "And there was nothing left to say about Morning Star. You told me you were going. Use this butter knife," Vanessa said as it became apparent that neither one of them was willing, at that moment, to run and get it.

"I'm just trying to move out of your shadow," Keisha said, standing with the flatware Vanessa had fished from her drawer to use for her meal.

"I support you, I do. The truth, I guess, that I wasn't trying to admit earlier is that I'm used to taking care of you."

"That's just it. I'm a big girl now," Keisha said.

Vanessa gave her a look like she heard that one before, but she decided to let the thought go. "Plus, I need you. I've been close to pulling my hair out with unification, and you know Willie doesn't want a bald-headed wife. I've never realized how much stress this whole ordeal would be. But I am determined not to let the devil steal my joy."

"You know what the true test is?" Keisha said poised as if ready to do surgery.

"Yeah, the first year after unification." Vanessa said.

"No, if my beef is tender enough to be cut with this toy knife you handed me," Keisha said painstakingly spooning miniature helpings of roasted vegetables onto both their plates. Vanessa watched as the blade of the knife disappeared into the valley of meat Keisha created with one slice. She clamped the thinly sliced beef between her knife and fork to serve it before cutting another piece for herself.

"What are we drinking?" Vanessa dared to ask.

"I got some iced tea, fruit punch or Tang in the fridge."

"I didn't know they still sell Tang." Vanessa said, getting up feeling it was only right for her to be the one to run back and forth to the kitchen.

"That's because you don't go to the grocery store," Keisha said as Vanessa re-entered with two cups full of iced tea and napkins. "Poor Willie, you've got to handle that sis. Imagine if word got out around the combined church about that, and people began to talk."

"I know I'm getting better." Vanessa rubbed her forehead while thinking that was just another job to add to her long list of things to do.

"Remember we used to play church? Daddy would say in his booming voice, 'Don't play with the Gospel. It's our bread and butter, not to mention our life and breath.' "

"Yeah, our moon and stars, he'd go on and on. Grandma Cecily didn't take too kindly to it either. She used to light our tails up too, remember?" Vanessa asked.

"Church was so ingrained in us that it was easy to fake it. Come in to church sit through Sunday school and worship, welcome new members and go home," Keisha said, not pausing to say grace before taking a bite. Vanessa did a short and sweet version of grace out loud before Keisha said, "I don't want to church-play a role that makes me more popular or get's me attention. I did that for awhile. That's over. I want to play my role. I feel my role is expanding my ministry and teaching."

"You sound as if you're ready to leave Mt. Pleasant."

Keisha looked very solemnly at her sister. "I'm in prayer about it now."

Vanessa remained calm although her heart was beating faster by the minute. It brought to mind the time she came home to find Keisha packing her bags. Vanessa didn't have to ask where she would stay. It had been evident for a long time that someone else demanded her complete attention. His name was Chris and he was waiting in the car for her sister. Vanessa went into crisis-mode calling on scriptures that would help condemn her sister's intentions to live with a man she wasn't married to. It did little to deter Keisha who despised anything church-related at this point, sighting the institution for robbing her of her father who was in an assisted living nursing home. Vanessa did everything but blockade the door. Then she said something that she has always regretted, "You know, this is going to kill daddy when he finds out." Three months later their father was dead.

This was different, Vanessa told herself. She didn't want to get into a heated debate fueled by her own opinion that would drive her sister away like it had the last time.

"What do you need me to do?" Vanessa asked.

"Nothing, Vanessa, this is not something I need you to rescue me from. I'm praying about it. It's a good thing, really," Keisha said, trying to convince her sister.

"Daddy taught me that ministry is not always about what you want to do, but most of the times, ministry is serving others—the real grunt work like serving as Unification Chair."

Vanessa noticed her sister was still not taking the bait and wondered what was going through her head.

"Don't worry, I will be around for unification," Keisha assured her.

"Good," Vanessa said, satisfied that at least Keisha wasn't making a hasty decision. She decided to change the subject. "This meal is incredible. I hope you don't mind me taking some leftovers home to Willie."

"Sure, I got plenty," Keisha said, playing with the remaining bites of roast beef on her plate. "You know when you told me that people were starting to talk about me, I felt hurt. I know for myself that I haven't been as reliable and committed as I can be. I just wish folks at Mt. Pleasant realize that we are not going to be the same. Like Mary and Martha, we minister differently."

"Umm," Vanessa said, partly because her mouth was full, but mainly because her sister raised a good point.

"I am a classic Mary," Keisha said, sitting back from her half eaten meal and rubbing her stomach as if she had eaten too fast. Vanessa was feeling the same way.

"Hold up, if anything I'm Mary. How else would I have caught this vision to combine churches if I wasn't at God's feet, heeding his call?"

"Whatever, Vanessa, this is not like when we were younger arguing over who was Electro Woman and who was Diana Girl. Martha was a servant of the Lord also. Remember she was the uptight one, always on the go, who snitched to the Lord that her sister wasn't helping her. Now if that's not you, I'd like to know who is. She was just different from Mary, but equally important to God."

Vanessa was about to make a case as to why she was Mary when she spotted a familiar picture on her sister's bookshelf nearby. It was a picture that used to be in her father's den. It was of Vanessa and Keisha, when they were much younger, standing on opposite sides of their father, standing proud in his preaching robe. She remembered they had just finished arguing and her father had stepped in between them and very discreetly pinched the inside of their arms to tell them to cut it out. The only thing considered worse than playing church to their daddy was she and her sister fussing and fighting in church. That's why they both looked near tears.

"How'd you get that picture?" Vanessa asked her sister.

"What picture?" Keisha said, looking over her shoulder.

"Of us with Daddy, when we were kids," Vanessa whined as if she were ten years old. "How'd you get that?"

"Momma told me to take what I wanted from his den

before she donated a lot of his stuff to the Bible College. I got that one and another one of just him in my bedroom."

"Gosh, where was I?" Vanessa heard herself asking for the second time that night.

"You were so busy being Pastor, arranging the estate funeral, and not allowing yourself to be the grieving daughter. You missed out."

Vanessa ignored her sister's comments that were snide but true. She had missed out. She now remembered receiving a few of her father's more expensive books piled in a box, but the photos of him were priceless. She would give anything to have her daddy back to see how Mt. Pleasant had flourished under her leadership and hear his ideas about unification. They both needed him still to break up their fights, and to tell them they were both special in their own way. She saw a lot of her daddy in her baby sister. Vanessa was beginning to think that Keisha was right; maybe Keisha was Mary and she was Martha.

Chapter 19

Basic Baptist Protocol

Keisha sat at the round table in Thelma Grant's house. She was grating sharp cheddar cheese for her macaroni and cheese casserole. She wanted to contribute something for the unification meeting since Thelma had volunteered her home, insisting that they always held meetings at one another's home at Harvest so they could fellowship and not feel rushed holding the meeting at church. Vanessa had gotten a list of people interested in working for the Unification Committee before she left Keisha's apartment that night and tasked her with at least calling everyone and setting up a meeting date, time and place.

This was suppose to be a pot luck dinner meeting but it felt more like Thanksgiving at Thelma's. Although it was a week prior to the holiday, she had ordered a honey-baked ham, prepared a tossed salad and cooked green beans.

Keisha had free reign of her kitchen and tried to keep her mess confined to the table top. Thelma came in to check the ham in the oven so Keisha asked to borrow a cup of milk. She had added the other ingredients and needed the milk to moisten her mixture.

"Here is a jar of mustard too. I got dried mustard if you prefer," Thelma said.

"Mustard in macaroni and cheese?" Keisha asked, holding the jar in her hands.

"Sure, mustard gives it that twang."

"Oh, thank you, but I don't use mustard in mine."

"Have it your way, honey," Thelma Grant said, laying the jar of mustard on the table. "Paul usually likes when I add a little mustard, pinch of salt, egg, milk, Colby and sharp cheddar cheeses. Everybody has got their own recipe, I suppose. Let me get out of your way. I'll be in the dinning room setting the table if you need anything."

Keisha waited for her to exit the room. She picked the mustard jar up off the table. *It's worth a try,* she thought. She flung a spoonful of mustard in the bowl before blending the brownish yellow glob into the already orangish yellow mixture. She evenly distributed the concoction into an aluminum baking pan and put it in the oven. She rinsed the spoon and bowl thoroughly before joining Thelma in the dinning room.

"Did you say Paul was coming to this meeting?" Keisha said. "Because he wasn't certain when I called everyone."

"I told him we were having a dinner meeting. Paul doesn't miss many opportunities to eat unless he is working."

The dinning room and living room were adjoining. Keisha walked around the living room looking at the pictures on the mantle. "Is this Paul's father?" Keisha said, pointing to several photographs of the same man.

"Yep. Paul Ulysses Grant, Sr." Thelma joined Keisha in the living room. She picked up an obituary from a collection that was fanned out on her coffee table and handed it to Keisha. "He died over in Vietnam when Paul was young. Ever since then Paul has been the man of the house."

"It must have been hard raising Paul by yourself all those years."

"I had God. I didn't know anything about raising a boy to be a young man. It is the most awesome job on earth, but Paul practically raised himself though. He brought home good grades and his paychecks from his part time jobs. He is a special person, but I suspect you know that," she said.

Keisha smiled politely, wondering what that last comment was suppose to mean before they both wandered back to the dinning room table to fold napkins. Thelma, as she insisted upon being called, had not stopped talking about her son since Keisha had been there. Keisha thought she might bring out his baby pictures after awhile if people didn't start showing up.

The other committee members began arriving with bags of entrees and other side dishes. Alice James had a homemade peach cobbler. Luella Banks brought potato salad. Lottie Freeman and Paula Simmons had four bags between them that Deacon Simmons helped carry in for them. There were collard greens, yams, fried fish fillets and cornbread. Even Buster Johnson brought a case of sodas. Keisha helped Thelma set the kitchen table buffet style so everyone could serve themselves.

Although Keisha had called everyone, she did not place the faces with the names. She did notice that the crowd had one distinct thing in common. Everyone was considerably older than her. Keisha took her macaroni dish from the oven and wondered when Willie and Vanessa were getting there.

Thelma started the meeting as Paul entered his mother's house with his own key. Keisha nodded to him and was startled when he began with her kissing the women hello around the table. His cologne lingered after he made his rounds. Thelma pulled a small Bible and reading glasses from the end table. She stood and read the 23rd Psalm. Alice James sang "Blessed Assurance." Her voice seasoned with age left the hymn writer's intention as clear as the dew in the morning air. Her soprano voice rendered an almost operatic version to the song as everyone joined in with the chorus. "This is my story. This is my song. Praising my Savior, all the day long." Thelma asked Clyde Simmons to lead them in prayer and bless the food. Everyone filed in the kitchen to help themselves to the food.

Keisha watched the door while they ate. It was silent except for the sounds of very hungry people smacking their lips and what she thought sounded like the rattle of someone's false teeth, which temporarily put a halt to her appetite, that and the fact that Vanessa wasn't there yet. Keisha waited for Vanessa to come prancing in with an overabundance of things to fit into the agenda. That's why Keisha had a hard time understanding why she even needed a chairperson for this event knowing her sister had a very specific idea of how the day should run. Keisha doubted if Willie even had a say so in it. A doorbell announced a latecomer, who Keisha thought for sure was the diva herself that turned out to be Lenora Rogers, her roommate from the retreat coming in apologizing for being late.

"You haven't missed anything since Brother and Sister Pastor haven't arrived yet. Maybe I should call them to see where they are," Keisha said, feeling as if she should apologize for her family's tardiness.

"Brother Pastor is preaching this week in DC and Sister Pastor more than likely is accompanying him, so they will not be attending. Either you or I will just report what we have decided to her. Paul is here to report to Brother Pastor," Luella Bates said.

Keisha looked around the room. *Wasn't that just dandy?* she thought. She knew Vanessa wanted her to be chairperson, but Vanessa could have at least told her she wouldn't be at the meeting instead of assuming that she would feel obligated, which she did, to give in to her sister's initial request to become the chairperson. How was Keisha supposed to know what she expected? Everyone seemed to be looking at her. "I didn't know that I was running the meeting. I just thought I was calling folks to come to the meeting," she said, looking at the phone list Vanessa had given her.

"It should be easy. We all know the scripture reference. Brother and Sister Pastor planned the unification date for January first. That's on a Saturday, right?" Luella said, referring to her planner.

"We cannot expect this young lady to run Unification Day," Lottie Freeman said

"She won't. We are her committee. It is our job to help her," Paul said, smiling in front of his second plate of food.

"If you want to be the chairperson, just say so Lottie. We just figured you might want to take a backseat after trying to run the Retreat Committee." Paula Simmons said. Lottie, who wore a look as if it didn't faze her either way, did not say a thing.

"Well, Ms. Chairperson, what is your first order of business?" Thelma said.

Once again, all eyes were on Keisha. She placed her purse beside her plate on the table and began searching for a scratch sheet of paper. She pulled out an envelope to take notes.

Thelma got up immediately to retrieve several notepads from beside the telephone for everyone to use. *Calm down*, Keisha thought to herself. She figured she had been in enough meetings at work to get through this one. She would just plan a few things for that day and kill her sister later. Keisha, recognizing her weakness for details, asked for someone to write down the suggestions for a report and was relieved when Luella volunteered.

"This shouldn't be a big deal. Sister Pastor said we would have a service that afternoon. Let's just have a nice reception afterwards. Then Sunday it's worship as usual with an additional Pastor on the pulpit and additional members in the congregation," Keisha said between bites.

"Are you for real?" Lottie said. "We got to do more than that."

"There are ceremonies that need to take place," Clyde Simmons said.

"Yeah, Brother Pastor needs to be officially installed as a Pastor of Mt. Pleasant church, as well as, us, deacons and trustees." Buster Johnson said.

"I remember when we installed Pastor Green at Harvest," Paula Simmons said.

Keisha wrote her own notes although Luella was writing the minutes. "Is this installation service written down anywhere so we can incorporate it into the service?" Keisha said.

"Sure, you always install officers. That is basic Baptist protocol," Clyde Simmons said, swinging a fork over a plate covered from edge to edge with food.

"We are not just installing officers. We are leaving our church home. Some of us have been at Harvest for twenty years or more. Deacon Pace has been at Harvest since he was a child," Thelma remarked.

"That is why it kills me what Charley Thompson is trying to do with the church. It will be like the Harvest church never existed," Lottie said, her lips greasy from the entrees.

"This is off the record, but can someone fill me in on what is happening with him? I heard about him on the retreat," Lenora said.

"He tried to stop the whole move. He is so determined to stay at Harvest that I hear he is going to get a new Pastor," Thelma continued.

"Pastor Green had to ask him to leave the church," Paula Simmons said, eager to share. "This whole thing has got to be like a slap in the face to Pastor Green. After all he has done for Charley."

"You mean a slap in Charley's face," Thelma said. Lottie, Paula and Thelma looked at each other before they burst out in laughter.

"Ladies, ladies," Keisha said. Although she was interested, gossip would only prolong the meeting.

"Obviously this Charley person is not the only one that disagrees with the move," Lenora said, ignoring Keisha's attempt to change the subject.

"Naw, all these quack leaders got a following. It will be a congregation of heathens. It's like the Pastor said, if you're not sure who you believe in, you can fall for anything," Lottie said, licking her fingers instead of using her napkin.

"In my opinion, Charley has always been a little off," Thelma started.

"And Charley got his poor wife mixed up in his foolishness," Lottie Freeman said.

"Well, that is to be expected," Clyde Simmons said.

"What is that suppose to mean?" His wife asked.

"I mean, she is the man's wife. She is just submitting to him. It's in the Bible," he answered.

Paula's head turned and slowly grinded to a halt in front of her husband as if the absurdity of his comment slowed down her motor. "So if you are defying God, am I supposed to follow you because we are married?" she said.

"I'm sorry, but that is out. Clyde Simmons doesn't have a Heaven or Hell to put me in, but God does."

"Let's get back to the matter at hand. We'll never get finished with what Minister Morton has to discuss if we keep getting side tracked," Paul said, leaning across the table. "You all know full well that Charley cannot take anything away from the Harvest legacy. God will take care of us and He will take care of Charley and his group also."

Keisha looked around the table at the apparent free for all that was going on. A few of the ladies left the table and went into the kitchen, no doubt to finish the conversation. She scooped up the last bit of macaroni and cheese off her plate, flattered that Paul spoke up on her behalf. Maybe this was why Vanessa didn't want someone from Harvest running the meeting. There wouldn't be any meeting. Well, it would not be said that they did not accomplish anything under her watch. Keisha looked up to find Paul smiling at her. He wore an expression that read, "what can you do?" and she returned the look. She waited awhile to start again.

"What other kinds of Baptist protocol can we think of that we can incorporate on Unification Day?" Keisha asked.

"How old are you?" Lottie asked. Her jaw extended like a drawer being open while she waited for a reply, displaying the shift in her dentures and the remains of her food.

"Lottie, please," Thelma said.

"What? I just asked the young lady's age. We are planning UNIfication," Lottie said as if they were all imbeciles. "Maybe she is too young to remember all the great services at her church, but I will always remember the services at Harvest, especially the one's I have chaired, like Sunday school pageants, Tom Thumb weddings, Carolina Day. This has got to be the service of all other services in the past."

"All those people we took to the water. My favorite time was around Easter, Seven last words service, Foot-washin' and Good Friday service," Alice Jones said.

"Foot-washin'? I admit that is a new one to me," Keisha said. "You all have way more services than we have at Mt. Pleasant."

"Y'all got anniversaries right?" Buster Johnson said.

"For choirs, sure," Keisha said.

"How about for the Deacons and Trustees, Pastor's Aide or Flower Club, Men and Women's Day or banquets?" Thelma said.

Keisha looked at Lenora and Luella before saying, "No." She was beginning to feel like she was in the line of fire.

"What is going to happen if we don't have Carolina Day?" Thelma Grant said, looking around. "I'm supposed to be chairperson this year coming up."

"So you all take the 23rd Psalms literally when it says, I will dwell in the house of the Lord forever," said Lenora.

"Yeah, we do little lady," Buster Johnson said.

"You all have to remember that Sister Morton grew up in church just like her sister. Their father was the pastor, for goodness sakes. All the services we spoke of were all well and good. They served the purpose to bless our souls at the time. My father was a deacon and he told me that there are only two sacramental services that a Baptist church should observe, and that is Communion and Baptisms. Everything else is a tradition born into the Harvest Baptist Church."

"Amen," Thelma said, getting up to get the trash can from the kitchen. Everyone sat quietly thinking about what had already been said. Keisha mouthed the words, "thank you," to Paul from across the table, thinking about the comment his mother made earlier. He had come to her defense twice that evening. He was indeed special and becoming more interesting by the minute.

"But we've got to march," Thelma said, returning to the table.

"March?" Keisha said.

"Yeah, it's a tradition when you move from one building to another for the whole congregation to march from one church to the other if it is not that far," Thelma said.

"Is this tradition written somewhere?" Keisha asked.

"Who knows? We've seen other churches do it," Clyde Simmons said.

"Lord yes, I remember when Holy Anointing Baptist moved into Maryland. They tied up Pennsylvania Avenue. There were so many people," Lottie said.

"Got to get a permit for that," Luella said.

"Wow, that's a long way to walk and it will be the middle of winter. What is the purpose?" Keisha said.

"To show what God has done. It shows the community that the church is coming to possess the land. The walk doesn't seem that long when you sing all the way. It's like a New Year's parade," Lottie said.

"Let me get this straight: we are planning a parade and we are all going to walk to Mt. Pleasant Baptist Church from Harvest Baptist Church?" Keisha said, chuckling at the absurdity of it all.

"We will get buses or something; let you young ones walk when we get within a mile of Mt. Pleasant. My knees won't take that," Lottie said.

"Your knees? My hip would pop out the socket. The other day when it rained, I could hardly get out of bed," Paula Simmons said.

"Well, I'm walking, bad back and all. I'll be singing too," Thelma said.

"Aww shoot," Paula and Lottie said in unison.

"Who is going to lead these songs? Do we need to contact the combined choir?" Keisha asked.

"Anyone can lead a song. It's like devotion. Hymns of

the church are sung, songs of determination. Everybody got a song that strengthens their faith. Songs like "Yes, God is Real," "By and By" and "Amazing Grace." Someone just starts it and everyone just backs them up," Alice Jones said.

"Well, if I could sing like you, Sister Jones, I wouldn't have any problem," Keisha said.

"We should all have a couple of hymns ready to start," Thelma said.

"Do we have a budget? We got to rent a bus," Keisha said.

"Just take up another collection at both churches," Buster Johnson said.

"Another collection? You mean tithes? How many collections do you all have?" Lenora said.

"Three," Thelma said.

"Three?" Luella and Lenora said in unison.

"One for the church, the benevolence offering and the plate for the pastor," Clyde Simmons said.

"Well, we give one offering and you're expected to bring your tithes. Sister Pastor is on salary," Lenora said.

"We heard," Lottie said.

"It's getting late. Sister Chairperson, are we adjourned?" Deacon Simmons said, trying to avoid another gossiping session.

"I think that would be in order," Keisha said. "Thank you all. I have learned a lot. You will be called when I schedule the next meeting."

Everyone began to leave after a tentative itinerary was set. Keisha made sure she wrote down the names of everyone who volunteered to do something before the next meeting in December. She could not believe she was thrust into this responsibility and only hoped she had what it took to pull it off.

In the days that followed, Thelma called Keisha everyday with something to think about for the unification. One idea was for Keisha to get in touch with the local newspaper and radio stations to publicize the changes for their churches. Thelma volunteered Paul to write copy for a press release. She also insisted upon Paul picking up the press packet guidelines Keisha had picked up from local newspapers in the area so that it could be returned before the Christmas deadline. *Why do I feel like I'm being set up,* Keisha thought, *and why don't I mind?*

Chapter 20

All in Good Time

Paul looked at the submission guidelines Keisha had given him as he sat at his desk at work. He had every intention on completing the article on the grand unification of their churches weeks ago, but was constantly distracted by work. He had set a personal goal with himself to complete a proposal of incorporation for a new company. Then he would assist Level II with the policies and by-laws for which the company would be governed since he had already met with the CEO. He had his eye on a Level II promotion and the corner office with the window view.

I will absolutely write the article draft tonight, Paul thought. He had called Keisha twice to get additional information for the piece since he missed the December meeting. That was the pretense anyway. They easily got off topic and chatted about other things. He had only recently admitted to himself that he really liked her. Ronny Miller interrupted Paul's thoughts with a phone message.

"Keisha Morton on line two," he said as he passed Paul's cubicle.

"Thanks, Ronny," Paul said as he found an empty desk with a phone extension.

"What's up, buttercup?" Paul said.

"Is that how you answer the phone at work?" Keisha snapped.

"Hold up, sister, I didn't rip your brand new dress. What is wrong with you this afternoon?"

"Sorry. I'm just a little frustrated."

"What's up?"

"My colleague at work forgot something he promised to do for me. He made me miss an important deadline," she said. "Then this unification stuff is consuming all my extra time and energy, but I didn't call you to complain. How's the article coming?"

"I was just looking at it."

"Good, you got it with you. I want to hook up with you before you leave work and get the article."

There was a pause. He saw no need to continue to lie to her. He wanted to maintain their relationship, not isolate her. "Um . . . Keisha, it is not exactly done. I need a little more time."

"And I need a man to do what he says he is going to do," Keisha said. Paul could tell she was struggling to keep her tone even. "That's okay, Paul. Your mother said you were always busy with work. I guess she was right. I can get someone else to write it."

"The deadline to have it in their office is Friday, right? That is three days away. I know that is no excuse for not having it done by the time we had arranged. Look, I will have it done by tomorrow and I will bring it over to you. We can look at it over dinner, my treat. What do you say?" he said.

"Well, I guess. I'm sorry I snapped at you earlier. I mean, it is no problem finding someone else to write it if you are busy."

He sighed with relief. "I'm not trying to get kicked off the Unification Committee by the chairperson."

"You're so silly," she said, laughing.

Paul got her address over the phone although his mother had told him exactly where she lived. Last week's December unification meeting had been changed from Lenora Rogers' house to Keisha's apartment. He had been working on an excuse to stop over there and see her since he missed that meeting, but kept telling himself to let whatever happens between them evolve naturally. Now he had asked her out. Actually, it was more like an outburst, he thought. Women he dated in the past usually didn't understand that his dedication to progressing on his job meant long hours. Since he didn't have a lot of time to devote to dating, he didn't want to lead anyone on, especially someone from his church.

The next day, Paul buzzed Keisha's apartment from the security door in the lobby. Keisha met him at the entrance to her apartment and they walked the short distance to the parking lot. She wore a maroon pantsuit that Paul suspected she had on all day because she still had her work badge attached to her lapel. She had to step up into his Isuzu Trooper.

"So, where do you want to go for dinner?" Paul asked her.

"I don't know," Keisha replied, adjusting the seat belt that was holding her too close around the neck. She noticed he hadn't started the car so she turned to face him.

"I'm waiting for you to decide. If you are anything like my mother, you will have me driving all over town and still would not have chosen a restaurant. There is your American cuisine served buffet style down the road, a seafood restaurant up the street, barbeque, Italian, Chinese, Mexican, Japanese . . ." he said.

"Okay, okay, how about seafood? Gosh, you sure know your restaurants," she said, laughing.

"That was just my abridged list for this area." He finally put the key in the ignition and drove out of the parking lot.

Paul chose a restaurant where they could get Alaskan crab legs, shrimp prepared five different ways and a Maine Lobster tail when it was in season. The wait was extremely long so they had to settle for a table instead of a booth. His long legs stretched on the side of her chair. Keisha poked his leg twice with her heel.

"These things are dangerous," Paul said, lifting her heel slightly off the ground with his outstretched leg. "I'm surprised you still got them on. A lot of women can't wait to sling those things off."

"I'm used to them. Plus, I wanted to be at least half your height," Keisha said.

"So tell me about you're family; do you have any other siblings besides your sister?" Paul asked.

"No, it's just me and Vanessa." Keisha raised the menu under the guise that she was still making a selection.

Paul could tell she was a little nervous. He wondered when was the last time she had a man's complete attention. "I'm the only child, as you probably have guessed."

"My dad was the only child, but my mom had three sisters that would come visit us when I was growing up."

"Do any of your aunts have any children?" Paul asked. "My cousins were like my brothers and sisters."

"Nope," Keisha said. "It's funny, but my mother was the only sister that got married."

"So what do you want?"

"What?" Keisha was caught off guard.

"What do you want?" He nodded his head slightly at his menu. He looked straight at her knowing the misinterpretations his statements held. He waited for an answer as if any answer would suffice.

"I can't make up my mind. I want it all," Keisha said.

Paul brought out his draft of the unification article for her to look at while they waited to place their orders. She nodded her approval as she read the copy.

"I like this part. This is so true," she said.

"Which part?"

"You said the unification required personal sacrifice. The saints of Mt. Pleasant and Harvest Baptist realize that once you come to know Jesus as a personal savior, everything else is secondary to his will. The congregations are willing to give up the autonomy of two independent churches to unite in one Spirit of Christ. This is excellent. You are a great writer. This will be good for the Metro. It's a small local newspaper so they depend a lot upon outside writers."

The waiter came to take their order as Paul accepted the compliment. He fought the urge to check her out as she spoke with the waiter. She was beautiful in a delicate sort of way, he thought. After the waiter left with their menus and dinner orders, Keisha caught Paul checking her out and shifted her attention back to what he had written,

"When did you really start to believe in God?" she asked.

"Gosh, I guess it was when I would read the Bible with my mother. She would tell me what things meant. That is when I fell in love with words. I looked at the Bible as an exhaustive guide book. You know how you hear atheists who say a group of scholars wrote the Bible to control people in ancient times and it's been passed down like an age old scam?" Paul paused to sweeten his iced tea. "No way. There is no one that smart who could write a book that covers every need, every want and every situation."

"Yeah, I know what you mean," Keisha said. "For me, it is how God seems to personalize his messages for me. The day I came back to Mt. Pleasant it seemed like he reached down to my pew and guided me up to the altar."

"Do you remember what it was that spoke to you so significantly?"

"It probably will seem irrelevant to you, but to me it was so personal."

"C'mon, you can tell me," Paul said, noticing that he was making her blush.

"Vanessa was preaching about how David became King. Samuel was sent by God to anoint one of the sons of Jesse, but he was a little depressed that his boy, Saul, was going to be dethroned. God told him, 'how long will you mourn for Saul, seeing that I have rejected him.' I just remember my sister saying, 'He is not the King I want for you,' over and over again. Besides the fact that Vanessa knew what I was going through in my personal life, I was filled with such peace thinking God was speaking to me through his word. Shoot, I reunited with the church, dumped my no good boyfriend and changed my life in the process."

"The word will shine a light on you."

"Tell me something, if you're always so busy working, how did you become so active in church that you became appointed the liaison on the Retreat and Unification committees?"

"I told Pastor Green that I was willing to help the church in any capacity he felt necessary, but that was before I knew how little my schedule would allow. So one day in church, he appoints me liaison out of the blue. I guess I was trying to follow my father's example. He worked hard before he died, but always had time for family and his church."

"So, it was sort of like me being thrown into chairing the Unification Day Committee."

"Yeah," Paul said, "you'll be great though. We have a good committee."

"You sound like Vanessa. She was so elated when I told her about the first meeting, as if I found my divine calling or something."

"I guess working within the church will help you find your way to that calling. Remember the message from the retreat on Hidden Talents? I was blown away. I guess you are used to Sister Pastor preaching like that."

"Yeah, Vanessa can definitely preach now."

"And I hear you can really divide the word of truth yourself," Paul said, letting the cat out of the bag that he had done a little research on his very attractive dining companion.

Keisha was careful to finish her mouthful before asking, "Who told you that?"

"I'm a writer. I can't reveal my sources."

Paul had to think that although she wasn't an only child, she was in her thirties, single and working for the Unification Committee. Could it be possible that God had a female version of himself waiting at the church his would soon combine with? He figured a calling was not all that a person could find when they got involved in church.

The waiter arrived with their meal. Paul blessed the table and immediately dug in. "I'm sure the union of our churches will make Brother and Sister Pastor stronger preachers," Paul said, finishing a bite of his fried flounder.

"And stronger as a couple," Keisha said, "although, when he first started visiting our church and preaching, I guess it was while they were dating, I felt she was taking a back seat to him. It would be different when any other guest minister would visit Mt. Pleasant. She would still give us prescription verses, and close us out in prayer. But when Willie Green was there, he carried the whole service, like it was his church. She was more subdued."

" 'Cause that was her man."

"So when she announced that they were uniting churches

after getting married, which I didn't find out until everyone else, I didn't know if I could take their lovey-dovey leadership. I think that they did a good job of showing everybody at the retreat that nothing has changed about their preaching since they got married or their personal style."

"I guess it's like your parents. Your parents are two unique individuals that join forces to raise their children."

"In many ways Vanessa helped raise me. I spent a lot of time being rebellious in my early adult years that took me away from the church when I needed it most. Vanessa was there to give me a reality check. She took responsibility for me and showed me that the love of God could wipe away my tears, pain and sins all at the same time," Keisha said, looking as if she wanted to leave it at that, but Paul's eyes told her it was okay to share. "I know it might seem silly, but although I grew up in Mt. Pleasant, it feels like Vanessa's church. I've been in her shadow all my life. Now I'm at a crossroads and I don't know whether to start the classes my job is paying for, or apply to divinity school. It feels like it's time, but I can't help but feeling I haven't been rooted long enough."

"What's wrong?" Paul asked, noticing her shocked expression.

"I can't believe I told you that. I haven't even told Vanessa that I may be ready to start divinity school."

"Well, I'm flattered."

"Every minister doesn't become a preacher, and every preacher doesn't become a pastor; but we all have a place."

"Well, I pray that you find your place."

Keisha and Paul changed the subject back to their admiration of their pastors and their relationship as they completed their meal. Paul tried to speculate what their home life must be like. He wondered how much of Keisha's own preference was she revealing as she shared

that a strong woman like her sister needed a kind generous man like Pastor Willie Green.

"Willie balances her out. She's like me, very blunt;
sometimes coming off as harsh." Keisha said, taking the
last stab at a few garlic shrimp left on her plate.

"I'd be interested to know how they met. I know everyone thinks that single Christians should have no problem
meeting in church, and I agree. Your religious beliefs
should be the most important thing, but not the only
thing a couple has in common," Paul said.

"Vanessa and Willie met in church, but that's hard
'cause in church you're focused on the word. It's not like
you can be on the prowl for a date like single people out
in the world. I don't remember exactly how the story goes,
but can you imagine your pastor trying to pick up my sister in the pulpit?"

"I guess the way we met on the retreat would be ideal
for someone who is looking for someone."

"Yeah," Keisha said, "if you were looking."

The waiter walked up to the table just then with the
leather billfold containing the check. Paul made sure to
grab it and signaled for the waiter to wait while he counted
out the amount due, plus gratuity.

"I'm sorry, what were you saying?" Paul said, helping
Keisha pull out her chair as she pushed away from the
table.

"No, I think you were saying something about looking
for someone."

"No not me, I've done my share of hunting and I've
even been hunted a couple of times. Lord knows my mom
probably has my name in the personal column, wanted:
sweet Christian wife for my hard to please son, so I can finally give her some grandkids."

"Your mom is ready for you to settle down, huh?"

"She's wondering what is taking so long. What she doesn't

know is that I have asked the Lord to help me find the one, not just someone."

Keisha looked at him and nodded as if he had said what she felt. They walked out of the restaurant side by side and he helped her into the passenger seat of his truck. Except for a disagreement about the best route to take home, Keisha and Paul were quiet in the car. Paul knew her suggestion was quicker, but he wasn't ready to take her home yet. He wanted to ask her to his company's holiday party. Since it was promotion time, he felt he had to make an appearance, and he knew Keisha would keep him from being bored to tears at the fancy social.

He pulled into the curved drop off area in front of her building. "I didn't ask you if you wanted dessert," Paul said, prepared to prolong the evening for another stop.

"That's okay, I am stuffed." She pecked his cheek.

"Hey, I got this office party. They do it a couple of days after Christmas before the New Year. I know you may be busy with the unification stuff, but I would like you to go with me."

"I'd love to go. Call me," Keisha said as she retrieved her purse and doggy bag from the truck and went inside.

Paul couldn't tell his co-workers much about his Christmas when asked, "How was your holiday?" He was even having a hard time telling his mother about the extravagant holiday party at ISC that he attended a few days ago with Keisha. All Paul could think about was their kiss. Men usually didn't make a big deal out of stuff like that. He had to remind himself that it wasn't like he was a teenager being kissed for the first time, but it felt as if it had been his first time.

He had been nervous when he had picked her up because he hated those required social events. As the night wore on, Keisha was able to get him to loosen up and they danced and laughed like everyone else. They stepped out on the veranda where they could see a panoramic view of the stars. Paul decided to put all his anxiety about his post-date doorstep expectations aside and asked her then, "Stop me if I get out of hand, but I think I'm going to kiss you now."

Paul leaned in as the thick lashes of Keisha's eyes fluttered in anticipation. Her lips were as ripe and sweet as the delicate skin of a Georgia peach. Compared to other kisses he had given on dates before coming to the Lord, that were laced with insincerity and carnal expectations, their kiss made him feel like she was the one. Now he had to just wait on God to confirm it.

Chapter 21

Substance of Things Hoped For

Willie had a trapeze of steel balls on his desk that swung back and forth like a pendulum clanking into one another creating a rhythm that was relaxing to him. His mother had given him this device when she replaced his hodge podge of desk accessories for those black and stainless steel to give his office a more executive feel. The clanking of the balls has been the background music for many of his prayers for the people of Harvest. Everything in his office was packed for the move to Mt. Pleasant except for his desktop. He had a feeling that there was something that he wanted to take with him to Mt. Pleasant that couldn't be packed in a box.

Paul had called to say he would be a little late for their last update meeting. Unification was a week away and he wanted to know the entire itinerary for Saturday as well as the persons responsible. Willie wanted to call those Harvest members that were involved personally to make sure they would be in place, because he knew Vanessa would be holding her members accountable to ensure a smooth transition into the final phase of the combining process.

Willie started the balls in motion. The closer it got to Unification Day, the more he thought about Charley Thompson and the others that had left Harvest. Even after all that had happened, he held out hope that some of them would have changed their mind and returned to the church. Last week, Willie bumped into Beatrice McGee, a member he hadn't seen in church since the night of the meeting to find that she didn't want to wait for an official unification date to start attending Mt. Pleasant. "I figured if we were going to move, then I better go on and go then." She had said. "I prefer my changes be swift." That prompted Willie to compile a list of everyone who walked out the night of the church meeting, and others he hadn't seen in Sunday Service a while in order to discuss a reclamation idea with Paul during their meeting.

The Harvest Baptist church building was another concern to Willie. Members inquired all the time about his plans for their soon to be vacant church home. He and Vanessa had talked about a community center to lend support for a neighborhood that had embraced the church for so long, but now they had more pressing issues before them to put any concrete plans in place. He knew his members had an attachment to that place, but he wanted to put a big "For Sale" sign on it because, besides taxes and insurance, they were still paying exuberant amounts for its general maintenance and upkeep when compared to its worth.

Willie held one ball suspended above the others before letting it go. He could hear Paul Grant calling his name as he rounded the corner to the back office. The nearly empty building gave a hollow echo of his call and Willie's response. Paul offered the same excuse he used on the phone for being late, but Willie was anxious to get down to business to admonish him about time.

"Grab a chair there, Paul," Willie said, silencing the

clanking of the balls by holding them stationary. "I'm sorry I can't offer you anything to drink, but as you can see we are ready to go."

"I see. You have done a lot in a week's time." Paul looked around.

"I can't take all the credit. A couple of members from the Pastor's Aide Committee were down here Wednesday packing the Sanctuary Bibles and hymnals. You should have seen them fighting over the altar flowers. I'm just sorry that was all I could give them to remember this place by."

"It's truly an end of an era," Paul sighed.

"So what's it looking like for Saturday? Will we have time to breathe? I tell you, Sister Pastor is so excited about this weekend."

"I bet. Keisha is starting to get excited also," Paul said, smiling at the mention of her name. "That would be your sister-in law Keisha, the Chairperson of Unification Day."

"Oh yes, you've been working closely together. Can you believe I'm going from a congregation that was barely a hundred to two hundred and fifty combined?"

Paul pulled out a portfolio from his worn briefcase where he had taken notes. Willie could see Paul searching through an assortment of papers for his notes, which either he or any of the five members from Harvest that were already on the committee could report to the congregation before Wednesday night Bible Study. He unfolded those notes now and balanced them on his crossed leg so he could reference them.

"Before we begin, Pastor and First Lady Rawls will be joining us for the entire weekend, not just on Saturday. They are getting in Friday evening and staying with Vanessa and I," Willie informed Paul.

"Okay, well, we're asking everyone to assemble at Harvest Baptist Church at eight a.m. on New Years Day. We are going to have a prayer hour of some sort, I don't know if you and Sister Pastor want to lead it or your guest preacher. You can then say your remarks before everyone heads over to Mt. Pleasant."

"I thought Vanessa said something about a bus to transport people," Willie said, pushing back in his desk chair to cross his legs.

"Yes, that's right. The members from Mt. Pleasant that want to join us for the prayer hour will be brought over in the two church vans. Keisha said something about a novelty double-decker bus that we can attach our banners to on the side. They use them a lot in parades. It will transport you and Sister Pastor, Pastor and First Lady Rawls, the Executive Board, the Mother's Board and the Unification Committee. Then the two vans from Mt. Pleasant and the rest, I guess, are going to trail along in cars."

Willie wanted to ask if it was too late to cancel all of the pomp and circumstance. He was feeling like Sister McGhee, now that the time had finally come, he wanted it to be over swiftly. Instead he said, "Vanessa will love it. She bars no expense or extravagance when it comes to the church. I just want to make sure that everyone knows what they are supposed to do."

"My mom, Sister Lottie Freeman, and Sister Simmons are in charge of the welcome reception so they won't be present at the prayer hour or the processional. You know you never have to worry about them, just point them in the direction of the kitchen. I may be helping them because I might have to leave early. Do you know Keisha suggested that we have the reception catered? I thought they were going to overthrow her position as chairperson."

"Keisha, huh?" Willie said, leaning in. "Is there something I should know?"

"No," Paul said quickly. "I mean yeah, but no. Let's

move on, Pastor. Then we will have a short installation service."

Willie had noticed his ever present sister-in-law had
been preoccupied lately, allowing him more quality time
with his wife and he wasn't complaining.

"I'll let it go, but that reminds me," Willie said, opening
his desk drawer and taking out a carbon copy of a receipt.
"I ordered these matching preaching robes for Vanessa
and I a while back, and well, Mae usually handles these
things for me. I picked them out of a catalogue but Mae
dealt with them directly. You ever heard of Grace's Custom Fit?"

"No," Paul said.

"I almost forgot about them because I was keeping it a
secret from Vanessa in order to surprise her before the installation service. I found the receipt on Mae's desk. You
can see from the receipt that we are paid in full. I just
need for you to see if they have the robes finished."

"Sure," Paul said, adding that chore to his immediate
to-do list that already seemed to be filled. He added the
receipt to the pocket of his planner.

"Doesn't look like your calendar can accommodate
much more," Willie said.

"It looks a lot worse than it really is. I have a lot of deadlines for each project at work so I back map each step in
my calendar." Paul placed his portfolio on the desk so his
pastor could get a better look.

"What are all those symbols for?"

"I have a symbol for meetings, phone conferences and
deadlines. Then each action item is categorize week to
week as microwave or back burner depending on whether
their immediate or not."

"Is that a trash can?" Willie said, pointing to the inked
icon.

"Yeah some ideas or engagements get canned," Paul said, sitting back in his seat and leaving the calendar on the desk as if he didn't want to see what he didn't get to last week. "Usually it's a lot of personal things that I want to do or work on but just can't get to in a week's time. I put everything on the calendar, but some of it doesn't ever get done. Why don't you let me hook up your personal calendar?"

"No thank you, it sounds way too complicated. I use to sit right here with Mae and she would shoot dates at me according to the church calendar. She'd throw in little personal things like buy your wife some flowers or go home and get a decent night's rest and I'd take her advice every time," Willie smiled. "I guess from now on I'll be working with Vanessa's, I mean, our secretary over at Mt. Pleasant. You just make sure none of your church events or personal study time gets canned."

"It won't, Pastor. Is there anything else?" Paul said, folding his portfolio.

"I did want you to take a look at something," Willie said, opening the desk drawer pensively to retrieve yet another slip of paper. He handed it to Paul to look at. "I want you to help me with the wording on this."

Paul read the heading, "Special Invited Guest," written in his pastor's handwriting. He glanced over the rest briefly before looking up at his pastor. "I thought I mentioned at our first meeting that the County Executive and Regional Representative have been formally invited. Their offices assure us that if they cannot personally make it, then they will send a representative from their office to read a proclamation."

"No, Paul, this is for Sister Connie Stewart, Bill Case, Greg Johnson," Willie paused, "and the other folks who walked away from the church. What do you think?"

"It sounds okay. These are folks you used to pastor, so I would not use such formal language."

"I mean, what do you think of the idea of inviting them . . . and Charley? Do you think I'm foolish? I mean Beatrice McGhee changed her mind from the time of the church meeting until now."

"No, it's not foolish. I think it is a compassionate thing to do. It's like the parable of the man and the sheep that I read last night. The man left all his other sheep in the wilderness to go and retrieve the one that was lost," Paul said.

Willie almost sighed audibly. He felt that it was his responsibility to offer the invitation just like he did every Sunday for those that didn't know Christ. Willie knew from years of counseling members that some people who perceive that they have been wronged only need the door of communication to be opened before reconciliation can begin. Willie knew he offended many people when he allowed Charley to bring him out of character.

Charley was another case entirely. Willie wasn't exactly rational when he put him out the church and he wasn't sure how Charley would be received by other members if he decided to come back. But if he did, it would be a powerful testament of faith and forgiveness for all to see, Willie thought.

"Well, I hope I'm not leaving them all in the wilderness," Willie said. "I just want them to know our doors are still open to them even though we're over at Mt. Pleasant. So you say it sounds too formal?"

"That can be fixed easily. Actually, I can take the invitation for the County Executive that Keisha and I worked on. I like the design."

Willie began to cough facetiously. "Keisha and I," he said, followed by more coughs and a pound on his chest.

Paul ignored his apparent ribbing. "I have it saved on my computer at work and can tweak it to sound more like a homecoming invitation," Paul said smiling. "If you have the addresses, I can send it out through our office mail system."

"Are you sure?" Willie said, pulling out the last piece of paper from his desk, which was the list he had previously prepared.

"No problem, now I have to go. I still have one more microwave item to attend to before going home."

"Hey, have you ever thought about being a deacon?"

"My dad was a deacon," Paul replied.

"I think you would make a good one. I'm going to recommend you. We're installing the present deacons on Unification Day, but we will begin training for new ones in early spring, maybe by then your schedule will allow it."

"Yeah, maybe I can thin it out." Paul pulled out his portfolio from his briefcase that was on his shoulder. At a glance he reminded himself to see about the robes and mail out the invitations, "What about you Pastor? Are you about done for tonight?"

"This is it," Willie said, laying his steel ball trapeze in an empty box with the rest of his desktop items. "That was the last official business to be conducted at Harvest Baptist Church. We move the last of this stuff tomorrow."

Chapter 22

Soon and Very Soon

The cold air, crisp with moisture, and wind assaulted anyone who was outside. It was the kind that burnt your ears and left your nose dripping automatically. Everyone assembled at Harvest made sure they layered themselves and appeared to be going on an alpine adventure. The attire was casual and the day promised to be a long one. Everyone was inside during the prayer hour trying to warm their bodies as they warmed their spirits before they began. It ran like a regular Wednesday night prayer service with members sharing sentimental prayers of thanksgiving for the length of time they could call Harvest Baptist their church home. Willie reserved his thoughts and comments for later in the evening. He kept thinking about the bags of trash standing alongside the church gate in the alley. Charley had been there. Willie wanted to believe he had picked up the litter like he always did in an attempt to tidy up for this very special church occasion—wanted to believe he'd show up for the festivities. Willie deferred the closing prayer to Pastor Benjamin Rawls.

"Give God some praise, church. I have heard from my

good friend here that the devil has tried to take you through hell and high water since your pastors have decided to combine. Let me tell you any church can praise God without being tested. You should have a new praise on your lips from Harvest Baptist church on over to Mt. Pleasant Baptist church; new praise 'cause he's taken you over a new hurdle," Pastor Rawls said, resisting the urge to take a topic and preach.

Every one was pumped for the day's events. Willie had mixed emotions. On the one hand he was sensitive to the fact that after today he had no reason to return to Harvest church, yet he was anxious to begin the joint ministry with his wife over at Mt. Pleasant. He expected more of a closure with the vacant building and discontented members, but like Vanessa said when he told her about Roy Jones preaching in abandon store fronts of the plaza without a home, "All loose ends don't tie up into a pretty bow like we want them to. Faith is knowing that God will take care of us all."

Willie looked out the window of the bus when he saw Bill Case, a former trustee, pull his car alongside the curb to park. Willie excused himself from his special seating and made his way toward Bill.

"Glad you could join us," Willie said, shaking Bill's hand.

"Well, I got your invitation in the mail. Linda and I were just talking about whether or not you had already combined," Bill said.

"We are just about to take off. Today is the day we make it official."

There was a long pause. "I guess we didn't trust your vision, Pastor. We let Charley Thompson convince us that the devil was feeding you all these ideas and things. I signed that petition of his because I didn't believe this day would actually come. Then when you put Charley out . . . well, I don't know, I guess I want to say I'm sorry."

"You don't have to apologize to me. I felt I needed to apologize as your spiritual leader. That was what the invitation was sent to do."

"We haven't been to church in a month. We didn't want to look for a new church and were too ashamed of looking hypocritical coming back."

"None of that matters now. I can't claim any of this for myself. This is God's will. Now, let's get you a seat on the bus."

"I have to go get Linda. It's amazing what God has done bringing everyone together. Look at all these people. I just came down here to see. It's amazing. I can't wait to tell Linda. We'll meet you all over at Mt. Pleasant," Bill said, getting back into his car.

Willie looked at the scene before rejoining the fanfare. Now he knew what all of this was for. It made a grand statement to get people excited about what was about to happen in the life of the church. The motorcade began with a police escort that traveled the route at thirty miles per hour because the novelty bus, originally designed for sightseeing, was semi enclosed on the top level and could not travel above forty miles per hour. Banners which read "Unification Day, Mt. Pleasant Baptist church: We are many members in one body of Christ," were attached to the side. They were a mobile billboard with balloons attached, and committee members waved and sang songs from the bus to a neighborhood burgeoning on a new day. Vans from Mt. Pleasant followed the bus. Some people opted to drive and blew their horns as soon as they were en route.

Onlookers began to honk their horns with support as well. A member of the committee made a suggestion to start a song. Willie was not a singer, but he loved the hymns of the church. They began singing "Soon and Very Soon." The choir would sing this every time they marched into the sanctuary and it seemed fitting for today. He remembered what Bill Case had said about not believing this day would actually come. Willie had no doubt this day would come. He just had no idea what it took to prepare for it. Their *soon* had finally come. The chorus moved like a wave through the bus until it sounded as if they were singing it in rounds as the song echoed from front to back.

Singing the songs must have made everyone feel much warmer. Vanessa appeared to be having the time of her life. Ever so often Willie would catch her looking at him with a worried expression. He realized that he was sitting stoically, neither clapping, nor singing. He decided whatever mood he was in that he would not ruin this day for her. Willie caught on to the second verse and continued to sing, "No more crying there, we are going to see the king." *There* sounded like his earthly interpretation of heaven. He pondered a Heaven on Earth when he got to where God called him to be.

They came within a quarter of a mile of the church to the corner of Ritchie Highway. The streets were lined with those Mt. Pleasant members who hadn't made the prayer meeting. By then they had started to sing "Sign me up for the Christian Jubilee." Paul Grant's ears were a bright red from standing in the cold waiting for them to get there. Willie watched as Keisha, who had been on the bus with him, reached up and tugged Paul's earlobe playfully as a greeting. They looked awfully cute together. They waited for Vanessa and him to lead everyone up the hill to entrance of the church.

"Everything seems to be going well," Willie said to Paul.

"Yeah," Paul said. "Is there something wrong, Pastor?"

Willie didn't realize it was that apparent that something had been bothering him since Lincoln Avenue. Like he and Paul discussed the night of the last meeting, he had sent out his invitation and God only brought back the one family that he knew of. Willie still wondered, had it reached Charley Thompson and could Charley find it in his heart to accept it?

"I'm just worried about some of the older members making it up the hill," Willie said.

"Like my mom, who is sixty-five years old. She been standing in a kitchen all morning, but insisted upon walking down this hill to meet you all and walk back up. She really shouldn't be out here," Paul said.

"Tell that to Deacon Pace or Judd Mason. They are happy to be here, and grateful to be alive." Keisha said.

"I'm just wondering who all these people are," Willie said.

"They are your new congregation, along with invited family members, guests, and dignitaries. There's even a news crew up there," Paul said.

They looked like a Civil Rights march in progress as they held hands some twenty persons across and at least that many deep at the base of the hill. Many people had joined the group since the beginning. Some were from the two churches and others just passing by. One man followed the crowd claiming to be looking for a church home.

Mt. Pleasant had a majestic presence to those who had not seen it up close. They stepped up the concrete stairs as if they were entering a palace. Many Harvest members took pictures outside for their memory books. They arrived at Mt. Pleasant ahead of schedule. That extra time gave the marchers enough time to rest and get acquainted in the fellowship hall before the reception.

Willie and Vanessa were served at the head table along

with Pastor and First Lady Rawls during the reception. A table was also reserved for the committee. Keisha, being the chairperson, presented awards to her committee.

"I would like to thank Sister Pastor for giving me an opportunity to serve as the Unification Day chairperson. Both Brother and Sister Pastor have been very supportive in bringing us together as a group. Until now I have felt Mt. Pleasant was the isolated entity doing the work of the Lord. God has enlarged our scope and I feel one in Spirit with everyone at Mt. Pleasant Baptist church," Keisha said with a tear coming down her cheek. "I'd like to thank my committee that worked tirelessly during the holidays to make this day possible. Please stand when I call your name: Deacon Buster Johnson, Deacon and Mrs. Simmons, Ms. Lottie Freeman, Mrs. Luella Bates, Ms Alice Jones . . . ," Keisha said passing down certificates to each of them. When she got to Paul's name he was gone.

The third phase of the unification, which was a short installation ceremony, began right after everyone was fed. Willie surprised Vanessa with her new robe and they changed into them for the ceremony. His robe was made of purple material accented with a Kente cloth trim around the collar and wrists. Vanessa wore a similar robe in royal blue. Willie was standing tall at the altar with Vanessa, smiling from ear to ear beside him.

They crafted together a ceremony for this unprecedented event. Deacons and Trustees from Mt. Pleasant welcomed their counterparts from Harvest. Pastor Rawls led the joint board in installing their new pastor. Finally, the combined congregation read the Church Covenant responsively and they all shared in communion.

Willie and Vanessa were exhausted at the end of the day. The adrenaline that carried them through most of the day had waned. They were one of the last people to take the van back to Harvest Baptist Church to retrieve their car. The Unification committee dwindled down to one person, Keisha, who was reflective in the front seat of the van. Vanessa and Pat giggled in the back corner like a couple of school girls, which left Willie and Ben in the middle.

"Tomorrow will begin your new life as a church family. I know you and Vanessa are itching to preach, but I'm the invited guest for the weekend," Ben laughed. "It's all mine."

"I can't believe it's finally over," Willie said.

"The work has just begun, my friend. You think the work was over for Dominion when we finished construction?" Ben looked at his friend closely. "I was worried about you earlier. You didn't seem to be present or enjoying yourself."

"I don't know what it is."

"You better snap out of it. Look at your wife back there, man; she's lively. She looks good and feels good because God has blessed her. You, on the other hand, look worn out."

"I guess I'm not satisfied at how I left things at Harvest. I know I'm holding on and I shouldn't."

"Think about all you had to go through these last couple of months. Holding on to Harvest was like holding on to dead weight. God could be trying to show you that physically, emotionally and spiritually, the church was dying out there. It's gotten so bad that it has robbed you of your joy. He wants to give you a rebirth here at Mt. Pleasant."

"I read the scriptures and interpret them for others, but I am ashamed to say I'm not getting what it is God is telling me to do. I keep feeling like telling God, 'alright Lord, I led the congregation, now what?'

"You may be looking for new vision when you should be looking for revelation on how to accomplish the vision you have. I'm afraid the first step is letting go."

Willie knew Ben was right. He had to let go, but it would be easier said than done.

"Pastor Abe Townsend, now how does that sound?" Charley said over the phone.

"Sounds like something I been waiting to hear all of my life, Uncle Charley. But I never thought I'd come by a church this way."

"Oh, this is going to be official. We have other candidates that are interested. Willie is just waiting for us to come up with our top choice. That's how Willie is. He's not going to turn over the church to just anyone, that's why we are meeting through the courts so it will be official. You got to be prepared to answer some questions."

"What kind of questions?" Abe Townsend asked.

"The questions will be about your background, and your plans for Harvest church. But I already told them you were keeping everything basically the same. Give me a signal if you get stuck. You know, Willie would nod his head when he needed me to get into position," Charley said, sounding as if he was demonstrating although he was on the phone. "You just got to be prepared."

Abe had been preparing for ministry since age seventeen. He had been called and he didn't ignore his call like some ministers who hoped God would change his mind and give up on them while they lived a life of sin. After graduation he had done what all seminary students do, he found a pastor to sit under. Abe found Philippians Baptist Church, a neighborhood church, but he fell from grace and he fell hard. It was one of those falls that when it is over, you avoided the spot altogether.

While teaching Sunday School he got too close to one

of his students. Marion Butler had always attended church alone and had sat up front in his class. She shook her head to his adages, said Amen in the right places and stroked his ego. He had not let his attraction to her interfere with his duties at church. Matter of fact, they had been so discreet that the pastor hadn't even known they were meeting after church.

Their dates had been innocent enough until meetings at a steak house led to a tavern inn. Abe had never felt the way Marion made him feel. He struggled with a way to make their relationship right in the sight of the Lord and still continued seeing Marion. He had plans to cut off their sexual relationship and make her his wife. That is when he found out she was already someone else's wife.

She had been a wife determined to hurt her cheating husband and anyone else in the process. When it was rumored that Tom Butler, Marion's husband had had several affairs at their former church, she stuck by him and planned her revenge. What better way to top her husband's indiscretions than to have an affair with the new younger minister? In the end, Marion confessed to the affair in a marital counseling session to her husband's devastation and Marion's pure satisfaction. Pastor Murphy had asked that Abe be relieved of his duties and it had seemed like everyone in the Baptist conference got the memo.

That is why it was ironic to Abe now that he could be the next pastor of Harvest church. It had been two years since his fall and he had been running from the Lord. Maybe this was God's way of restoring him, bringing him full circle, he thought. Now he would pray for forgiveness and do everything to cleanse himself outside of joining a monastery. Now he would prove to his family that he hadn't wasted his time at seminary.

"When and where should I meet you, Uncle Charley?" Abe said, ready to do God's work—again.

Chapter 23

The Battle is Not Yours

Willie and Vanessa had to extinguish the fire in Mt. Pleasant. Fiery gossip was spreading throughout the church. Even those who never knew Charley Thompson carried his name on their tongue like a household word. Willie almost fell out his chair when Vanessa said from the pulpit during one of her sermons that church folk wouldn't have half the problems if they stayed off the phone, stayed out of each other's business and stayed prayed up. *Sure, blame the latest worries on gossip,* he thought. To tell the truth, if it wasn't for the gospel grapevine, he might not have heard about Charley's latest antics.

Charley Thompson found a minister to head up twenty or so people who refused to leave Harvest Baptist church. Willie still had the deed, the church treasury, and more importantly, the keys to the facility. Willie did not know exactly what he wanted to do with the Harvest building, so he waited for a word from the Lord to proceed and had no intention of turning over the church.

In the meantime, Willie was ready to call members of the deacon board to go to talk to Charley intervention style to resolve the matter. Then he remembered most of those deacons that served with Charley at Harvest were less than pleasant or reasonable at the last church meeting before coming to MT. Pleasant. Of course, Vanessa had another take on it. Forget taking him in front of the elders of the church; she wanted to hire the best lawyer money could buy and sue the pants off him.

Willie and Vanessa were in the Pastor's study, which sat adjoining to Vanessa's office. Willie's private office was down the hall. The study was redesigned to accommodate both of them and it was where they usually ate lunch together. Luella announced they had a group of members that wanted to discuss an idea with them.

"Do they have an appointment Luella?" Vanessa questioned over the telephone intercom system.

"No, Sister Pastor. Shall I tell them to come back next week?" Luella asked.

"We got time to talk to a few members," Willie grinned. "Give us about five minutes then send them in Luella."

Willie placed his lid back on the sweet and sour chicken with lo mein they had ordered for lunch. "Hopefully, it's not an emergency," Willie added before wiping his fingertips with his napkin. "And for God's sake, act like your listening this time."

"I don't know what you are talking about, Willie Green. I always listen to my members," Vanessa said, clearing her takeout container from the table.

"How about the time that nice young lady, I forget her name, but she is a teacher."

"Carmen Ray, I remember precisely," Vanessa said with her hands on her hips as if she took offense to what Willie said to her.

"She came in here and told you that one of her students had been murdered down there in DC."

"Yes," Vanessa said.

"She was having a hard time coping with the loss."

"Well, didn't I help her?"

"Vanessa, I sat there and watched you interact with her. You sat at your desk and wrote out verses." Willie said, lowering his voice, figuring their five minutes were up and Luella would be escorting members in the lounge at any moment. "That's what you do. You're like a walking concordance. Sure, you listen for keywords, and spit out prescriptions, but sometimes you have to deal with people's emotions. Let them know you understand where they are, then tell them how God's word can elevate them."

"Well, I'll just watch the maestro at work and keep my Bible quoting, non-feeling mouth closed," Vanessa said with a wounded expression. Willie pulled her into him and kissed the bridge of her nose when they heard the knock on the door.

The group, all ladies, came in and sat around the small round table in the back of the spacious room. Linda Reed, Lillian Armstrong and Carla Jordon were all originally from Harvest Baptist.

"Brother Pastor, Sister Pastor, beg your pardon, but I know at Harvest you had an open door policy. Always willing to hear new ideas," Lillian said.

"Certainly," Willie told her.

"I mean like the time when we wanted to have a toy drive for the children at Christmas. We just came right in and you listened to us," she continued.

"That was a real nice idea," Linda Reed said.

"Look, ladies, what's on your mind? If you'd rather talk it over with Brother Pastor, I can step out of the room," Vanessa said, getting up from her desk. Willie shot her a look and she sat back down.

"No, Sister Pastor. We have an idea for the combined church," Carla said.

Vanessa sat back down at the desk while Willie brought water over to the table to encourage them to get out whatever it was they wanted to say.

"Descendants of Harvest Baptist were worried about the good name of the church they left behind. For a long time I've been . . . I mean, we have been associated with the name of that church," Lillian Armstrong said.

"What descendants might that be?" Vanessa asked. "This wouldn't have anything to do with Deacon Charley Thompson and the people who chose to stay at Harvest?"

"Now, Vanessa, let's let these ladies finish what they have to say," Willie said.

"No, no we are not with that group. It's just that a group of us at the Women's Auxiliary meeting last Thursday thought that you both would consider renaming Mt. Pleasant to reflect the heritage of both churches."

Willie held up a hand to silence Vanessa who was ready to respond.

"We have a list of names you might want to consider. The Greater Mt. Pleasant Baptist Church," Carla Jordon read ceremoniously.

"Now that is a nice name," Linda Reed said.

"Lillian came up with New Mt. Pleasant church, or the New Union Baptist church."

"May I see that list?" Vanessa asked. She had to read them over for herself. She chose to remain quiet and let Willie handle this situation.

Luella knocked lightly on the door before entering.

"This letter came certified mail addressed to Brother Pastor." Luella said handing it to him.

"Thanks, Luella. Ladies, I think you came up with some awfully good choices, but we don't have to worry about Harvest Baptist church or its good name. It's not the name of the church we are concerned about; it's the name of

Jesus. Sister Pastor and I will continue to pray for direction of this church. Will you pray with us?" Willie said, helping Linda Reed out of the chair.

"Oh yes, you know I pray for you and Sister Pastor and the whole church everyday," Lillian Armstrong said.

"Good, good. If the Lord leads us to rename the church, then we will let you know. Okay?"

"Okay, Brother Pastor, I'll just hold on to this list in case you need to see the names again," Carla Jordan said.

"You do that. Thanks for stopping by," Willie said, ushering the ladies to the door.

Vanessa waited for the door to close before saying, "You're good. You make a denial sound endearing."

"They make a good point, Vanessa. We might want to think about it," Willie said, going again for the takeout. He placed the carton in the microwave and read the cover of the envelope Luella had given him.

"I've barely had time to think since unification, let alone pray over names."

"How about the New International Harvest Fire Baptized Mt. Pleasant Church," Willie said, getting tongue tied.

Willie's grin slowly left his face when he read the letter Luella had brought in for him. He extended an invitation to the unification celebration to Charley, now his response was a certified letter from Morgan and Brown Associates for an arbitration session in the interest of the Harvest Baptist Church. He showed the letter to Vanessa who became outraged.

"Arbitration is one step away from suing someone in court and is no way of settling a dispute for the children of God. Remember telling me that?" Vanessa said.

"I had no idea it would come to this. Obviously, Charley is still harboring resentment over the unification."

"What are we going to do?"

"Pray that we handle the situation in a Christian-like manner."

Willie had not told anyone at church about the arbitration. Vanessa and he attended alone. She wore a tailored pinstripe suit that made her look more like his attorney than his wife. He didn't even know what to bring to the session. They prayed before they left the house.

Morgan and Brown Associates was housed on the third level of the Suitland Professional building. They arrived early for their 2:30 appointment. The receptionist escorted them into a small conference room with an oval shaped table that took up most of the space. A tray of ice water sat in the middle of the table beside some documents. Willie and Vanessa took a seat facing the door. They sat in silence for ten minutes until the moderator entered the room with Charley, and two other men. Willie rose to shake hands with the attorney on the end that introduced himself.

"Mr. Green, I'm Daniel Williams, an attorney for Simms, Craft and Foster. This is Reverend Abe Townsend and of course Mr. Charley Thompson," He said.

"That's Reverend Green," Vanessa said from her seated position.

Mr. Williams nodded his acknowledgment before taking his seat. Willie looked at Charley who had painted on a blank expression to shield himself from Vanessa's icy stare. Abe Townsend looked scared to death. Willie could not help but feel sorry for him. *No doubt, Charley has talked him into taking his place,* Willie thought. Willie decided he would try to reach Abe. This arbitration was proof that there was no reaching Charley.

The moderator, Bill Jenkins, took over the proceedings. He explained that arbitration was a step to go over the circumstances of a potential case to reach a settlement and also see if the evidence warrants an official court case. He also explained that the members of Harvest Baptist church, represented by Charley Thompson and Abe Townsend, wanted to remain at that church and elect Abe as new pastor. They had Willie portrayed as a delinquent pastor who neglected his duty and absconded with the church funds, Willie thought. Mr. Jenkins gave each side time to share before making a recommendation on how to proceed.

Mr. Williams, a young looking man, pulled a legal size pad from his briefcase. He stood and paced while he talked as if he were in an actual courtroom. Mr. Jenkins even frowned at his formality. "Let me review some facts before I share my client's views. The church at 8901 Lincoln Avenue is chartered as Harvest Baptist church. According to the church roles, there are 112 members, roughly 93 are active members. I have a petition of about thirty signatures that can be matched with the church roles of members who would like to remain at Harvest Baptist as their place of worship," Mr. Williams said, growing tired of walking. He took a seat next to Charley.

"Reverend Green, is it true that you are the pastor of another church?"

"Yes," Willie replied.

"Reverend Green, were you shown the petition from the members who wanted to remain at Harvest Baptist?"

"Yes."

"Churches are not regulated on a daily basis under local or state rule. Usually religious institutions have by-laws according to denomination whereas, they have their own system of selecting and installing a leader." Mr. Williams motioned for Charley, who handed him a newspaper clipping. This was passed to the moderator along with the petition. "Reverend Willie Green has been installed Co-Pastor of the Mt. Pleasant Baptist church, leaving the office of pastor vacant at Harvest Baptist. The afore-mentioned names on the petition simply want to exercise their right as a congregation to elect a new leader. Reverend Green has the deed and access to the church building and church funds. The church has two accounts at Citizens Bank of Maryland. The members I represent cannot proceed with their right to install a pastor and hold worship services until this matter is taken care of. It comes down to the willingness or unwillingness of Reverend Green to turn over the property of Harvest Baptist church to those who remain there."

Willie tried to focus on the arguments presented by Mr. Williams, but he felt disoriented as if he were in darkness. Memories of services at Harvest Baptist flashed in his head like a side show. The souls of the saints that worshipped there seemed to radiate to the outside and painted a welcome smile on the façade to the outside world. He thought about his own wedding held at Harvest months earlier and how the small sanctuary was filled to capacity and overflowing into the lobby. Then he thought of how the building looked once they departed for the unification march. It looked desolate then. Willie wondered would it ever look lively again.

Willie kept being drawn back into the session with the word "petition" and talks about the church accounts. Willie could not believe how accurate Mr. Williams had been considering Charley had not attended a Trustees meeting since October. The church checking account was off by 550 dollars used toward the unification efforts. He was days away from transferring the entire budget over into Mt. Pleasant accounts.

Mr. Jenkins asked Willie and Vanessa to share their side. He put his notes in the file and pulled out a fresh sheet of paper. Vanessa waited for Willie to start.

"We don't have counsel," Willie said.

"It's not necessary. What we are looking for is anything that would help resolve this matter," Mr. Jenkins said.

Vanessa sat to the edge of her seat waiting for Willie to begin, and Willie waited for a cue from God. She put her hand on his to prompt him to begin speaking.

"Harvest Baptist Church and that whole community will always be in my heart. We have plans to use the building to benefit the community," Willie said.

"Willie tried to discuss this matter with you. I don't think it had to come to this." Vanessa spoke directly to Charley. Willie put a hand on her forearm in a feeble attempt to stop her. He knew his wife was about to blow.

"What is it, Charley? I don't fit your image of what a Pastor should be? Or do I not fit the image of what a woman should be, quiet and timid? I am not trying to be a man or take a man's place. I'm trying to be the woman God called me to be," Vanessa said.

"Mrs. Green, please," Bill Jenkins said.

Charley did not address Vanessa, but instead looked at Willie. "I should have seen it coming. First you had Mae Richardson up in the office practically running the church. Now you got your wife running the pulpit." He trembled and spit shot from his mouth as he spoke.

"I knew this whole thing wasn't about you and Willie. It's about me. I intimidate you." Vanessa said.

"Mr. Thompson, awh Mrs. Green," Bill Jenkins said in an attempt to get order.

"Vanessa," Willie said. Something she said confirmed what he must do, but Vanessa was on a roll.

"I'm sorry the move of God inconveniences you. It disturbs your five minute drive and your one hour and fifty minute church experience. You're not concerned about the church or your religion, you worried about your routine. I suggest you take a look at your motives." Vanessa stated.

"Vanessa, hush." Willie said harshly.

Everyone was silent. Vanessa stared at Willie in disbelief. He stood up and took out his key ring. He disengaged a bundle of keys and laid the rest in the center of the table.

"You have to have a strong relationship with the Lord to be a pastor. You got to be willing to take His directions. It's not about being in charge," Willie said as he pulled out Vanessa's chair and helped her with her coat. "Reverend Townsend, I assume you went to divinity school like my wife and I did. You ought to know when the Lord is telling you to stop the madness like he's telling me right now."

Willie gripped Vanessa's hand and led her out the door. He suddenly felt lighter.

Chapter 24

Ask Not What the Church Can Do for You, But What You Can Do for Your Church

Willie could smell that Vanessa had started dinner when he got home from a Saturday evening Men's Fellowship meeting. He wouldn't consider his wife a great cook when compared to the women of the church, but, at least she had been trying recently. It was a step above his cooking out of necessity days. Vanessa was pan frying chicken in their deep cast iron skillet when he went in to greet her.

"Good, you're home. Taste this," Vanessa said anxious to serve him a piece of chicken from the batch lying on a napkin covered serving tray.

Willie knew that what she really meant was, is it as good as Mae Richardson's fried chicken. She placed a piece of chicken in front of him with an ear of corn, a heap of boil in the bag rice, and a glass of lemonade. She waited for his reaction before serving her own plate. Willie, not wanting to prolong her agony, took a bite.

"Umm yummy," he said.

"Oh you," Vanessa said, throwing her dish towel at him

before turning to fix her plate. "I just don't get it. How does she get her coating so crispy?"

"Your coating is fine. It's the seasoning that makes yours different. I don't taste it through to the bone."

"But does it taste alright? I mean really?" she said, hovering above his seat with plate and glass in hand.

"Yes," Willie said motioning for her to sit down. "You got to get serious like those ladies in the church kitchens. You got to prepare to get dirty, get a little grease popped on you. Where's your apron and hair net? That's when you know you are serious."

"So, what you're saying is I need to study under Henrietta Davis or should have studied under Mae Richardson before she passed?"

"Speaking of Henrietta Davis, she and a couple of members from the quilting circle were up at the church dropping off those quilted tapestries for the fellowship hall. They wanted me to ask you something," he said, finishing off the last spoonful of rice.

"I know, they want the church to create a new logo for the sign out front, offering envelopes and correspondence stationary for the combined church."

"No, it wasn't that."

"Sometimes I want to go to these women and ask them for their list of demands so they won't have to introduce a new one every week," Vanessa said exasperated. "I know what; I'm going to write a list of things I would like for them to change like popping up during church service to share a testimony or introducing a visiting relative. Then, they send little messages for you to give to me. Do you realize they put you in the middle when it comes to things that might dramatically alter Mt Pleasant?"

"What about Harvest?" Willie said. "And I'm not saying

we have to go with everything they suggest or tolerate everything our members do, but think about what it is they are asking. They wanted a plaque in the main vestibule with all the Harvest members' names on it to commemorate the unification. They suggested raising money and dedicating new pews in honor of our coming together."

"Nothing is wrong with the old pews," Vanessa said, "but then I sound like the bad guy when I say no."

Well then I was the pushover, Willie thought. He knew Vanessa's father built their church from the ground up when he was just starting out in ministry, and after fifty years he passed the legacy on to her. So it was natural to want to protect it. She had to realize that the people at Harvest had a fifty year history as well—a history that was now being furthered by a disgruntled deacon and his nephew.

"You might want to consider their suggestions, like renaming the church, for one because you know what's already begun to happen?" Willie said before draining his glass of the remaining lemonade.

"What's that?"

"We have unofficially changed the name of the church. I have not heard neither you or I call the church anything other than the combined church since January." He watched her peel the skin and meat off the chicken bone with a fork before eating it.

"What did the ladies want?"

"They were wondering when we were going to have a fellowship dinner or church bazaar."

After several minutes without offering a reaction, Vanessa asked, "What do you think?"

"Well like I told the ladies that were betting, by the way, that you would say no, that it seems like a good idea."

"They must not have heard my sermon last week about

expectations and faith, oh I forgot, those women only come when you preach."

"What are you talking about?"

"Don't act like our members don't have their preference of pastors," Vanessa said, pushing her plate away. Willie, taking that to mean she was done, began finishing her leftovers.

"I did notice in the beginning when we used to alternate Sundays that there was a trend in attendance."

"That is why I suggested mixing it up a bit and letting the Holy Spirit lead and help us to decide who would preach the night before," Vanessa said, gathering empty dishes, glassware and pots into the sink. "I can understand members preferring to talk or counsel with you or attend my Bible study class. But it kills me that on Sunday when the word has been sent from the Lord, that they are wondering who will be preaching."

"It's not that bad, baby," Willie said, placing his plate into the sudsy water.

"It's been three months and I am still waiting to have church. Each time I stand up to preach I may see two or three new faces other than my old Mt. Pleasant members. A few more women from Harvest that have come out to a women's fellowship and are just getting the notion that it doesn't matter who is preaching. It's like I'm preaching my trial sermon every time and waiting for approval from the congregation."

"I know. I'm annoyed that there is still gossip going around that we are personally being sued by Charley and company. That news is late and wrong." Willie opened the insert advertisements for Sunday's paper delivered a day early by his postman.

"Yeah, well I guess you can't do anything about gossip."

"Sure we can. I say we take our complaints to the people

since they have been bringing their complaints to us during our first church-wide fellowship dinner and deliver the State of the Church address."

"You will have to do all the talking because right now, I come off like a villain. Plus, you'll find a tactful way to tell folks they can't keep calling here whenever they feel like it." Vanessa said

"If they don't call, how do we know if it's an emergency?"

"We would know it was an emergency if your members would only call when it actually was an emergency."

"Oh, now they're my members. Put it on your list." Willie folded up the paper he was looking at. "I'll get a crew of fine church ladies to fry you some chicken," Willie said, attempting to duck another blow from the dish towel Vanessa was now using to dry dishes with.

"Oh no, we can have the fellowship, but you are not going to have the church smelling of fried chicken like this house is now. That smell lingers for days."

Willie looked at his wife as if he was seeing her for the first time. "You know you are such a snob." This time he dashed out the room to avoid her blow.

The members of the combined church originally from Harvest Baptist were craving an opportunity to get together besides the four sacred services of, Sunday School, Sunday Morning Worship Service, Prayer Meeting and Bible Study. They were used to a church where pew mates were their best friends and the church was their social club. Willie only had to inform a few choice people before the word spread through the network that the ladies were cooking and they would be as foolish as Lot's wife not to show up.

Vanessa, who preached the very next day, took the

topic, "The Fellowship of the Saints," before announcing the dinner. She had a prescription of verses prepared on the topic, and just to seal the deal; she added a touch of guilt. "Now you can't say as a pastor that I ask you for much. Just that you love one another, study the word of God and support the church through your tithes. We have been united into one church for three months, but we haven't quite gelled as a congregation. So Pastor is asking you, no, I am charging you just like the Lord is through His message today to join us next Saturday for our fellowship dinner."

Willie and Vanessa were their own committee and facilitators. They put together ice breakers, door prizes and a southern style feast courtesy of the Kitchen Committee. There were over a hundred people in attendance. For this occasion, Willie and Vanessa decided to change roles so that their membership would be forced to see them in a different light. Vanessa gave Willie pointers, this time, on being assertive. He would stay aloof, no smiling or greeting people at the door, remaining in character until he was ready to hit them with his corrective speech. Vanessa donned the hospitality hat; her job was to make sure everyone mixed and mingled. The congregation didn't know they were being set up.

"The Bible says, how good and how pleasant it is for brethren to dwell together in unity, Amen!" Vanessa said, waiting for the crowd that had just eaten their choice of fried or baked chicken, macaroni and cheese, green beans, rice, pasta or tossed salad and an assortment of desserts to reply in kind. "We are here for just that purpose. Open your mouths and give God praise for the wonderful women of the Kitchen Committee. That delicious meal was worth the time of you coming out here on a Saturday evening, but we have more in store for you. Brother

Bobby Campbell, a Christian disc jockey that has been playing music for your enjoyment this evening, will help me in our first and most important activity."

Vanessa led the group in one round of musical chairs. Everyone was required to get out of their seats and walk around the room in any pattern until the music stopped. At that point they were to take the seat closest to them and remain there for the entire evening. New seats, with new neighbors they were required to get to know. Willie and Vanessa came up with this activity to bust up pre-unification and even retreat cliques that began to solidify. Willie had to go over to a table of women who refused to move during this game and lead them to another seat, uprooting some who had been obedient to the original rules before it was his time to address the crowd.

"Brothers and sisters, some of you I've known quite a while, some I'm just getting to know. Sister Pastor and I are your spiritual leaders put here by God to help you on your Christian journey. We are painfully aware of what our role is and we pray about it all the time," Willie said, not offering the wide generous smile he always wore when speaking.

"What are you here for? Have you ever stopped to think about that? I know your mama and your mama's mama went to church and busied themselves in the activities of the church, but what is *your* role in God's kingdom? You are not the pastor. You are not the husband or the wife of the pastor. Say amen somebody. The Lord put the pastor in the position of authority and respect and as much as I love everyone here, it's not respectful to call my house all hours of the day and night."

Willie noticed the expressions on some of the member's faces who started to question where this address was going while others shifted uncomfortably in their chairs.

"This reminds me of a coach I had in college, a Mr.

Bernie Latell. Many of you may not know, but in my earlier days I was a distance runner. Coach Latell urged me to do other track and field events other than just running cross country. I was hesitant, because as a distance runner, I had the pace down, the rhythm, the stride."

Willie began moving away from the podium so he could mimic some of the movements of his earlier days. Vanessa found the story interesting, but wondered herself where he was going. She knew her husband had more anecdotes than a motivational speaker, but she wanted him to get to the point before he lost his audience.

"Coach would always say, 'Green what are you here for?' Now I'm asking you." Willie watched the faces as he moved through the crowd stopping at Paul Grant. He lightly put his hands on his shoulder. "What are you here for, Brother Grant? He's one of our new deacons-in-training."

"To glorify God," Paul said, caught off guard.

"And you Sister Morton?" Willie asked Keisha that was right beside Paul.

"I'm here to learn more about Jesus," Keisha replied.

"Great, thank you. Cute couple, you need to split up." Willie waited while Paul reluctantly moved to the only available seat at the table with Vanessa and Keisha rolled her eyes. "Notice they didn't say to be a busy body or to take over every committee. Our primary focus should be to glorify God, learn about Jesus and help to bring others to him. Get rid of those hidden agenda spirits that want you to be in charge of everything, know everyone's business or make you unwilling to change," Willie said, looking specifically at one of the ladies from earlier who did not want to give up her seat.

He moved toward Vanessa who was taking notes. He had prepared this address like a sermon with three points minus the introductory scriptural reference. He knew she had his back if he needed a scripture to prove his point.

"My coach said, 'Willie you're here to run. It's just that simple; no matter whether I put you in the fifty or the hundred meters or whether you win or loose, you just run.'" He snapped his fingers in the general direction of his wife as if he was asking her to help him remember something. "This Christian journey is like a race. We happen to be completing this lap at Mt. Pleasant, but the Bible says the race is not given to the swift or the strong, but to the one that endures to the end."

"Ecclesiastics 9," Vanessa offered.

"Yes, and if we are all in this race together, we should all be going in the same direction. Tell someone pay attention, he's going somewhere." Willie's command was met with a few amens. "My coach believed so much in my natural ability, but he knew I lacked discipline. Say lack discipline."

Willie dropped the pretense and began to preach. He felt the unction of the Lord leading him to elaborate his second point, and just like Vanessa urged, he couldn't be concerned with who he was offending.

"Discipline is following a set of rules and coming under authority of your leaders. The Lord wants to take us to higher heights, but we have to have discipline. The sanctuary is where we draw closer to God through worship and Sunday service is reserved for worship, prayers and praise. We must stop conducting business and jumping up in service to interject. We're so concerned with trying to be seen. You don't know if you're hindering someone from coming to the Lord. We need discipline in our prayer life as well as the study of the word of God. Everyone who came here today to socialize or eat should be the same ones in the pews on Sunday, no matter who is preaching. My wife and I pray for you all and are willing vessels to receive the word from the Lord for your lives, and you miss it because you're waiting for a certain person to deliver it. Tell someone that's stupid."

Vanessa was shaking her head in agreement with everything Willie had just said. She caught a glimpse of a few women at the table next to her who stared at her as if to say, "I know you put him up to this." She made sure to give the ladies her warmest smile.

Willie took time to take a sip of the ice tea left on the table from earlier. He was ready to go in for the kill.

"I went from cross country running, to metered events indoors, to hurdles. Each was a different discipline that helped me train and stay in condition for the other. Coach Latell wanted me to be a well-rounded athlete, compete in indoor and outdoor events in different seasons, but I had a hard time when it got to the high jump."

Willie kept everyone's attention as he explained the science of the high jump. He demonstrated the leap of a high jump athlete by pacing toward the back buffet table, that was now cleared, and raising up in slow motion on and over the table, the way one would do over a cross bar.

"I wasn't getting it. I would choke right before the leap, sometimes passing underneath the bar and landing right on my face in the pit. My coach would say, 'What's wrong with you, Green?'" Willie said, grabbing a member nearby. "He said it just like that. What's wrong with you, Green? You've got to get over it!"

Willie still had the member by the shirt shaking him. Vanessa was up on her feet as if she had been let in on the punch line early and everyone else was on the edge of their seats waiting for their revelation.

"We're here!" Willie said, making a spoof of the famous *Poltergeist* phrase. "Harvest Baptist has invaded Mt. Pleasant as some of you feel. Get over it! My wife is a dynamite preacher of the Gospel, but a woman, Oh my God. Get over it! Yes, Harvest Baptist no longer exists the way we knew it. There are about twenty people who went to extreme lengths to have services there, and since then, more stories have been told about my wife and I and the Harvest dispute than those passed around at a folk tales convention. Guess what? You'll get over it like I had to. If your mad and feel like you want to leave the church because I'm saying this to you, guess what? You'll eventually have to get over it when you get to where you're going. Get over it, people. Get over your issues and get on with the work of God."

Willie got the wide eyes and stunned expressions he had anticipated. Even the ones who usually nodded their heads self righteously had tight jaw lines and cheeks red with embarrassment.

"So guess what I did the next time I was faced with the cross bar?" Willie said, bringing his tone down.

"You got over it," mostly everyone shouted out.

"Actually no, it was hard for me, y'all. It was so hard. So my coach said, 'Green, I'm going to lend you some support. Instead of the high jump, let's try pole vaulting.' " Willie said grinned for the first time that night. "Come on over here, baby."

Vanessa joined her husband. She had written a sermon outline of her husband's address to be added among the collection of his greatest sermons.

"The pole vault is just like the high jump. You've still got to get over it, but you have the support of a flexible fiberglass rod, or, in some cases, bamboo reed. You land on the cushion of the pit when you've made it over. Sister Pastor and I are here as your support, whether you think of us as the stick you lean on to form your arch, or the pillow you land on; we are there. You are the one that has to get over it. We need members that know why they are here, members that are disciplined disciples and members that can get over their issues." Willie turned to Vanessa, "What is that one about the babes in Christ with their milk and the adults eating meat?"

"The scripture my husband is referring to says that the time has come that you be teachers, but you wind up having to be taught again like a baby still on milk. Can you say prescription time, if that's alright with Brother Pastor? We're going to get this thing right," Vanessa said.

"I'm done. Hopefully I didn't bore you with tales from my track and field days. After Sister Pastor gives you those verses let's look to the Lord to be dismissed," Willie said.

Willie let Vanessa close the assembly in prayer. The Lord never failed to amaze him as to how he brought the fragments of his messages together. There were many times when he was asked to speak with only ideas in his head. The Lord always provided the context.

"It's funny that I didn't know you were such an athlete," Vanessa whispered to her husband as everyone dispersed. "I mean, running cross country, high jumping and pole vaulting. You're a regular Olympic star."

"Please, with my puny behind and chicken legs?" Willie whispered as they joined each other in laughter.

Chapter 25

Practice What You Preach

Vanessa tried to interpret the automotive jargon from Willie's one sided telephone conversation with the mechanic to find out what has been ailing her BMW 325i convertible and what damage it would cause to their bank account to get it fixed. She was using his computer to pull up the notes from the last joint board meeting because it was her turn to hold this month's meeting.

"What did they say?" Vanessa said.

"They're finished. I can pick it up today if I can make it in the next half hour," Willie said, checking his watch.

"So much for me working late on the budget for the board meeting."

"No I'll just pull Deacon Simmons to drive with me down there," Willie said, "plus, I need you to meet with Paul Grant for me. He called a little while and said he needed to speak to me; he sounded upset."

Vanessa resisted the urge to let out a long annoyed sigh. "What time is he supposed to be here?"

"He told me seven," Willie said, grabbing his suit jacket

from the hook on the back of the door. "If the car is really done like they said, I should be right back."

"It's seven now." This time she checked her watch and confirmed the time with the wall clock over the door. "Didn't Keisha say she was waiting for him as well when we saw her sitting in the Sanctuary twenty minutes ago?" Vanessa thought how ironic it would be if Paul made this appointment with Willie expecting to talk to him about Keisha and their apparent love affair. Although Keisha had been surprisingly discreet about her social life instead of her usual candid self, Vanessa and Willie had long since figured out that they were an item.

"Yeah, I think that's what she said," Leaning in close for a goodbye kiss, he could see she was less than enthused with her new assignment. "He's probably running late. I don't know, Vanessa, just . . ."

"I know, just listen to him," Vanessa said before he gave her a peck on the cheek.

Of course she would listen to him, she thought. She had listened to Lottie Freeman when Vanessa had accepted her proposal to let the missionaries go to a Foreign Missions convention. She had also listened to her husband's good friend, Buster Johnson, talk at length about nothing in particular; both of which were Willie's appointments that for some reason or another he couldn't keep. She was beginning to believe he was deferring his appointments to her on purpose.

Vanessa went to her office down the hall to get her pad while she waited for the print out from the computer. Her good friend, Pat, had an actual doctor's prescription pad printed with her name on it. She wrote Paul's name on it where it said patient's name in anticipation of his visit, but was reminded of what Willie had said to her about writing while people were talking. She decided that she would save the prescription writing until they were done talking.

Paul was standing in the open reception area as she came down the hallway. The office was vacant except for her since Luella got off work at five each evening.

"Mr. Grant, so nice to see you," Vanessa said, embracing Paul. She led the way into Willie's office.

"I didn't see Brother Pastor's car or your car for that matter." Paul said sitting on the edge of one of the chairs opposite Willie's desk. "I thought maybe everyone had gone."

"My car has been having some trouble and Willie went with Deacon Simmons to go pick it up from the shop, then they'll drive it back here."

"Oh," Paul said.

"Willie thought that you could meet with me instead," Vanessa said, noticing that he looked confused. "Is that okay with you?"

"Oh yeah, yeah. It's nothing really."

"Did you see my sister waiting for you in the sanctuary?"

Paul slapped his forehead with the flat of his hand. "God! Oh sorry, Sister Pastor," he said, "Oh well, she'll be furious, but she knows exactly where I was; tied up at work again, as always."

There was a lull in the conversation. Paul yanked the briefcase strap from his shoulder and slumped down in the chair as if the strap was the only thing holding his body erect. He held a paper in his hand that was face down so Vanessa couldn't see what was on it.

"Willie said when you called you seemed upset. Whatever it is, it's over. You're in the Lord's house now."

Paul let out a stifled chuckle as if in hindsight whatever was bothering him was now funny. "I got passed over for a promotion. All day I've been watching the corner office more than I was watching the monitor on the computer I was using. There was gossip that the partners of the firm were going to make the announcement after their meeting, so I wasn't actually working. I was too nervous for that, plus I should have been gone an hour ago to meet up with Keisha," he said as if in a trance. "Then, Stan Browning had called a meeting of all the department heads into his office. Everyone knew an information leak would come out at the conclusion of this closed meeting divulging the names of the people who got promotions before they were officially notified. When Adrian Slatter, the Level II manager, passed my desk to leave an envelope on Ronny Miller's desk, a wave of nausea came over me because I knew what that meant. I knew. That's when I called Brother Pastor."

"I don't know how long you've been at this job, but more than likely it wasn't your time."

"I wish I had known it wasn't my time before I spent all those extra hours in the office, missing deacon's training and missing dates with your sister. I keep thinking if I just had more time before promotion season to prove myself, then I'd be out celebrating now instead of wasting your time."

"Number one, you're not God; you can't make more time. This delay does not mean a denial if it is a desire of your heart and you've made that known to the Lord," Vanessa said, empathizing with Paul who now had his head in his hand looking like a forlorn child. She knew full well how it felt to want to rush your destiny and being denied by God while he prepares you for the right time. "But God is sovereign; He knows what's best for you. Are you sure this is where He wants you to be?"

Vanessa's mind began to bring up scriptures about calling, God's sovereignty and timing. Like Galatians 6:9, that says "for in due season we shall reap, if we faint not." She didn't want to appear as if she was taking her attention away from him now that he was opening up and apt to share more.

"I don't know anymore," Paul said. "Just like I was prepared to come in here and tell Brother Pastor when I got my promotion that I wanted to cease deacon's training, but now . . . I guess I will continue on."

"Whoa, I've missed something. You want to be a deacon, right?"

"My father was a deacon," Paul was fast to say.

"That's all well and good, but that is not what I asked," Vanessa said. She could not hold out any longer. She brought the prescription pad front and center on her desk. "One of the greatest scriptures can be found in James five, verse twelve that says, "let your yea be yea and your nay nay." That means be a man of your word. Now, I don't want to have to read you before I write this prescription."

"I need it because I'm a mess." He smiled in spite of himself as if admitting his calamity was freeing.

"I can't believe this is the Paul my husband was bragging about being so organized and so together. How is it that we are training a man that doesn't really want to be a deacon? I mean, making all kinds of concessions for the times you've missed training."

"I wouldn't say; *doesn't want to be.*"

"Shall we say is in no position to be or hasn't made this position his number one priority? God said my yoke is easy. Serving God should not be a burden if God is telling you it's where you need to be."

"I've been so stressed, giving all my time to this thankless job that I was honored when Pastor recommended me," Paul said, his hand suspended in mid air as he thought of a way to express his predicament. "I think when I helped him with unification, Brother Pastor learned that he could depend on me. He knew my schedule was ultra tight, but I think he wanted me to be a deacon so I could sort of replace Deacon Thompson."

"Say no more," Vanessa said, knowing Paul's explanation was highly probable. "I want you to know that this still doesn't get you off the hook. You knew your schedule was ultra tight yourself. A simple, 'I'm flattered but I can't,' would have worked. I'm going to let you handle that with Brother Pastor."

"Okay," Paul said.

"Is that something you want to give to Brother Pastor? You've been holding it since you've come in." Vanessa said, pointing at the sheet of paper in his lap.

Paul sighed loudly as if the despair he had come in with had returned. He hesitated before passing the paper to Vanessa to read.

Transplant—A poem for Keisha
by Paul U. Grant Jr.

I came upon a clearing
and couldn't help but stare
at an amazing little flower
I never noticed there

Her petals were lovely
Bursting with color in full bloom
But her edges were browning
Because it was plucked up to soon

Upon further inspection
I became painfully aware
That her roots were starving
It hadn't been rooted anywhere

How beautiful this flower
Standing all alone

How I long to love and nurture her
And make her my own

"Wow." Vanessa cleared her throat. "I don't exactly know what it means, but that was nice. I had no idea that you and my baby sister were all that close."

"Yeah, Keisha's great."

"Is she the one?"

"Yeah," Paul said, looking up in the air like he was just realizing how important she was to him, "but I think I might have messed that up too."

Vanessa was reluctant to go down the road of romance and relationships with Paul or any couple other than with those considering marriage; especially someone dating her sister. Her premarital counseling sessions led couples on a long journey, looking at them individually and their relationship with Christ before they began to assess their love for one another.

"Why do you say that you've messed up?" Vanessa asked Paul.

"I had to cancel a couple of dates, trying to make deadlines. I knew Keisha was getting tired of it, so we agreed to talk about it. I told her I didn't know if I had time to be idle, especially during promotion season," Paul told her.

"Idle?"

"You know, silly and in love." He sighed. "Bad, huh?"

"I'm going to pray for you, my brother."

"So, she's put up this barrier that she has only recently dropped to talk to me over the phone. I called her at work and told her to meet me here because I thought for sure I would have news of a promotion to share with her." Paul interlocked his fingers, forming a cap to rest comfortably on the crown of his head. "I printed out this poem, but when I wasn't going to be the one promoted, I totally forgot about it and my arrangement with her. You know Keisha, Sister Pastor, have I totally messed up?"

She waited a while. "Can I be real? You've seen me in the pulpit. I shoot straight from the hip. If I was her, I would toss that poem in your face because it doesn't mean a thing when measured against how you've treated her. I say that because just like deacon's training, you haven't made her a priority. You got her on the back burner," Vanessa said, leaning across the desk. "Oh yeah, Willie's told me about your system. Men are definitely a different breed when it comes to romance. You like to keep quiet about your feelings and intentions until you are certain and have every detail in place, but guess what?"

"What?"

"A good woman is only going to sit around and wait but so long for you to decide she's important, especially if she's a Christian and has been used to being spoiled by God."

His mouth opened several times to respond before he actually spoke. "But it's only been four and a half months. It's scary that I am so sure about this woman in that short amount of time that I have known her."

"In less than a year and a half, Brother Pastor and I met, courted, got married and combined churches."

"So what can I do to make amends?" Paul asked.

"I'm not going to tell you. I'm looking out for my baby sister, as always, to make sure this is not another situation where you didn't get the promotion you wanted, so now you are going to concentrate on your girlfriend. You've got to think about it." Vanessa handed Paul the one scripture on his prescription from earlier. Vanessa raised an eyebrow after he read the prescription as to say, "so, what did you decide?"

"Yea, Sister Pastor, my answer is yea."

* * *

Paul sat with Sister Pastor until 8:30 when Brother Pastor returned. Brother Pastor was surprised to see them chatting like old friends. Paul declared before both of them that first thing the next morning, he planned to put in for his first week of vacation leave since he has been at the company.

Paul had a lot to think about as he drove into Keisha's development and found a parking space. He knew that Keisha was ready for a commitment, or at least consistency from him. He thought back to when he accepted God into his life for the first time. He had been about twelve in his hometown in North Carolina. All week long they had been in Camp Meeting Revival. A couple of women from the church had caught him kissing Mary Thomas in the back of the church. The elders of the church, including his grandmother, had been convinced that he would lose his soul to the devil. Every day he and Mary both had been on their knees at the front pew called the mourner's bench praying that God would save their souls. The saints had been determined not to let them up until they were saved. His grandmother and the other woman had cried and had prayed and had laid hands on them. Paul had been scared to death. He remembered getting off his knees and facing the crowd. Everyone had asked him, "Are you ready son? Are you sure?" Paul hadn't been completely sure what they were pressuring him about, but he was raised learning about God, and just like now, he knew God had been offering him something he did not want to go without.

He pressed the buzzer to her apartment after being let in the security door by a resident. Keisha answered the door with a sullen expression. She greeted him, but did not yield the way to let him in.

"Can I come in?" Paul asked.

"Yeah, sure," Keisha said as she turned and walked away, leaving him to close the door behind him.

"How have you been?"

"Fine," Keisha said, picking at her sweater. "How's Miss Thelma? I heard she had the cold or flu."

"She's doing well. She is as stubborn as ever; not wanting to take it easy and begging to go to church."

She sat across from his chair on the love seat. They did everything to avoid each other's eye contact.

"Look, I know I've been busy and unavailable," Paul started. "I got passed over for a promotion at work and forgot about our date. I want you to tell me what my punishment will be so we can go back to the way it was. So, what's it going to be? Will a week or two weeks of this silent treatment suffice?"

"You're not some child, and it doesn't matter anymore. I can't make you feel the same way about me that I do about you. I've been through that before. So, it is best that we set parameters so I won't expect anything from you. I mean, you're never available. Then you call me and tell me everything is going to be different."

Paul was angry at himself for trying to make light of the situation. He could tell as he let her finish her last statement that she had wanted to say that to him for a long time. She sat there with her legs crossed. Her top leg bobbed up and down out of frustration.

"I mean, I'm tired of uncertainty," Keisha continued. "I've been struggling with whether or not I'm going to business or divinity school. I've had time to spend with God and really get focused. If we are going to be friends, be a friend. If we are going to date, then be a boyfriend."

Paul noticed how quickly she changed from being in control to totally vulnerable. "I need you," he confessed, praying that he wouldn't mess up yet again.

"Yeah, well I couldn't tell."

"I'm having a hard time right now. I didn't get the promotion I've been busting my butt for at work and I miss you."

She wanted to reach out to him but resisted. "And you need me because you didn't get the promotion?" Her voice was laced with sarcasm.

"I need you because I love you. You're the one."

Keisha got up from the couch and walked to the window overlooking the parking lot. She was suddenly angry.

He got up to join her. "Keisha, I know the day will come when I will have to take care of my mother. I dread it, but I know it will come. I've been in the mindset so long of working to establish myself in my field so I would have the resources I need to support her."

Keisha turned to face him. "The greatest gift you can give your mother is your time."

"I also knew the time would come when I would find a woman whom I wanted to share my life with. I wanted to be secure enough in my job so I could have the extra benefits to start a family."

"But sharing your life means just that. I'm sure she would want to support you through your disappointments and celebrate your victories along the way. Not wait until this magical day when you attain something because there will always be things to attain. When you have the possibility to attain a loving relationship, it is something you can not put off."

"I'm sorry," he said, pulling her to him.

"I'm sorry also," Keisha said. "I realize that I have been selfish, too. Whining about me; who is going to help me get into grad school? Who is going to help me with my ministry? I especially owe Vanessa an apology for putting up with me. She has always been supportive and given me a place where I can grow and mature in the Lord. Then when she asks me for a little help, I accuse her of holding me back."

"I owe your sister too. Recently she helped me see things more clearly."

"I think I've always known I was led to follow in her footsteps, but I was rebellious at the same time because I thought that this was her blessing. Where was mine? Where was my niche? Then she fell in love and got married to Willie. Just like that, she had found what I was out in the world looking for and I was jealous. I was like, 'Lord, who is going to love me?' " Keisha slapped a palm on her chest and looked to the sky as if she was asking the Lord right then, right there.

"I love you," Paul stated.

She shook her head back and forth as if warning him not to use those words casually.

He grabbed her shoulders. "I do. I love that you are feisty and full of conviction and all that strength is wrapped up in a delicate package. I love that you make me think and challenge me to do better. And, you make me laugh. Even when I am alone, I think of something you said or did and laugh," He said, appearing to laugh as he spoke the words.

The spark in her eye told him that she could see the sincerity in his eyes. "I love you too."

They spent the next couple of hours talking about her goals and his fears and the wisdom that both Willie and Vanessa had shared with them through the years. Paul no longer had any excuses or hesitations that made her doubt his love for her. Their conversation was filled with the possibility that soon they would get what they were hoping for in each other. He made her believe.

Chapter 26

Sooner or Later

Easter was the main event in the Christian calendar. Every sermon preached throughout the year could be tied to Jesus' death, burial or resurrection, and just a prelude leading up to this commemoration of Christ's ultimate victory. This was one of those eventful years where God seemed to redirect his people by bringing Easter early. Everyone was heading home to the church seeking acknowledgment, redemption, salvation, but most of all, an available seat for the most popular day in the life of the church.

Willie and Vanessa were robed and listening to the service in progress on the intercom in the joint lounge before being escorted out by the charge deacon. Passages were studied, the text was marked and tithe checks were written, which left Willie fishing for a handkerchief and Vanessa fidgeting with the upsweep hairdo her sister pinned up the day before. She hoped the tendrils left dangling in the front for style sake would not be a hindrance throughout the service.

A knock on the door at 11:15 let them know that either something was wrong, or they had a visitor. Neither one of them could imagine the latter because preachers didn't normally go visiting on Easter.

"Brother Pastor, I got someone out here I think you might want to see," Buster Johnson said through the closed door to conceal the person's identity.

Willie shrugged at Vanessa, who he knew objected to anything that disrupted the sanctity of their meditation time even if they were done mediating.

"Who is it?" Willie asked.

The door opened as a reply, and a familiar face of a woman stood on the opposite side minus Deacon Johnson who was waiting in the hall to escort them all into service.

"Hi Pastor," the woman said. Turning toward Vanessa, she mouthed "hello."

"Sister Thompson, it is so nice to see you," Willie said. He looked over her shoulder, hoping to catch a glimpse of someone. "Baby, this is Elaine Thompson, Charley's wife."

Vanessa nodded and took that as her cue to grab a seat at the table to give her husband and his guest privacy.

"He is not here with me, Pastor. I haven't given up though. I keep praying," Elaine said. "He can't substitute the Harvest experience and he can't find anyone to take the place of his pastor. He's beginning to see that."

"Has he got a congregation over there?" Willie asked.

"A few of them that were on the petition and a few that wandered in. Roy Jones is there every Sunday preaching on the steps before anyone gets there. Charley runs him away from there every time. " She smiled faintly. "This morning he sat on the side of the bed to lace up his shoes; must have taken him over an hour. I left out before him. I'm not even sure he left. It's getting harder and harder for him to keep it going, but you know how stubborn Charley can be."

"I'll pray for you both," Willie said, reaching out to squeeze her hands.

"Well, I didn't mean to bother you before service. I just came to say I'm praying that it's only a matter of time before we both are here," Elaine said quietly before waving and walking through the door.

Willie didn't have the heart to tell her before she left that he had stopped praying that prayer. He had come to realize that just like his beloved Mae Richardson, everyone was not meant to go with them to Mt. Pleasant. Now his prayer was that God's will do his will.

The ushers had begun to put down folding chairs in the side aisle anticipating the sanctuary would fill to capacity. The only rows with available seating were up front as if the ushers had begun seating everyone from the back of the church first. Members were forced to give up seats they were reserving for guests and close the space left to ensure their Easter ensembles wouldn't wrinkle.

Keith Fischer played an organ prelude that added to the pageantry of Willie and Vanessa's entrance into the sanctuary. The joint board stood as a reverent welcome to their leaders. They could see a rainbow assortment of outfits including, suits, ties, dresses, hats and hairdos that screamed out, "I'm brand new," from their seats in the pulpit. One of the Deaconesses went to the microphone to welcome the visitors. It seemed like over a quarter of the church stood. Those were the faces that most pastors fixed in their minds as the main recipient of their message and invitation to Christianity. They capitalized on the opportunity to make a difference in a visitor's life because they never knew who may need to accept Jesus.

An eager Willie Green approached the sacred desk and answered the question on every member's mind: which of their pastors would bring the Easter sermon, until Vanessa took place beside him.

"Let the church say Amen. Jesus said I am the resurrection and the life. On this Easter Sunday, there is a word from the Lord for us today. I know you got on your Sunday best. Some of you who haven't been here since last Easter, Christmas or Mother's Day, must be a little perplexed right now as to who I am, Amen. Look at you neighbor and say, stay in church, you might miss something. Oh say amen somebody. You know I'm telling the truth." Willie looked at a smiling Vanessa beside him. "Well, I didn't come to badger the wayward. No, we have a word so that someone's heart may be pricked and come saying, 'what must I do to be saved?' Let us pray," Willie said.

They had mutually agreed that Willie should bring the Easter sermon until he came into their home office and tossed a scripture at Vanessa and said, "What do you make of this?" It was understood that he would run the field and she would assist. Just like when they stood together the day they met in the pulpit at Dominion Baptist, their message would be fresh, spontaneous and unrehearsed. He had his outline and she had hers.

"The book of Hebrews, tenth chapter is where we find our text. That's in the New Testament to those who haven't cracked a Bible since the last time they were here, but I am not here to shame the backslider. I was telling my wife one night while studying this passage that I felt the Lord was leading me to start a series of messages on the book of Hebrews. In it is the key to Christianity and the way we should be conducting ourselves in these latter days. Brother Johnson read for me from . . . oh let's see, all of it is so good. Sister Pastor, have you heard of anyone taking a sermon from an entire book of the Bible?"

Vanessa shrugged. "No I haven't, Brother Pastor, but you're the man."

"You hear that," Willie said, finding his place in his

Bible. "I am humbled everyday I wake up with this woman by my side. Praise God. Brother Deacon, start with the thirty-second verse and read until I say when."

"*But call to remembrance the former days, in which, after ye were illuminated, ye endured a great fight of affliction.*"

"That word illuminated can mean when you were first saved or when you were called. Remember that time when you were busting the door of the church down just to hear the word. No one had to call you and remind you about prayer service or special events of the church. Even during trying times you remained faithful."

"You're preaching already," Vanessa said.

"Skip down to verse thirty-five, Brother Deacon," Willie instructed.

"*Cast not away your confidence, which hath great recompense of reward.*" Buster read.

"That's right, reward. Continue."

"*For ye have need of patience, that, after you have done the will of God, ye might receive the promise.*"

"Stop right there, Brother Deacon. Say, sooner or later I will receive my reward."

The time between when the preacher takes his or her position at the sacred desk until he or she shares the sermon title was the last call for sanctuary seating at Mt. Pleasant. The ushers allowed another wave of worshipers to enter before taking a seat themselves and roping off the main aisle. Many of the latecomers had visited another church for an earlier service and were making their rounds to fellowship with relatives and friends. Others just decided it would be too much of a sin to sit home on Easter. Vanessa noticed Paul and Keisha coming down the aisle to the deacon's row and smiled, knowing that the fact they were together, God had given Paul his reward.

"Patience and reward, Sister Pastor, does this remind you of anyone?" Willie asked her.

She smiled at his inquiry, "You mean besides us during our season of unification?"

"Testify," Willie said.

"This may not be the traditional Easter message some of you were hoping to hear, but it is the message God wants you to hear. How many of you know that all of this didn't just happen? God knew that we would be sitting here in our finest; but it was a journey paved with stress and pain. Can I speak for my husband and myself?" Vanessa said. "We lost some people along the way and broke some ties. The Book of Hebrews encourages us to persevere in our faith, even when we are facing great stress and pressure. Verse thirty-five and thirty-six says don't loose confidence in the Lord that no matter what happens, he has great rewards for you if you remain faithful. So the question becomes, how strong is your faith?"

"We are talking about faith that brings you to the house of the Lord more than once a year," Willie added jokingly. "Let me leave the once-a-year saints alone."

Vanessa shoved his arm playfully. For the first time in a long while he realized that he was having fun, in church. This wasn't disappointment or frustration; reprimand or correction. His joy had returned and he looked forward to running the gamut of emotions with his congregation, knowing that this is where God wanted him to be.

"How many people are willing to admit that things may not be going your way right now, but you are resting in the faith of what God has done for us in the past and trusting in what he will do for us in the present and future?" Vanessa said.

"I say to you, don't get weary in well doing. You feel you are the only one not receiving, not prospering, and not getting any. God will give you your reward. I need my scripture here," Willie continued.

Buster Johnson walked up to the microphone. Thinking his part was over, he had retired to the front pew with his Bible. "No, Brother Johnson, if you don't mind, I need my wife to read this one," Willie told him. "The Bible says he who findeth a wife, findeth a good thing. I declare I can be down sometimes. Some of you didn't know, like my wife just indicated, that during the unification, I was hurting. I would pray to God for relief. God sent me comfort by the way of Vanessa Morton Green. She would open the Bible and read a scripture or pray with me and the pain would begin fading away. Glory. Come on, darling; tell these people my scripture with feeling."

"The text says have patience. That means wait. Some people say the harshest words the Lord can say to you are to wait. We want to hurry up and get our breakthrough, and get our deliverance. We have to pray like the old gospel tune, 'Lord help me to hold out, until my change comes.' The Bible says in Isaiah 40, 'They that WAIT, upon the Lord shall renew their strength.' Psalms 27:14 says, 'WAIT on the Lord: be of good courage and he shall strengthen thine heart.' So you see, Christ has given us a self renewal system. I may remind my husband of the scriptures, but God adds the power," Vanessa said. She was feeling the power of the Holy Spirit.

They shared the sermon like they shared their lives. Some saw their joint sermon as entertainment, like a comedy team or a radio program with two co-hosts. Willie and Vanessa thought of it as a dance where they swayed naturally to the rhythm God provided. She no longer was the fire breathing dragon who had to prove herself with every breath, and he was not the good-natured pushover; but they were a little of both, and not quite either.

"Thank you, Sister Pastor. Wait doesn't necessarily mean sit back and do nothing. Continue in Bible study. Continue praying without ceasing. Here is the guide book," Willie said, holding up a Bible. He paused when he locked eyes with Elaine Thompson who had stayed for this service. "There are some basic truths in the guidebook. Jesus is Lord. That is a basic truth. We can't make it without him. I have tried life on my own and have filled my days with pain and sorrow. Point to yourself and say, I will ultimately mess up!" Willie waited for the crowd to respond.

"If you want to do the will of God and run the race with patience until God sees fit to bless you, then you still must follow the one true example which is Jesus Christ. He was born into this world for this season we celebrate right now; to die on the cross for our sins. He spent a short time on this earth, but while he was here he left a legacy for us to follow. If you are not following Christ, seeking to be like him, how are you planning to prosper, to be delivered, to win souls to Christ?"

Vanessa pointed to her outline to indicate that she had a point that would fit perfectly at that spot. "Another basic truth is if you serve him, he will reward you. He will also lead you where you need to be. He will lead you to that car, that house, that job, that man or woman. You think I would have found Brother Pastor, as perfect as he is for me, if it wasn't for God? It would be like finding a needle in a haystack. We are all unique, quirky, and down right crazy individuals looking for the perfect mate out of all the billions of people." She looked out in the audience, and found Paul and Keisha. She temporarily lost her train of thought as her sister dropped hands with a smiling Paul, and began waving as if she was just crowned Miss America Vanessa was able to make out the sizable diamond as her sister wiggled her fingers on her left hand.

"Sisters used to come up to me all the time and say, they need to get out more, maybe visit other churches to find that man. I would tell them, what you need is God. God is so awesome He will bring your mate and sit him next to

310

Sherryle Kiser Jackson

you in church one day. Say amen, Minister Morton," Vanessa said, overjoyed for her sister.

Willie allowed his sister-in-law to revel in the moment, standing to her feet and sporting her rock before the congregated souls. *Hallelujah*, he thought. He was sure his sister-in-law would be spending a lot less time at his home. Their spontaneous engagement announcement gave witness to how God will reward those who were committed to him, or in Paul and Keisha's case, at least trying to be. Willie continued to explain the rewards of being examples of righteousness. Men and women were filled with the Holy Spirit and moved to tears.

"We have talked about some basic truths. Does that mean that those people who know Jesus is Lord devote their whole lives to him? Or, the people who know they cannot live without him, do they serve him diligently? Do those people who serve him diligently, ultimately make it to the promise land? Do they have all they desire? We know the answer to the questions are no. Another basic truth is found in Ecclesiastes; to everything there is a season. Some people's season of being saved, of growth, of prosperity is now. Some people's season is soon. Unfortunately, if we do not shine our lights round about us, some people will never know the full extent of God's love and grace."

"Brother Pastor, do I have time to give a prescription?" Vanessa asked, turning her Bible to where she tabbed it earlier.

"We are all here together; we have nothing but time." Willie yielded to her.

"You know where I'm going with this don't you?" Vanessa asked playfully, testing just how well her husband knew her. It was easy to forget she was working when she was with him.

"Surprise me," Willie said, knowing Vanessa could pull a related scripture out of a hat.

"Hold that thought. I do have a surprise for the entire congregation, but let's get back to homework. The next chapter of Hebrews is commonly called the Faith Hall of Fame. It starts with a definition of faith and has examples throughout the Bible of people who showed extreme faith: Abel, Enoch, Noah, Abraham, Issac, Jacob, Moses and the children of Israel. Ladies were not left out; Sarah and Rahab are mentioned also. Theologians suggest quite a few authors for this particular book, but whoever it was gets an attitude with us by verse thirty-two and asks, 'how many more examples do you need?' I haven't even told you about Gideon, Barak, Samson, Jephthah, David or Samuel. Now I'm saying it to you, how many more examples do you need to hear before you are convinced that it takes Faith to run this thing here?" Vanessa put her hands on her hips in a sassy manner causing her robe to blouse out. "To run this church, to run your relationship or marriage, and to run your life, you need faith."

"So the ultimate question, Sister Pastor, is would your name be listed in the Faith Hall of Fame?"

"Woo, that's a good one, Amen." Vanessa said. "I think we should close on that one."

"I think we should close on that one too," Willie agreed.

Vanessa knew she tested the patience of her congregation by holding them for this special presentation after the end of the message when everyone's thoughts were on the Honey-baked ham and other dishes prepared for Easter dinner. She had been in quiet contemplation since the fellowship dinner and kept this secret from her husband. For a long time, Vanessa thought being chosen to succeed her father as Pastor of Mt. Pleasant Baptist church was her greatest accomplishment until she married Willie and God blessed them with this vision. Thanks to God, she helped her husband get over a difficult time and grow as a pastor and she wanted to do something to show the combined church that she also had grown through this transition.

Vanessa had Willie stand beside her as several members who were privy to the surprise held a huge sign covered with a sheet at the back of the sanctuary for all to see.

"First of all I'd like to thank Deacon Johnson, Deacon Simmons and the ladies you see here in the pulpit for not divulging my secret to anyone; especially my husband, your pastor. I am overjoyed at what God is doing in the church. He brought us together to do good work but also to shake us up. I needed to be shaken. As much as I have told my congregation to get serious and stop playing church that was actually the advice I needed to take for myself. I was thinking my way through and not feeling." Vanessa paused with tears in her eyes as if the Lord was revealing this to her as she was sharing. Willie put his arms around her.

"Now we are here together, and we know we have to get over the past to get on with our new collaboration," Vanessa said. "As much as my husband was holding on to Harvest Baptist, his first love, I was holding that much tighter to Mt. Pleasant as if it were mine. The Lord says it's ours, and it's time you start acting like it. These ladies and I have formed a committee to think of a name for our church that reflects the best of what God has joined together.

Surprised gasps could be heard through the assembly. Even Willie placed his hand over his mouth and shook his head in disbelief. Keith Fischer took over the drums and was prepared to sound out the ceremonial drum roll.

"Now I know some of you are thinking, isn't that something you vote on at a church meeting? How many of you know that God didn't hold a church meeting to vote when he changed Saul's name to Paul? He was in authority then and He has put me in authority, along with my husband, right here, right now. We have one name to present and what better day to hold a special church meeting to vote on that name than the most attended day of the year. Drum roll please," Vanessa said.

The deacons uncovered the sign for the signboard outside that read, *The Pleasant Harvest Baptist Church* in huge Old English style letters with a slogan, *The Blessed Union of Mt. Pleasant Baptist Church, Harvest Baptist Church and the Holy Trinity* in custom style block letters underneath. The new logo bore two doves whose head and body formed a heart with the Holy Bible in the center.

"Okay let's make it official," Vanessa said above the crowd that was already rowdy with excitement. "All those in favor say yeah!"

"Yeah!" the congregation raised as one voice.

"You've been extremely patient with us, not only this day, but also the past year. Let's be about the business of serving God, and my wife and I will try not to cast any more visions for our church anytime soon." Willie said, hugging a smiling Vanessa.

"Let's not make any promises," Vanessa urged. "Beloved, let's look to the Lord and be dismissed."

Epilogue

Alexis Montgomery, the local assignment reporter, inserted her ear piece and waited for a countdown that would indicate it was time to start her live report. She handed off a bottle of Spring water to her production assistant in exchange for a blue insulated microphone with the channel 7 logo. She picked the location at the corner of Lincoln Avenue with her cameraman for two reasons: she wanted to be out of earshot of the apparent praise-fest that was going on, and she wanted the camera to pan in slowly to the devastation on her cue. Her cameraman began mouthing the countdown signal he was receiving from the station's remote broadcasting van.

"After the break, we have an interesting story of faith this Easter afternoon. A fire at a local church sends previous parishioners into exuberant praise in the streets of Capitol Heights," Alexis said.

"And three, two, one clear," Alexis heard through her ear piece.

"Okay, I want the Pastor and the Fire Chief nearby

when I walk up," Alexis shouted to the station workers who immediately raced on the scene to set up the next shot.

Alexis waited for Rebecca Lane, the anchorwoman reporting from the station, to lead back into her story. She had only gotten to the scene herself twenty minutes ago after receiving a call from the fire house. She was used to it being slow on Sundays. This Sunday she was preparing for her coverage of the annual Easter Egg Roll on the White House lawn scheduled for the next day. She could see the production assistant talking to a man with a knit cap. He put up the number one to indicate that she should interview the eyewitness first before talking to the pastor and the fire chief.

"Thank you, Rebecca. Praise and worship is not uncommon for a Baptist church on an Easter Sunday, but it is a little unusual for a church that only a short time ago was smoldering with fire," Alexis said, walking a short distance to her next location. She flipped the page of her notepad to read over her notes while her voice track played to the footage shot earlier when the fire trucks were still on the scene.

"It happened in the 8900 block of Lincoln Avenue in Capitol Heights, Maryland. Shortly after noon, flames broke out in the back office at the Harvest Baptist church. The fire spread setting the roof ablaze, sending beams and debris into the sanctuary below."

The cameraman signaled that they would be back to her live. *I hope I have enough time to cover this story thoroughly,* she thought. It would be a tremendous boost to her career.

"I'm standing with Louis Crenshaw who was passing by the Harvest Baptist Church and saw smoke. Tell us about it," Alexis said, putting the microphone to Lois' mouth.

"Well, my cousin and I were walking to the corner getting ready to take the bus down Florida Avenue," Louis said.

"So there were people inside for service this morning?"

"Yeah, I know I saw somebody go in there this morning. Lately, not many people attend this church. I mean, the parking lot back there isn't as crowded anymore on Sundays," he said, somewhat distracted by a man who looked as if he was going to enter the shoot. He did a backwards nod to signal something to his friend. "My cousin told me, you know, the pastor done moved to another church."

"Tell me, did you see the flames?" Alexis said, trying to wrap it up with this witness. She was receiving instructions in her earphone telling her that in the interest of time to cut to the minister. She could see the production manager getting information from the fire chief who apparently had been cut for a live interview. The fire chief interview will have to be read at the latter part of her story, she thought.

"Yes, see we had missed the bus and just walked to the plaza to get some breakfast. It must have been a short service, 'cause on the way back we seen smoke. I ran up to the door to see if anyone was hurt, but the door was locked. I knocked on the door while my cousin ran toward the back. When he came back around, he told me to get the hell out of there, oops, to get out of there 'cause the whole back wall was on fire."

"Thank you, Mr. Crenshaw."

"Yo, it might be this dude that be camped out on the front steps all the time. It's mighty funny he's nowhere to be found today. He get up there preaching, 'you're gonna burn in hell. If you don't find Jesus, you're gonna burn.'" His yelling sent feedback into the headpiece from Alexis' microphone.

"Thank you, Mr. Crenshaw," Alexis said, turning her attention to the pastor off to her left. The producer was telling her to continue coverage since it was a slow news day. Louis also turned his attention to Pastor Green.

Alexis stepped quickly over to the left so the camera could pan over her shoulder at the crowd to avoid further comments from Louis. Men and women still in their Easter outfits were singing and waving their arms at the brick face building that was still standing under a charred roof.

"Willie Green is the former Pastor of this church. He is the leader of this group that is here today. Tell us, Reverend Green, what message are you sending today by being here?" Alexis said, standing in front of Louis who was still in the shot.

"We just thank God today that no one is hurt. We got a call shortly after service at Mt. Pleasant that the building was on fire here at Harvest Baptist. It was the strangest thing, I don't even know who called. My wife and I and several other members of my congregation came over in a hurry. When we saw that no one was hurt, well, we just thank God today," Willie said, waving his right hand over his head.

"I hear you have a history with this church, although you are a pastor of another congregation?" Alexis said.

"Yes, I was called to lead my congregation to unite with the Mt. Pleasant Baptist church with my wife, Vanessa Morton Green. Traditionally we would be gathered in this place for an Easter Sunday service followed by what we called a Love Feast; but God knew better. Lord knows I had plans for this building, other people had plans for this building, but God had other plans. We have brothers and sisters who still carry on service at this branch of Zion. God spared them all. Thank you, Jesus!" Willie said, drifting away, caught up in praise.

"Reverend, I have just one more question. Do you know of anyone who might have intentionally set this fire?"

"Whether someone set it or it caught fire itself, God allowed it. All we can do is wait for revelation from the Lord," Willie said, suddenly serious.

"There you have it. While church members wait for revelation from the Lord, Fire Investigators will be on the scene to see just what caused this fire. Fire officials say it will be a couple of days before anyone from the church will be allowed inside. Fire Chief, Terrie Levins, told news 7 that behind the brick front stood an old stucco and wood frame that might have added to the blaze. Investigators will also inspect the grounds for the possibility of arson since the cause is still unknown at this point. It was not long ago that a Pentecost Baptist church in downtown DC was intentionally set on fire. Fire investigators found magazines and rolled up cardboard wedged in a doorway. We've also been reporting on Minister Paul Lovett of After-life Christian church, also in the District, who is now facing charges for collecting $125,000 in insurance money for a 1997 arson fire he allegedly set that destroyed his church. So, this fire here at Harvest Baptist church could very well turn into a criminal case. Chief Levins estimates over $400,000 in damages to this church. For a church this size and with considerable damage to the church structure, it may have to be demolished and rebuilt. I am Alexis Montgomery reporting. Back to you, Rebecca."

Alexis had to thank God herself for that report. That was the kind of live coverage producers looked for when they needed a new anchor. She was impressed at how she was able to patch the summary from the Fire Chief into her report. Alexis was about to tell the people over her shoulder that they could go home, but then realized that they weren't a prop or staged by the station. They weren't trying to be seen by anyone but God. Their praise was real.

Charley's heart raced as he sat slumped behind the

wheel of his wife's car long after the fire trucks and the remote broadcasting van were packed up and gone. He
managed to remain undetected by his former church
members amongst the chaos of the fire scene. Soot and
ashes covered his suit jacket and pants as he clutched the
heavy metal lock box he had risked his life to retrieve
from the church's back office.

Charley observed the ravaging demolition of his
church home and felt as if he were in the pit of hell. He
thought he might relinquish himself to the flames with
the church he loved so much, but was sure the fire would
reach him before he could repair the breach he had made
with the Lord. A huge wooden beam licked with flames
fell across his path nearly missing him. He ran blindly to
the back entrance, the smoke, this time wrapping tightly
around his lungs, choking the life out of him. When he finally got outside he had run faster than any 63-year-old
should be allowed to move, and it took a moment to convince himself that he wasn't having a heart attack; he was
okay—the church was not.

Now he took peeks through the alley. Every now and
again he'd catch a glimpse of Willie at the base of the
church, consoling some, and encouraging others as he had
done so many times before on the inside. *I thought he was
through with this place,* Charley thought. He held on tighter
to the box that contained the deed, insurance papers, and
other important documents of the church that Willie's
lawyers had recently demanded that his name be removed
as pastor relieving him of all obligations at 8901 Lincoln
Avenue. Charley undid the lock and stared at the documents as if they were gold. *Well, Pastor Green, I guess we'll be
seeing each other again, soon.*

Reader's Group Guide

1. What specific challenges did Vanessa face being a woman preacher and pastor, and how did she combat them? Do you believe these challenges present themselves to woman preachers today?
2. Discuss the validity of Vanessa's stages of spiritual growth and development. Do you think a person must go through all of the stages to be primed for their spiritual purpose?
3. How would you characterize Willie and Vanessa's preaching styles? Did they compliment each other?
4. What do you think about Willie and Vanessa's debate on tithing versus service when they first met in Chapter 3-A Spiritual Hook-Up?
5. Deacon Charley Thompson was so entrenched in his routine of tending to and caring for the Harvest Baptist Church building that it hampered his spiritual growth. What were some of the routines of the other characters that hindered them as well?
6. What characteristics made Keisha a good choice for Mt. Pleasant's Minister to the Singles? What characteristics made her an unlikely choice?
7. In chapter 16-A Charge to Keep, Keisha commented that her roommate, Lenora, was either naïve or a mature Christian. What did she mean by this? How was Lenora a mature Christian?
8. How did Vanessa learn to balance being a competent Co-Pastor and First Lady?

9. Read the Abigal story in the Bible in I Samuel 25. How did Vanessa's actions in chapter 13-In Abigal Mode compare?

10. Read about Mary and Martha in the Bible in Luke 11:38-42. Do you agree with Keisha's assertion that she is more like Mary and Vanessa is like Martha?

11. Re-read the epilogue. How does this apply to the characters and events in *Soon and Very Soon*?